A SLIPPERY SHADOW

Gary D. McGugan

A Slippery Shadow
Copyright © 2022 by Gary D. McGugan

Cover and book design by Castelane.

ISBN 978-1-7779049-1-3 (Paperback)
ISBN 978-1-7779049-2-0 (eBook)

1. FICTION, THRILLERS

For Allen,
Warm Wishes!
Gary M.
06.11.23

Also by Gary D. McGugan

Fiction
Three Weeks Less a Day
The Multima Scheme
Unrelenting Peril
Pernicious Pursuit
A Web of Deceit

Non-Fiction
NEEDS Selling Solutions
(Co-authored with Jeff F. Allen)

ADVANCE PRAISE FOR A SLIPPERY SHADOW

"What an incredible story. Exciting, suspenseful, and thought-provoking, A Slippery Shadow by Gary D. McGugan is one of the best stories I have ever read. The numerous characters with their different personalities keep the story interesting. Gary does a fantastic job of describing the various scenes and locations around the world, making it easy for the reader to form a visual of the many places and events that take place. I especially enjoyed the way Gary uses dialogue to carry the story forward without giving away too many secrets. The story is filled with twists, turns, and surprises, making this novel a page-turner from start to end."
~ *Natalie Soine for Readers' Favorite*

"An astonishing three-way story that merged to form a satisfying whole. I enjoyed everything about this novel, from the unique plot to the excellent storyline and character development. Gary also employed stylish writing that hooked me so much that I didn't want to miss anything. The author was so meticulous in his narration that the events felt realistic."
~ *Jennifer Ibiam for Readers' Favorite*

"Filled with suspense, mystery, and intrigue, A Slippery Shadow keeps you hooked throughout the pages with an entertaining plot and twists and turns you never see coming. Author Gary D. McGugan maneuvers an intricate story spanning multiple continents and involving international crime syndicates, corrupt governments, and powerful corporations that at times might threaten to overwhelm you, only to come together in the end to form the perfect completed jigsaw puzzle. McGugan's writing is exemplary, and the narrative feels more like a Hollywood blockbuster than a conventional crime novel."
~ *Pikasho Deka for Readers' Favorite*

"A Slippery Shadow is a riveting revenge thriller."
~ *Tammy Ruggles for Reader Views*

 "I highly recommend all of Gary D. McGugan's books. Though all the stories stand nicely on their own, please do yourself a favor and start at the beginning. The road from the first novel Three Weeks Less a Day to his latest release A Slippery Shadow is an incredible journey."
~ *Sheri Hoyte for Reader Views*

"This rich, vibrant tale offers all a reader could possibly want, and more, from an edge-of-your-seat thriller!"
~ *Amy Lignor for Feathered Quill Book Reviewsv*

A shout-out to the creative crowd who make up the Writers' Community of York Region for your encouragement, support and camaraderie along our writing journeys.

ONE

Flashing blue lights caught her eye first. A security van pulled up in a hurry and stopped abruptly below the window of her private jet. She froze. It had been a tumultuous two months since Fidelia Morales seized control of The Organization and was still far too early to ignore any abnormality. Her stomach knotted, and she shuddered as four large men jumped from its doors.

All were heavily armed. Each dashed in a different direction, probably surrounding the plane. Another vehicle screeched to a stop behind the van as her pilot stepped from the cockpit and headed toward her.

"Apologies. I know it's been a long flight. However, ground control notified me immigration authorities want to interview everyone on board. They've asked that you remain seated."

His face telegraphed no apparent worry, but pilots were notorious for masking their facial expressions and tones of voice to dispel concern.

She nodded, then shot a glance at her companions. On the right, Howard Knight sat stoically with his belongings in his lap. Already, her former lover had closed all his devices and retrieved his backpack from a storage compartment. Up front, the young IT expert loaned to her by Singaporean country boss Stan Tan still dozed in his seat. His head drooped downward toward his chest, limbs sprawled in various directions.

The guy's fatigue was understandable. He'd worked most of the night performing sophisticated stock transactions that had increased her net worth by several hundred million dollars that morning.

She'd grown accustomed to nosy authorities. With her former line of work, it had happened often. In thirty years recruiting women for the escort game, she'd attracted her share of unwanted attention. Immigration had never detained her for more than a few minutes. Still, she couldn't be sure.

When the co-pilot opened the aircraft door, a cool early morning breeze flowed into the cabin. Her nose crinkled. The air wafting in also carried the acrid odor of jet fuel. Still, it was refreshing on her skin after the long flight from Sydney. She covered her mouth and inhaled deeply to settle herself as one of the uniformed men from the van below poked his head inside.

"Good morning," he said. "Welcome to Singapore. We'll inspect your passports and ask a few questions here on the plane. Then we'll drive you to the arrivals area." His posture projected authority, but his manner looked impassive. His penetrating dark eyes shifted methodically from one passenger to another. He turned toward the pilots. "Please take a seat in the cockpit and prepare your passports. My associate will join you there."

Once the crew re-entered their area, a short woman appeared in the doorway, scooted into the compartment, and closed the door behind her. Right after, the man in charge motioned for the Singaporean to step forward. Groggy, but awake, the young man complied. In Mandarin, the officer demanded a passport, took a five-second cursory look at the document, and then pointed for him to leave the plane.

Fidelia watched warily in silence. The knot in her belly swelled when the agent next looked beyond her to Howard and motioned for him to approach. Why did they process the men first? Which fake documentation was Knight using? That made her more nervous; she couldn't recall immediately which name might be on his documents.

He scanned Howard's passport without question or comment and handed it back. "Okay, Mr. Bartoli. Your documents appear in order. Ride to the terminal in the vehicle at the bottom of the stairs."

Another glance out the window. Now a military jeep stood parked on the runway where Knight headed. She turned back to the officer. His expression hardened. Hostile eyes glared at her while his jaw jutted out further. He said nothing for what seemed like an eternity. A second woman entered the cabin doorway and looked toward Fidelia.

"Show your documents to her." The immigration representative pointed, his lips tightening and his voice rising with authority.

Fidelia complied and watched the agent for any sign of danger. She clasped her hands in her lap to stop their trembling and breathed deeply and slowly. The inspector didn't glance up from the documents until she'd checked every page of the passport issued by the Republic of Uzbekistan and scrutinized both sides of the attached visa issued by Singapore.

"Do you have a driver's license or some other form of photo ID, Ms. Morales?"

"No. I never learned to drive," Fidelia said and forced a smile.

The agent didn't return her gesture. Instead, she glanced at her superior and delivered a few words in Mandarin.

The leader spoke next. "We'll take you to the terminal now, Ms. Morales. We need to validate some of your passport details. We will process you in a facility where we have better technology."

Fidelia nodded, tried to smile again, and reached for her belongings. Her left hand shook noticeably. She used it to grip the top of the seat next to her and pulled herself upward, then followed the departing agent with short, tentative steps.

The ride took longer than expected, at least five or six minutes. An unwelcome urge to use a bathroom grew, so she squeezed her knees more tightly together. No one asked questions or made a comment. If their silence was designed to intimidate her, it was working.

Their destination turned out to be at the extreme end of Terminal Four, near an area reserved for cargo flights and warehousing. As they all stepped from the van, the impatient leader dashed a few steps toward the building, followed by one female agent gripping Fidelia's right elbow. The woman who had checked the pilots strode to her left, with little space between them. Sweat formed in her armpits, and the air turned oppressive.

Inside, they led her to a private room. Once the woman released her elbow, she told Fidelia to turn around and put her hands behind her back. She froze at first—sensing what was coming—and looked desperately for an escape. There was none. So she extended her arms behind her while plastic ties tightened around her wrists. For only the second time in her life, despair of captivity enveloped her.

The leader turned and stepped closer, face-to-face. They were almost the same height, though her low heels gave a modest lift. He adjusted his eyeglasses, cleared his throat, and read with a forceful tone from a sheet of paper he held with an outstretched arm.

"The Government of Italy demands your immediate arrest, detention, and extradition to Milano. There, you must answer serious criminal charges. You will stay in a cell in this building until they process the required legal documents and arrange for your transport."

Shock registered like a punch to the side of her head. Blood drained from her face and her body trembled. This unexpected detention came at the worst possible time and dread weighed heavily. With resolve, she mustered courage and corralled her exploding thoughts. Her law degree from Columbia didn't count for much in the tiny city-state. Still, after another deep breath, she forced herself to remain polite, her demeanor calm.

"I am not certified to practice in Singapore, but I'm sure your laws allow me to make a call for advice. I'd like to do that now."

TWO

Florida, Tuesday March 17, 2020

St. Patrick's Day started badly for Suzanne Simpson and plunged downward as the morning unfolded. Sharp, throbbing pain around her temples grew more intense by the hour. Despite air conditioning in the office, she wiped a damp brow with tissues alarmingly often. This time, she couldn't chalk it up to the onset of menopause.

By noon, dozens of messages jammed her email inbox. Some carried an exclamation icon. Others used jarring caps in the headline. All expressed urgency and concern.

Multima Corporation's share price had collapsed in a terrifying freefall right from the stock market's opening bell that morning.

As she peeked at an oversized monitor on her office wall, the latest price displayed was down a staggering 30 percent from the previous day. Stock exchange authorities had already issued a 'stop-trade' order once, but allowed the financial massacre to resume after a half-hour delay.

"It's a disaster, whichever way we look at it," Edward Hadley mumbled, his tone barely above a whisper. It was hard to read his face as he peered downward, hands spread across the top of his head in angst. His body was almost motionless, his usually buoyant spirit crushed. Could her vice president of corporate and investor affairs burst into tears?

"Don't blame yourself. Suicide is never easy to accept or explain. I think you chose your words carefully, as always. The stock market jocks never want to read a media release telling them a company's just lost the leader of a division. That ours killed herself rather than deal with the damning fallout of poor personal decisions only exacerbates their frustration."

"I know you felt awful yesterday when you heard the news," Hadley said, raising his head and looking at her, but not directly. "We should have scheduled someone on CBNN before the market opened this morning. We could have broken the story more gently and given investors more guidance. I should have expected this."

10

"If you couldn't offer me up for a network interview, who could you credibly put in front of the television cameras to announce Wilma's death? And only weeks after I thrust her into the added role of Chief Financial Officer? After all, she plugged that CFO hole only because someone murdered Heather Strong. Don't beat yourself up. We have serious problems to face in the coming months. Investors realize that. Some might bail out."

"Do you have replacements ready to fill the two vacant positions? At least temporarily?"

"I have some irons in the fire, but it'll probably take another couple days to finalize."

Her timeframe reflected the urgency but avoided any unrealistic expectations for an immediate solution. The truth? She hadn't even had a preliminary conversation with her preferred short-term replacement. He had been on a commercial flight all morning. Suzanne glanced at her watch, checking how soon he would land.

Hadley's gaze drifted off to the wall-mounted monitor, and he grimaced again as a news commentator on CBNN speculated about how much further the company's value might drop that day.

The guy described Multima's dire gaps in crucial leadership positions with exaggerated animation and almost theatrical eloquence. Could those issues prove serious enough to prompt a Securities and Exchange Commission investigation? The attention of the Federal Reserve? His advice was to get out of Multima investments right now or prepare for a long haul to recoup losses.

Eileen buzzed before either could comment. "I reached James and he's on the line. Would you like me to put him through?"

"Give me a moment to finish with Edward, please," Suzanne told her executive assistant. She nodded toward Hadley to signal the end of their meeting, then issued instructions. "Do your best with the institutions. Try to keep them onside. Retail investors will need to wait for now. I'll call you as soon as I have something more for the media."

Hadley signaled his understanding and left with a thumbs-up and crooked grin of feigned optimism.

"Can I assume you've heard the news, James?" Suzanne started out in a tone just above a murmur and with none of the usual pleasantries.

James Fitzgerald was a retired Multima executive who now served on its board of directors and was unquestionably her most trusted advisor.

"About Wilma? Yes, I read Hadley's media release on the plane. I saw you tried to reach me earlier too, but I was already in the air. Those cursed commercial flights really should allow phone calls."

"I agree. When I learned about her suicide last night, I was too distraught to call. Thanks for getting back to me. Are you in Virginia now?"

Only yesterday, James had officially notified Suzanne of his intention to resign from the board of Multima at the end of the year. He pined to move from Chicago to Virginia, setting up home with a newfound love, Angela Bonner.

"Yes, we've got a day of condo hunting planned. Angela's thrilled about her upcoming job with the FBI, and she's found a half-dozen potential locations near Quantico for us to visit."

It struck Suzanne as odd that Angela had landed a position at the Bureau so quickly. She had training as a forensic investigator but had never mentioned law enforcement as a career goal. But now wasn't a time to digress.

"You know I'm going to try to put a kink in those intentions, right?"

"How so?" Always a wily negotiator, James used few words, but his tone suggested curiosity.

"I need you to modify your plans. No doubt you're aware our share price is tanking this morning, and I can't describe the anger and concern inundating my email inbox at the moment. Candidly, Multima and I desperately need your help."

"I'll always listen. You know that. But I'm firm about starting another chapter in my life. I've given over three decades to Multima. If I'm lucky enough to live that long, I'm giving the next thirty to Angela." James's tone was soft and polite as ever, but there was no mistaking his conviction.

"I get it. No one has done more for the company than you. And I wouldn't be where I am today without your support," Suzanne chose her words delicately. "Here's my request. You said you wanted out by the end of the year, and I respect that. But I need to ask you to modify how you'll spend those last nine months with us."

"If it's manageable from Virginia and it's legal, you know I'll help any way possible."

"I'm not sure you can do it entirely from one location, but we'll see. I'd like you to become Multima's acting chief financial officer *and* acting president of Financial Services until we name permanent replacements for both positions."

Suzanne paused, giving him time to process. When he didn't reply after a bit, she said, "Frankly, I think you could still live in Virginia. If you accept, I'll assign a company jet to you exclusively. Each week, you can spend a couple days here in Fort Myers, one or two at Financial Services in Chicago, and have weekends in Virginia, for example."

"And if I decline?"

"I think you know the answer to that already, James. I don't have anyone inside the company ready to assume either role. If you can't pitch in for a few months, I'll have to appoint lesser-known people and try to weather the storm while we undertake searches for both positions." She paused again to emphasize the gravity of the situation. "We'll both see our holdings in Multima decline. I would do my best, but the next few quarters promise to be ugly."

"What terms do you have in mind, other than the company jet?"

"What would it take to win your support?"

"I don't know for sure. Whatever we discuss, I want to run it past Angela." James's tone hardened. "Her preferences determine whether I jump in. But let's start with a million-per-month salary and options on 250,000 shares at a strike price of today's close."

If Multima equities held at their current twenty-dollar-per-share level until the end of the day, James would have an option to buy them with an investment of five million dollars.

If he exercised that option, then sold them later at stabilized market prices, his payday could be spectacular. Should prices recover to where they started that day, his gain might be as much as two and a half million dollars. If the shares climbed to where they had traded before an earlier collapse, his haul could be almost nine million!

Either way, he demanded a steep price for a few months of work. But that wasn't the point. Since the stock market opening that morning, Suzanne's personal holdings had dropped by more than a billion dollars. That was the measurement that counted. She and her fellow investors were far more interested in the value of their shares than the exorbitant fee James Fitzgerald wanted for plugging the holes at Multima.

Of course, he knew that.

THREE

On the flight north from Sydney, Howard had paid attention to Fidelia Morales's instructions.

"Before we get to the arrivals area, split off and clear immigration with Tan's guy. I wanna to go through the formalities alone."

She promised to contact him the next day to discuss his planned departure, including the more-than-minor detail of getting him some money so he could be on his way.

Their odd greeting by the authorities, followed by separation at the aircraft, came as a surprise.

It was also extraordinary for immigration officials on the plane to give his passport so little scrutiny, but that happened sometimes. Things became more bizarre when the first van disappeared with the young Singaporean, leaving Howard to follow moments later in another one. However, the intense interviews inside the arrivals area were the most perplexing of all.

An agent had escorted him into the massive hall, then to an office halfway to the central processing point. For about an hour, three separate officers had peppered him with questions. The weird thing? All they wanted was information about Fidelia. How long had he known her? Where in Australia did she go? Why were they in Singapore? Where was she planning to stay?

Of course, he just created a string of lies he knew he could remember if tested again, without giving the agents a single piece of valid intelligence. When they let him leave the office and wend his way out of the airport, he couldn't contain his smile and was almost giddy by the time he reached the limo area.

It appeared Fidelia would undergo a significantly more extended interview. That probability boosted his spirits. It felt like poetic justice. With all the power of The Organization at her disposal, she shouldn't be far behind him. He expected it would be one of those life experiences she'd be furious with while it was happening, but laugh about a few years down the road.

So he followed her instructions, gave a taxi driver the address for Stan Tan's residence, and respected her orders to wait there for her call.

He woke up mid-morning after sleeping almost five hours. Before getting out of bed, he glanced around the now-familiar surroundings. He'd already spent a few days in Tan's guest house. Since he'd been a prisoner there for a week or so in February, nothing had changed.

Back then, Tan's hoodlums had captured Howard in Cambodia in the middle of the night and spirited him across two national borders. It seemed like years ago, not weeks.

It was all to help Fidelia execute her outrageous plan to steal several hundred million dollars from some unknown foe. That enemy might have been the Russian mafia, but he couldn't be sure.

He shook his head a couple times with a mix of exasperation and disbelief, then crawled out from the bedsheets. First, he checked the locks by wandering to the front door and turning the knob. Surprisingly, it opened effortlessly to a bright sunny day outside, already warm and humid.

He peeked out and drew in a deep breath of fresh air. A slight breeze gently swayed the nearby palm trees, and several birds chirped melodically as he surveyed his surroundings. Professional gardeners had recently trimmed the thick green grass, and the lawn's rich color contrasted dramatically with beds of brightly colored pink and purple orchids in full bloom. Tall, dense, and meticulously groomed hedges surrounded the property, dampening background sounds.

Like the last time he was here, none of the usual annoying hums of urban traffic penetrated this oasis of tranquility in the heart of the bustling city-state.

As he reached to close the door and step back inside, an unexpected movement caught his eye. He turned toward the main residence. Although a colorful mask covered her lower face, he recognized the same young woman who'd brought his meals when he stayed here the last time. Again, she walked barefoot and wore knee-length beige denim shorts with a brilliant white T-shirt. She also carried an oval tray stacked with covered dishes that looked as if they might conceal breakfast.

He held the door open and couldn't miss a sparkle of welcome in her eyes after he motioned for her to step ahead of him into the house. As before, she said a few words of greeting in Mandarin while she set the tray on the only table in the spacious living area. Then she bowed and backed out of the room, closing the door behind her. He rechecked the doorknob and sighed with relief when it still opened from inside.

Breakfast was unremarkable. Western-style cereal, boiled eggs, and English muffins without butter were identical to the breakfasts the woman had brought him the other time. But he'd eaten only salty snacks and a few pieces of fruit on the private jet during the previous twenty-five hours. So he wolfed down the delivered food. Moments after he poured a second cup of steaming hot coffee from the carafe, a sharp knock on the door interrupted his thoughts. He watched it swing open from the outside.

"Welcome back, Howard Knight." Ever polite and formal, Stan Tan bowed deeply. He wore a face mask and displayed a mischievous glint in his eyes. When Howard motioned for him to enter, the lithe Singaporean strode confidently toward the sofa before sitting down with his slim arms and legs crossed comfortably.

"Have you heard from Fidelia?" He made the request sound as offhand as possible. His long-time former lover probably wouldn't be up that early—particularly after the unbelievable day before. Considering immigration's unusual interest in her, she likely hadn't arrived at her suite at the Five Seasons Hotel much before five or six in the morning. The thought prompted an involuntary grin again.

"Only yesterday, before you left Australia. She asked me to prepare the house for you and said she'd drop by today. How did everything go down there?"

It was an odd question. Stan Tan had a financial stake in their mission. Didn't Fidelia tell him about their success when she spoke with him the day before? How much did he know about the details of the escapade? And what percentage did he earn from the project's success? Howard couldn't answer any of those questions, so he divulged as little as possible.

"Fidelia only shared with me what I needed to know to do my part of the job, but she appeared satisfied with the results."

Tan smiled behind his mask, his black eyes animated. He said nothing at first but continued to look directly at Howard, assessing.

"Is everything alright with your temporary home? Do you need anything else?" Stan Tan broke the gaze as he raised himself from the sofa, perhaps seeing no point in pursuing more questions at that stage.

Every guest knows it's essential not to alienate a powerful man, so Howard stood as well, formed namaste politely, and reciprocated Tan's bow of exit. "Everything is fine with your charming house. And I appreciate your warm hospitality."

As it turned out, Fidelia didn't call at all that first day. But that wasn't unusual. Since their breakup a couple years earlier, he'd noticed a tendency for her to play mind games with him on the few occasions they'd met.

In fact, three more days passed with his sole visitor the quiet young woman delivering food and refreshments. Fortunately, the Wi-Fi worked this time, so he surfed the Internet with a fully charged burner phone he found on a shelf.

The news was bleak everywhere. The COVID-19 pandemic had disrupted travel, and many countries warned their citizens to return home while it was still possible. Their messages implied governments would soon seal borders and ground airlines. It made little sense to stay in Singapore any longer than necessary. Although Fidelia had promised some money for expenses, it was also essential to have enough to tide him over for several months. A visit to the TVB Bank's local branch was crucial.

After five days, he still waited for Fidelia's call, but he used his time well. He checked the pandemic situation in multiple potential destinations, surveyed flight schedules, and calculated travel times. Most important, he weighed his alternatives from every perspective he could imagine and developed an outline of a strategy to finally put The Organization behind him.

Equally important, he also memorized the address and phone number of the TVB Bank, called to learn the local manager's name, and plotted a route there on Google Maps. The app calculated sixty-two minutes' walking time, but Howard was taller than average and still physically fit—he might shave a bit at a quicker pace.

On the sixth day at Tan's compound, he left the guest house, knocked on the door of the main residence, and asked to speak with his host. The young woman who served his meals signaled for him to wait while she went for her boss.

Tan arrived some minutes later, slipping a colorful face mask into place as he approached. He gave his usual bow of greeting. "Still no word from Fidelia. Is everything okay with your stay?"

"That's curious. Have you tried to reach her at all?"

"Yes. I called the hotel every day, including just a short time ago. She hasn't checked in yet."

Behind his face mask, Howard scowled at first, then caught himself and smiled to brighten his eyes and appear more nonchalant. Something was amiss. It was one thing for Fidelia to make him wait a few days for whatever underhanded purpose she might have. He'd prepared for that.

But why would Tan not share that she'd failed to check in to the hotel until almost a week after her expected arrival? He tested the local crime boss.

"I'm feeling a little cooped up here. Do you mind if I wander off and walk around the city for a couple hours?"

"Not at all," Tan responded without a moment's hesitation. "Fidelia asked me to provide you shelter and hospitality until she connected with you, but she made no request to limit your freedom."

"I'll bring the phone you left in the house. You can reach me should she call and want to connect immediately."

"Of course." With that brief response, the Singaporean crime boss bowed, formed namaste, and closed the door.

With Tan's renowned technology expertise, he'd probably connected the burner handset directly to a monitoring device inside his primary residence. It was possible he'd also arranged a discreet tail or shadow to report Howard's movements. To avoid generating any suspicions that Tuesday morning, he walked for exercise only.

The following two days—still without a word from Fidelia—he stretched walking distances, and time away from the guest house, to about four hours. Emboldened, he plotted a different route on Google Maps each day. He also varied his pace, constantly changing directions and looking back over his shoulder to see if someone might be tailing him.

By the end of the third day, the lingering pinch of worry in the pit of his stomach disappeared. Either Tan's spy was impossibly good, or no one was following him.

Friday, Howard walked toward the TVB Bank. Three blocks before reaching his destination, he shut off the phone before making a couple extra turns onto side streets to check again if someone followed. Then he approached the entrance. As expected, it was locked, but an inconspicuous sign identified a button just below the bank's name.

"Hello, this is Mr. Smith," he said after a female spoke a few words in Mandarin over an intercom.

"How can I help you, Mr. Smith?" she asked.

"I'd like to make an appointment with Mr. Lee for a brief meeting tomorrow, please."

"Do you have an account with us, Mr. Smith?"

"Yes, check your voice recognition software." He had moved closer to the intercom, spoke clearly, and used a confident tone.

"May I ask at what time you prefer to meet Mr. Lee tomorrow?"

Her tone, while formal, had become friendlier. The app had probably confirmed "Mr. Smith" among the most valuable customers of the offshore financial institution in Grand Cayman. TVB Bank employed voice recognition in all its branches precisely because many of its highest net-worth customers were reluctant to show identification to the bank's employees. Or, like him, their travel documents bore no resemblance to the information the bank held in its files.

"Will eleven o'clock be convenient?"

"Of course, Mr. Smith. Please have a wonderful day, and we look forward to serving you tomorrow."

A block away, he turned on the phone again. It didn't matter if Tan saw a gap for a short distance and a few minutes. Back at the residence, Howard stopped again to knock on a door at the main building. The same woman who brought the meals responded once more with a smile, and promptly fetched her boss.

"I heard from Fidelia this morning," the Singaporean said before bowing or greeting him. "She's delayed. She apologized for not letting us know earlier, but she asked me to give you this."

He handed over a large, bulky, sealed brown envelope as he spoke, pausing only long enough for the transfer to occur. Something about his appearance was different, too. It took a second to register, but his right eye sported a nervous tick that hadn't been there before.

"She requested I let you stay in the guest house here for as long as you choose but emphasized you were free to leave."

Howard processed that. Something didn't compute. He knew Fidelia well. They'd been lovers for over two decades, after all. She wouldn't take days to make contact if everything was okay. The envelope Tan handed him was almost certainly stuffed with American dollars, probably in large denominations. And the crime boss showed no concern. It deserved a tiny probe.

"Did Fidelia say when she might be able to meet?"

"No. She left a message with apologies and instructions on my voice mail. Unfortunately, I was preoccupied when she called." Tan's tone had once again become exaggeratedly polite as he raised his hands in namaste to convey an apology.

That, too, was out of character. Howard's heartbeat increased slightly as his internal antenna sensed danger. Fidelia never left requests or instructions by voice mail. She considered it too risky and insecure. Tan was lying, but why?

"Thank you for sharing that information and the envelope." He formed namaste as he bowed and backed away, then headed to the guest house. Inside, he opened the package and started counting hundred-dollar bills. They totaled precisely five hundred—fifty thousand dollars.

Minutes later, Howard set off again, leaving the phone behind this time. He set off toward the Great World shopping center with a handful of bills stuffed in a front pocket of his faded blue jeans.

It took over three hours and almost twenty of the hundred-dollar bills. It also required stops at several stores and boutiques before Howard accumulated enough clothes for warm and cold climates. Then he needed a piece of carry-on luggage with wheels to store it all, plus a knapsack to sling over his shoulder to carry new socks, underwear, and toiletries. He made his last stop at an Apple Store for a laptop and an iPhone loaded with unlimited international minutes from SingTel.

After dragging it all back to the guest house, his online research resumed. One flight left about two o'clock. A check of the seating plan showed a few spaces available in either first class or economy. The connecting flight showed space as well. Immediately after Tan's servant brought his evening meal, Howard shaved and packed up for an early departure the next morning.

The new iPhone alarm sounded at seven o'clock. Within thirty minutes, he dressed, tucked the burner phone Tan had provided back on a shelf, and rushed out to the street, dragging his carry-on and backpack. He walked to the Great City shopping center once again. There, he found a spot for a leisurely breakfast, read the morning *Singapore Straits-Times* newspaper, and shopped for more incidentals he'd thought of the night before.

At precisely ten thirty, he headed toward TVB Bank. After a brief hello and a phrase or two to let the voice recognition software do its job, he sat opposite Mr. Lee—the most common name in the city-state. Both kept their face masks in place and both said as little as possible during their brief meeting. Mr. Fernando from the bank's headquarters in Grand Cayman had already instructed Mr. Lee to provide whatever funds or services Mr. Smith needed.

In less than thirty minutes, Howard left with a new Mastercard, pre-loaded with a one-hundred-thousand-dollar spending limit, showing the name Mario Bartoli to match his fake Canadian passport.

Dragging his carry-on luggage along the sidewalk for a short distance from the bank, he arrived at a station for the Downtown Line headed toward the Expo MRT Station. Following his telephone's GPS guidance, he transferred to another train for the Changi Airport. Both lines had few riders, and the entire trip took only about forty minutes before arriving at Terminal Three.

He spotted the EVA Airline check-in counters the moment he glanced around the lobby area, then indulged a few moments to look upward and admire the building's architecture one more time. It was magnificent. With its gleaming glass, sweeping roof supports, and live vegetation everywhere, it was easy to understand why many visitors scheduled time for sightseeing within the Singapore airport itself.

However, that day, Howard's priority was an orderly exit from the country. Only minutes later, he purchased a first-class ticket to Toronto with another wad of cash. He'd have a short layover with time for a meal in Taipei, Taiwan, before boarding a subsequent fourteen-hour EVA flight to his destination in Canada.

For a second or two, his thoughts drifted back to Fidelia. There could be little doubt she was in some sort of jam, either with the authorities in Singapore or The Organization. Maybe both.

He felt a twinge of guilt leaving this way, but it didn't last. She was no longer his problem.

As he headed toward the departures lounge, Howard's conscience was clear. He owed her nothing. His posture and manner reflected the weight that had lifted from his shoulders. With a bit of luck and another few hours, he'd start a journey to find a complete and final escape from all of it—Asia, Fidelia Morales, and The Organization.

FOUR

The son-of-a-bitch had double-crossed her. No other explanation fit. For the first two days after calling Stan Tan to describe her predicament with the Singaporean authorities, Fidelia blamed bureaucracy or administrative glitches. The local crime boss said he was shocked by her arrest and promised to spring her loose "as quickly as possible," but a week had passed already with no sign of an attorney.

Normally, the head of a powerful crime syndicate would simply call her security team. They'd spring her from custody—one way or another. But Luigi Fortissimo, her primary protector, had been trapped in a violent ambush that had probably claimed him and a dozen of his best men in a hail of gunfire. She'd heard the massacre two days earlier, before their phone line suddenly died.

The American consulate was also out of the question. She'd burned that bridge with an earlier refusal to cooperate with the FBI and they'd destroyed her passport, following up with a *persona non grata* notation in her US passport file, according to sources. That's why she traveled with Uzbekistan documents.

Her captors knew she had money. Someone must have counted the fifty grand she carried in the bag they confiscated, but offers to share some or all of that cash with three separate guards proved futile. Someone had planted intense fear of retribution and none had wavered.

Anxiety grew by the hour. Sleep became elusive and erratic. She remained stuck in a single locked cell in some remote corner of Singapore's Changi Airport. Nobody else nearby. Immigration officials brought food and refreshments three or four times a day but seldom shared more than a used newspaper and a few curt words.

After Fidelia had politely asked to make a second phone call, an officer promised only to enquire. That was days ago, and the woman hadn't returned since. Making a proposition a person with her stature and power in The Organization should never need to make, Fidelia had tried another, more desperate, plea with a male agent yesterday.

He leered suggestively in return, then remembered the tiny cameras mounted high in each corner of her cell and refused the suggestion.

Last night, her tactics had become more urgent; she pleaded for help with gushing tears and cries that her detention was all a big mistake. She'd resolve it quickly with the aid of a lawyer, she insisted. The guy said he'd see what he could do.

Finally, another unfamiliar face delivering breakfast that morning announced someone would visit her later that day. That news prompted a flurry of speculation about the visitor and how she could best leverage the opportunity.

Stan Tan wouldn't make an appearance, even if the authorities allowed it. Almost certainly, they were holding her with his permission and maybe on his orders. His role with the leaders in Singapore was complex and precarious. He'd never jeopardize his connections and the firewalls around his criminal activities to spring her from custody. He might send an attorney, as promised, but after the long delay, she'd have trouble trusting that lawyer without good reason.

Perhaps the promised visitor represented the Italian government. That country had requested her arrest and detention. Maybe their plodding legal system had produced some sort of document the immigration guys could take to a court to have her expelled.

What were the criminal charges the Italians were pursuing? They couldn't relate to escort services or human trafficking. She hadn't recruited or managed women in Italy for over five years, not even indirectly. No trail of evidence remained from those days.

Other than a single weekend shopping trip while hiding out in Uzbekistan, she didn't even remember visiting Italy before the Lake Como matter in January. Any criminal charges must relate to eliminating The Organization's crime boss in that country during her consolidation of power.

But it would be difficult to pin anything on her. Luigi and his minions had done the actual deed. Inside the cabin, she'd touched only the wine bottle they used as a distraction. They took that bottle with them when they left, and one of Luigi's men pulverized it before disposing of the dozens of glass fragments in a waste bin in an industrial area of Milan.

Chances the *Carabinieri* had found hard evidence connecting her to the guy's murder were low, but loose lips somewhere in The Organization could've tipped them off.

While she weighed the possibilities for the hundredth time, a slight noise from the darkened corridor caught her attention. A short Asian woman poked her head around a corner, locked eyes, and then bowed deeply as she executed namaste. She wore an expensive business suit and sported a Hermes handbag.

"You're Fidelia Morales, right?"

"Yes. And you are ...?" It was always better to offer only minimal information initially.

"Of course, I apologize." The woman smiled politely before she again bowed with hands in prayer position and said, "Namaste. I'm Sheri Wong, with the legal firm Wong and Associates. Mr. Tan asked me to meet with you."

The woman's downcast eyes did not instill confidence. Fidelia always had a hard time accurately guessing someone's age, but this woman looked young and inexperienced. Although her wardrobe appeared expensive, she wore the designer brands with neither panache nor style. It felt too early to test her legal knowledge or vent frustration at the week-long delay. Instead, she tried to put the woman at ease with the most charming smile she could muster.

"Thank you for coming. I really need your help. Can you tell me what's goin' on?"

Sheri raised a finger, signaling to wait a moment, then abruptly dashed away for several seconds. When she returned, an immigration agent carrying a folding chair followed her. It was the same officer who'd leered the day before. Now, he projected only boredom as he unlocked the cell. Sheri entered the opened door, accepted the offered chair, and set up facing Fidelia about three feet away.

After confirming the guard had left the area, Sheri leaned forward and spoke in a stage whisper.

"Sorry it took so long. Mr. Tan called me last week, but the authorities refused to let me see you until today." The woman started a music app on her phone and adjusted the volume of some hip-hop tune to a moderate level. "Whisper. Assume they are listening to everything we say."

Fidelia nodded her understanding and suppressed annoyance. The vaunted Singaporeans had one of Asia's most advanced legal systems, yet attorney-client privilege didn't exist. She scrunched up her face in curiosity as Sheri unwound some earbuds and plugged them into her iPhone before handing them to Fidelia, motioning for her to use them.

"Listen to my questions in the Voice Memos app, then write your answers on this notepad. I'll destroy your notes after I read them."

Fidelia listened to one question at a time for the next hour. After writing her answer, she passed her scrawled response to Sheri, who studied it intently. As the lawyer finished reading answers, she shredded each into tiny pieces and stuffed them into the bottom of her bag, taking care to mix them all up. Not a foolproof covering of her tracks, but creative.

"Okay. I understand your answers and your contention of innocence," Sheri said when their exchange finished. "Now, I'll need to get Mr. Tan's approval to engage with an attorney in Italy. I already spoke to the embassy here, and they're deferring all responsibility to the court in Milan."

Time to test her new lawyer's legal prowess. "What sort of appeal process does Singapore have for extradition requests?"

"None. The authorities here assume you're guilty of the charges unless a court from the extraditing country finds otherwise. Unless we can convince the Italian *Carabinieri* to drop the charges before the end of April, my country intends to honor their request and put you on a flight to Abu Dhabi with a connection to Milan. The embassy has already booked the flights."

Blood drained from Fidelia's face, and she stood up and took a deep breath to compose herself. This wasn't the time to appear weak.

"Call this number," she whispered as she jotted it on the notepad she'd been using. "It's in Germany. The woman's name is Klaudia Schäffer. She's a friend of mine. She'll know someone in the *Carabinieri* who can help. Ask her to handle it personally."

The lawyer looked into Fidelia's eyes, then diverted her gaze toward the floor before she mumbled, "I'll ask Mr. Tan's permission. He is our firm's client. If he approves, I will call her."

"I want to engage you as *my* attorney. I have more than adequate means to pay your fees." Fidelia used a tone that left little doubt about her financial strength and intentions.

"I'm sorry." The woman's voice trembled. She kept her gaze cast downward and said, "Our firm works only for Mr. Tan. I'll need his approval first."

The woman summoned the guard to let her out. She backed away from the cell, bowing, her eyes never meeting Fidelia's. The moment the lawyer and guard disappeared, she grabbed the folding chair and flung it violently against the locked doorway with all her force. A string of silent obscenities followed, cursing her stupidity for making a deal with Stan Tan to use Singapore as a home base.

In dozens of other places, she could easily make a call and be out of custody within hours, not days. And the likelihood of ever appearing in court to face charges in those other countries would be negligible. Not on this island, though. Here, Stan Tan controlled The Organization's operations with an iron fist.

When her blood pressure returned to normal a few minutes later, Fidelia took stock of her plight. Luigi was missing in action from a screwed-up mission in Chile. He hadn't answered her dozen calls from the plane, and he'd set his phone to never accept voice messages. The immigration authorities in Singapore still refused to let her make any more calls. Sheri Wong was clearly beholden to Stan Tan, who may have nefarious intentions.

As the guys in The Organization would say it, she was fucked.

Only one person came to mind who was both nearby and might help if she could reach him: Howard Knight. The guy was a bit of a wild card, but odds were high that he was still waiting for her in Stan Tan's guest house. She just needed to get a message to him.

Reverting to habits she'd first formed as a youngster in her parish-school days in San Juan, she used a tool that worked best in these circumstances. She unbuttoned her top, took it off, and removed her bra. When she slipped the shirt on again, she closed only the bottom two buttons and carefully parted the fabric before shouting out for the immigration guard who'd leered the day before.

He wandered back to her holding cell. Since the authorities in Singapore had few requests to hold air travelers in transit, the cell had no toilet or shower. Her overseers had grown accustomed to her occasional shouts. Each time, one or another would amble back at their own pace and priority to escort her to a facility typically used only by the office staff.

The restroom was only a dozen steps from the cell. The guards would unlock her door, walk down the hallway just past the employee room, and wait for Fidelia to follow them. On each trip, she'd searched the nooks and corners above to be sure they hadn't mounted cameras anywhere in that hallway. While she took care of her needs, a guard would stand outside the doorway, blocking escape.

This time, after she called out, she bent over to slip on her shoes and let the guard have a long look inside her top. She chose an angle that exposed both firm breasts and stood up slowly, teasing. As hoped, his gaze locked on her nipples. He didn't try to mask his interest—or even look up—as he backed down the hallway to the staff room and waited for her to advance toward him.

It was primitive, but many men in this part of the world still thought more with their penises than their brains, so she considered it fair game.

After a lifetime of practice, she made every movement titillate and lure. She positioned each foot before the other, like a model on a runway. Before reaching him, she tossed her long hair, then showed the tip of her tongue through her lips and smiled suggestively. At last, the mark looked into her eyes and grinned like a teenager.

"Can I use your phone to make one call?" she asked.

"You know the rules. No calls," he sputtered, shaking his head for emphasis.

"I know the rules, but you're alone. Who would ever find out?" Fidelia undid another button and stood more erect, watching his eyes dart back to her cleavage and stay there. "It's local. I need only a few minutes."

The immigration guard thought about it before he answered. While he considered, she gave him some more motivation and undid the last button of her shirt, exposing the full outline of her breasts.

"It's too much risk. I'll lose my job if they catch me."

"You're alone. Who's gonna know? Let me use your phone for one call, and I'll make it worth your while." She almost spat out a laugh at the directness of her ruse, but the guy still stood across from her, fixated on her nipples. "Just five minutes on your phone, and I'll give you my *full* attention."

When he glanced upward, Fidelia looked into his eyes with practiced seductive temptation. He took a step back, as though willing her to release him from her spell. His voice was hoarse when he said, "Only if I can fuck you."

She knew she had him and murmured, "I'll do anything you want, but it has to be after the call. A girl can't be too careful, you know."

He thought about it for a moment and told her to wait where she was. "Not one step," he ordered with a warning wag of his forefinger. With that, he dashed toward the front of the complex. She listened for a rattle of keys and the click of an outside door locking. Then, a bonus. All the lights and the fans of an air conditioner stopped at once. He'd cut the power. No cameras.

Fidelia removed her top and leaned against the doorway to the staff room with an inviting pose. As her mark turned the corner, she pasted on her most seductive expression, enticing him closer with slow, deliberate moves. He stepped forward and passed her his handset, then laid both hands on her breasts possessively as she punched in the numbers for the phone she had loaned to Howard Knight.

She heard the initial ringing as the guy fondled her breasts and started pinching her nipples as if checking fruit for ripeness. Fidelia smiled in encouragement. On the fourth ring, there was an unexpected recording in Mandarin.

"The mailbox is full. You can't leave any message," the immigration guard translated nonchalantly, still fondling her breasts.

"Let me try again. Maybe I dialed the wrong number." Her haste telegraphed her despair, so she flashed a smile of promise as she meticulously keyed in each of the digits once more.

On the fourth ring, she got the same recorded message. The guard laughed this time.

"You still have to take care of me," he taunted, leering.

"Let me try one other number, please." She formed a playful pout to hide her desperation and reached to unhitch a snap. Her jeans fell to the ground while she dialed the new number, then she snatched off her panties one leg at a time while she listened for the first ring. Distracted, the guard started to play with her pubic region with one hand, while the other massaged her left nipple.

About ten in the morning in Düsseldorf, Fidelia guessed, as she prayed for an answer to this call. She almost cried out when a voice said, "Schäffer *hier. Guten Morgen.*"

"Klaudia, it's me. Don't hang up!"

The immigration guard took an interest and pulled both hands away to better listen. She tried to shoo him off to speak privately, but he was having none of it. Instead, he stood more erect and tilted his ear at the handset, trying to hear both sides of the conversation.

"I'm in trouble. I need your help urgently."

"You swore Australia was the last time. Sorry, but I just can't." Exasperation punctuated every word. Fidelia pictured her friend already moving the device away from her ear to cut the connection.

"Singapore immigration has been holding me incommunicado for a week. I need you to reach our mutual friend in Uzbekistan. He must call his contact at the *Carabinieri* in Milan. Get the charges against me dropped. They're trying to deport me to Italy to face charges of murder. Please Klaudia. Do it today. Luigi is missing. Howard isn't answering. Stan Tan isn't cooperating. You're my only hope."

The immigration agent snatched the phone from her hand and hit the end button with an authoritative flourish. Then he crudely motioned downward for her to complete her part of their bargain in the darkened building.

FIVE

After Eileen's discreet prompt, Suzanne drew her telephone conversation with an aide to the governor of Florida to a firm but diplomatic close. Then she headed from her office toward the large conference room where other senior executives waited. As she passed her assistant's desk, Eileen handed her an agenda, briefing notes she might need for the meeting, and a plain white face mask.

Well before its competitors, Multima had instructed all its employees to wear masks to protect themselves, their co-workers, and their customers against the raging coronavirus. Suzanne waived her own directive while working alone in her office but took care to have one in place before every personal encounter. Eileen kept a few spares handy for those rare occasions her leader became distracted and forgot. Times like this morning.

In deference to directors operating in various time zones, they scheduled the session with the board to begin at eleven. It was their first meeting since a rushed video conference to gain support for James Fitzgerald's temporary appointment. As expected, the directors approved him becoming the acting chief financial officer of Multima Corporation and the temporary president of its financial services division. It seemed like far more than a week had elapsed.

Running a major corporation in the first stages of a global pandemic had been an experience like no other. Suzanne had worked from her office every day since returning from Montreal while the rest of the executive team hunkered down at their homes. Starting before six each morning, she'd toiled at her expansive desk on the fourth floor and hadn't once left before midnight. Still, the company's shareholders expressed displeasure with the poor performance of Multima shares in a tumultuous stock market.

Before she stepped into the conference room, she smoothed the front of her outfit to catch any stray wrinkles, checked her posture, and put on her most charming smile. Then she took long, confident strides toward her usual spot at the head of the table. Smiles—and seemingly cheerful hellos—greeted her from those already seated and others gazing down from a massive screen mounted on the wall facing her chair. She got down to business right away.

"Thanks for all your support, everyone. These past few days have been extremely stressful for the entire team, and you've all performed masterfully. You directors joining us from across the nation have done a tremendous job rebuilding investor confidence. When I checked the markets on my way to our meeting, our shares were trading about ten percent higher this morning. We're still far off our real value, but it's gratifying to see our share price stabilizing."

She scanned the faces in the squares on the screen. There were nods and an occasional smile.

"James, I want to welcome you to your first meeting of the board in your new capacities. I know I speak for all of us. Thank you again for bailing the company out. My agenda tells me you're prepared to start with updates on both roles."

"Prepared might be a little stronger descriptor than I'd choose, personally, but I'll share what I have," James replied.

She suppressed a grin at his characteristic display of self-deprecation and listened as he spoke for his allotted fifteen minutes without notes.

The information he shared wasn't exciting, but it was vital. He walked the board through each division's profit-and-loss performance and estimated how the first quarter of the year should finish. Business in Supermarkets would exceed even the wildest estimates of stock market analysts. While sales had surged, expenses had increased too, but the amount left after paying costs was still staggering.

James's review of the financial services division was equally impressive. He knew it intimately and spoke with his usual poise and authority. The directors' worry lines faded, with smiles tugging to escape the lips of even the most hardened. They realized it immediately. While the stock market might not reflect the same comfort level about the company's eventual performance, there was little doubt the foundation was solid. Confidence would eventually return.

"In conclusion, I recommend we take action to moderate expectations in the outlook." James's tone dropped an octave. He gave everyone around the table time to catch up before he slipped in a bombshell. "Although the operating results for Financial Services look good for this quarter, I propose the board elect to triple our loss reserves. We have to prepare for how people might default on their credit card debt should we have massive unemployment while offices and factories are closed."

She watched her directors' faces, maintaining a poker face herself. It took a moment before one director, who was also the president of Bank of the Americas, allowed himself a tiny smile before speaking with a stern voice.

"I think that's prudent, James. We're doing the same thing at the bank this quarter. If we don't need it, we can always shift the reserves from losses back to income later."

Chuck Jones, a director from the Midwest, immediately nodded in agreement. "That will create a quarterly loss on paper and reduce total reported Multima Corporation profits by how much?"

"About five hundred million for the quarter," James replied with an entirely neutral expression and matter-of-fact tone. "About the same as the unexpected windfall from Supermarkets."

Chuck Jones proposed to accept James's recommendation with essentially no further discussion. One director wondered out loud if the share price might fall further with a reported loss in the financial services division, but the proposition passed unanimously.

"After such brilliant fiscal workmanship, I'm almost embarrassed to ask," the Bank of the Americas president said. "But how are we doing with the search to find a replacement for our acting CFO?"

Uproarious laughter greeted his query, eliminating all tension. In fifteen minutes, James Fitzgerald had assuaged any concerns about the financial health of the company. He'd saved a couple hundred million in corporate income taxes. And he'd set the stage to optimize the generous bonus negotiated with Suzanne. Only a wily, skillful executive could perform that kind of magic. She tipped an imaginary hat to him as she prepared to answer the question.

"We've divided our search into two buckets. James will lead the effort to find a new president for Financial Services. I'll oversee the hunt for a Chief Financial Officer." She glanced at the faces on the screen, searching for any signs of concern. When she found none, she continued.

"Let me lay out the strategy. In the package Eileen sent you before the meeting, we provided a detailed job description for the CFO's role. It's the same basic framework we used for both Wilma Willingsworth and Heather Strong, but we've added a requirement for broad global management experience." She hesitated an instant on both names— their violent deaths still too recent. She took a sip of water and a deep breath before she continued.

"In the info package, we included a proposal to use the executive search firm Fencer Duart. Are there any objections to this choice?" She scanned the faces in the room and on the conference room's massive wall-mounted screen. No hands rose.

"The managing partner in New York, Gustaf Duart, will lead the search. But I've also asked an acquaintance named Stefan Warner to be my emissary as they work to identify the final candidates." At this stage, there was no need for the board to know she'd slept with the guy a couple times and thought of him as much more than an acquaintance.

"Stefan is a highly regarded professor of international business at the prestigious French University, École Polytechnique. You also received his resume in the information package. He has agreed to accept this assignment for a token fee of one dollar." It was also unnecessary to share that Multima's security department had checked his background and cleared him with glowing recommendations.

When she paused, Ruth Bégin, an independent director from France, found it important to comment. "Stefan is surely a great business scholar, but why is he undertaking this important project for a reward of only one dollar?"

"He's sensitive to his stature at the university and prefers to make sure there's no appearance of personal benefit from that respected position. He is also an acquaintance of mine. Does that create any concerns?"

"No. I just think it unusual for such an expert to consult for a major corporation like ours without demanding six-figure compensation. Are we at least paying his travel expenses?" The question generated a murmur of laughter, and Suzanne joined in before she replied.

"Candidly, with that pesky pandemic causing grief everywhere, I doubt Mr. Warner will generate many travel expenses. But we'll reimburse any he incurs. Are there other questions or concerns before we move forward?"

Two board members requested minor clarifications, but a motion to engage Fencer Duart and Stefan Warner passed without objection.

James Fitzgerald's outline of the strategy for finding a new president for Financial Services followed. However, his fellow directors were not as receptive to his proposed delegation of the legwork.

Suzanne had anticipated some pushback and had cautioned him in advance. But his proposal to have a mid-level manager from his former division lead the search drew several questions posed in a scathing tone. After all, Natalia Tenaz had been James's favorite resource in his business intelligence group less than a year earlier.

"So let me get this straight." Cliff Williams was a director from Chicago. He often used hand gestures, but this time feigned restraint. "Am I correct in understanding your choice to select candidates to hold the position of president of our financial services business is a young woman? And did I read correctly from her resume that she's thirty-three and has held the title 'Leader of Risk Management' for less than a year?"

She watched silently as James Fitzgerald skillfully handled his long-time friend's skepticism and sarcasm. It took a few minutes, but he remained relaxed. Patiently, he walked his audience through Natalia's history of progress within the financial services group and closed with a challenge.

"I trust her judgment. She knows every potential internal candidate for the job better than anybody else in our company—including me. I have found no one who identifies an individual's personality and values faster, and risk management is an important skill we need in our new president. I also like the way she challenges usual assumptions and accepted norms. Does someone around the table have a more qualified name to put forward?"

Moments after his challenge met with silence, the company's secretary asked if there were any objections to accepting James's proposal as submitted. There were none, and that left just one other relatively minor issue to complete.

"The last item on our agenda has to do with Michelle Sauvignon, and that's the reason she's not taking part today. You all know her, and some of you have shared with me informally that she may be one of the best assets we got when we bought Farefour Stores." Suzanne chose her words carefully to avoid a lot of discussion. "She has accepted our request to re-locate to our Montreal office and manage the worldwide Supermarkets' operations from there. You've seen my proposal in the meeting package to promote her to chief operating officer for Multima Supermarkets."

Although the appointment was a foregone conclusion, she invited questions and comments about her choice, the remuneration scheme, or other issues. She scanned the screen and waited for the briefest decent interval.

"Okay. If there are no objections, we'll ask Michelle to assume the new role with her relocation to Montreal as soon as the COVID-19 pandemic restrictions permit."

She was just about to move to "other business"—the last item on the agenda—when a woman leaned over the shoulder of her division

33

president for Supermarkets in the US and passed him a note. Gordon Goodfellow's head recoiled almost instantly, and he blanched with an expression of horror. Eyes bulging and his face turning a brilliant shade of red, he pushed back his chair and rose from the table as he announced the problem.

"They just found a bomb in our Naples, Florida, store. I have to go."

SIX

Singapore, Saturday March 28, 2020

Howard inhaled deeply to counter his sweaty palms and quicker-than-expected heart rate, then applied advice his father had offered decades earlier. "Just act like you belong there."

From the EVA Airlines check-in counters at Singapore's Changi Airport, he followed signs to Immigration Control and Security. He handed a passport to the officer, nodding politely with a smile behind his mask. The agent motioned for him to remove it and took a moment to match Howard's face with the photograph in the document.

Then he started turning the pages. The officer squinted and pulled the passport closer to his eyes as he inspected the contents, often shifting it to check some detail from another angle. It was hard to keep a blank and unconcerned expression.

There shouldn't be a problem. Fidelia had already realized they needed to update his fake information before their trip to Australia. Of course, he had entered Cambodia illegally from the Mekong Delta. Then The Organization had kidnapped him from a guest house in Siem Reap and smuggled him into Singapore with stops in Thailand and Malaysia. Any cursory inspection could've raised questions about how he got to the city-state from Vietnam with no exit and entry stamps.

The moment Fidelia had noticed that gap, she'd called Stan Tan. Within an hour, the crime boss had introduced Howard to a visitor—a youthful, well-dressed, and polite Indian lad—who requested the fake document for some quick modifications. There was little choice. If he hoped to leave the country and go anywhere unchallenged, the passport needed to show a credible entry trail. Later that morning, the same young man had returned with a passport sporting official-looking dates, and neither Singaporean nor Australian officials had questioned the document before. So why was this particular agent now inspecting every page?

"Why are you leaving?" the fellow asked, after at least a minute of scrutiny.

"Our government has recommended all Canadians return home as soon as possible because of the pandemic."

"What was your reason for coming to Singapore?"

"I'm a retired businessman. I traveled here as a tourist."

"Since COVID-19 started to spread, you've traveled from Barbados to Canada, then almost immediately to four Asian countries and Australia. Why didn't you stay in your country when you were there last month?"

He swallowed but dared not clear his throat. He should have expected this question and hadn't prepared a well-constructed response. Meanwhile, the immigration official said nothing. Instead, he inspected every detail about Howard's appearance from head to toe.

"I know it may sound foolish, but I read Australia and Asia had better control of the pandemic. Thought I'd be safer over here. Now, I realize that's not the case so I'm returning home."

The officer nodded as he listened, but the gesture probably signaled understanding more than belief. He motioned for Howard to stay put while he strolled over to the next station and consulted with a colleague. The new fellow went through the passport as thoroughly as the first and glanced over several times as they chatted about the situation.

"Do you have any symptoms of the coronavirus?" the original agent asked upon his return to the podium.

"None. They tested for a fever when I entered the terminal and I feel fine. I'm in excellent health."

That appeared to satisfy the man's curiosity. Handing the passport back, he waved his hand to move forward and said nothing more.

Howard's hike down long, spacious corridors with massive ceilings and bright natural light flooding in from outside was uneventful. Security at the gate was routine and boarding the aircraft relaxed. It appeared fewer than fifty people headed toward Taiwan that afternoon.

Only one other person sat in the well-appointed first-class section of the EVA jet. Someone in charge noticed their assigned seats were closer than necessary and suggested the Chinese woman choose a seat two rows back on the other side of the aircraft.

They served dinner soon after take-off, and a courteous flight attendant catered to every subsequent need for food and refreshments. Twice, flight attendants inquired about the onboard entertainment system he wasn't using like everybody else, concerned about his technical aptitude. Otherwise, the crew was polite, welcoming, and masked.

He stayed in his seat and feigned sleep, except for brief intervals to eat or drink.

The layover in Taiwan also passed quickly. As passengers debarked from the plane, a group of uniformed officials welcomed them in at least three languages and ordered everyone to form a line to have their temperatures checked. He was first out of the aircraft and at the front of the queue.

An official waved him forward when a satisfactory reading displayed on the electronic gadget pointed to his forehead. Then he found the departure gate for Toronto and settled into a coffee shop to kill time between flights. Although eligible to hang out in the first-class lounge, Howard wanted to avoid any potential companions for the next flight. For whatever reason, chance encounters in a waiting area sometimes led new acquaintances to assume continued friendship on board. The last thing he wanted on a fourteen-hour flight to Canada was a chatty seat mate.

It worked out okay. After submitting to one more temperature check before boarding the jet, he found only a handful of passengers in the plane's first-class section. He read, ate, and then slept almost eight hours in two segments during the trip. As the aircraft touched down, he looked refreshed and cheerful as he prepared for scrutiny from Canadian immigration.

Along the path toward an exit, several uniformed agents repeated the same questions about his health and symptoms before he reached the massive processing center. The lines were surprisingly long given the late hour. People jammed themselves much closer together than the recommended six feet. Whether or not it helped, he tried to avoid breathing more than necessary behind his mask.

"Where are you arriving from?" The female immigration officer posed the question with a stern expression tinged with boredom. Her shift probably ended soon and a cheerful demeanor wasn't a requirement for the role anyway.

"Singapore."

Unconsciously, the agent pulled her face covering a little higher over her nose and intensified her scrutiny of the document.

"You've been to several countries over the past few weeks. Any symptoms of COVID?"

"None. I feel fine and have no fever." He always followed the advice of experts who suggested giving as little information as possible at immigration, answering questions directly, and volunteering no details.

"You don't have an address recorded in your passport. Where do you live?"

Oh shit. Howard quickly manufactured a partial answer, picturing landmarks he knew, trying to avoid creating suspicion while giving himself a second to put together a better response. He hadn't spent time in Toronto for years.

"Toronto. Downtown Toronto. For the next few days, I'll stay at the Tiantang Hotel. Then I plan to rent an apartment for a few months until this pandemic passes and I can travel once more."

She listened to his answer, then peered down at the document with increased interest and thumbed through a half-dozen pages. She shook her head at one point, glanced up at Howard again, then diverted her attention to her terminal, keying in or retrieving data. Her expression didn't show which it might be.

"You'll either need to do your apartment hunting online or stay in the Tiantang for at least two weeks. You know the federal government is requiring all returning Canadians to self-isolate for fifteen days, right?"

"Yes."

"Do you have a number where we can reach you?"

"No. I lost my mobile phone while I was traveling. I'll have to buy a new one," he lied.

A look of exasperation with the reply created another slow shake of the agent's head and more data keyed into the computer.

"Do you have a copy of the reservation confirmation you received from the Tiantang Hotel?"

With an internal sigh of relief, Howard scrounged in the pocket of his backpack until he found the sheet of paper he'd printed at Stan Tan's guest house just in case. He showed it to her as she keyed more information from that page into her terminal.

"Expect to get a call from public health. Make sure the receptionist knows to put it through to your room, or you'll draw a visit from the RCMP," she said before returning his documents and waving him on.

There was no "welcome back" to Canada this time.

SEVEN

Something positive finally happened.

After confinement for ten days in a tiny cell in an immigration building at Changi Airport, Fidelia Morales heard her name mentioned as people approached. One voice sounded like Sheri Wong's, the attorney sent earlier by local crime boss Stan Tan. The other was unfamiliar. Perhaps an additional guard.

"The news isn't great," Sheri began after a custodian unlocked the cell and she had set up a folding chair across from Fidelia. "We got word from the *Carabinieri* in Milan. They refuse to drop the charges. But they also won't let you travel to Italy for trial. COVID-19 is raging there, and they're shutting down all flights from Asia."

"So I'm supposed to sit here quietly and wait for the pandemic to pass?" She tried to mask her annoyance politely, but a tinge of sarcasm surfaced and her voice rose an octave.

"That's what the Italians might have hoped. But the immigration authorities won't stand for it. They're releasing you to the police force for detention in a station cell."

"You're right. Your news isn't great. And you don't expect me to be satisfied, right?" Fidelia looked the attorney directly in the eye before she asked the obvious question. "So what are you gonna do now?"

Her brow first furrowed with the demand, then a smile may have formed on Sheri Wong's lips as her eyes widened and sparkled above her protective mask. She whispered her words while glancing upward to remind Fidelia authorities might record their conversation.

"Once the police take custody, they have only forty-eight hours to bring you before a magistrate. That judge will decide if there's sufficient evidence to hold you. So far, the *Carabinieri* in Milan has sent nothing."

Sheri Wong nodded twice and winked. Fidelia took a deep breath and processed the tidbit of news. Her attorney appeared confident that the evidence for them to continue holding her in custody wouldn't materialize. Perhaps she had more smarts than it first appeared.

"The immigration people have already called the police, and they should transfer you this evening. Law enforcement won't make their formal request to the *Carabinieri* in Milan until tomorrow morning. We rarely see authorities respond to requests until the next working day." Sheri nodded again.

Fidelia did the math. Suppose the *Carabinieri* performed as predicted with a six-hour time difference. In that case, she'd have her hearing with the judge before they sent off any evidence to Singapore. Odds were, they'd release her—unless Stan Tan mucked up the process as she now feared he might.

"Is *anyone else* aware local law enforcement is taking custody?" Fidelia raised her brows as she asked, still whispering.

Sheri Wong shook her head twice.

By seven-thirty that same evening, she posed soberly for police photographs and tried to avoid dipping her manicured nails into a vile-colored pad for fingerprints.

About an hour later, someone led her to a cell she'd share with two other women. Both looked like illicit drug users by the marks on their arms. Their appearance made her want to recoil, but she smothered her angst, assuring her unease didn't make it to her face. Then it occurred to her that Singapore's penalty for trafficking in drugs was death, and the unexpected thought caused her to shudder despite her efforts to appear nonchalant.

As predicted, nothing positive transpired for the following forty-eight hours. Neither cellmate spoke English, and both suffered from the early stages of withdrawal. At times, they sweated and thrashed in agony. None of the cellmates had an appetite. Fidelia forced herself to eat fresh fruit each time the guards brought some, while she ignored the hot, sticky slop they doled out in bowls. Detention in Singapore offered no pleasure and little comfort.

She avoided counting the hours by reading old newspapers the jail staff passed on after they'd finished. Concentrating, though, was difficult. Rising case counts and dire predictions about the coronavirus spreading throughout the world filled each newspaper. On the second day of her confinement, she abandoned the tabloids entirely after finishing a lengthy article describing some COVID patients' horrible last moments.

Sheri Wong didn't visit the police station, but Fidelia remained optimistic the court session would unfold as her attorney described. She maintained that ray of sunshine until she sat in a courtroom late on Monday afternoon, where a female magistrate glared down at her scornfully.

"Murder is a serious charge, Ms. Morales. We need to allow the *Carabinieri* a few more hours to produce their evidence." She then switched her focus to Sheri Wong. "The timing of your transfer from immigration to the local police seems contrived to thwart the Italian authorities."

Fidelia resisted the temptation to glance sideways and measure her lawyer's reaction. She also forced herself to maintain a blank expression. She didn't even blink until the judge looked down at her papers and declared her decision.

"Ms. Morales will continue to be held for another forty-eight hours, and I want to see a copy of a follow-up email to the Italian authorities within the next hour." With that, she stood and dashed from the courtroom.

The court police officers respected Sheri's murmured request to have a few minutes in private with her client and ushered them into a tiny room just across the hall.

"Sorry, Fidelia. I thought you were home-free. Someone must have figured out our strategy and informed the judge. It surely wasn't me!" She whispered, but her exasperation was clear. "But there's some good news. Your friend Klaudia told me she has already spoken with Uzbekistan. No evidence will come from the *Carabinieri* to Singapore."

"So I have to be patient for another two days?" Fidelia leaned in to be sure her attorney understood the question wasn't idle curiosity. Her body language, tone and scowl conveyed a clear but implied threat should Sheri Wong's second promise fail.

EIGHT

Fort Myers, Florida, Monday March 30, 2020

Suzanne Simpson listened to the summary wordlessly. The entire matter felt like a giant vice, pressing progressively tighter with every detail.

An alert Multima Supermarkets cashier had noticed an odd package under a display featuring chewing gum and candies at the store's express counter. When she picked it up, she detected an unusual noise. She described it as a whirring hum rather than the ticking sound often portrayed on TV or in movies.

Without panicking, the woman gently placed the box on the floor again, taking care to slide it under the desk. Evidently, she hoped a heavy piece of equipment would reduce the damage should it explode. Before alerting her superior, she dialed 9-1-1 and asked for immediate help, waving away customers in the area.

Once emergency services got the information needed to respond immediately, the cashier tracked down her manager, who instantly acted to evacuate the store. To avoid a customer stampede to the exits, the supervisor kept her tone calm as she made a PA announcement. There was a safety concern and all customers and employees must leave by the back doors immediately. She asked Multima staff to implement the evacuation plan and guide the patrons in all the aisles to the rear without delay.

Within minutes, police, fire, and paramedic vehicles converged on the supermarket with sirens screaming, then stopped abruptly outside Multima's location in North Naples. The last remaining employees and customers squeezed out of the warehouse door or jumped down from loading ramps as emergency crews congregated in front of the store.

Someone on Dan Ramirez's team had been monitoring a police scanner at the time and alerted him. Multima's security chief reached the scene just after law enforcement deployed a robot to seek out and retrieve the suspicious package.

"Thankfully, we don't have any casualties," he concluded after relaying the information to Suzanne and the Supermarkets team in

Atlanta. "But you should probably get Hadley managing the media. At least a half-dozen TV and press vehicles are here already."

"He's on the call with us now." She nodded toward their vice president of investor and corporate affairs.

"Do you need me there, Dan? Or would you rather hand out my contact details?" Hadley's default style was to manage a message from afar.

"I'll let you decide, Edward. But reporters are interviewing some of the first responders just hanging around waiting for the robot to do its job." Ramirez was not a fan of the press nor the attention they drew to emergencies like this. "Maybe it would help to get out an immediate release, noting that all customers and employees evacuated safely and emergency teams have the situation well under control."

Competition in the retail supermarket business was among the most intense of any market sector. It was easy to lose customers and painfully costly to win them back. With a brisk nod to Edward, Suzanne agreed.

It took a few hours, but the police retrieved and detonated the package. Quickly, they confirmed it was a live bomb—timed for detonation after the store's closing. It would have caused severe damage if the alert cashier had not acted but probably would not have injured or killed many people, if anyone.

It was that odd timing characteristic that intrigued both the local police and Dan Ramirez. Terrorists usually scheduled their bombs to kill or maim as many as possible. Extortionists sometimes planted fake devices to get attention and impart fear. A bomb designed to explode and do serious damage without significant human casualties raised both questions and concerns.

By mid-day Saturday, Ramirez learned the FBI's operating theories from his contacts there. The explosive used materials and techniques most often originating in Japan or the Koreas. However, someone in the US assembled the device, likely a novice. Traces of the apparatus revealed a high probability it might not have exploded—without some help—because the digital timer had multiple defective parts.

Sunday morning, Edward Hadley made the rounds of the TV talk shows and calmly explained how brilliantly store staff had responded when they discovered a suspicious package. He repeatedly assured interviewers and their audiences that Multima Supermarkets were safe environments where conscientious employees looked out for their patrons and colleagues.

Sunday afternoon, Gordon Goodfellow called in. The Supermarkets division president wanted to report that in-store traffic at most locations across the Southeast had returned to normal. The Northeast felt no impact from the incident, nor had stores in Canada or the Midwest. Customers there either didn't know about the situation or considered it too far away to be of concern.

However, sales receipts for the past week had plummeted in both Florida and Georgia.

Compared with the same period a year earlier, the company had lost over twenty-five million dollars in revenue. During a pandemic where customers were still hoarding goods and buying on fear, the team in Atlanta pressed hard to ensure those losses were only temporary. Goodfellow had them working overtime to create special incentives for purchasers to return to Multima supermarkets in droves the following weekend.

But it was his last concern that prompted their latest worry.

"Did you receive the email I shot you about my call from David Jones at Jeffersons Stores?" he asked.

The mammoth Japanese conglomerate, Suji Corporation, owned the aggressive competitor outright. Suzanne had indeed read Gordon's message sometime earlier. And she deleted it after the first sentence. Their competitor had proposed to Gordon Goodfellow that they get together to explore the synergies of joining their companies.

Years earlier, Dan Ramirez had warned that Suji Corporation was a legitimate business front for the Yakuza—a Japanese organized crime outfit. It also controlled that country's popular pachinko parlors, prostitution, and drug trafficking operations. She wanted nothing to do with them anywhere in the world.

"You recall Dan Ramirez's opinion of Jeffersons Stores, right?" Suzanne's tone softened the harshness of her query.

"I do. And I told Jones I didn't foresee any scenario in which we'd be able to work together." Gordon's manner was firm and convincing. "He backed off at that point. But over the past few days, I recalled an odd remark he made. I realized I should share it with you."

Goodfellow paused as though trying to recall the precise comment.

"Just before we signed off, I asked Jones why he hadn't called you directly like he had the last time. He said he knew you would be a hard sell, so he'd try to get me onside first. Then—almost as an afterthought—he added that since neither of us shared his vision, he'd have to consider less subtle ways of attracting our attention."

"And you're thinking a bomb in one of our stores might be his idea of less subtle?" Suzanne took a deep breath as she processed the possibility.

"I didn't initially, but that kind of malicious mischief may not be out of the question."

She made a meeting with Dan Ramirez her first agenda item of the week. He shook his head in disbelief after she recounted her conversation with Goodfellow and the concern he raised.

"It's hard to say. Jeffersons Stores belongs to people who play by some nasty and unconventional rules. But planting a bomb because an executive showed no interest in a merger? It doesn't sound like a good way to lay the foundation for a smooth company integration with all the synergies you corporate folks always look for." He managed a rueful grin to accent his attempt at levity. As a former FBI deputy director, he also correctly realized humor was not his strong suit.

"Have your contacts in Naples got any theories about motive or any leads?"

"They're drawing blanks so far," Ramirez conceded. "Although the materials used in the bomb seem to be sourced in Asia, they are all readily available here in the US as well. We can't leap to any immediate conclusions about Yakuza or Jeffersons Stores' involvement."

"Regardless, I think we'll need to update our security procedures manual for the retail outlets and conduct some training with personnel to be alert. We can't assume staff in all stores are equally adept. Agree?" Suzanne's sigh and grim expression telegraphed her concern about the well-being of Multima's staff.

"That's a good idea. Shall I work with Hadley and his team to develop something?"

"Yes. Let's do that. Meanwhile, I'll talk with James Fitzgerald. Maybe he can ferret out information from the financial markets that might have led Jeffersons to become more aggressive."

Eileen signaled an end to their discussion with a wave to get her attention and a polite reminder the Prime Minister of Canada was on line two.

NINE

Howard Knight assessed the landscape in downtown Toronto far more attentively than before. The cursed pandemic was rewriting all the rules. A sense of fear had enveloped Canadians. Their Prime Minister had shut down the border with the US except for essential services. Airlines had canceled flights to the Caribbean and Europe for weeks into the future.

He'd toyed with ignoring the self-isolation the immigration agent had ordered him to follow but decided that path was too risky. Canadian governments usually seemed moderate and steady. Now, all levels appeared spooked. Their fears transformed into heavy-handed legal orders and forced massive closures, making it hazardous to attract unwanted attention. His fake passport got him into the country, but misbehavior might well get him thrown out, or worse.

After hanging around his suite in the Tiantang Hotel for five days, Howard made his first call to a secret, memorized FBI number. It took several calls and messages before the agent he'd connected with from Singapore returned his call.

Yes, Interpol had withdrawn the Red Alert. Yes, they remembered the Justice Department undertakings in the agreement for him to enter the witness protection program. No, they couldn't get the process underway immediately because COVID-19 had closed offices and borders.

Howard pressed further with another call a day later and more desperate attempts after that. His official handler finally relented. An FBI agent inside the Toronto facility had adequate security clearance to meet with him and get him into the US consulate. There, they'd have impenetrable communication connections and would listen to his ideas and figure out what might be possible.

Officially, all the offices at 360 Avenue Road in the heart of the sprawling metropolis were closed. But Howard's contact had guided him to a rear entrance used only by employees and provided an access code to get inside the building. He found it easily, keyed in the numbers, then waited for the door to open outward. He stepped into a narrow entryway blocked by another locked door.

Inside, cameras pointed from all four corners, suggesting they monitored his every movement.

His contact had warned of surveillance for at least the initial entry and along the hallways. So Howard wore a plain wool tuque on his head, pulled down to his eyebrows. The collar of his ski jacket covered his throat, plus the bottom third of his face and chin. Behind it, a face mask concealed his mouth and nose. He cast his face downward and dealt with questions from the intercom with the fewest words possible.

"Agent Bronkowsky," he replied when a male voice inquired who he wanted to see.

"Smith, John Smith," he responded when asked his name.

There was no reply. No request to be patient for a moment. Nothing. Howard stood there with his hands deep in the pockets of a warm jacket he'd ordered online for delivery to the hotel. He kept his face lowered, breathed slowly and deeply, and willed himself to stay calm.

Over five minutes elapsed before a door from the entry foyer opened and a short black woman with tightly wound dreads poked her head around it.

"Your code?" she asked, still showing only her unsmiling face and hair.

"Thirty-three fifty-seven."

"Follow me." She swung the door wider to allow him inside and offered a polite but restrained smile. "You can call me Barbara, Barbara Bronkowsky."

Howard trailed the middle-aged woman down a long, pale green corridor on the ground level, noting video cameras mounted every few feet. He kept his gaze fixed on the woman's low heels and rather shapely legs below her knee-length black skirt.

They stopped at an open door to a large, barren and unoccupied meeting room. She led the way in, pulled out a chair at the end of the table, whirled it toward another on the side, and pointed where Howard should sit facing her.

"It's doubtful we can make that work," Agent Bronkowsky pronounced almost instantly after listening to Howard's pitch. It was an aggressive ask but doable despite her initial reluctance. He set out to convince her.

"I beg to differ, Barbara. You're sure you don't mind if I call you Barbara?" He waited for her nod. "We already know your hierarchy will back a foreign refuge for the witness protection program. They supported me and a companion for two years in the Netherlands. It worked fine until The Organization penetrated your internal security and discovered our location."

"Yes, I heard about that. It was unfortunate, but they've plugged that leak now. The foreign aspect of your request isn't what concerns me; it's the scope of your request. It would take far more resources than the Bureau typically spends—human and financial—to harbor you in Canada." Her expression conveyed some empathy, even sympathy, but her manner remained firm.

"I'm not seeking any financial support," Howard insisted, with a tone more brusque than intended. He softened it when he continued. "I have cash. I'm not prepared to share with you where it is or how I access it. But I have more than enough money to buy a luxury suite on the Toronto waterfront and live with no burden on the public purses of either the US or Canadian governments."

"We realize that. Your offshore accounts are not a concern, and we know you can take care of yourself financially," she countered. A smirk, or perhaps a hint of a smile, appeared. "Unfortunately, we don't have enough people in this country with adequate security clearance to manage your case. You're a tough one. There are only two of us—me and a counterpart in Ottawa. We've tried to get more resources for years."

"Again, I have the financial means. You won't need to spend a lot of time on arrangements."

"We can't do anything right now anyway," she said. "The country's shut down. There are no cosmetic surgeons open. Non-essential travel is prohibited. I've left dozens of voice mails over the past few days and no one is returning my calls. It's like the people here decided a pandemic was excuse enough to ignore everything else."

She snorted, then broke into a full-throated laugh at her observation. Howard leaned forward conspiratorially and tacked in a different direction.

"Was the cosmetic surgeon in the south of Costa Rica the internal leak?" He remembered Janet Weissel, his companion in the Netherlands, traveling to a private clinic near Quepos for minor surgery before taking refuge overseas.

"No. It was a systems glitch in the US that someone hacked. The boys in IT think they've eliminated any recurrence." Her tone was just short of sarcastic, perhaps not entirely convinced despite her earlier assurance they'd fixed the problem. "But it's unlikely you'll get a flight there. They're shutting everything down. Only bringing back stranded Canadians."

"Private jets are still flying. Worst-case scenario, I stay in Costa Rica for a few weeks while this pandemic thing blows over, but I can think of more unpleasant places to hang out."

"That part might be easier. I agree. What's more problematic is your idea of us building you a totally different public profile. Do you realize how many person-hours we'd need to create a new background and bio for you?" Barbara asked, shrugging her shoulders and extending her arms in exasperation.

"I'm still a relatively young man," Howard started. He leaned in again and lowered his voice an octave for emphasis. "I'm entitled to a full life using my skills and knowledge to benefit investors. The US government—especially the FBI—owes me. I provided valuable information that led to the arrest and conviction of dozens of my former colleagues in The Organization. The Bureau screwed up and allowed sadistic scum to find me and Janet. Now, she's dead. And I've been scrambling to stay alive and out of their hands for more than a year."

Agent Bronkowsky relaxed her posture. She crossed her short legs at her ankles and leaned back in her chair for a moment, considering. The woman had read his file and appeared to realize Howard's case was compelling. After thinking about it for a minute, she looked directly into his eyes, assessing him. When she spoke, there was just a touch of surrender in her reply.

"It's still high risk. If we could find the resources and expertise to rebuild your history to make you a wildly successful, previously unknown investment guru, facial or voice recognition software might still betray your true identity." Her demeanor turned negative again. "You want to be a public figure while simultaneously hiding your identity in the FBI witness protection program. Hiding in plain sight—the idea is weird, yet kinda bold at the same time."

"I've thought of that." Howard cleared his throat to assure a most convincing tone. "I'll agree in writing never to grant a TV interview. I'll use voice distortion software on my phones. I can set up physical and digital barriers. Let's suppose your surgeon in Costa Rica can make me look fifteen years younger with slightly different features and hair coloring. I'll take my chances with facial recognition by the thousands of cameras spread around the city. With surgery, a hat, and sunglasses, I like my odds."

Bronkowsky was a veteran of the Bureau. Experience showed in her manner, tone, and body language. She'd only move forward in baby steps with extreme caution. Again, she considered Howard's arguments and passion for more than a minute before she spoke.

"I'll run it up the flag-pole. No promises. No expectations. I'll see what they say and get back to you." She stood up to end their interview. Her expression was dour, and her posture rigid.

TEN

Singapore, Wednesday April 15, 2020

Temper tantrums, offers of sexual favors, pleas of innocence, promises, and threats. Fidelia had tried them all over the past few weeks, and still she sat in a tiny jail cell with two other women.

They'd moved the drug addicts to another facility and replaced them with two illegal immigrants from Bangladesh. Neither spoke English.

Her treatment had been civil. They allowed her a daily shower. The food ranged from passable to just plain awful, but they served it twice a day in sufficient quantities. Still, Fidelia had probably lost a few pounds because she exercised as much as possible.

She'd always treated her body as her most valuable asset and used the long hours of boredom to stretch, practice yoga, and do exercises using the walls and floor. Her cellmates never joined, but occasionally offered smiles of either sympathy or curiosity. Those routines had helped bring Fidelia to a place of benign acceptance of her current circumstances. It was impossible to determine precisely what was going on with her case.

Sheri Wong never returned. They met up in court for Fidelia's second appearance. It lasted less than five minutes. A new male judge was now handling the matter of her extradition, he had explained nonchalantly. He had read the evidence received from the Italian *Carabinieri*, and he concluded there was more than enough to honor their request to extradite her to Italy as soon as possible.

With a rap of his gavel, he declared the issue decided, then ignored Fidelia and her attorney as he swung around and left the courtroom.

"I'm shocked," Sheri had claimed when she shifted toward her open-mouthed client. "Your friend Klaudia said the Italian authorities wouldn't send any evidence. The judge didn't share any documents with me, and I've never seen a case like yours decided without an opportunity to ask questions or debate the merits of the facts presented."

Their entire exchange had lasted a mere two minutes and ended with Sheri's promise to investigate and circle back with Fidelia in a couple days. There was little doubt now the local strongman of The Organization was pulling some strings in the background. She had underestimated Stan Tan to her peril.

His influence and finesse with the city-state's government had appealed to her when she sought a secure, long-term location to live and manage The Organization once she solidified power. Clearly, she had misjudged his initial quick acquiescence. He'd projected loyalty and submission to her self-proclaimed authority. He even loaned her an IT specialist and contributed financially to her brazen attack on the Russian mafia from Australia. Now, what might he be up to with her behind bars in a country where he wielded demonstrable sway?

As she stood up from her latest meditation session, a clacking of leather soles on a cement floor warned of approaching visitors. There were enough footsteps that Fidelia turned with her cellmates to check out the commotion. Four male military types in uniforms. Strangely, none appeared Asian, and their demeanor was decidedly different from the usual police representatives in the building. The contingent stopped directly in front of her cell with a command, a synchronized turn, and a loud clamp of their heels.

The men remained in tight formation. One called out Fidelia's name just before a regular guard appeared from behind the group and entered an electronic code on the door, opening it. He disappeared before the military leader looked directly at her and spoke again.

"You are Fidelia Morales?"

She nodded.

"Follow me."

When she walked from the cell trembling, her only option was to assume the space between the speaker and two large, heavily armed men. The experience was terrifying at first.

On a signal, the lead pair strode forward in a formation. Another pair pushed her from behind. They marched down the hallway toward an open area, with Fidelia awkwardly trying to match the length of their strides and pace while forcing herself to breathe deeply.

From behind a counter, in a larger greeting area outside the cells, a uniformed police officer handed her a plastic bag and a list of its contents.

"Check that we returned to you each of the items listed and sign the document at the bottom," the official commanded.

"Who are these people and where are they taking me?"

"These are members of the Uzbekistan military from their embassy here in Singapore. They have agreed with the Italian government to take you into custody and transport you to Milan as soon as possible." He waved a document but offered no opportunity to read or discuss it as he pointed again at her personal effects and the list he wanted her to sign.

Fidelia maintained a blank expression, but allowed her hands to tremble noticeably as the police officer probably expected. She took only a cursory look at the plastic bag's contents before signing and dating the document. Satisfied, the police officer waved her on with no further comment.

Outside, two black Lexus limos dominated the tiny station parking area, and doors of each swung open as Fidelia approached with her military escort. The leader motioned for her to sit in the rear of one with him while the other three climbed into the other automobile.

As soon as the doors slammed shut, the driver spurted out of the lot into the road.

She spun in her seat to look behind them. The second car followed, but they were almost the only vehicles on the roadway. Before she'd left for Australia at the beginning of the pandemic, she'd already noticed significantly reduced traffic. Now, the city looked like a ghost town, with no pedestrians on sidewalks and only a few delivery trucks on the roads. Her escort still said nothing.

With so few vehicles on the streets, they arrived at the Concorde Shopping Mall after only minutes and turned into a driveway. Fidelia knew the location and allowed a smile to form as soon as she saw the sign. Embassy of Uzbekistan. The cars dropped their passengers in front of a secure, discreet entrance. There, the military guard resumed its formation around her—this time without the commands and synchronized marching.

They showed her into a meeting room a few steps later, where two men sat comfortably in oversized leather chairs. Each stood as she entered. It took every ounce of self-control to maintain her composure as a powerful crime boss should. An overwhelming sense of relief and joy swept through her body as she recognized Luigi Fortissimo with her friend, Zefar Karimov, Uzbekistan's deputy minister of finance.

Both men started toward her, but it was Luigi, her primary protector, who spoke first. She'd hung that label on him when they plotted to overthrow Mareno, and it had stuck.

"Great ta see ya, but there's no time ta chat. We'll take one of those cars out front." He held her elbow and guided her back outside. Her friend from Uzbekistan stayed a moment to thank a colleague, then trailed behind them.

"It took you long enough," Fidelia said when she and Luigi were comfortably settled in the rear seat, with the finance minister riding shotgun. She used a tone of gratitude, not complaint. And a warm smile let him know just how glad she was to see him. It also masked her prior assumption he was dead after the shoot-out in Chile. Seeing him was beyond surprising. That he had somehow survived was amazing, pleasantly amazing.

"It took a while ta get back to New York and several days 'fore I found out where ya was." The pulsating vein on his neck signaled his anger, though he kept his voice controlled and without emotion. "Your friend Stan Tan was no help at all. When ya decide ta take him out, let me handle it."

"We're headed to the airport?" Fidelia focused on her most immediate concern. She nodded slightly as she asked the question.

"Yeah, we'll use the government jet ta get ya outta here," Luigi confirmed. "There aren't many planes flyin' right now 'cause of the coronavirus, even the private ones. Zefar will fly us into Tashkent, and ya can hole up at the compound until this pandemic thing blows over."

Fidelia took a moment to process that information and think it through. Zefar Karimov was certainly well connected. The main airport in Uzbekistan carried the name of his distant relative—a former president of the country for about twenty-five years. The guy had helped her several times in the past. She could rely on his discretion and power to ensure no one found her at the compound she owned in Muynak, a small town near the border with Kazakhstan.

She was grateful for the offer, but a significant worry lingered. With the pandemic raging across the globe, what sort of medical treatment might there be in an underdeveloped region? She leaned forward and spoke over the shoulder of her friend.

"Zefar, you know I appreciate your help and love your country. But this coronavirus terrifies me. Are the hospitals in Tashkent ready for it?"

He shook his head twice before he turned sideways in the front seat and looked back at her. "No. I was on a Zoom call at the embassy while we waited for the security detail to bring you over. The cabinet decided today to ignore the virus and treat it like a seasonal flu. We have neither the human nor financial resources to cope with it, so we'll let nature take its course."

"Can you help me get into another country?"

Karimov wasn't officially part of The Organization, but his name and previous line of work earned him his current influential role in the government of Uzbekistan. He was the country's unofficial contact with both the underworld and high-ranking state officials around the world.

Her friend thought for a moment. His face brightened as he thought of something. "Would you consider Vietnam?"

ELEVEN

Ocala, Florida, Monday April 20, 2020

Three days earlier, at the Multima Supermarkets location on East Silver Springs Boulevard in the small city of Ocala, a clerk who stocked shelves in the home goods section felt unwell. The store manager, Jodi Albright, immediately sent her employee to be tested for the coronavirus. Late Monday afternoon, she locked the doors to the store and gathered her staff for a quick announcement in the large storage room at the back, reminding them to stand six feet apart before she spoke.

"Public Health requires me to tell y'all one of our employees tested positive for COVID-19. Now, that same policy forbids me from disclosin' the name of that employee, but y'all know anyway 'cause she told everybody she wasn't well. Regardless, we have ta close the store to customers immediately. Y'all need to go get tested too. Then we have ta thoroughly clean the store overnight."

Jodi studied their reactions. The assembled nineteen people looked at each other uncomfortably as she shared the news, some shuffling their feet restlessly and gazing downward to avoid eye contact. She took a deep breath, drawing her five-foot-four-inch frame as tall as possible, and upped her usual high level of enthusiasm for the sell.

"Headquarters has authorized me to pay double your hourly rate if you'll go get tested right away, then work an extra shift tonight, cleanin'."

None of the crew truly wanted the assignment, so she shouldn't feel disappointed with the response. When she asked for volunteers, only seven raised their hands. It was no coincidence all were recent hires. They were also all recent immigrants from Latin American countries, folks who needed money desperately.

Among the seven volunteers, all were men except one young woman from Guatemala who'd just joined the team. Her name was Kamila and her husband hadn't found a job yet, so she was the family breadwinner. Although Kamila had married just a few weeks earlier, she was also three months pregnant. She'd divulged that to Jodi in her interview to avoid any misunderstandings later. She'd also been the first to raise her hand and probably embarrassed the guys into following her good example.

Reacting to pressure from Multima headquarters, Public Health had agreed to rush test results for the store volunteers so cleaning could start as quickly as possible allowing the store to reopen the next morning. All seven tested negative and were cleared to clean the store. They started their second shift at eight that evening after eating the pizzas Jodi ordered before she left for home.

Most would probably agree no task is more boring than washing shelves and wiping down the goods on them with sanitizers. So the team worked in a cluster, completing two aisles at a time. They made the task more interesting with chatter, loud music, and good-natured kidding.

At first, Kamila enjoyed the kibbitzing. It made her feel comfortable with her new team and gave her new reasons to laugh—something she'd missed recently with the strains of leaving behind her family, emigrating to a new country, and learning she would have a baby. After the first few hours, though, she felt tired and listless from lack of sleep.

About two in the morning, her team of three had advanced about halfway along the paper goods aisle where Kamila prepared to wipe down a section of paper towels. As she squatted down to remove a row of packages from the shelf, she lost her grip on one roll. It tumbled backward and struck an object at the back she couldn't see. Before Kamila could bend her knees further to check, a deafening roar sprayed small parts of her body in every direction.

∽

Suzanne's phone showed 2:23 a.m. when she reached to answer its insistent rings. Usually, she woke on the first or second one, but this morning she was still groggy. Dan Ramirez was calling.

"Sorry to wake you at such an ungodly hour, but we have another crisis." Her chief of security's tone was calm and flat, but there was more to come. "Someone planted a bomb in one of our stores in Ocala. This time, it detonated. We have a lot of damage."

He paused again as Suzanne braced for more news, and a frisson of alarm shot up her spine, causing an involuntary shudder. Before she could bring herself to ask a question, he carried on.

"We have casualties, too. My contacts in the police department tell me we have seven victims—three died, with four people injured."

Suzanne gasped heavily in both horror and shock. It had been almost five years since she'd received a similar call about their supermarket in Kissimmee, Florida. That time, The Organization had planted the bomb, working in cahoots with Jeffersons Stores, trying to intimidate her into a merger of their two companies. Was the same despicable outfit at it again?

"According to police at the scene, it looks like a different device than we found in Naples last month," Dan continued. "They'll need a few days to analyze fragments. Forensic experts are at the site already."

"I'll connect with Eileen to reach the pilots and Edward Hadley," she said. "We'll fly up on the jet to meet with the injured and deal with the media. Will you join us at Page Field in about an hour?"

As they had with Multima's founder, John George Mortimer, after the earlier incident, the three executives spent their twenty-five minutes flying time developing a strategy to work with the media and police.

Dan Ramirez spent most of his time talking with law enforcement contacts to identify the command-and-control structure on the ground, understand the scope of the damage, and determine the best entrance for them to use at the damaged building to avoid a media crush.

Suzanne and Edward focused on what they should share with the press before she made a formal statement. Anger, frustration, and shock about coping with a fatal bombing for a second time underlay their conversations. The incident was real to them, but both had trouble processing the horror. Nothing they'd studied at business school had prepared them for this.

A police car met the group on the tarmac of Ocala International Airport once the plane came to a complete stop at the private jet section. With lights flashing and siren blaring, the officer had them at the scene of the disaster within minutes and dropped them at an undamaged entrance at the rear of the building.

Acrid smoke attacked her senses first. Even in that warehouse section—more than a hundred feet from the actual detonation—the odor was overpowering. She coughed several times as her eyes watered. She gagged after realizing part of the horrible smell was human flesh burned in the fire after the explosion. Someone handed her a bottle of water and a package of tissues.

It was the store manager, she realized, as her blurred vision slowly cleared. Suzanne had met the woman before, during her visits to retail stores in the years she'd managed Multima's supermarkets business, but didn't recall her name.

"Jodi Albright," the manager said. "I'd be honored to shake your hand again, but with this coronavirus around, we're better to keep our distance."

Suzanne nodded and tried to smile behind the mask she'd slipped into place the moment she'd slid into the police car. After sucking in a deep breath, she began her mission.

"So sorry you have to deal with this, Jodi." Her voice broke, and another pause to inhale deeply became necessary. "Have they notified the families?"

"The police handled that right away. It was impossible to identify a few of the bodies, but I had the shift records for everyone scheduled, and one of the injured workers confirmed the names I had were all there when it exploded. They've reached every family."

"Are the survivors' injuries serious?"

"Two are in critical condition at Kindred Hospital just down the road. The other two have minor burns, hearing issues, and are suffering from shock, but should recover. They're all at the same clinic."

For another few minutes, Suzanne posed questions of both the manager and the police officer in charge, slowly regaining her composure and managing the impact of the trauma. Dan Ramirez filled in her gaps with queries about how the event unfolded. Had there been any threats? Demands? Calls of warning? Any labor issues? Any other recent incidents in the community?

After about thirty minutes in the smoky warehouse, Suzanne was ready to meet with the press gathered in a corner of the parking lot at the front of the store. Dan called Edward Hadley, who was attending to the impatient herd of journalists, and learned they now numbered over twenty-five. Multima's vice-president for corporate and investor affairs had persuaded them to place their microphones in a row and stand at least fifteen feet back. Police established a cordon to assure compliance and stationed more than a half-dozen burly officers behind it.

Edward Hadley had already introduced her before she arrived. He explained Suzanne's title, role at Multima Corporation, and other basic biographical information the press might find helpful as they prepared their news stories. When she stepped up to the dozens of microphones in the bank, the cacophony of shouted questions died down. She cleared her throat and looked directly at the cluster of TV cameras.

"The police have already told you what they know about the horrible incident that took place here tonight. They are much more capable of describing the explosion and its aftermath. What I would like to do is offer my heartfelt condolences to everyone affected. We are heartbroken three of our colleagues lost their lives in this terrible blast. We're concerned about the four employees who survived the attack but have suffered injuries. Our sympathies go out to all the family members of the victims."

Suzanne took another deep breath and let the TV audience think about the significance of her words when they watched the video sometime afterward.

"We don't know why someone planted a bomb in one of our stores, killing and injuring innocent workers. We also don't know who might be behind this tragedy and want to assure you Multima Corporation will cooperate with the authorities in every way possible to apprehend and bring those responsible to justice. This store will be closed indefinitely, and we'll reopen it only when we are sure it is entirely safe for employees and customers."

Surprise registered on Hadley's face when she thanked the reporters and walked away from the podium, uncharacteristically leaving him to deal with the barrage of questions that followed.

Dan Ramirez summoned the police driver who'd brought them from the airport. With a blast of a siren to alert the media crowd, and blue lights flashing brightly in the still-dark Florida morning, the officer whisked Suzanne off to Kindred Hospital.

She dreaded meeting the families, but had no alternative. Following the earlier tragedy in Kissimmee, victims' relatives had sent her letters and cards for weeks, expressing how much her visits and concern helped them cope with the traumatic experience.

Jodi Albright was already there; she'd left the bombing scene while Suzanne spoke with the media. Now, she stood in the corner of the waiting area, hugging and consoling two women. Both were spouses of the more seriously injured employees whose condition remained critical. They were all crying, with loud sobs and gasps for air as they struggled to find words to express their anger, shock, and grief. Suzanne joined them.

"I'm truly sorry about your husbands. They'll get the finest medical care as they recover. Doctors do marvelous work these days, and we all have to hope for the best." Tears formed in the corners of her eyes even as she gritted her teeth for more strength.

"And don't worry about the expense. I'll speak with our insurance company later today. We'll make clear they should deal directly with the hospital. I'll also be certain we deposit their regular wages in your bank accounts until longer-term benefits kick in. We want you to think only about helping them to recover fully."

The more mature woman sobbed and tried to express her gratitude but failed. Instead, she swung further around and clutched Suzanne tightly by the shoulders, drawing her closer as she buried a tearful, pained face just above Suzanne's chest. With her other arm, she drew in the younger wife and shared an embrace with both women. Tears trickled down her cheeks, but she ignored them and whispered further condolences.

Jodi Albright waited an appropriate length of time until she murmured to the huddled women that they needed to make more stops that morning.

They had agreed Suzanne's next visits should be to the two employees with relatively minor injuries; the hospital had already discharged them. Jodi directed the police driver to the residences of both workers, following in her own car, while Suzanne touched up her make-up and wiped away the residue of grief.

She briefly visited their homes, expressed her displeasure that they had to deal with this incident, and declared relief that their wounds were not more severe. Again, she provided assurances of any needed financial help.

Three agonizing visits to the bereaved families followed. One family thanked her at the doorway for coming but insisted it was too soon, then closed the door before Suzanne could finish expressing her condolences. The second was grateful for the visit and praised her for reaching out even as the distraught woman wiped tears from red eyes and grimaced with pain. Her last stop was to a newly married husband.

Jodi explained the victim, Kamila, was just into her twenties, pregnant and had only worked at the store a few weeks. She was a legal immigrant from Guatemala. The youthful man who greeted them at the door was timid and tearful. He spoke English poorly but was clearly distraught, and his eyes pleaded with Suzanne for answers as he tried to respond to her questions.

The police officer noticed the language barrier and immediately said a few words in Spanish with a reassuring hand on the fellow's heaving shoulders. After prompting, he invited his early morning guests inside.

For a few minutes, Suzanne shared her expressions of condolence as the policeman translated. Her message seemed to comfort him. Tears subsided, and his breathing became calmer as he listened, nodding his understanding and glancing at his visitor with eyes more trusting and grateful.

Her duties completed, Suzanne thanked Jodi and wished her well. Then she slipped into the police car before collecting Dan Ramirez at the scene of the bombing. From there, they headed back to the jet. He waited until they were airborne to share his news.

"It looks as though one of our employees may have planted the bomb." His brow furrowed as he said the words and looked away from Suzanne's eyes as she recoiled in shock. "The doors were all locked when the first responders got there."

"Didn't they plant it with a timer to delay detonation, as they did in Naples?"

"Perhaps. The forensic specialist found the remnants of a timer, but it wasn't activated. It appears this bomb exploded as it was being placed on a shelf. Explosives planted by amateurs are often so unstable they blow up prematurely. The police are currently working on a theory that one of the injured or dead planted the device but wasn't quick enough to escape before it exploded."

Suzanne was skeptical. For the first time she could recall, her intuition collided with her security chief's opinion. The suggestion an employee might become so disenchanted they'd plant an explosive device—designed to hurt both people and the company—was difficult for her to accept.

For the rest of their flight back to Page Field in Fort Myers, Suzanne traded hypotheses with Dan Ramirez and grilled him on the evidence that led police to believe the attack began with someone inside the store. Even as he drove from the private jet airport to their office, he continued to argue his case.

"Let's keep in mind the possibility the blast wasn't in any way linked to employee dissatisfaction or unhappiness. Sometimes it's greed or desperation. Among Multima's thousands of employees, odds are, more than a few of our people might live with issues of concern."

Dan Ramirez let Suzanne consider that possibility. His dark eyes glanced over to her face for signals, then swung back to the road as he threw out the clincher. "Most likely, we're dealing with a criminal element again. The Organization, or some other nefarious bunch, will always find a crack—a weak link they can penetrate with either threats or avarice—it's human nature. Wilma Willingsworth was a prime example of that."

The raw and daunting memory of her former CFO's suicide—only weeks earlier—powerfully gripped her attention. A woman she had trusted unequivocally had fallen prey to The Organization and had betrayed Suzanne's confidence. It made her more wary and suspicious. There was little doubt Dan Ramirez would remember her recent demands for full background checks on Michelle, Stefan, and James before moving them into new roles. Still, she wasn't convinced of his theory.

"Okay. I get it. We can't rule it out. Where do you think we should go from here?"

"I can talk with my people at the FBI. Only they have the resources and technology to penetrate the underworld. Sadly, the current administration is starving the Bureau of funds for investigations into organized crime. I doubt they'll give it much priority if we can't find an incentive."

"No. I don't agree. I remember when you convinced John George to do that once before. I find it repulsive, no better than a bribe. You're asking to use Multima's money to tip the balance of justice in our favor. I don't support that direction."

She'd scolded her father when she discovered what he'd done, but he'd persuaded her Dan Ramirez knew how the FBI worked better than anyone alive. Again, there appeared to be few options. A bomb threat in one part of Florida, followed by an actual detonation elsewhere in the state only a few weeks later, could be disastrous for the company. Pandemic or not, if customers didn't feel safe visiting a Multima supermarket, sales would plummet.

"Let's see what James Fitzgerald thinks," she said after a long moment.

Once they reached headquarters, Suzanne and Dan stopped in the interim CFO's office and pulled up chairs around his desk. Within minutes, they'd summarized the situation, including Dan's proposal to "incentivize" the FBI to make the investigation of their case a priority.

James's initial reaction mirrored hers. As she had earlier, he argued strongly that payment for services from law enforcement was a slippery slope, and he wanted no part of the scheme.

Ramirez persisted—articulately and forcefully—countering each objection the savvy financial executive raised. After more than an hour of resistance, James and Suzanne both acquiesced, seeing no other viable option. Later that morning, they ordered a wire transfer of five million dollars, a donation to the US treasury, earmarked for research into "organized crime in America."

TWELVE

Quepos, Costa Rica, Monday June 1, 2020

Howard studied his reflection in a large bathroom mirror with bright mid-day light flooding in. An entire month had passed since extensive cosmetic surgery on his face. The expert who performed the procedure and removed the last of the bandages had issued a strong warning. Stay out of direct sunlight as much as possible. So far, he had complied.

It was time to inspect the doctor's work. At first, Howard fumbled clumsily as he inserted tiny contact lenses. They did nothing to improve his vision but changed his eye color from dark brown to a sparkling bright blue. Successful after a couple tries, he slipped on prescription eyeglasses as well. Instead of the previous nearly invisible thin metal frames, his new ones were thick, essentially black, round, and deliberately oversized.

He looked like a pale Steve Urkel from the TV show *Family Matters* in the nineties. That was the look the FBI had instructed the surgeon to create. Computer modeling showed the more Howard resembled that youthful television star, the more likely a mismatch between facial recognition software and file photos of Howard's former face.

He grinned at his unfamiliar mug and noticed his lips were thinner, now almost an outline sketched around his mouth. And his jaw was noticeably larger where the doctor used implants to increase the volume of his chin. It made his face fat compared to its earlier hollow contour.

He also inspected his changed hair color. Previously a naturally fading black with gray speckles, his new light brown dye included subtle highlights that made the current tint look almost auburn. Already, his mop was longer than he remembered at any time in his life. He hadn't cut it for over six months and it curled up at his shoulders. Still, the FBI recommended another few months before getting only a trim, except around the ears. There, he should keep it short.

With a tilt of his head, he inspected those ears. The surgeon gave them more mass and formed them to protrude out conspicuously. Howard thought they resembled the comedian Stephen Colbert's, but one couldn't be choosy if the goal was to avoid detection. Trimming his hair above the ears to draw more attention to them seemed odd at first, but the FBI claimed it did wonders to confuse facial recognition apps.

Worry lines on his forehead had disappeared, along with the tiny wrinkles that used to form around his eyes when he laughed. Now, his healing red skin looked taut and youthful. Perhaps it resulted from shrinking the bags below his eyes and raising his drooping eyelids. Regardless, the surgeon followed the advice of the FBI experts precisely. People and apps should find it more difficult to detect his true identity.

He wandered down the stairway to the main living area in his rental condo, opened the windows and doors, and then savored the fresh, warm air from a gentle breeze. Because his skin was still healing, it was too early to venture outside in the sun. Instead, Howard stood in the doorway and took pleasure in the rustling palm trees, the brilliant colors of dozens of flowering plants, and a cloudless sky. It relaxed his mind and soothed his spirit.

A ring of his high-security FBI phone interrupted the pleasant reverie after only a moment or two. The caller identified himself with a numeric code confirming he was an agent from the US Embassy. He said he'd flown down from San Jose earlier that morning and was in a taxi just outside the condo complex. He needed Howard to let him in to deliver a package from headquarters.

With the lock-release button doing its job, he waited in the unit's doorway as the enormous metal gate swung open slowly. Moments later, a tall, dark Latino strode confidently inside the compound toward the ground-floor entrance and to the first condo unit on a corner. He displayed a badge cupped in one extended hand as he approached, a hint of a smile fixed on his face.

"You must have left San Jose early today," Howard commented in greeting.

"Good morning." The agent's manner wasn't curt, but it was all business as he lifted a small box toward Howard's outstretched arms. In a more polite tone, he added, "Actually, I got away less than an hour ago. It's only a twenty-five-minute flight directly over the mountains."

"Would you like to come in for a coffee?"

"Thanks, but I should stay outside. With this coronavirus circulating, we don't want to take any chances. Be sure you use only the document inside and destroy any others. I'll text you a four-digit number after I leave. Use it to open the laptop, then change your password immediately."

"Will I find any info on the computer?" Howard arched his eyebrows as he asked, expecting a positive reply.

"Two pdf files. The first covers about ten years. The other has background information for your part of the deal. Headquarters said they'll send more after the fourth of July. They want the initial feedback on your assignment then too."

With that explanation and no further comment, the agent touched a finger to his forehead in dismissal and turned on his heel. He set off at a brisk pace back toward a cab waiting outside the open gate.

It might have been nice to enjoy the fellow's company for a few minutes, but Howard understood the drill. The guy was only a delivery service. In a unit of the Bureau where they shared information strictly on a need-to-know basis, Howard's case was much further up the command structure than that fellow would likely ever reach.

The package contained more than a laptop computer and a new passport identifying him as Stuart McGregor, a Canadian citizen. The information inside that laptop was truly the key to his future, but he resisted the temptation to jump right into it. Instead, he fingered the passport.

A genuine travel document was a good start. Within seconds of scrutiny, Howard noticed several tiny differences compared to the fake he was about to destroy. He paused, held up both at different angles to the light, and shook his head. It was a miracle none of the numerous immigration agents who'd checked it over the past few months had caught the minor variances in the one he'd had forged in Barbados.

Over the kitchen sink, he lit a match to set the phony passport aflame. At the last second, he doused the flame and carried the bogus document to the wall-mounted safe. The FBI guy meant well, and his instructions made sense, but Howard knew too personally the limitations of the Bureau.

With the documentation issue settled, he prepared a cup of coffee, took it out to the shaded patio surrounded by shrubs and flowers, and leaned back in a lawn chair. He had to find a way to complete his new assignment.

Negotiations with the FBI hierarchy had been more brutal than Howard had expected. Barbara Bronkowsky first reported her superiors wanted nothing further to do with him. Memories had faded among the Bureau chiefs. The valuable information he'd provided to support convictions of dozens of leaders in The Organization a few years earlier meant little to the bunch currently in charge.

"We have a new regime," she complained. "They're tough on crime with black folks and left-leaning protesters. Truly dangerous criminals like The Organization have no fear under this administration."

"But we have a binding legal agreement," he protested, his tone lamer than intended, so he ratcheted it up a notch. "Have your guys at the top thought this through? Doesn't someone realize the integrity of your so-called witness protection program depends on strict adherence to the arrangement? Do they think they'll get anyone to step forward to help the FBI in the future if they leave me to the vultures now?"

Bronkowsky finally relented and reached out again to her masters at Quantico with Howard's arguments. Every time he followed up with her, the answer was always the same—no interest or progress. He continued to press her to do more.

That routine carried on for days before she called him with an invitation to visit 360 Avenue Road in Toronto once again. When he entered the code she provided, the door opened, and a voice instructed him to use the same room as the last time, just down the corridor from the entrance. When he stepped into the meeting area, there was no one else in the room. A massive monitor on a wall came to life with a face he'd never seen before. The fellow with a mid-west accent spoke at a quick pace. No hello or opening pleasantries. He got right to the point.

"We're not recording this conversation and there will be no follow-up email or any other communication. Candidly, the Bureau couldn't care less about your fate. The jobs of the guys at the top are so precarious in the current administration they expect any help they give you could worsen your exposure. Someone in the justice department— with connections close to the White House—has already been poking around, asking questions to see if anyone knows where you are. Do you understand what I'm saying?"

Howard swallowed hard and nodded once.

"Further down the food chain, a few of us know precisely how you feel and agree we need to intervene. We've got a unit that operates with different policies and less visibility. They're prepared to help you on two conditions. First, everything is off the record. If you accept their rules, all future communication will be with them directly. No more going through witness protection channels. Is that clear?"

"Maybe. It depends on your second requirement and whether they agree to deliver what I outlined to Agent Bronkowsky." He kept his tone even but looked straight into the camera above the monitor with lips pursed in determination. "What else does your ambiguous unit ask of me?"

"They need your help with an investigation into two bombing incidents at Multima Supermarkets. Someone thinks it might involve The Organization and that you have the expertise they need."

"I know nothing about bombs. I'm finished with Multima, and I'm done with The Organization too. I have no interest in working on anything that involves either."

His tone was too defiant. The large monitor on the wall simply went entirely black, completely silent.

He sat there staring at the unlit screen for several minutes, deep in thought. Nothing was as it once seemed. Back when he'd served Giancarlo Mareno in The Organization, they'd laughed and joked about the impeccable morals of the FBI hierarchy. They all mocked the rigid adherence to strict policies and the rule of law, and they'd complained how hard it was to penetrate the Bureau's veneer of upright enforcers of rules and regulations.

It took The Organization several years to worm its way into the lower echelons of the Bureau. But the new administration in Washington tilted the culture with its Justice Department appointments. He cursed his earlier stupid mistake in trusting the FBI. Fidelia had the right idea when she refused to cooperate with the bastards. She'd shrewdly demanded they send her to Europe instead, letting her sell out key figures in the criminal element over there.

Interpol rewarded her with anonymous freedom in Central Asia. At the same time, Howard coped with incompetence and corruption within the Bureau that had endangered his life multiple times in the past year alone. He felt trapped, as if a massive noose tightened around his neck. With Fidelia missing in action, Stan Tan probably up to no good, and the FBI absolving itself of any responsibility for helping him survive with another identity in a different environment, things looked bleak.

Barbara Bronkowsky slipped into the room after a few minutes, carrying two cups of steaming coffee. She smiled sheepishly as she offered one to Howard.

"You gave the wrong answer to his question. You still don't seem to understand. You have no negotiating leverage here at all. None. Zero. Zippo." Her smile had disappeared, but her voice remained calm. "There is only a single correct response to their demands. Either you accept the conditions they establish and help them with Multima, or I've served you your last cup of FBI coffee."

He hadn't responded immediately. Years of watching how comfortable Giancarlo Mareno was using silence as a tool had rubbed off on him. So Howard took several quiet minutes to dissect every phrase employed by that anonymous face on the screen. Barbara Bronkowsky used the time to check emails or something on her phone.

"Your guy didn't make any mention of my requirements," he muttered after a while.

"No? I wasn't on the call, so I don't know what he said. What I received was a text from somewhere in the Bureau asking me to notify them if you accept both conditions—or show you the way out if you decline."

They all had him where they wanted him. It was only a matter of time before someone in The Organization evened the score. Dozens of the guys he'd betrayed had spent millions of dollars defending themselves and still ended up in prison. They would never forgive or forget. The Feds held all the remaining cards. If he stood any chance of surviving more than a few years, a new identity and appearance were essential. And only the FBI had the expertise and power to make it happen.

"Let them know I'll accept all their conditions if they take mine," he had conceded.

$\backsim$

The ace team in the back rooms of the Bureau had done an impressive job. Inside one computer file, Howard found ten years of his new life laid out and ready to memorize. Stuart McGregor had been an average student, ranked in the middle of his class, and graduated from the University of Stirling in Scotland as an expatriate.

The identity they'd created was unremarkable and buried in the archives of a college listed in the intermediate tier in the United Kingdom. Curious minds would soon lose interest if they tried to piece together his educational background. No awards for achievement or distinguishing grades. No quirks or behavior that a fellow graduate might try to recall.

Inside the university's archives, visitors to the yearbook for 1987 would eventually find a younger version of the photo displayed in Howard's new Canadian passport above Stuart McGregor's name. They'd read he was an exchange student from Canada whose parents had emigrated from Glasgow to Toronto after the Second World War. They would also discover the football team he followed, his favorite foods, and a penchant for studying alone. Those were the details about his newly created identity Howard needed to memorize.

Fortunately, his memory was almost photographic. If he focused adequately, he remembered nearly everything he read. And the timing for that kind of mental exercise was perfect. He couldn't spend time outside for a while with the harmful, intense sunlight of the tropical region. His accommodations were comfortable. Few other units in the complex were occupied because of the rainy season and the pandemic. All it took was a brief phone call to summon food and refreshments. And there were no distractions from TV or other forms of entertainment.

For a month, he could learn all about his days at university, followed by the first two jobs he held with Canadian banks. That would probably be the straightforward part.

The other term of the deal was far more problematic. Contacting old sources in The Organization would easily betray his new identity, so how was it possible to satisfy the FBI's cursed demand for information about Multima Supermarkets and the bombs?

THIRTEEN

Hue, Vietnam, Monday June 1, 2020

Two weeks into her temporary refuge in the charming mid-sized town about halfway between Hanoi and Ho Chi Minh City, Fidelia reasserted her authority within The Organization. Her day started by meeting with Luigi.

"Did the European money all arrive okay yesterday?" She had a deal with each of the heads of the criminal element in Europe. It required them to deposit her 10 percent of their monthly take digitally into a numbered bank account in Basel, Switzerland. There were no exceptions allowed, and she showed no tolerance for late transfers.

"Thirty-five million and change in euros from all but Italy. My guy in Gibraltar tried ta find out what's goin' on in Italy, but Sargetti is outta the box today." Alphonso Sargetti was the new country head she had installed when she'd consolidated her power a couple months earlier.

She reached for a nearby burner phone and hit the speed dial code for his private line. It rang several times before switching to voice mail, but she didn't leave a message.

"You have anyone closer to Italy than Gibraltar?" Her tone was just hard enough to convey a tinge of anger. Her primary protector couldn't miss the warning.

"I got a runner in Lyon an' 'n enforcer in San Marino. Either should be able ta get ta Milan within a few hours." Luigi sat straighter, his lips tightened, and his black eyes focused their full attention on hers as he waited for her instructions.

"Send your runner to find out what's goin' on. Sargetti's no dummy, but there might have been a screw-up somewhere. Let your enforcer know we may need him in a day or two. Be sure he sits tight in San Marino."

It was already approaching evening in Europe, so she gave Luigi time to start his calls. She contacted her friend Zefar in Uzbekistan, where he was probably turning his attention to his wife. She didn't bother with greeting formalities.

"How close is Nguyễn to Stan Tan?" Duc Nguyễn was the well-connected Vietnamese cabinet official who'd granted her permission to stay in the beautiful apartment overlooking the Perfume River.

"You're working early this morning," Zefar said with a casual laugh. "Having second thoughts about how secure you are there in Vietnam?"

The deputy finance minister had urged her to return with him to Uzbekistan, but Fidelia had insisted she could take care of herself. That was still the case.

"No. I'm more concerned with finding out precisely what role Tan played in my arrest and confinement in Singapore."

"You want Nguyễn to work it into a conversation somehow?" Zefar appeared reluctant to share information until he understood the end game. This time, he'd need to wait to satisfy that curiosity.

"No. I'm more interested in knowing if he deals with Tan directly or uses an emissary. I suspect he rarely likes to leave a trail back to himself. Sort of the same operating philosophy as you."

"I get it. You'd like me to discover who that intermediary is and how you can connect with them." Zefar was quick. She liked that.

"If possible. Luigi tells me they're watching us here. I'd prefer to create a little more distance between what we're doing and Tan's ears. Be a love and let me know what you find out."

While her primary protector finished talking with the Italians, she rechecked her panoramic perspective of the river. One thing was sure. Nguyễn had considerable influence. Their suite on the thirty-eighth floor of the Vinpearl Hotel was immaculate and separate from other guests. It also had the best view of the city in every direction.

Five or six blocks from the intersection of the Perfume River and a smaller stream called sông Như Ý, she could see the historic Kinh thành Huế, or Imperial City. It was once the capital of Vietnam and remained a source of pride for the local people. She'd jogged past the massive complex earlier that day and every morning since they'd arrived. The first time, she tracked her distance around its circumference at about seven miles.

"Accounts 'n Cayman just updated," Luigi announced, breaking her focus on the city below. "Almost fifty-three mil. 'Bout half the usual take. Must be that damned pandemic."

They had noticed the impact of the coronavirus everywhere they operated and the Americas were no exception. Escort business numbers were way down. Casinos were closed, eliminating the skim there. It was pointless to steal anything because there were no buyers, even if they penetrated any of the thousands of locked warehouses. Because the government was throwing money at anyone with a pulse, even deadbeats were paying their debts. Only drug sales continued to thrive.

"It's a good thing our little job from Australia worked out, isn't it? We'll need to plan another heist if the cash flow from regular operations doesn't improve."

"If ya do it again, let's find an easier mark." Luigi's tone was uncharacteristically sarcastic. "I lost a dozen men in Chile with that last ordeal. Guys I haven't been able ta replace. We're more exposed than ever."

Fidelia took a moment to weigh the severity of his comment. Of course, he was bitter. Those twelve goons killed in South America by a group they'd not yet identified were also enforcers, and all close to Luigi. Plus, the mystery assailants had almost got him, too. Her primary protector had been lucky to escape with his life. Then it had taken days for him to make his way home clandestinely before teaming up with Zefar Karimov to spring her from the Singaporean authorities.

"Maybe we should get you back to New York." She tossed out the comment casually, then homed in on his reaction. His gestures would tell her more than his words.

"Ya need protection here. I know that guy Nguyễn loaned ya a couple bodyguards, but I don't trust him or his two gooks. If my knees weren't givin' me so damn much trouble, I'd even go with ya on those mornin' runs. I oughta stay here in Vietnam. I can still work on recruitin' new guys from here, and I gotta trainer back there who'll get 'em up to speed."

She noticed first the resigned shrug of his shoulder with his opening sentence. Then he spread his hands in frustration as he mused out loud about his apprehension about Nguyễn's assigned men. Finally, he had used a crude slur against Asians. Together, they signaled his concern was more intense than his words suggested.

"I've got Zefar working on a little exercise that will test Nguyễn. In another few days, we'll know if you're right. Did you find a private jet and a place we can tuck it away nearby?" she asked.

"Yeah, it's costin' ya a buck or two, but I found a plane in Alaska. Used ta be leased by the Red Cross. Still has all the markin's on it. Even came 'cross a few ventilators the pilots can donate ta the hospital here. Give ya some cover for a few days if ya need it. We can park it at Phu Bai airport. 'Bout twenty minutes from here. Could probably see it off'n the distance if it weren't so damn hazy out there."

"What's the flying time from Alaska?"

"Thirteen 'r fourteen hours. Depends on headwinds 'cross the Pacific."

As usual, Luigi had done his homework. She valued that characteristic as much as the smarts he showed by contacting Klaudia Schäffer to track down Fidelia in Singapore. Despite some initial reticence, her friend in Germany had provided the information about her plight to Zefar and Luigi. The tip had sprung her from that horrid jail cell.

Reluctant or not, it was time to tap that remarkable, resourceful woman again.

FOURTEEN

Sainte-Agathe-des-Monts, Quebec, Friday June 5, 2020

They shouldn't be in Canada. But two days earlier, Dan Ramirez had interrupted Suzanne's early morning video conference with Michelle Sauvignon in Paris. He whispered in her ear that the FBI had learned of a credible threat to her life. Within minutes, they'd all agreed she needed to be somewhere else until the Bureau could check it out thoroughly.

Michelle had planted a further seed. It would be inconvenient for Suzanne, but it would be a great way to get her friend physically into her new leadership role in Canada, and get some face time with Stefan as an added bonus.

By noon, an elaborate scheme had taken shape. Eileen wangled a "special visit" permit from Canadian authorities for Suzanne to have a brief stay in the country without the fifteen-day self-isolation requirement the federal government had imposed. Her creative executive assistant had also convinced the immigration authorities to grant similar permits for Michelle Sauvignon, her fiancé, and Stefan Warner.

By early afternoon, Suzanne was aboard Multima's Bombardier Global 5000 corporate jet headed toward Paris to collect them. As if a death threat wasn't enough to contend with, the past few days had drained her energy. The supply chain for Supermarkets' businesses around the globe showed signs of fraying, with some producers shut down entirely and others operating at reduced capacities. All those factors had robbed her of many nights' sleep. However, the hum of the engines was hypnotic, and she slept for much of the nine-hour flight.

When she awoke, her brain raced again. The word stress had taken on new meaning. Her unease usually began from the time she rose and continued until well after she turned off her lights at night. That morning, an all-too-familiar concern sprang to the top of her wall of worry.

Almost three months had elapsed since Stefan set out to find her a new chief financial officer. During the early stages of the pandemic, the task had proven challenging for him on all fronts. Dozens of potential candidates for the role were unwilling to consider a job change because of the climate of uncertainty. As with her, some were besieged with problems that needed constant attention to keep their companies afloat. Others simply preferred to see how things sorted out after the lockdowns, travel restrictions, and government COVID-related policies all ended.

Regardless the circumstances, pressure from her board and investors mounted steadily because she had nothing new to report on finding a permanent CFO.

However, she didn't dwell on the issue. Instead, she willed herself to refocus on Stefan and their first in-person reunion in months. As a result, her spirit soared as the jet touched down smoothly onto the tarmac at Orly.

It was about three o'clock in the morning at the almost empty international airport on the outskirts of Paris. She reached for her make-up kit and popped into the jet's restroom once they came to a complete stop. The others would take a few minutes to walk from the private terminal to the plane, and she was eager to touch up her appearance before they arrived.

Despite the ungodly hour, her heart rate bumped up a notch as Stefan poked his head through the doorway, a crooked smile broadening by the second. Two steps into the jet, he paused awkwardly. She stepped forward with her arms wide apart and face tilted upward for a delicious kiss and a long, tight hug. Were they reckless given the pandemic dangers? Perhaps. But her body relaxed more with that welcoming embrace than it had with dozens of late-night yoga sessions in the weeks before.

They all broke into laughter as Michelle and her fiancé, Guillaume Boudreau, squeezed through the doorway behind them. All sensed—at the same instant—the prevailing dominance of the pandemic. It touched every aspect of their personal relationships.

First, Suzanne tried namaste and bowed, but realized that didn't quite work. She followed up quickly with a step forward, hugs and traditional French pecks on both cheeks, regardless. When their greetings were complete, their co-pilot asked politely if they were ready to sit down and prepare for takeoff or needed more time.

They headed to the padded swiveled leather recliners forming a circle around an anchored table. Suzanne grabbed the same spot she'd used for the flight over. Now, a welcoming bottle of water sat in a discreet holder at the front of each seat arm. It took mere seconds for everyone else to stash their carry-on bags and get comfortably settled in the plush beige seats.

They'd caught up on small talk before the jet engines roared to thrust them along the runway and into the air. No one spoke as they gazed out the windows, taking in the lights of Paris as they climbed to cruising altitude. Michelle Sauvignon broke the silence.

"Twenty-five of our supermarkets and the regional warehouse in the city of Guangzhou were all affected by testing today. Seven new COVID cases were detected in the surrounding area, so the local authority commandeered corners of our parking lots to conduct hundreds of tests. They started with our employees before each location opened, then stopped every customer entering our stores, and also diverted cars from the streets into the parking areas to test occupants. It was chaos."

Weeks earlier, the government appeared to have contained the coronavirus to the Wuhan region. But over the past few days, they'd detected over eighty cases in southern China. Local governments had reacted with almost draconian urgency.

"On the flip side of the coin, we're still seeing thousands of positive tests every day in Florida, but Disney plans to re-open its parks in Orlando. It might be good to escape the constant barrage of bad news at home for a few days," Suzanne replied with a sigh. "Does that Guangzhou issue impact more than our stores there?"

"Only in the sense that I expect Western politicians underestimate where this pandemic is headed," Michelle continued. "If we can't limit the spread of COVID-19 in the country with the world's most stringent controls, what makes people think we're finishing up with the coronavirus in countries like the US, where millions of people still take no precautions at all?"

"You didn't, but if you were to ask my opinion," Stefan began with a grimace and a shake of his head, "even if they develop a vaccine by the end of the year, I imagine we'll deal with closures and lockdowns for many months and in lots of places. The epidemiologists seem unanimous there will be a second, and perhaps third and fourth waves."

For two hours, the four bandied about ideas, rumors, and speculation about the pandemic and the impact it would have on their businesses. Then her companions faded. Unlike her, they hadn't had the benefit of sleep earlier, so she let them drowse off into slumber one by one.

Until the dull whining drone signaling the plane's descent woke the others as they approached Montreal, Suzanne plowed through a stack of reports, summaries, and emails. Unfortunately, the Multima jet didn't have a flight hostess, so she'd eaten only a few snacks and fresh fruits during her seventeen-hour odyssey across the Atlantic and back.

Her stomach growled in protest, and a headache formed just above the bridge of her nose.

Eileen had instructed the pilots to land at Montreal's Mirabel airport, used mainly by cargo flights, because it was close to Sainte-Agathe-des-Monts, a town in the Laurentian Mountains north of the city. There was an added benefit to arriving there at four o'clock in the morning. When the captain led the way into the lounge for private jets, they didn't see a soul. Immigration authorities? Police? Terminal manager? There was no one in sight.

The pilot found an exit door to a parking lot, where he spotted a running vehicle with no lights. He called out, and a voice answered from the other side of the van. A man pulling up the zipper of his pants appeared as he came around the front fender into a beam of overhead light from a high pole.

"Madame Simpson?" he shouted toward the terminal.

The pilot gave a thumbs up, and the driver dashed over to collect them at the door. Within minutes, the entire entourage, including the crew, headed northward to the house Eileen had rented for a month. If Suzanne found it possible to return to Fort Myers earlier, Michelle Sauvignon could still use it while searching for a permanent home for her new assignment to the Montreal office.

Travel on winding Highway 15—as it climbed through the mountains from the airport to beautiful Sainte-Agathe-des-Monts—was quick. During the last few minutes of the drive, the dark night faded with a promise of light. When their van came to a stop in front of the house, a short, plump, neatly dressed woman waited for them at the entrance with her arms outstretched and a smile beaming radiantly.

Speaking French, she introduced herself as Florence Carpentier, host and custodian for their stay.

They all made their way into the elaborate dwelling, sorted out bags, and wandered through the magnificent home to one of four separate bedrooms. Each had adjoining bathrooms, Florence had announced as she assigned accommodations with animated hand motions.

By the time they settled in, a brilliant sunrise peeked through the mountain caps with hues of daffodil yellow and fiery orange. Everyone temporarily forgot their fatigue as they stood together on an outdoor terrace and traded glowing comments about the majesty of the location and their good fortune in catching such a beautiful sight.

Only moments later, friendly Florence sang out to them that breakfast was served.

They ambled from the stoop and followed their host toward an alluring combination of scents, including bacon, toast, and home-fried potatoes. As they entered the living room, every head instinctively tilted upward to a massive wood ceiling that rose to a sharp peak over forty feet from the ground. Knotted pine floors, walls, and ceilings all generated a warmth that relaxed the group, leading to repeated murmurs of appreciation and awe.

From the living area, they stepped into a country-style kitchen where Florence magnanimously pointed with an outstretched arm toward a counter laden with food. Beyond it, a tall square wooden table, where eight adults could comfortably sit and eat, looked prepared for a feast.

Clusters of fruit overflowed gigantic bowls. Warm, fresh bread and toast covered an oval plate while their wheat aromas teased taste buds. Another large bowl barely contained a heaping portion of muesli. Beside it was an array of assorted cheeses with colors ranging from white to brown. Suspended over a burner heating its bottom, a single tray extended almost halfway along the counter. In it were eggs prepared three different ways, along with stacks of bacon, ham, and home-style fried potatoes.

Florence grinned from ear to ear as her hungry guests found their plates piled high after sampling each choice from her buffet of culinary delights. For about an hour, they ate, shared stories, relaxed, and rejuvenated their spirits after the long trip. When their host offered everyone a third cup of coffee, the pilots excused themselves and retired to their rooms at the top of the luxurious cottage.

Michelle suggested she and her fiancé walk outdoors. They left hand in hand, casually swinging their arms as they set off, giggling and laughing along a stone path from the house toward the road.

Suzanne also took Stefan by the hand and guided him into the living room, where she avoided the alluring sofa and instead plopped into an armchair facing a matching one where she pointed for him to sit. There, she established the initial ground rules.

"We'll have some "we" time over the next few days. Lots of it, I hope. But first, we have to get some traction on the CFO role. We're running out of time; the board is losing patience."

Stefan nodded his understanding, stood up, and crossed the room to a briefcase on the floor, then theatrically spun on his heel, opened the case, and pulled out a thick stack of papers. He looked at her with a barely suppressed grin before he said, "I thought you'd never ask."

For over three hours, they studied resumes, letters of reference, and notes Stefan had added to the margins. Suzanne quizzed him about his impressions, concerns, and preferences, drilling down on mundane details as thoroughly as highlighted achievements. They'd packed up the inconclusive scattered documents and huddled around the coffeemaker for a break when Michelle and Guillaume returned from their long walk.

"You guys were gone a while," Suzanne exclaimed.

Michelle's smile evaporated. She looked at her fiancé then took a moment to answer, her voice quavering at first.

"I spent most of the time on the phone. Poor Guillaume got most of his exercise doing pushups on the grass beside the roadway." Michelle tried to smile before her expression became somber. "The Chinese government called our country manager, Amber Chan, on the carpet this morning. It didn't go well."

"What happened?" Suzanne probed her memory bank for recent news out of China.

"It's the pro-democracy riots in Hong Kong. Somebody in the Communist Party suspects our employees' union is harboring dissidents, creating all the havoc in the streets. They ordered Amber to attend a meeting in Beijing where they harangued her for hours." Michelle's usually bubbly manner was subdued, her expression grim.

Suzanne gave her a moment before she asked the obvious question. "How did it turn out?"

"They threatened her with arrest twice in the so-called interview. In the end, they let her return home, but they shut down all pork shipments to our stores everywhere in the country. They canceled deliveries scheduled for today. They ordered trucks already on the road back to warehouses. The government officials gave her seven days to ferret out dissidents from the union and turn them over to the authorities in Hong Kong. If she doesn't, next week they'll stop all poultry shipments. I don't need to tell you those are staples in the Chinese diet. Customers will abandon us in droves."

"What are you going to do?"

"Amber's meeting with the union leaders now to see what light they can shed on the allegations. It's late in the evening there. Riots are raging in the streets again, so she had to hold a clandestine meet up in Shenzhen just across the border with the mainland. She promised to circle back with me after they finished, but she wasn't optimistic about getting much."

Multima's operations in China were among the fastest growing and most profitable in the world. But doing business there came with risks. The thought of appearing before ruthless bureaucrats with blind loyalty to a powerful dictator caused Suzanne to shudder and squirm nervously. Michelle had managed her father's businesses there for a decade and knew some of those government officials personally. Stefan's and Michelle's assessing gazes fixed on Suzanne, waiting for some form of reaction.

"Amber has always had a good relationship with the union over there. Let's see what she's able to find out. In the meantime, how will the stores cope without pork for at least a week?"

"I'm not sure I agree entirely with her strategy. But Amber's management team is buying all the beef it can find and offering it at special prices. It should keep the numbers up, but I hope that doesn't further anger the powers that be in Beijing."

"I expect you'll keep a close eye on it and let me know about any developments. In the meantime, will you have a word with Edward Hadley and figure out the best messaging for us to use with both the media and investors?"

Mere minutes elapsed. They hadn't even finished their freshly brewed cups of coffee when Suzanne's mobile alerted her that Dan Ramirez was on the line.

"Brace yourself. It's bad." Her chief of security used a calm tone and let her prepare before he delivered a message that left her shaken. "Someone planted a bomb at your house in Atlanta. It leveled the entire structure a few minutes ago. First responders report they've seen nothing like it."

She remembered only screaming in horror.

FIFTEEN

Quepos, Costa Rica, Monday July 6, 2020

Not surprisingly, they didn't observe the Fourth of July weekend in the Central American country. As promised, the guy from the FBI office in San Jose called from the gate, asking Howard to let him in for the latest delivery.

"I'll hook it up for you," the young fellow offered when he arrived at the door to the rental unit.

"It" was an optical encryption line card. A twenty-thousand-dollar tech toy that improved the security on his Apple computer immeasurably. He made no claims to technical prowess. However, he realized the assignment the FBI had given him was hazardous and he had little alternative. The unpleasant job was their non-negotiable requirement for arranging cosmetic surgery and creating his new identity.

They wanted him to play on the dark web. He knew the difference between the deep web—harmless data and digitized records—and the dark web for criminal activity from his days with The Organization. When the same guy delivered his laptop computer a month earlier, the FBI had already connected the Onion Router. That let him access TOR servers that evade search engines and supposedly offer anonymity to users.

But Howard hadn't bought the anonymity part. He'd refused to use it until they installed an additional layer of privacy. It made little sense to endure the lingering discomfort of rearranging his face—and the ongoing effort of learning to be Canadian Stuart McGregor—only to be found out. Trying to identify whoever had planted bombs in Multima stores increased the odds of discovery. To make matters worse, the SOBs had now also blown up Suzanne Simpson's Atlanta home.

Someone in the FBI came across clues that may have connected the bombs to The Organization. While they couldn't trace specific names, secret software linked word associations and patterns to users the Bureau believed were operatives of some part of the criminal element. Howard's job was to engage with the people they'd identified and learn more.

"It's ready to go," the young technician announced after toiling studiously for about an hour. "You want to try it?"

Howard had no way of knowing if the encryption filter was actually working. He'd have to trust the FBI and this guy they'd sent to install it. More importantly, did it now impede his access or create any other challenges?

While the technician slipped outside to smoke a cigarette, Howard punched letters and numbers into the keyboard, testing a few of the sites pinpointed as suspicious by the guys and gals at Quantico. He had to make those references gender equal now. They'd just assigned a new liaison for his assignment—Angela, no last name offered.

Before the guy finished his smoke, Howard found the upgraded equipment did nothing to block or impede his access to either the regular or dark web.

"We're good," he said to the technician. "Care to stay for some lunch?"

As expected, the fellow declined the invitation and phoned for a cab. Once the gate opened, he let the guy out, seeing him off with a hearty wave of farewell as the taxi left the compound. It was time to prioritize one other matter before returning to the drudgery of research for the FBI or memorizing copious details about his supposed life as Stuart McGregor.

He lathered on sunscreen, entirely coating his face, ears, and neck, then vigorously rubbed it into his skin for a couple minutes. Today was the first time since surgery that he'd venture outside the condo.

He put on a long-sleeved shirt that covered his arms and slipped into jeans like the locals rather than his touristy shorts. He laced up the Nike shoes he'd bought on his shopping spree in Singapore. Looking into a mirror, he gently positioned a broad-brimmed straw hat that flopped casually over his upper forehead. His final touch: wrap-around dark sunglasses.

Grabbing a bottle of water from the refrigerator, Howard locked up and stepped away from the condo. From the front gate of the complex, he crossed the street and headed on foot toward the downtown area of Quepos. He walked facing oncoming traffic in the mid-day heat and intense sunlight, allowing lots of space between his path and the roadway. There was no point tempting idiots who drove like they owned the highway.

A gradual uphill climb for about thirty minutes brought him to the edge of town, where homes clustered. He surveyed his choices. If he continued to follow the road, he'd walk another half mile downhill, but winding gradually to a point directly below where he was currently standing. He also faced another narrow roadway. It was much steeper but cut the distance by at least half. He cautiously headed down the steep direct route.

Shops and houses lined the quiet street. A few people took a second look at him, not only because he was a stranger, but also one wrapped up like an Egyptian mummy. No doubt they found him a curious sight in the intense heat and high humidity. At least they couldn't see the sweat oozing from more pores than he knew his body had.

Arriving at the bottom of the hill without mishap or interference, Howard resumed his path toward the town center. About two hundred yards later, he spotted a car rental outlet with a half-dozen vehicles strewn about a compact, fenced compound. None of the cars appeared new, but a white Toyota Rush SUV caught his eye. It looked good from the exterior and of relatively recent vintage.

Within an hour, he had tested the car, completed the required paperwork, paid the seventy-five-dollar rental fee, and was driving up the meandering route back to his condo. He didn't stop when he arrived at the complex. Instead, he continued to follow the same winding course for another three miles—just as the GPS instructed—until he reached Highway 34. With an abrupt right turn, he headed toward Panama.

Howard rolled down all the car windows and let a warm breeze blow through. He turned on the radio and found a station playing Spanish rock music. He cranked the volume almost to its maximum with a dramatic twist and boomed along the two-lane road like a carefree teenager. His grin grew broader with every mile.

For the first time in more than a year, he experienced genuine freedom. Tapping his fingers on the steering wheel to the beat, he hummed at times. Often, he laughed out loud and even tried to sing along using his less-than-perfect Spanish. That produced more guffaws as his delight increased.

Threats on his life hadn't entirely disappeared. But the Interpol red alert was gone; the FBI had confirmed it. Cosmetic surgery, a new environment in Costa Rica, and a sense someone had temporarily clipped Fidelia's wings, all combined to create absolute joy. Even if the elation lasted only for a day, he'd take it.

A few miles along the route, the GPS instructed him not to follow the roadway toward Dominical Beach at the intersection. Instead, it advised him to turn to the left, continuing onto another two-lane highway numbered 243. He climbed into the mountains, always wending upward with zig-zag curves overlooking deep ravines with palms, banana trees, and other more exotic vegetation at the bottom. The views and colors proved spectacular.

Drop-offs several hundred yards down moderated Howard's merriment—but only slightly. A wrong move and the vehicle might plunge down sheer cliffs mere feet away from the side of the road. Threatening clouds rolling in from the Pacific Ocean behind him darkened the sky and added mystique to the mix. Happiness, jubilation, apprehension, and no sense of what lay ahead fermented emotions that simple words couldn't adequately describe.

After an hour, the roadway became more level for a few miles, suggesting he had reached the summit of the mountain range. A roadside sign showed mileage to San Jose, which confirmed he'd traveled far enough for the day.

He stopped at a snack bar beside the highway with only adequate space between the building and the pavement to park the Toyota Rush. The bright rental company identifier beside its license plates boldly warned locals he was a tourist, so complaints about his parking were unlikely.

He tried the front door but found it locked. A handwritten sign in Spanish said COVID-19 was the reason.

As he headed back to the SUV, a soft voice called out in English. "*Señor*, would you like a drink?"

Howard turned toward the voice. It was a young woman, probably still in her teens. She wore a T-shirt tied tightly above her waist and shorts as short as any he'd seen. She flashed a mischievous smile and waved for him to follow her.

"We have to close because of the pandemic. But we have a nice spot outdoors at the back with a beautiful view. I can serve you there." Her tone was casual rather than conspiratorial. "Nobody will bother you."

He followed her to a small wooden picnic table like those found beside secondary roadways in America many years before. Its stain had faded to a dull gray, but it looked stable enough.

"I'll have a beer, thank you. What do you have?" Howard inquired.

"Because we're closed, no one can deliver to us. So Imperial's all we have."

"No problem. Imperial will be fine. With a glass, please."

The young woman was correct. The view was spectacular. Across the horizon, mountain tops were entirely green, with foliage right up to the summits. The sky became more overcast and darker clouds hovered low, almost touching the trees. It was the rainy season in Costa Rica, with precipitation almost every afternoon. Likely, in only an hour or two, rain would arrive in a deluge. Air heavy with humidity suggested it might come even earlier.

The young woman left him alone with his introspection and beer, disappearing inside after her delivery. His mood became more somber as his thoughts shifted to the FBI project and their almost unreasonable demands for help with the Multima bombings. The folks at the Bureau had become more desperate for a solution after Suzanne Simpson's home in Atlanta was destroyed.

He didn't doubt the bombings and fire had occurred, but he questioned whether the dots really connected the culprits with The Organization. Giancarlo Mareno was no longer head of the criminal outfit, and it had been a few years since Howard had been part of the gang. But the *modus operandi* still didn't fit.

Mareno had always preached the same message. Keep threats on a business level, not personal. The long-time crime boss insisted company executives rationalized payoffs and extortion demands as a cost of doing business. With private pressures, it became more likely they would run to the police and demand protection.

But the FBI folks suspected it had something to do with the Japanese wing of The Organization that controlled Jeffersons Stores in the US. That posed a more significant problem. He knew the former leader of the Yakuza. But Suji-san had died after Howard went on the run, and he had learned nothing about the guy's successor. Fidelia claimed she had complete control of the Asian arm of the criminal element. Still, it was impossible to know if the Singaporean Stan Tan had as much influence over the Japanese as she thought. And considering Tan's behavior, did Fidelia even have adequate control over him?

He glanced at the time on his phone just as the young woman came back outside. She had changed her outfit. Now she'd put on a sheer, frilly, pink button-down top with no bra. Howard could see the outline of her nipples from a distance, and she had only buttoned it partway. She had also slipped on a skirt, a very short skirt. In fact, his first impression was that it covered no more than the shorts had.

"Would you like another Imperial beer?" she asked with a flirtatious smile.

"No, I'm driving. I need to be careful on these mountain roads. Thanks. I'll just take the bill when you have a moment."

Her face was crestfallen. For an instant, it looked as though she might cry. "Can we prepare you some food? You're the first customer we've had today. It's tough for us with this pandemic. We have no money and no help from the government. Can we cook you a nice Casado? We have fresh fish, and my mother is a wonderful chef."

"I'm sure it's delicious, but I've already eaten," Howard lied. "I'll just take the bill, please."

Rather than wander off right away to fetch an invoice, as he expected, she lingered and wanted to chat. Where was he staying? How long had he been in Costa Rica? How did he like her country? What did he think about its women? He indulged her politely for a few minutes, then glanced at the time on his phone again.

"Are you sure you wouldn't go for just one more beer?" Her tone reflected growing desperation, but he shook his head.

Was that sound a sob as she spun around and headed back inside for his bill? It took longer than expected before she returned. Her eyes were red. She sniffled slightly as she passed him the check and leaned forward enough to expose one breast entirely.

"Would you like some company at your condo?" Her voice was little more than a murmur, inviting but not luring.

She tempted Howard. She was indeed a beautiful young woman, and it had been more than two long months since the last time. Instead, he shook his head, stood up, and reached into his pocket. He pulled out a one-hundred-dollar bill and passed it to her with a smile more reassuring than sympathetic.

"Thank you for your great service. Don't worry about the change."

Her shock turned quickly to an expression that was difficult to assess precisely. She smiled tentatively, but promptly wiped a single tear that appeared in her left eye. In return, he looked away to make it easier for her and headed to the rented SUV out front.

"*Gracias, señor*. Thank you so much," she murmured as he passed.

Howard's drive back down the mountain ridge toward Quepos was as exhilarating as the climb. Occasionally, he gazed down on rain clouds from above, then watched refreshing rainfall nourish the forests below. At other times, showers pelted the windshield furiously for a few moments, then suddenly evaporated into a mist. He met few cars on the way and became increasingly at ease driving through the towering slopes while peeking down into deep valleys as he navigated dozens of hairpin curves.

There was only one major highway on this side of the country, so he retraced his path back toward the town of Quepos. He turned up the volume again as soon as he hit the main thoroughfare. Joy returned as he sang along with the radio and soaked in his tropical surroundings.

Howard silenced the music as he approached the left turn for the route down to the condo and car rental spot. After turning, he popped into a gas station on the corner to top up the tank. Inside, he noticed a wide variety of groceries and snacks, so he also picked up a few things to save ordering from a local store.

He stashed three bags of supplies in the rear compartment, filled the tank, and set off toward town. Logically, he stopped en route to leave the bags at the condo so the ice cream wouldn't melt. He encountered no problem using the big gate's numeric code for entry and parked the car in a spot directly facing his unit.

Cautiously, he surveyed the townhouse from the automobile and found nothing amiss. Carrying the supplies, he unlocked the door, but one of the plastic bags slipped and a box of ice cream tumbled away as he stepped inside. The distraction led him to gather up the wayward dessert and put it in the freezer. Already started, he stashed away the rest of his supplies. Within minutes, he had tucked everything away in an appropriate place.

Before resuming his trip to the car rental station, he finally got around to a check of the apartment. He'd started the habit years earlier and maintained it rigorously. Upstairs in the master bedroom, he headed toward the safe mounted in a wardrobe closet. He'd secured the laptop there.

Howard sucked in his breath the instant he noticed the strip of dental floss on the floor. He'd carefully installed the thin plastic strip on the inside of the nearest doorknob, the one a stranger might pull first. It was no accident. Someone had opened that door after he left the condo. He turned to the bureau and opened the top drawer. There, he found his shirts and shorts rearranged, and the bottom drawer on the left side was ajar. Empty, that drawer had been closed completely. Furthermore, his rental contract didn't include a cleaning service.

Quickly, he moved back to the closet and keyed in the six digits required to unlock the safe. He released a long sigh of relief when he saw the silver tint of the computer.

Gingerly, he fingered the circumference of the device and found nothing. He eased it from the vault and slowly lifted the lid. The screen came to life as usual and his password worked. Howard tilted his head back in careful deliberation. The complex manager had provided two keys to the condo and sworn no others existed.

Next, he checked all the windows and both doors and detected no signs of forced entry. Someone had another key. He brought up Google on the laptop, made some quick inquiries, and then keyed a note on his phone app before closing the device and slipping it into his backpack.

Within ten minutes, Howard had stripped all the clothes from hangers and in drawers, then scrunched them tightly into his carry-on bag. He gathered all the shaving and oral hygiene products in the bathroom and stuffed them into an outside pouch. After one last look around the unit for anything he may have missed, he headed out. With a slam of the door and a check to ensure it was locked and secure, he stowed everything in the rental Toyota and sped toward the compound gate.

As he eased the SUV onto the street, he silently cursed the wasted food he had to leave behind. Especially, the chocolate ice cream.

Returning the vehicle was painless. He was early. The return inspection went quickly, with no attempt to generate additional income by claiming new scratches or dents. As soon as he finished the formalities, he walked out of the office and turned left. Dragging his carry-on, he followed the street from the rental agency as it wound toward the ocean. He'd been to Quepos years earlier and knew precisely where he wanted to go.

Halfway to the beach, he spotted the bus terminal. He headed directly into the tiny station and bought a ticket, then walked to the bay indicated by the clerk. The right bus was parked in its assigned space, its door open, and the driver smoking a cigarette outside. He showed his ticket; the fellow nodded once, and Howard climbed in. At the last row, he stashed his possessions in an overhead rack and settled in for the four-hour trip to San Jose.

The euphoria of only a few hours earlier had disappeared completely.

SIXTEEN

Hue, Vietnam, Saturday July 11, 2020

Fidelia noticed how anxious Luigi was to make someone in Italy pay for her incarceration in Singapore. The guy was as restless as a thoroughbred horse at the starting gate. That kind of default reaction was typical of The Organization and men in general. She intended to change that tendency. Not only with Luigi, but throughout The Organization. At times like this, leaders had to analyze and not react with blunt force.

No matter how many victims Luigi took revenge upon, chances were low he'd ferret out who had masterminded the miserable affair. No, her problems wouldn't end until she tracked that person down.

Of course, her friend Klaudia had been reluctant to get involved again. Too soon after the nonsense in Australia and Chile, she'd protested. But Fidelia had few options other than intensifying pressure. After an hour of coaxing, her German friend once more relented and agreed to use her technology prowess to tap into the private conversations of the guy Fidelia had appointed to lead her criminal operations in Italy.

It took eight days for her to plant digital software on the guy's phone. Then almost another week passed before she heard the exchange between Stan Tan and Alphonso Sargetti. Klaudia played it for them over a landline. The men were trying to be ambiguous. However, since English wasn't the first language of either, it was comical.

"Has the lion come to feed?" the Italian asked.

"Do you mean the lioness?" Tan replied. "I think the lion died in South America."

"They have lions in South America?"

"They used to. The New York lion was slaughtered with some other animals a couple months ago." Tan's curious, oblique reference drew Luigi closer to the speakerphone. "In English, the female of lion is lioness. As far as I know, our lioness is out in the jungle somewhere—despite the evidence your guy produced."

Fidelia smiled dismissively at the amateur attempt to talk about her without using her name. Luigi held up a finger to his ear, silently

90

suggesting she wait to hear more. It took a moment for Sargetti to ask his next juvenile question.

"How do lionesses travel during a pandemic?"

"I don't know. I've scoured every corner of this country. She's not here. I put out the word and heard nothing back."

"Is everyone following the new order?" Sargetti demanded.

"So far. Only the bitch in Australia resisted. We fixed the problem for now but we might need a longer-term solution."

"Yeah. But sit tight until we get more from the Shadow."

"You'll have some contact soon?" Tan's tone of voice displayed a tinge of impatience or annoyance.

"I hope so. You know I have to wait for his call. He'll have my balls if I try to reach him."

On that note, Stan Tan hung up, and Sargetti swore in Italian before the connection broke entirely.

Her friend had played the recording, then listened in with them, and her insights were usually correct.

"What do you think?" she asked Klaudia.

"You know both guys better, but it sounds to me like they're taking orders from this guy they call the Shadow. It seems all kind of eighties movie stuff to me, but they did it without laughing, so they're probably serious."

It took only another few moments for her to persuade Klaudia to continue monitoring Sargetti's calls. It helped that the woman had a natural curiosity, but it had also required a million-dollar retainer fee to seal the deal.

Her next call was to Aretta Musa. Fidelia used her phone with the app that scrambled both sides of the conversation, and they got down to the issues after only the briefest of greetings.

"What's goin' on up there in Singapore? I've bin tryin' to reach you for weeks!" The Organization's Australian country boss sounded genuinely alarmed, but it was too early for her to learn the whole story.

"I had some problems with immigration. They kept me incommunicado for a bit. Didn't Stan Tan tell you?"

"Yeah. That's what 'e said, but 'e wouldn't provide any details. You know 'e changed the payment rules, right?" Aretta's tone blended annoyance with a touch of fear as she posed the question.

"Did you follow his orders?" she inquired. Luigi leaned closer to the phone to hear a confirmation he expected since the recorded conversation between Tan and Sargetti.

"Not at first. I informed 'im I made the deal to share income from the technology heists with you, not 'im. Told 'im I'd follow your instructions until you told me otherwise. The day after I was s'posed to remit the payments to Macau, all our telephone and Internet connections failed. All my people. Everywhere in the country."

"He shut down everything? All at once?" Fidelia expressed appropriate shock to encourage more.

"Yeah. Even the restaurant in front of m' office. I finally had to borrow a cellphone from one of its delivery drivers to connect with Tan in Singapore. He told me our technology would magically start workin' again the day after he confirmed receipt of your twenty-five percent in Macau. Of course, we transferred the money the same day, and it's been okay since."

Luigi's face reddened as he listened. He slammed his fist into the sofa. As he turned sideways to vent his frustration, she saw a vein on his neck pulsating erratically. They finished the conversation by assuring Aretta she should continue to follow Tan's instructions. Fidelia would explain it all to her later.

Luigi pined to set the wheels in motion to take out Stan Tan immediately. He argued Mareno wouldn't tolerate this kind of insubordination for even a day, and she shouldn't either. Regardless, she calmed him down and persuaded him instead to talk with the runner he had dispatched to Milan while she got their Vietnamese protector on the line.

It turned out Duc Nguyễn didn't use an intermediary when dealing with the Singaporean crime boss. That's what he had told Zefar, and he made that point strongly once again to start their conversation. Satisfied, she expanded upon the background for her concerns and her suspicion Tan had caused her imprisonment in Singapore. That unleashed more anger from the Vietnamese.

He absolutely resented the need to involve Tan. What was his value? Why couldn't he just deal directly with Fidelia when Vietnam needed a favor?

Fidelia's pulse slowed, and her body relaxed as the official explained Vietnam's tenuous relationship with the Singaporean. She hit the speaker icon and listened.

"My government resents the amount of cash we send him. Every month, I have more trouble justifying the expense to my colleagues, but we see no alternative. We need his technology, but you can be sure we deliver only money to him."

That meant there was no oath of loyalty. Fidelia arched her eyebrows at the nugget of perspective he had volunteered. Luigi was back and heard it, too. He shrugged and shook his head, also unsure to what extent they should believe him. She tacked in another direction.

"How much are you sending him monthly?" It never hurt to cross-check reported receipts before divulging confidences or extending trust.

"We send about one million each month. We use him only for technology protection, you know."

The number seemed accurate. Tan aggregated the money each of the Asian crime bosses sent to his account in Macau, then forwarded her share to a bank in the Cayman Islands. As she had initially feared, her share for June hadn't shown up yet, but that vital detail was none of Nguyễn's business.

"Has he asked any questions about me?" she probed.

"He said a friend wants to reach you and asked me to let him know if I heard from you or came across anyone who mentioned you in my travels."

"And you didn't tell him anything?"

"I reminded Tan I'm a servant of the government of Vietnam. I don't normally interact with The Organization's other country bosses, only him. We don't need his associates to control our people." His tone was emphatic and raised an octave. Then he added one more snippet of information.

"I didn't understand Tan's meaning, but he said the Shadow wasn't a country boss of The Organization. He was a politician. Then he hung up."

As they said goodbye, she thanked him again for providing refuge. Then she restated her request he not share her whereabouts with anyone. Finally, she told him she'd make it worth his while in a few weeks with an implication the source of friction with his colleagues might go away.

"If we can bypass a middleman, I'm interested in considering whatever you ask," Nguyễn said.

"Any idea who Tan was referring to when he used the name the Shadow?" It was unlikely but merited checking anyway.

He chuckled nervously before he answered.

"I hear that expression only around our government offices. They use it to talk about the dark shadow cast across the globe by your unpredictable American president." Nguyễn laughed again, this time with greater confidence.

"That kind of speculation isn't very helpful," Fidelia said dismissively after she hung up.

Hours of strategizing with Luigi followed. They compared notes about their calls. Next, they digested the implications of Tan's overt attempt to seize greater control of The Organization in Asia. Then they argued about what role her primary protector should play in the subsequent steps and whether she should remain in Vietnam or seek safe harbor somewhere else.

In the end, they decided Luigi would summon the special jet standing by in Alaska. He'd also send for two of his best American bodyguards to stay with Fidelia. For the moment, they'd trust Nguyễn.

Their plan called for Luigi to take the leased private plane on to Europe. He had located a small airfield in a relatively remote area of Slovenia with enough asphalt runway to land the jet secretly with no immigration formalities. His guy in Milan would drive over to pick him up, and together they'd check out the Italian crime boss, Sargetti.

She slept with her primary protector for the first time since he'd sprung her from Singapore. It was odd he hadn't requested their usual romps in bed. In the past, he had panted like a dog in heat, but this visit he was subdued, too shy to ask. Could it be he was losing interest? Fidelia offered him the reward, anyway. It would be timely to remind him how good she could be.

Luigi left a delighted man. It took longer than she expected and initially required more coaxing to bring him to arousal, but he gained enthusiasm and reached a climax. For her, it was a chore. She had one minor orgasm, but the earth didn't shake and there wasn't enough to bother storing it away in her memory bank.

His sexual appetite sated for a while, they slept until minutes before he needed to leave to meet the jet. He scrambled to clean up and finished dressing just as the driver called from downstairs. She passed him his stuffed backpack as he dashed out the door, much like she remembered married American women in TV reruns handing their guys a lunch as they set off for work.

All the right pieces seemed well in motion until five hours after Luigi left. From the jet, he called to tell her the shocking news.

There was chaos back in the US. Overnight, the FBI had quietly arrested over fifty of The Organization's people in Florida, Georgia, and New York. He didn't have all the details yet, but it had something to do with bombings at Multima Supermarkets and Suzanne Simpson's Atlanta home.

SEVENTEEN

Sainte-Agathe-des-Monts, Quebec, Wednesday July 15, 2020

Hiring a new chief financial officer wasn't as easy as one might think. Suzanne was coming to terms with the reality. The best potential CFOs weren't usually folks sitting on the sidelines or looking for a job. Instead, they tended to be already employed in rewarding positions with lucrative bonuses and a dazzling array of company-paid benefits. That's why it was generally easier and less costly to promote a candidate from within. It was a shame she didn't have someone already groomed to fit the need.

More than a month earlier, when she'd reviewed their progress with Stefan Warner, they realized acutely how slim the pickings were for the caliber of person they sought. He and the executive search firm Fencer Duart had toiled diligently for weeks to identify a dozen potential candidates around the globe. All held positions with legally binding contracts, often with non-compete clauses or "golden handcuffs." The contenders were spread across different countries. All spoke English and most were fluent in at least one other language.

Gustaf Duart, the search firm's managing director, had personally screened each of the names Stefan put forward without divulging that Multima was the company interested in speaking with them. Those two expert judges of qualifications and character had narrowed their list to the select dozen. By the end of their discussion, they had pared another three from consideration.

Suzanne, Stefan, James Fitzgerald, and the company's human resources director interviewed the remaining nine individually via Zoom and compared notes. From those discussions, they had trimmed the roster to three. All were impressive. Two were men. None were American. Any of the three were acceptable, and she had no hesitation putting each of the selected candidates before a committee of the board of directors.

The director from Bank of the Americas, one from the Midwest, and Michelle Sauvignon's director friend from France, Ruth Bégin, formed the decisive selection panel. Abduhl Mahinder from the bank was their spokesperson.

"Kudos to Stefan and the folks at Fencer Duart. The quality of the candidates was outstanding. We all agreed on that. And I can tell you we'd be happy to have any of them at Bank of the Americas, too!" He laughed as he made his opening comment to dampen any tension before his follow-up. "Our only apprehension is a lack of diversity among the contenders. Mindful of the current uproar over Black Lives Matter and the civil protests across the country, is Multima setting itself up for criticism about its diversity policies?"

Suzanne had expected that concern. She'd voiced the same observation as they discussed the selection, whittling the number of competitors from nine to three. Two black aspirants from that group hadn't made the cut. They'd agreed Stefan should handle the question when it came up.

"It's a valid consideration. We were mindful of the race issue from the start. We had it high on our list of desirables. But the pool of contenders was limited. There are racialized candidates out there, but few had international experience, one of our prime requirements. Among those who might fit our desired profile, few were interested in making a move right now—a combination of unease about the timing and adequate satisfaction with their current employer."

The human resources director added her comment on cue. "Suzanne asked Edward Hadley to consider how we might best manage the public relations angle should we name one of the three candidates you interviewed. One is Asian, and that would help portray diversity should you select her. However, we also think we have a candidate ready to become CFO in the Supermarkets division. There's a retirement coming up and we need to announce a new finance leader there. The person we're planning to promote is a woman of color. Hadley suggested we try to synchronize those announcements to quell any negative concerns about opportunities for diverse candidates within the group."

All three directors nodded their heads, seemingly mollified by the answer.

Ruth Bégin asked a follow-up question. "It might sound odd for me to say it, but the female candidate seems to have the weakest people skills. We all noticed that. Aren't expert interpersonal skills a vital prerequisite for the position?"

"They are," Suzanne responded. "We all interviewed her individually, and she impressed each of us one-on-one. However, if she didn't handle the group interview well, that's a showstopper for me. Meetings with analysts and investor groups are a crucial component of the CFO's role.

If our woman failed to impress on that characteristic, let's strike her from the list."

Suzanne's reply was designed to remind everyone around the table to focus on the single best candidate for the position. Color, gender, nationality, and a multitude of other factors were secondary to their mission. Multima needed to select the most capable person for the job. Full stop.

Cliff Williams from Chicago raised his hand next. "Between the remaining two candidates, it was almost like splitting hairs to choose a better one for the position. They're both great. But I think we agreed the Canadian was probably the better choice." A grin formed as he paused.

"His experience with Multima's accounting firm, OCD, in America and Singapore, is an excellent asset. The fellow's current job with one of Canada's big-five banks earns him some marks. And his interpersonal skills charmed us all. Plus, he's currently living in Montreal, near our new global headquarters. We won't have to figure out how to get him into the country with this damned pandemic or pay relocation expenses!"

Williams laughed uproariously by the time he got to the end of his statement. They all knew the cost of relocation was the most minor of factors in the equation.

By noon that day, Eileen had scheduled the next meeting of the entire board of directors to approve a management and committee recommendation to finalize an employment agreement with Pierre Cabot.

Michelle Sauvignon slouched on a comfortable sofa in the corner as Suzanne stepped back into the living room of the rental house in the Laurentian Mountains. She had a phone to her ear and her face was chalk white. As she said goodbye, she broke into tears. "Someone has kidnapped my father from his home in Provence. They're demanding we transfer fifty million dollars to an account in Macau before midnight tomorrow or they'll start to remove parts of his body. The *gendarmes* recommend we consider paying it."

EIGHTEEN

Jaco, Costa Rica, Wednesday July 15, 2020

It made little sense to Howard. The graphic scrolling along the bottom of the TV screen broadcasting a CNN news feature confirmed police in France had reported the kidnapping of business tycoon Jean-Louis Sauvignon. The story was probably accurate, but the FBI woman who had pressed him for information for the past half hour couldn't possibly have it right.

Angela was her name. Her manner seemed decent enough. Her voice had an appealing lilt, and she certainly knew financial forensics. He could tell that by her description of a money trail her colleagues at Quantico had discovered. But kidnapping just wasn't a game The Organization played.

When he'd worked for Giancarlo Mareno, the crime boss had drilled it into subordinates around the world that kidnappings were nothing but trouble, no matter how attractive they appeared financially.

"It's too personal," he always said. "Police become far more serious about an issue when it affects people personally. If you want to get rid of a guy, do it. The cops will pay much less attention than if you ask a few thousand for his return alive."

Of course, Mareno was gone. But Fidelia had learned from the master. Howard had seen nothing in her manner or behavior while they'd traveled together in Asia that suggested she might stray far from the crime model Mareno followed. One of the country guys might have turned rogue. Still, it was hard to imagine a guy in France taking the risk of ignoring The Organization's unwritten rules.

Angela wanted him to surf the dark web some more and reach out to her again before morning. She asked politely, but her tone of voice signaled she was under considerable pressure to produce leads she could pass on to the French *gendarmes*. The intensity of her tension was puzzling at first.

After a while, Howard drew on his memory bank to recall Sauvignon's connections and why his kidnapping had escalated so high, so fast, within the FBI. He was the founder of Farefour Stores. His daughter Michelle was a close friend of Suzanne Simpson from college days. In fact, he read somewhere that Multima had bought Farefour a few years earlier.

Dan Ramirez, the chief of security at Multima Corporation, was a former Bureau guy and maintained tight relationships with the hierarchy. Bingo! A couple calls to the right people probably made Sauvignon's kidnapping a new FBI priority even though it all took place in France.

So, Angela and the issue weren't about to go away. The hour was late, but the tiny dining area off the lobby stayed open around the clock. If he was going to work through the night, he'd need some coffee. Howard put on a cap that covered half his face and the wraparound sunglasses. It looked bizarre at that hour of the evening. However, he'd already established a lie with the staff that he had severe vision issues and needed to wear shades all the time.

Outside his room at the end of the second floor, he let his eyes adjust. He gripped the railing that ran along the walkway overlooking the brightly lit twin pools. A couple groups still swam and lounged with drinks nearby. His walk measured about a hundred yards to the stairwell, and his gait had normalized by the time he skipped down the steps to the sidewalk into the motel-style lobby.

Josephine had occupied the front desk when he arrived. Howard had first noticed her French accent the moment she greeted him the evening he'd checked in and laid on his charm. She showed unusual curiosity about his abnormally late check-in.

"We don't see many guests arrive at this time of night without a reservation," she had said. Her tone implied a question rather than a statement as she tilted her head to underline she expected a response. He complied with a hastily construed lie.

"We were staying down in Quepos, but my wife and I had a quarrel and she threw me out." He shook his head remorsefully to emphasize his desperation.

"Couldn't you find a room in Quepos until you patched things up?" Her smile suggested empathy, but the eyes conveyed suspicion.

"She wants a divorce. Told me it was over and I should go home and wait for a call from her lawyer. I didn't want to make things worse, so I took the bus headed to San Jose but then decided to stop here instead. If you have a suite, I'd like to stay here tonight and call her tomorrow. Maybe she'll change her mind."

Josephine had appeared satisfied with his good intentions. However, this was now his ninth night at the little inn beside Jaco beach, and during each interaction, the desk clerk subtly checked to see if he was making any progress on reconciliation. The time had come to shift the story to avoid creating more suspicion.

"*Bonsoir*," Howard greeted her with one of the few phrases he knew in French. "How is my favorite hotel director tonight?"

"If I'm already your favorite administrator, I understand better why your wife threw you out." She pursed her lips flirtatiously, then smiled. "Will you be leaving us soon, or is she still mad at you?"

"There's no progress. I'm going to wait another day to see if she'll talk to me. But if I don't connect with her by tomorrow, I'll know it's all over. She's scheduled to return to Canada."

"Okay. I have a sizeable group of German tourists coming in on the weekend. It might get a little loud. You're welcome to stay, but consider yourself warned." She shrugged and disappeared into a room behind the counter.

As Howard filled his cup with strong coffee, a giant white rooster wandered past. At first, he found it strange to meet a chicken wandering about a reception area, but in this hotel, people accepted it. The proud bird oversaw an entire family of chicks who had the run of the place. Still, it felt odd seeing the little guy there so late at night when his insistent crowing usually woke guests at the light of dawn.

Howard glanced at his watch. He would probably still be working on the damned FBI assignment when the rooster next reported for morning duty.

Only a few minutes had elapsed since leaving his room, but he carefully studied the security markers he'd staged. Behind the door, on the floor, he noticed a clean facecloth he had hung on the inside doorknob as he stepped out. Alarmed, he scrutinized the suite quickly and efficiently—under the bed, in the wardrobe, anywhere a person could hide.

He found no one. Then he dashed back to the wall safe in the closet. It still sat there on a shelf, but someone had tried to steal it. When he went out, the safe had faced outward to an alcove. It now sat crookedly near a ledge, with its electrical cord unknotted and drooping down toward the floor. Nevertheless, its door remained firmly engaged.

He walked back to the toilet and inspected the open window. The screen on the outside looked off-kilter as well. Someone had been in his room during the few moments he was away and left by the bathroom window in a hurry. He locked the window again, then verified the security latch on the front door was engaged. His gut told him to leave right away, but the FBI gal was pressing hard. If the intruder hadn't taken him out when he returned to the room, he was probably okay for a bit. He went to work.

He retrieved his laptop from the safe and dove into the dark net as Angela had requested. He started by searching for references to Farefour Stores. Nothing of interest appeared. He refined the search to the chain's supermarkets in France, Jean-Louis Sauvignon's name, and the *gendarmes*. Nothing significant appeared in either English or French. Of course, with his limited French capability, there may have been something significant, and he just hadn't realized it.

Regardless, after two hours of fruitless searching, Howard leaned back in his chair, raised his feet to the desktop, and racked his brain for other potential avenues to explore.

It was essential to remember the kidnapping of the tycoon was only the latest violent incident involving Multima. It began with the thwarted threat in Naples, then the bombing in Ocala, and the destruction of Suzanne Simpson's house in Atlanta. Should he consider those incidents somehow related?

He pursued that line of thought for some time. If The Organization masterminded those actions, what did they want? It couldn't be money so soon. Fidelia had already stolen hundreds of millions with phony stock trades. Could it be another criminal element like the Russian mafia? They'd become more aggressive in Europe and America and had certainly attracted Fidelia's ire.

After more than an hour of reflection, he thought he might shift from crime to political interests. Suzanne had never shown an interest in politics before. As a dual Canadian and American citizen, she had always carefully maintained a neutral posture publicly. Had her position shifted? Was it possible she had new enemies?

Howard leaped into action again. He abandoned the dark web and started searching on the open web instead. He used keywords he'd heard on TV newscasts or talk shows, words like Antifa, QAnon, right-wing, or left-wing. Of course, pages and pages of references appeared with each inquiry. After he'd scanned through several dozens of lists, one caught his eye. He studied the brief, poorly written article attached initially to a tweet. The diatribe claimed Suzanne Simpson was a secret close friend of George Soros, the international financier despised by the political extreme-right in America.

Moments later, the morning crow of the hotel rooster sounded outside Howard's open window. He grinned and glanced at his watch, then reached for his secure phone and hit the speed dial number the FBI woman had instructed him to use. It rang three times before a woman's groggy voice answered.

"Sorry to disturb your sleep, Angela. But I think you're on the wrong track with The Organization."

She listened for fifteen minutes while he presented his case. They couldn't exclude The Organization because of the apparent internal pressures, but he laid out all the reasons it was unlikely. He summarized his initial research. He described his thought processes. Then he revealed the political angle and why he felt it deserved more focus by the FBI.

Angela listened silently until he finished. Studiously, she asked a few questions to be sure she had it right. She still insisted they couldn't discount The Organization because of its past record of interference with, and intimidation of, Multima. But Howard's new theories merited attention. She'd get folks on it as soon as she reached the office that morning.

Promptly after finishing the call, he began. First a shave, next a shower, and after throwing his few clothes into the carry-on, he set off for the front desk to check out and be on his way. He had nothing against German people, but he should probably avoid a large group of revelers of any nationality.

And if someone had tried to steal his wall safe, it was already past the time to leave. A bit of a shame, really. He would have liked to get to know Josephine better. At any rate, she'd probably buy the story that his wife had called.

NINETEEN

Hue, Vietnam, Thursday July 16, 2020

"It's worse 'n we figured."

Fidelia drew a deep breath to prepare. Luigi liked to ease her in. He thought it made hearing awful news easier, but this call from Europe caused a surge in her heart rate, regardless. She stood and looked out the floor-to-ceiling window of her apartment in Hue at the bustling streets below as she listened.

"Sargetti's hidin' out in the mountains near the Swiss border. *Carabinieri* in Rome arrested a dozen of his men three days ago. Acted on a request from Interpol. Who was acting on a request from the FBI. The guys 'r all out for now, but the interrogations were about those bombings at Multima and a kidnapping. A French guy somehow also related to Multima."

"Sauvignon's his name. I saw it on the BBC news. He used to control Farefour Stores before Multima bought them. His daughter's high in the corporate structure. Seems I read somewhere she was just promoted. Why do they think the men from Italy are involved?" Fidelia asked.

"Talked to one of the guys. He thinks Sargetti's outta the loop. But it's not only Italy. Local police picked up 'bout a dozen men in France, Spain, Portugal, 'n Germany, too. Our fuckin' lawyers are makin' a killin' this month."

His language telegraphed the intensity of his frustration. She changed the subject. "Anybody know anything about the kidnapping?"

"One of our guys in Germany heard some chatter on the dark web out of Belarus, of all the godforsaken places. Didn't mention Multima or Sauvignon, 'course. But referred ta ransom in the conversation. Thought the guy in Belarus might be connected ta Russia but couldn't be sure."

"Yeah, the Germans always suspect someone in Russia. It's like they live in constant fear the Russian mafia will eat their lunch." Fidelia's voice projected more scorn than necessary. So she toned it down when she asked her next question. "How much might this have to do with our heist from the Russians' brokerage accounts back in March?"

Fidelia and her team had stolen over 500 million dollars from the Russians in retaliation for its attempts to infiltrate The Organization. Two of her most trusted technology experts had turned against her at their peril. One was now buried somewhere in Chile, the other in Australia. Luigi continued to search for another rotten apple in the US, in the DC area, specifically.

Could the Russian mafia mistakenly believe Multima had been the culprit? Or might this whole scenario with Sauvignon be an elaborate ruse to suck in The Organization for some other form of retribution? Or could the Russians be trying to make it look like The Organization was involved?

Luigi answered after a long pause to think it through.

"This guy they call the Shadow worries me. We know it's not Sargetti or Tan from their conversation. Whoever it is wields a ton of power over both of 'em. Those Russian bastards aren't just ruthless, they play a mean game. And a half-billion dollars ain't small change. We have ta assume they're behind it 'til we get some evidence they're not."

Fidelia took her turn to consider it. She paced silently along the length of the window. A moment later, she moved a few steps and looked out the other window toward the river, dotted with dozens of little boats carrying people, or boxes of cargo, or piles of recently harvested fruits and vegetables. The diversion slowed her heart rate and gave her time to better process Luigi's assessment.

His rationale made sense. They had expected retaliation—they'd even prepared for it. But their preparations had focused on a technological response. Russians were better at hacking computers than almost anybody. Before the heist, Fidelia had Wendal Randall build a defensive wall he doubted they could penetrate. Part of the reason she had eliminated her technology genius was her strong suspicion Wendal might eventually share those secret defense tools with the enemy.

So far, no one had tried. He probably took the information to his grave.

Suzanne Simpson had played a minuscule role in their heist, and had done it unwittingly. All she did was buy equities for her personal account at a price Howard Knight had planted in her ear. The Willingsworth woman did the actual work, buying back thousands of Multima shares at inflated prices. Then she blew out her brains.

It would have been helpful to know if she took that drastic action out of fear or simply realized that the discovery of her involvement would destroy her career. There were too many loose ends to be sure.

Fidelia changed course again. "Did you get any news about the American guys they arrested?"

"Very little." Luigi drew in a long, deep groan of exasperation before he elaborated. "Our guy at the Bureau 'n New York said some secret rogue element outside the mainstream FBI made the arrests. Those guys have limited oversight 'n operate deep underground."

"Have any of them seen lawyers yet?" Fidelia asked.

"None. Not even sure they're still in the country. Our guy 'n New York thinks this under-the-radar faction spirited 'em offshore. Ta Guantanamo or someplace else no one in the Bureau hierarchy can penetrate."

She shivered at the name of the notorious Cuban site where the American government hid suspected terrorists and a few criminals whose evidence of crime was marginal but suspicion high. She'd spent a couple unpleasant months there and cringed as memories flooded back from the deep recesses of her brain. But Luigi must never know.

"Have your guy keep tryin'. If they've moved them offshore, one might eventually break and spill a lot of information. You'll have a pile of shit to deal with really fast."

"Already workin' on it. He's callin' another one of 'r guys in Florida. Dude's bin to Cuba and knows somethin' about the rogues."

"How about you? Are you still proposing to fly to New York tonight?"

"No. Plannin' to lie low near my grandparents' old house for a while. One other bit of bad news. My guy at the FBI tells me they've posted agents outside all four private airfields 'round Manhattan. Not only do they know I'm alive, the sons-of-bitches plan t'arrest me if I show my face at any of the airports."

Eventually, they decided he'd stay in Milan for a few days and try to bring Sargetti out of hiding for a chat. The enforcer he'd brought in from San Marino had a lead on where they might find him.

Her next call was to Duc Nguyễn. She reached him in Hanoi, where he had finished a meeting with several colleagues to discuss the fees Vietnam paid to Tan every month for technology protection. He was prepared.

"They agree. We'll send the July payment directly to your account in the Cayman Islands and see how he reacts. Our technicians think we can manage for a while should he shut down our computer operations. They backed up everything, everywhere. They'll add a layer of security to our firewalls, and they'll have a supply of personal computers loaded and ready to use for several days if necessary. It could get messy, but I have a consensus to do this to help you. You owe me."

"And if he shuts down the country's systems, will your guys cave and pay him?"

"No. We're confident we can reboot everything in a short time. Some Vietnamese people might be inconvenienced and unhappy for a few days, but we'll manage them."

"It sounds like using a sledgehammer to kill a mouse for twelve million dollars a year. How did you get them to agree?" Fidelia asked.

"I told them the story about Tan shutting down operations in Australia. They realized he could do the same to us if we don't meet his demands one day. We all agreed it's better to face the pain now rather than continue to pay increasing amounts and become ever more dependent on his protection."

"So someone will visit him if there's a blackout?"

"An elite team is leaving for Singapore tonight via Malaysia. They'll be ready to deal with Tan immediately."

"And if there's no outage? If Tan takes no action?"

"Our preference is not to wait. We'd rather eliminate the middleman. If you insist, we'll stand by and dispose of him afterward. But if you give your okay, we can do it before the end of July and send you a bill. You can pay later."

The Vietnamese official sounded like he was about to laugh at his cleverly worded offer, so she stayed silent on the line. This guy was just as anxious for her to order Tan's elimination as Luigi. Men. Regardless of their nationality or race, they all found it too easy to wipe out enemies who complicated their lives.

"Have your team ready, but wait a few more days. If you get rid of Tan now, we might not learn who the Shadow is. That could make everything more difficult. Give me some time to dig deeper and see what we can uncover."

Nguyễn wasn't in on the extent of the Shadow's influence, and it could take a while for Luigi to locate and break Sargetti. She'd have to find another way to penetrate Tan's security wall. When she needed technical expertise, there was no one better than her German friend Klaudia.

She reached for her phone and started calculating how much she'd need to pay to get her support this time.

TWENTY

Sainte-Agathe-des-Monts, Quebec, Thursday July 16, 2020

For the past two days, Suzanne had hardly slept. News out of France was dismal. The *gendarmes* were getting nowhere in their efforts to find Jean-Louis Sauvignon, and there had been no further word from the people who snatched him from his home in Provence. No one had any idea where he was or had any information about his welfare.

Michelle Sauvignon had been distraught from the moment she first learned the news and appeared not only emotional but irrational. When her fiancé first proposed they ask Suzanne to borrow the corporate jet for a flight home, Michelle had strongly resisted, insisting there was nothing she could do. They had quarreled until Stefan intervened and persuaded her that she might be more effective closer to the *gendarmes*. There, she could pressure them in person, he had pointed out.

Ultimately, the pair had left the previous night on Multima's corporate jet to join Michelle's family. Although flights between Canada and Europe were officially prohibited because of the pandemic, her fiancé had found a French government official willing to order an exception under the circumstances.

Many of Multima's moving parts wobbled. While dealing with the crisis in France, negotiating with her insurance agent and police about her destroyed house, and talking with Dan Ramirez periodically about the bombing investigations, Suzanne still had a company to run. And the pandemic created new obstacles to success from every direction.

As she prepared for her first meeting of the day, she enjoyed a mug of coffee and reviewed the agenda Eileen had emailed earlier. Her list of tasks was long and would take from seven that morning until at least eight in the evening. Her thoughtful executive assistant had carefully carved out fifteen-minute gaps in the morning and afternoon, with about thirty minutes for lunch.

She had also attached links to the series of Zoom calls she'd scheduled. All Suzanne had to do was click on the link and concentrate on the subject on tap. Still, no simple task on only a few hours of fitful sleep.

James Fitzgerald's face popped up on the screen first. He was in Chicago at the Multima Financial Services offices to discuss the progress Natalia Tenaz had made in her hunt for a new president for the group. His hand-picked choice to lead the search hadn't produced any acceptable recommendations after almost four months, and Multima's directors were growing impatient. Natalia's image appeared next, followed by the director of human resources for the division, Nancey Willson.

Suzanne casually studied their faces as they greeted each other with practiced informality. When she finished her quick assessment, she got right to the point. "So, where are we in the search?"

James leaned back in his chair with his arms folded, a clear deferral to one of the women, but probably carefully rehearsed.

"I won't make any excuses," Natalia began. "The candidates we've talked with just don't make the grade. We've set the bar high. You've all seen the job description and position requirements." She looked up from her notes, checking that everyone nodded. Satisfied, she carried on.

"At Suzanne's suggestion, two months ago we met with her friend Stefan Warner from France, and he arranged some meetings with Gustaf Duart of Fencer Duart, the executive search firm. Although we don't have a contract with them, they looked at our parameters and found them tough but reasonable. Gustaf Duart even ran our criteria through their database and turned up only a few names that fit the bill. Unfortunately, none of them were ready to entertain a job change right now."

"Where do the interested candidates come up short?" Suzanne asked.

Nancey Willson answered her question. "Entrepreneurial tendencies, mainly. We have several who meet all the education and financial literacy requirements. Most of them have our desired level of practical risk management experience as well. Some also had the people skills we're looking for. Of those, two or three had successfully completed international ex-pat assignments. None showed any intellectual curiosity for the unexplored, and we all agreed that was paramount."

For another half hour, Suzanne asked questions. Natalia or Nancey responded. Meanwhile, James Fitzgerald leaned against his chair back, with his arms crossed, and listened. She signaled their discussion would soon end with a glance at her watch and directed her last query to James.

"You heard the comments at the last board meeting. They're understandably impatient. What do you suggest?"

"It might be time to get more innovative. If our usual processes and channels aren't producing results, maybe we should find fresh ones that might work. This nasty pandemic isn't helping us, but we need to demonstrate precisely the characteristics we're looking for in a candidate. Let's think like entrepreneurs. Let's design a different search model." James spoke the words with a tone of encouragement and scattered a couple smiles among his sentences, but his advice was clear. She had little to add.

"And let's do it fast. I need something concrete for the next meeting of the board. Shall we circle back by month-end?"

It turned out that was only the first line in the sand Suzanne drew that day. Her agenda included virtual meetings with a trade association that lobbied governments on behalf of the food industry, another with an organization representing banks and other lenders. Supermarkets had also requested she join calls to lean on a handful of reticent suppliers who had repeatedly missed delivery deadlines. And Financial Services needed her help for a meeting with the European Central Bank.

Squeezed in among those tasks, she had brief interviews with business magazines in Belgium and China arranged by Edward Hadley, a half dozen individual conversations or meetings with her direct reports, and more than one call from Michelle Sauvignon.

The latest conversation with her grief-stricken friend in France had created another unplanned meeting before she finished their talk. She slipped off her shoes and popped a couple Tylenol to deaden the pain shooting across the region just above her increasingly heavy eyes. One more virtual meeting with Dan Ramirez would probably carry more bad news, and she needed to be prepared before she hit the connect button.

"The *gendarmes* think they're dealing with an amateur," he said, as his face appeared on the monitor. "The latest demand note sent to the Sauvignon family was cut-outs of newspaper articles. Like something the guys saw in a movie. It didn't even mention a specific amount, just 'millions'. My people at the FBI concur. This is amateurish."

"What do they recommend?" Her voice conveyed fatigue too clearly and her posture had slipped. She straightened her back, looked into the camera and added a follow-up with more vigor. "Is there any way we can speed up resolving this?"

"Not yet. The *gendarmes* haven't connected directly. They want to get their expert negotiators involved, try to talk the guys down. They still must find a way to do it. They've got forensic investigators checking every aspect of the messages received, including what kind of paper they used and where they may have bought it. So far, the only thing they're sure about is where it came from—a smallish city called Grodno in Belarus. There's nothing to suggest Sauvignon is anywhere near there though."

"Michelle's a wreck. Is there anything I can share with her to ease her concerns?" Suzanne asked.

"Not really. If we find out the kidnappers are holding her father in Belarus, it will only get more worrisome. Things will become exponentially more complicated. Their government connects tightly to the Russians. More particularly, to the Russian mafia. We won't get any help from the Belarussian regime, and it might create insurmountable roadblocks. It's happened before."

"What more can you tell me about the investigations here? The bomb incidents. My former house?"

"I'm using two channels. You know Angela got assigned to the incident, right? James Fitzgerald's new lady?" Suzanne nodded into the camera. They'd discussed this earlier.

Dan Ramirez received the message and carried on. "She called to get my opinion on something, so I probed a little. She and the people working the case still think some part of The Organization is behind both the domestic and French attacks. Although the bombings seemed less than professional, they think The Organization might have intentionally staged them to divert attention. It's always possible someone else is involved, but that gang's history makes them prime suspects."

"James maintains Angela doesn't indulge in pillow talk about her job at all. Is she close to the action on these investigations?" Suzanne asked.

"Very tight. They've given her another resource. She thinks it's probably somebody in the witness protection program, so she doesn't even know where he lives. He's reputed to have a background in the gang, but they claim he's also an expert about goings-on in the world of commerce. She likes him and listens when he speaks. He's also creating doubt about The Organization's involvement."

"Someone from The Organization?" Suzanne arched her eyebrows inquisitively, then added a bit more. "Knows a lot about business?"

She didn't expect an answer and just left the questions dangling. It was indeed not an appropriate time to mention the name Howard Knight. Nor her surreptitious early morning telephone conversation with him days before the massive Multima share buy-back a few months earlier. That might raise uncomfortable questions.

The timing also wasn't opportune to ask Ramirez to investigate Angela's background as Suzanne had a few weeks earlier for her direct reports and Stefan. She also found it strangely disquieting that an FBI employee would share so much information with her security chief.

She made a mental note to circle back with Dan when the timing worked better.

TWENTY-ONE

Cartago, Costa Rica, Friday July 17, 2020

San Jose had been his original destination. When Howard stepped out of the beach hotel in Jaco that morning, he fully intended to head toward the bustling capital and get lost in the crowds of the big city for a few days. He executed the first part of that plan well.

He had no trouble locating a bus stop for San Jose and didn't wait long for one to arrive. Aboard, it relieved him to find it almost empty with all the windows open. In Costa Rica, drivers seemed to have only two speeds: completely stopped or as fast as the engine would allow. Within moments, the operator achieved the engine's highest output and roared along the coastal road, honking at humans or animals who dared think about crossing his path.

Outside the towns, buses made stops wherever people chose to get on or off. The driver screeched to a momentary halt whenever someone flagged him down or a passenger shouted out to stop. At that time of the morning, the operator made dozens of starts and stops as the sun climbed higher and the heat intensified.

The last bit was the worst. Howard expected the trip to end within minutes after leaving the major Highway 27 for a secondary road. It didn't.

In fact, to travel the mere two or three miles from the highway to the terminal had taken over an hour. Twice, he'd moved to the front of the bus and used his passable Spanish to inquire about their lack of progress. Each time the driver had shrugged with dramatic exaggeration and complained it was always that way in San Jose. Pointedly, he first blamed the chaos on tourists, then the government, then on the *policia*.

From his seat, Howard watched an officer leaning into a front window of a car stopped in the middle of an intersection. In leisurely turns, the uniformed fellow took a drag from a marijuana joint held between a woman's two fingers and then kissed her open mouth to recirculate the smoke. All the while, cars honked, drivers yelled in anger, and traffic advanced at a pace only marginally faster than a turtle he spotted in a gutter beside the road.

While they crept towards the bus terminal, he decided San Jose wasn't his kind of town—even if he might escape into some obscurity. With both thumbs operating at optimum speed, he consulted with the experts at Google to find an alternative.

It was close to noon when they came to an eventual stop with a jolt at the Terminal de Buses Rápidos Heredianos. The moment he stepped down, he looked for the signboard displaying transit schedules. Within an hour, he sat in the back of another bus, headed away from San Jose and toward Cartago this time.

Once again, Google proved correct. Cartago was a beautiful, quiet city—large enough that tourists didn't attract attention and small enough to avoid the cacophony of a metropolis. He asked the driver to stop on the outskirts and walked along the same roadway, looking for a hotel. It took about five minutes to find a place with Wi-Fi, a comfortable bed, and in-house dining. Howard paid cash in advance for a week and started work shortly after settling into his new accommodations.

Angela had already sent three messages to his secure email address. Each included current information and fresh questions or requests for more research or input. Of course, she also needed those responses "without delay."

First, she sent him down The Organization rabbit hole. She didn't seem to realize the criminal element resembled society itself. It kept changing. People came, and people went. She didn't grasp how fluid the criminals could be. Take those arrests the FBI made last month. They snatched fifty of The Organization's guys. Did they think someone had not already replaced those men with new, willing recruits who started their new jobs with fresh enthusiasm and ambition?

He scrutinized the list of a dozen people she wanted more information about. As expected, he recognized only a couple and couldn't shed significant light on either. When Howard had been in The Organization a few years earlier, the guys she named were runners—players so low on the totem pole he knew them only by name. He doubted he'd even recognize them.

Still, he took her requests seriously. She had influence with the Bureau, after all, so he dared not blow off her queries. He thought a few moments for each name, tried to visualize a face that might match it, then wrote one sentence to let her know he could not help. He changed the wording each time so she'd hopefully sense the sincerity of his intent.

For the two he knew, Howard extended the explanation to a paragraph, probing his brain for any potential link to either Multima or its management. After about an hour, he closed the laptop, locked it in the digital safe, and left his room for a walk. His response needed more thought while he strolled along the street to ensure he could add nothing more. He'd press the send button when he returned.

Traffic was light in the streets. Few people walked on the sidewalks, and most of the storefronts were closed, both rare circumstances on a Friday evening. He wore his mask for identity cover and public health compliance. Temperatures were warm, the air still humid from a daily afternoon deluge that came with Costa Rica's rainy season. Perspiration formed on his brow within minutes, and his steps grew just a notch heavier. He covered about a mile before noticing a seafood restaurant on the other side of the road with customers entering and leaving.

He scampered across the roadway and stepped up the cement stairs to the doorway. A burly woman with a hand on her hip and a scowl on her face guarded it. She opened the door but immediately raised her palm, motioning for Howard to stop. In Spanish, she wanted to know if he passed the COVID-19 screening protocol.

"No fever. No symptoms of any illness. I've been in Costa Rica for almost two months, and I'm staying at Hotel El Guarco." He delivered his reply with a relaxed smile. Of course, he left out the part about traveling by bus from Jaco and San Jose that day and lied about the hotel name. He wasn't staying there. He had just passed it a few minutes earlier on his walk.

The woman sprayed his hands with disinfectant, then waved him in, reminding him he could only order food for takeout and to always stay two meters away from others inside the restaurant.

Howard looked for a menu but found nothing displayed. He asked the person ahead of him where he could find one and learned they didn't use menus during the pandemic. Instead, the fellow explained how it worked. When they arrived at the front of the line, the server would tell them what was available that day for a fixed price of twenty US dollars. He could either order it to take away or leave, whichever he chose.

Fried *dorado* wouldn't have been his first choice, but a man had to eat. It had already cooled when he arrived back at the hotel, but a basic microwave oven on the counter resolved that issue while he checked around the room for any signs of intruders. He wolfed down the food with a bottle of water and opened his laptop again while the meal digested.

For a few hours, he searched the Internet and dark web, trying to piece together bits from his own memory bank and the mountain of information he scrolled through repeatedly. Sleep grabbed hold of him, ultimately. Sitting in a wooden straight-backed chair at the desk, he remembered only leaning forward to rest his head on his arm.

When his eyes opened next, a faint outline of dawn penetrated a corner of the curtains on the window above. He stood up, fumbled around the room to find a light switch, and instinctively searched for a coffeemaker. With a steaming hot cup of jet black Costa Rican java arousing his senses, he sat down again in the same chair.

He glanced at his email answers to Angela's questions one more time. After a couple minutes, a single name registered more clearly. Juan Presivo. During Howard's era, the guy worked in the Miami area as a drug runner, bringing stuff into the country from Latin America. He was a loner and his boss didn't trust him with much more than carrying drugs. But Howard remembered a nugget of information.

The top man in Miami noticed Presivo had some interest in politics. In The Organization, guys learned early that politics didn't matter. There was always a way to reach a politician, regardless of party or affiliation. And politicians kept changing on the fickle whim of the American people. Giancarlo Mareno had constantly preached that guys shouldn't wed any ideology or develop a loyalty to one political party or the other. The local crime boss adhered rigidly to Mareno's outlook and highlighted Presivo's penchant for right-wing activity in a conversation. It cost the guy an opportunity to advance.

A tiny morsel of information perhaps, but Angela at the FBI might find it of some use. He added the note to his email message and pressed send.

Howard moved on to her second channel of inquiry. "What sort of network did The Organization have in Belarus?" He read the question three times, each with greater incredulity that she didn't already know the answer.

Opportunities had opened up for the criminal element in Eastern Europe when the Soviet empire collapsed in the early nineties. But the FBI knew well that Russia's notorious secret services morphed into a lethal form of organized crime. The Russian mafia had quickly and viciously established its presence in several of the former satellite states of the USSR. As a result, The Organization—and other Western-based criminal consortia—avoided Belarus.

The reward simply wasn't worth the chase. Poor, with little economic promise for the immediate future, those countries were best for nabbing unwanted or surplus women to feed the prostitution rings.

Gangs preferred to pay a pittance for the girls to thugs supported by the Russian mafia. Forget about collecting loans or selling drugs that western societies were willing and able to buy in far more significant quantities.

The quick answer to Angela's question? None that he knew of, no network at all. And there was little likelihood that had changed since he'd run from The Organization.

Still, Angela deserved a reply, so he summarized his thoughts and then pressed send.

He needed more sleep. Yesterday had been an insufferably long day with all the stressful travel from the beach hotel in Jaco. But habitually, he liked to check out the world's crises *du jour* before he turned in. Howard reached for the TV's remote control and clicked until he found CNN International. He hadn't yet set the device back in its stand before a bright red banner slowly crossed the bottom of the screen:

French billionaire Sauvignon's forefinger received today at Farefour headquarters

TWENTY-TWO

Hue, Vietnam, Friday July 17, 2020

Even after Duc Nguyễn agreed to test Stan Tan's intentions, Fidelia knew she still had to leave the country. With this threatening Shadow character pulling strings from somewhere and a pandemic raging, where could she safely go?

For days, she had mined data on websites tracking the spread of COVID-19. It all terrified her. At night, sometimes she broke into a sweat, unable to sleep. The concept of a virus so infectious and malicious caused a quiver down her spine every time it popped into her head. Just thinking about a ventilator with tubes and who knows what else forced down her throat made her gag in disgust.

Klaudia had finally agreed to come on board for the next crucial stage and Fidelia proposed to meet her in Germany. From there, they'd travel together to a safe location in Uruguay. She calculated the risks. The bodyguards were a problem. If she sent them ahead to Punta del Este, she'd be without security for two days. They'd need at least that long to get to South America on scheduled commercial flights. It might take even longer with the fewer flights available from some airlines.

On the other hand, the Vietnamese watched her all the time. If she forgot about exercising outdoors and stayed inside the apartment, she'd probably be safe. Tan surely couldn't find her location in the secretive country and muster any action so quickly.

The guys would almost certainly let her primary protector know about her new destination. That would raise his questions about how she planned to travel and a myriad of other security details. The solution was simple. She'd bring him into the equation first. As expected, he resisted.

"I get why ya wanna leave Vietnam, and I get that ya think Uruguay's safer and wanna fly there sooner than later. But ya need protection all the damn time. We take a risk even when ya touch down to refuel a private jet. Let me send a squad from New York ta South America. They can scout the place. When they give ya the all-clear, I'll send ya back your Red Cross plane. I'll travel commercial."

His intentions were good. He truly treated her safety with greater care than his own. Still, she had to win this one.

"No. We lost a dozen of your best men in Chile. I'm not comfortable with your B-team. With the crap Tan is causing and the FBI arrests in the US and Europe, I need to shelter in Punta del Este. Period. And I demand your finest guards—the ones right here—to get the place ready." She paused for a moment to let him absorb her insistence. "I'll stay inside the apartment here until it's safe to leave for Uruguay. Nguyễn's people are watching me anyway. Either you tell your guys to get the first flight out of here, or I will."

His team left in a car destined for Ho Chi Minh City a little more than an hour later. From there, they'd take flights to Singapore, then to Haneda, Japan. After, they would travel to Los Angeles, connecting to a flight for Panama. From Tocumen airport to Uruguay. They'd need the better part of two days for the entire trip.

When Fidelia was finally alone in her apartment in Hue, she phoned her friend in Uzbekistan. He, too, resisted at first.

The instant he heard her request, he claimed the plan was too risky for him right then. But she coaxed him a bit, and he eventually succumbed. His capitulation came after she suggested he not just send his government's plane but also travel to Germany with her.

"Google tells me it's 5,803 miles from here to Düsseldorf. With that fancy jet of your government averaging about six hundred miles an hour—and a few minutes on the ground somewhere to refuel—I'm guessing that would give me about half a day to make you a very happy man."

She used her most sultry voice. Zefar Karimov was unbelievably easy to control for a couple reasons. His wife was a traditional Muslim woman. For her, sex was a four-letter word. He also had a wicked fetish for unabashed intercourse on a plane. He was the only guy she knew who not only proudly proclaimed his membership in the mile-high club, he tracked his experiences up there with a spreadsheet on his phone.

Less than eight hours later, Fidelia grabbed her fully packed carry-on bag, took an elevator to the ground floor, and hailed the first taxi she saw. She showed the driver her screen where Google had translated her request to take her to the airport. He asked her a question in Vietnamese, probably aware there were no scheduled flights at that time of night. She flashed him the most charming smile she could muster and displayed the phone again.

With a resigned shrug, he set off. Fidelia noticed another car pull away from the curb immediately after the taxi passed it, and she hit a speed-dial number.

"I can't talk right now, but call off your guys. I appreciated your refuge these last few days, but I'm moving on. Let me know when you hear from Tan."

He laughed. "I expected you. Your friend from Uzbekistan phoned to assure clearance into Hue. We gave it. Sorry you're leaving so soon, but remember you owe me one."

She was ready to end the conversation when he added, "By the way, your mysterious Shadow guy called. Offered me a million-dollar reward if you showed up in Vietnam and I turned you over to Tan. Refused to tell me how to reach him. Just to call Tan."

As the taxi approached the airport, she saw the lights of a descending jet at the same time as her driver. He turned his head to glance at her in the rear seat and grinned, showing three gold teeth. The fellow nodded several times with enthusiasm. He probably sensed that a tip looked promising.

She rewarded the man generously at the front door of the tiny terminal. He waited to see if the doors opened and gave a hearty wave and toothy smile when she stepped into the dimly lit building. There was no one in sight. She checked all around the interior but found only deathly silence. No music. No air conditioning. Nothing.

Fidelia picked up her pace as she walked toward the rear of the terminal. She needed to flee this country before Nguyễn yielded to temptation.

A dozen steps from the exit, she noticed a human form seated on a hard-backed chair slumped over a short counter. A few pieces of paper lay strewn across its surface, maybe casualties of a gust of wind.

She cleared her throat and the armed security guard jumped to his feet, startled and ill at ease. He growled something at her in Vietnamese, so Fidelia pointed toward the jet landing on a runway in the distance. She prayed silently that the aircraft displayed the markings of the Republic of Uzbekistan.

The attendant raised a hand abruptly in a universal signal to halt and muttered a few more words. She stopped.

Satisfied with her reaction, the man pulled a device from his pocket and scrolled. It took only a few seconds for him to find what he was looking for. He held up the phone and squinted at the screen for a few moments with his brow wrinkled and facial expression tense. Then he looked up and nodded once before he reached for a set of keys on the table.

Fidelia stepped out of the terminal doorway as the huge plane approached. From out of the shadows, two figures dashed across the tarmac. Each carried a battery-operated signal light to guide the pilot to an appropriate parking space. As the pilots shut down the engines, a fuel truck appeared on the far side of the airstrip and sped toward the jet.

She stood beside the aircraft, leaning on the handle of her carry-on while the fellows with the warning lights shifted their focus to a portable staircase and tugged it to the airplane. A pilot tested the stairway before he bounded casually to the ground to greet her.

"Welcome aboard," he said in perfect English, reaching forward to take her bag. He motioned for her to climb the steps ahead of him and shared more information. "We'll still be another thirty minutes before departure. Make yourself comfortable in the meeting area until takeoff. Mr. Karimov is in the sleeping compartment. He asks you to wake him after we're in the air."

As they stepped through the doorway, the captain continued. "There are refreshments and fresh fruit in the refrigerator. In the cupboard you'll find some Western snacks. Help yourself to anything."

"Do I need a password for the Wi-Fi?" She knew the drill. It wasn't her first time on the state jet of Uzbekistan.

The pilot showed her a laminated card. The code he gave her was not secure, but it would do for her immediate purposes. He stowed her carry-on bag in a cupboard next to the kitchen, and Fidelia settled into a leather reclining lounge chair that swiveled in a complete circle. She pushed a button, elevated the footrest, and leaned backward to relax for a few minutes.

When the plane reached cruising altitude and was flying smoothly, she went to work. She washed herself as thoroughly as possible in the tiny toilet, brushed her teeth, and gargled mouthwash from the large bottle next to the sink.

Back at her seat, she slipped out of her bra and dabbed on some expensive perfume. As she approached the enclosed sleeping area, she unfastened the top three buttons of her shirt and knocked on the door. Zafar shouted for her to come in.

As expected, he sat on the king-sized bed, propped up against a stack of pillows in front of the headboard. He was entirely nude, his legs spread wide apart, a devilish grin radiating from his bearded face. His eyes sparkled with anticipation. And his penis stood fully erect.

He reached toward a nearby table where a bottle of champagne chilled behind two brimming glasses. He offered one to Fidelia, clutched the other, and proposed a toast.

"To a flight of magnificent delight." He downed about half the glass in a single, long gulp, fiddled with the controls over the bed, and activated some sultry music all in a practiced motion. Without a hello, a hug, or any other gesture of affection, he was ready to begin. "Please take off your clothes for me. Nice and slowly. You know the way I like it."

With her most seductive smile, Fidelia went to work. He wanted her to tease him with her lips and staged peeks at her body as she temptingly revealed small glimpses of her private parts. Greedy anticipation further hardened his erection and gradually transformed his grin into a hungry leer, his eyes never leaving her partially exposed nipples. Sooner than expected, his hand stroked his cock lovingly, and she shed her clothes more quickly.

Zafar might practice restraint and observe the tenets of his religion scrupulously on the ground, but he was a different man in the air. It had been that way since their first time.

After a few minutes, he masturbated furiously, desperately squeezing and tugging for lust-filled gratification. She took off her top and posed temptingly as his eyes grew wider and more animated.

In one practiced motion, she slipped out of her jeans and displayed herself completely naked. Within seconds, Zafar erupted with a yelp of joy and satisfaction as he reached for the towel at his side.

She cleaned him, as always, arousing him again with her tongue after she wiped the sloppy sperm away. It was invariably the same. His erection returned minutes after Zafar wrapped his arms around her. Then he put his mouth over hers and predictably penetrated two orifices at the same time and with the same urgency.

Typically, Fidelia's thoughts drifted while Zafar satisfied his needs with a passion she never understood and never experienced herself. But she performed with feigned enthusiasm, precisely in the way he expected: a muffled groan of delight with unusually deep penetration; a light touch to the bottom of his testicles; her index finger delicately arousing the nerves on his neck or stroking the inside of his thigh.

Welcoming his tongue so deeply he needed to gasp for air, she brought him to climax again. The man was like a machine. He defied the laws of physiology. While most collapsed in a heap after a single ejaculation, an orgasm rejuvenated and stimulated him anew within minutes. A couple hours passed before he signaled he wanted a break and would rest awhile.

That pause proved longer than expected. She had time to shower, file her nails, brush her teeth, and check her email.

Luigi reported more problems. They'd learned where Sargetti was hiding out in the Lake Como area, but someone had tipped him off, and the Italian crime boss had escaped before her primary protector and his enforcer broke into the cabin. The smell of food and cigarettes was fresh, but they found no sign of him when they searched the building and surrounding property. Luigi's email tone showed annoyance, and he had headed back to Milan to regroup.

Duc Nguyễn had left a message, too. His people in Hue reported two unusual occurrences. About an hour after she vacated the penthouse apartment, a woman called from an American number and said only, "The Shadow is not pleased." Minutes later, a fire started in the suite she had used.

His guys extinguished the flames before they spread widely, but they found a broken living room window and some sort of projectile engulfed in flames on the floor. Whatever it was, it'd burned almost entirely before they could extinguish the fire and inspect the device. They'd get it to a lab for analysis but didn't expect to learn much. One other bit he thought she might find of interest, experts traced the mysterious call to a burner phone in Washington, DC.

She cringed at the news and let out a quiet gasp of shock and concern.

Still naked, she looked up and noticed the cockpit door slowly opening. One pilot stuck his head into the main cabin, spotted her sitting in a comfortable position, and promptly slammed it shut. She smiled and moved to find some clothes.

Suitably covered up, she knocked on the door to the cockpit and waited for someone to answer. The co-pilot responded this time and peeked tentatively outside before he swung it fully open.

"I wouldn't wanna see you fellows squirming about up there. Come for whatever you need. I promise to keep my clothes on." She grinned as the fellow nodded, looked away quickly, and dashed into the toilet without a word.

Fidelia curled up in the same swivel chair and had a nap after the pilots had done what they needed to do in the main cabin. A gentle hand on her nape awoke her sometime later.

Zafar was now fully dressed. He touched her cheek as she woke up before he mouthed, "Thank you." His grin combined gratitude with sheepishness.

An unsmiling pilot stood a few paces behind, and he stared at Fidelia for a moment more than necessary before he headed back into the cockpit again. Moments later, the jet began its descent into Düsseldorf.

"I received a message while we were sleeping." Zafar lost his grin and wore a frown of concern. "One of our operatives came across some information she thought our government needed to know."

"What do you mean? An informant, or a spy?" She still smiled, but her voice hardened a touch.

"We treat them the same," Zafar replied coyly, grinning again. "Our girl accidentally overheard an exchange. One party in the conversation was drunk or high, but he was crowing about an animal he had in captivity. The phrase caught the attention of our person, and she listened more carefully. The guy bragged to the individual she was with that he'd be rich in another few days."

Zafar paused and walked over to a boiling teakettle on a counter, poured steaming water into two cups, then brought both over to her swivel chair. He handed one to Fidelia, sat down facing her, and took a sip before he continued. "Our woman feigned sleep, but kept her ear close to the guy she was with and listened. They talked for quite a while, and when he pressed the other for an explanation about why he'd soon become rich, the voice on the phone said he had a French billionaire in his basement. Some company was going to pay millions to get him released."

"You assume that person is Sauvignon?" She was wide awake now.

"It is. The guy our woman was with asked the same thing, and his caller confirmed it was him."

"Fair enough, but why did your girl think this would interest you?"

"The guy she was sleeping with is a well-placed bureaucrat in Russian politics. With all the rumors flying around that someone had spirited Sauvignon out of France to Belarus, it's not surprising they would keep the Russians informed. But here's what you may find curious. Our woman was bedding down with that Russian government representative at their embassy in Washington."

"Do you think the Americans are aware of the conversation?" Most thought the CIA or FBI intercepted all calls into rivals' embassies. She expected a confirmation, but not the shocking news he delivered.

"There's no doubt," Zafar replied too quickly. "Our person also reported the Russian guy's next call was to the White House. She recognized the distinctive voice that answered."

TWENTY-THREE

Sainte-Agathe-des-Monts, Quebec, Saturday July 18, 2020

The ringing phone showed 1:48 a.m. on its screen as Suzanne punched the green icon to accept a call. Groggy, she leaped almost clear of her bed after a piercing cry from her friend Michelle Sauvignon.

"They severed a finger and mailed it to our office!" Her short sentence took an eternity to get out.

Amid heaving sobs, gasps, and someone wailing in the phone's background, Suzanne strained to understand Michelle's comments, then struggled to interpret them. When it sank in, she gagged. Tears flowed from her own eyes, her brain deadened from the shock. She didn't know how long it took for her to respond.

"I'm so sorry, Michelle." The inadequate sentiment was all she could manage as she grasped for words and meaning. A hand touched her shoulder and gave a gentle squeeze of support. She realized it was Stefan. He pulled a blanket up around her and moved closer as the initial trauma abated.

"I don't have the words. I'm so sorry ..." He reached to take the phone from her and punched the speaker icon.

"It's me, Stefan. I didn't hear what you said to Suzanne, but I realize it must be bad. Can you tell us again?"

They heard another series of sniffles and deep breaths before Michelle could go on. This time when she spoke, she'd regained enough composure to better articulate.

"Our security people in the Paris headquarters called me a few minutes ago. They told me the mailroom received a suspicious envelope in the afternoon mail delivery. They immediately alerted the police but didn't report it to me because they didn't want to cause me further alarm." Michelle's tone hinted at either sarcasm or despair. Suzanne couldn't be sure. Her friend took another gulp of air before she carried on.

"The *gendarmes* did their forensic tests. A few minutes ago, they came to my apartment and told me the news. The left forefinger is my father's. There is no doubt."

"We can't even imagine how you must feel," Stefan said in his soft, reassuring tone.

"It gets worse. Just before I called you, I received a message on my personal email. They demand fifty million dollars, or they'll sever his entire hand." Her sobs, gasps, and wails escalated as she forced the words out. "I don't have that much immediately available. And we'll need my father's signature to sell any assets. I need you or the company to help me raise the funds.

Suzanne bristled. She knew Multima's policy about ransom intimately. Her father, John George Mortimer, had argued with her for hours about it in the weeks and months before he died. He'd been adamant. Multima management must never succumb to threats or extortion. To give in—even once—could lead to the gradual death of the company. No matter who. No matter how horrendous. She mustn't capitulate.

"This is a horrible situation," she said. "I feel for you and your dad. Neither of you deserves this kind of hell. I know it probably sounds heartless for me to say, but you and I can't decide this on our own. It has immense implications for the company and our employees. My father always cautioned that if we give in to ransom or extortion, no executive or employee of the corporation would be safe."

"This isn't a corporate issue," Michelle spat out. Her tone was the most vehement Suzanne had heard in their many years of friendship.

"It's my Dad, goddammit! They're cutting him apart and you're worried about company policies. Fuck you! We'll raise the money privately if Multima won't help. And you can shove my job up your ass!"

The total silence that followed cut deeper than the words.

Stefan put both arms around her as Suzanne cried once more with heaving sobs. He pulled her tight and held her without saying a word. In response, she leaned her head against his chest and let tears flow with no attempt to stifle them.

Sometime later, the tears dried up, her breathing returned to normal, and her brain processed the situation more rationally. She reached for her phone and called Dan Ramirez. He answered on the first ring.

"I heard. Already asked Eileen to prepare the jet. I'm flying up there with reinforcements. You'll need a full contingent of security 'til we sort this out." His tone left little room for negotiation.

"We should get some support for Michelle in Paris. She's extremely upset and planning to raise the ransom they're demanding. We should at least slow her down until we have time to talk it through. Have you got anyone nearby?"

He had someone available, only minutes from Michelle's apartment near the Champs-Élysées, and promised to have her there within the hour. Suzanne questioned the need for more security for herself and met Dan's cold, unyielding tone.

"This is non-negotiable. Eileen will find a way to get entry exemptions from the Canadian government for me and at least six people. I think you're probably safest right where you are, and we can build a protective wall around the place. But, it's your choice whether to hang out in Canada or come back here until this is all over. Either way, I must insist on heightened security for you."

Four hours later, two SUVs pulled up to the magnificent country home in the Laurentian Mountains before Dan Ramirez's unit poured out like a synchronized team. They fanned out from the vehicles, surrounded the house, and combed the wooded areas and fields of grass and flowers to clear, then secure, the place.

Florence Carpentier fussed about the kitchen early that morning, making coffee and preparing a mountain of food for everyone, including the new arrivals. There were suddenly so many. Where would they all eventually sleep?

In the meantime, Dan's resource in Paris got to Michelle's house, emphasizing her need for extra security and Dan's insistence she stay until further notice. Once inside, the woman had no success in softening either Michelle's determination to pay the ransom or her adamant refusal to speak with her long-time friend.

Stefan tried her fiancé. Friends for ages, he hoped to leverage their relationship to help repair the widening gulf between Suzanne and her close confidant of over thirty years. Hours of coaxing and conversation were to no avail.

Throughout the day, Suzanne went through the motions of negotiating with Dan Ramirez, the *gendarmes* in Paris, and Multima's Board of Directors. Only the French police considered payment a viable option. Everyone else remained adamant. Negotiations may be desirable, but they should make no payments or concessions.

Stefan diplomatically straddled the fence. He told her he understood the intellectual argument that any payoff opened a dangerous door. The company might never recover from setting this precedent, which could encourage others to emulate the successful attempt.

He also realized that the debate tore at Suzanne's soul. "It must be a terrible burden for you. Michelle's been a great friend forever. I'm sure she's never talked to you that way before, and you share her pain. Still, consider your own safety. If these thugs succeed with Sauvignon, you'll become an alarmingly alluring target. If the company pays millions for a 'has been' tycoon, imagine how much you would garner."

Stefan immediately regretted his choice of words and reached to console Suzanne, but she twisted away. She thought of the man who'd lost a finger, and might soon lose a hand, almost as a father. Her times with the old gentleman were as enjoyable, loving, and rewarding as her moments spent with John George Mortimer. After all, she had known Michelle's dad far longer than her own.

The only concrete decision they made that day was to push the FBI to use its influence and insist Interpol issue a Red Alert.

Of course, Dan Ramirez pressed the right buttons with his former colleagues in the Bureau hierarchy. Before nightfall, Interpol issued its global alert and urged police forces worldwide to redouble efforts to locate Jean-Louis Sauvignon. With the Bureau's clout and finesse, they also convinced the agency to permit an American forensic expert to join the team.

Amid Suzanne's tears, gloom, and fog of despair, James Fitzgerald called to say Angela Bonner had just boarded an FBI jet for Paris. He couldn't provide any other details.

TWENTY-FOUR

Cartago, Costa Rica, Monday July 20, 2020

Angela revealed her relationship with James Fitzgerald in a cryptic email on Sunday night—probably trying to further pressure Howard to produce some useful information.

He found the message among a few junk emails as he downed his third cup of strong, black Costa Rican coffee. His brain didn't know whether to grin or grimace. The result was a sputtered shower. He wiped up the desk with a damp towel from the bathroom.

On her way to Europe to be closer to the action, Angela appeared to be the FBI's designated heroine. Her email left out where she was going, who she'd work with, or how she expected to save Sauvignon from France—since rumor had it they'd stashed him somewhere in Belarus.

Angela's involvement wasn't entirely surprising. Dan Ramirez's clout with the FBI hierarchy was legendary. It was the reason Multima Corporation paid him a salary higher than any division president. If she was sleeping with James Fitzgerald, it made even more sense.

Howard had read about him moving into the CFO job after Wilma's suicide, and he had tons of respect for the financier. The guy was probably more instrumental in the phenomenal success of the company than its renowned founder.

But the woman remained fixated on The Organization and appeared to discount the other suggestions he'd fed her from his research on the web.

She sent several queries from the jet en route to France. Each requested more information about the notorious criminal element. Dutifully, he answered them one at a time. He hit the send button as he finished, then scrolled down to the next and repeated his steps. Occasionally, he had to check a name or address, but data flowed unfiltered from his memory, and that concerned him.

Howard had been away from The Organization for over five years. That he could answer so many queries about specific names was not a positive. He should have found it challenging to deal with dozens of questions because he simply shouldn't know newer, younger guys.

If Angela and her FBI cohorts were focusing on players who had been around for that long, they must not have the scoop on the latest batch. And if there were goons from The Organization mixed up in the Multima mess, it was most likely they'd find their culprit among the newbies. He shared his thoughts with Angela, then stepped away from the laptop as he pressed a decisive "send" with a theatrical flourish.

It was mid-morning. Outside, the heat was sweltering and clouds gathered, but Howard needed to clear his mind and get some exercise before the afternoon rainfall. He also grabbed a couple bottles of water, just in case. He slid them into the outside pouches of his backpack and slid his phones and laptop inside for good measure. There might be some new inspiration along the route.

With his oversized sunglasses, floppy hat with a wide brim, and mask on the lower half of his face, it would be hard for anyone to pick him out of a crowd. After the cosmetic surgery, change of hair color, and other minor tweaks to his appearance, Howard felt relaxed as he wandered the streets of Cartago.

He walked at a brisk pace for almost two hours. Sweat dripping from his brow, he stopped every mile or so to take in more water from the plastic bottles he'd taken from the honor bar in his room.

When they were empty, he headed back toward his hotel with a spring in his step and his mind clear of clutter. He used a key for the rear entrance of the building. That measure avoided talking to the woman guarding her front counter like a fortress rather than a place to engage with guests. Her inquisition could wait for another day.

Howard tiptoed along the corridor, listening for sounds and watching for any unusual movement. At the door to his room, he leaned in and listened as he inspected the handle. Its position had changed. The narrow end now pointed upward. It had angled down when he locked it earlier.

He pressed an ear to the doorway once more and glanced down the hallway. There was no sign of a cleaner, and with the pandemic, none was expected. He slid his plastic card across the electronic pad, and the lock freed with its usual clank. Gingerly, Howard twisted the handle and nudged open the door. Halfway through, he stopped and peered in horror at the mess.

His meager wardrobe lay strewn everywhere on the floor. Upended chairs. Emptied drawers perched upside down among towels, pillows, and sheets yanked from the bed. He dashed into the bathroom to be sure it was empty. Satisfied no one was in his room, he ran back to the door to lock it and block the view of any curious gawker who might pass by.

First, he checked the wall safe. Its door swung limply by a hinge. Someone had forced it open using a drill and some tool with a sharp edge. The box was empty except for thin foam padding on its bottom. The envelope where he stashed what remained of the cash Stan Tan gave him in Singapore was gone—about twenty-five thousand US dollars.

His wallet, phones and computer were all in the backpack still slung over his shoulder, so Howard instead checked clothes and shoes strewn about the room. Every piece was torn into shreds. Nothing remained wearable.

He scrambled to clear space on the counter and furiously worked the laptop keyboard. It took about an hour to complete his mission. Then he tallied a final inventory of the other items in his backpack. He checked both the fake and real passports and fingered the credit card in his wallet. Tucked in a hidden compartment, he found about five thousand dollars in cash he'd hidden away in the event of just such a disaster. With people reluctant to touch cash during the pandemic, he'd have enough to manage until he located a safe ATM.

His assessment complete, Howard calmly strode down the hallway to the hotel's rear entrance and slipped outside unnoticed—at least as far as he could tell. He chose a street away from the hotel and main road, then wandered off his desired course several blocks before he gradually wended his way back to the primary thoroughfare. It was within a hundred yards of the spot where he'd stepped down from the bus days earlier.

He stayed in the shade of a large tree and watched the clouds grow darker and more ominous. Every few moments, he glanced around the tree to his left, watching for an approaching vehicle. Otherwise, he looked forward, his eyes slowly scanning both directions for anything unusual.

Within five minutes, the sounds of a diesel engine broke the neighborhood's tranquility as the driver raced along the suburban road. A familiar screech of brakes and wheels welcomed him aboard after Howard stepped out from behind the tree and flagged down the bus.

Fortunately, there were few other passengers. Still, he gave each a careful glance as he trudged warily toward the rear. At the same time, the driver sped off with a thrust, determined to catch any vehicle on the road ahead of him.

Once seated, Howard pulled out his phone and checked the route of the Lumaca bus he'd boarded and paid two US dollars to ride. He confirmed it went directly to his destination, then strapped the backpack to his chest, snapping the straps together behind his back in case he should doze off en route.

One hour and thirty-three minutes later, the operator dropped him at the main entrance to the San Jose International Airport. He knew the way. Rather than walking toward the terminal, he headed off to the right and walked alongside the congested roadway for about two hundred yards.

There, he spotted the squat building beside—but apart from— the primary terminal. However, Howard marched past the entrance. Instead, he continued to meander along the sidewalk until he reached a trash bin. Discreetly, he pulled the FBI-supplied phone from a pocket and dropped it on the ground behind the container.

Then, he stomped his foot on the device until its glass screen and outer case shattered. Gingerly, he separated the fragments and broke them into even smaller pieces. He scattered one handful in the waste bin. The other half, he threw on the roadway as a large truck passed, crushing what remained.

He returned to the squat building, walked up the winding sidewalk, and cleared security. They didn't check for tickets or boarding passes there. With most flights, either short commuter routes or private planes, the concern was illegal weapons. The inspector looked surprised he carried no luggage, but waved Howard through without comment.

The jet service he'd reserved appeared well organized. It had a counter like the big airlines and a single attendant. She beamed when he stopped in front of her cubicle.

"I'm Mario Bartoli. Is the plane ready to leave?" He passed her his prepaid Mastercard from Singapore. He hadn't had an opportunity to load a Mastercard with his new identity yet, but if they approved the amount, she wouldn't ask for other identification.

"Certainly, Mr. Bartoli." She swiped the card in her machine and handed it to Howard to enter his PIN. Her smile broadened as she heard a beep confirming TVB Bank would soon transfer thirty-five thousand dollars into the company's account.

She slipped around the counter and asked him to follow her. With long hair blowing in the outdoor breeze, her hips swaying confidently with each step, the woman chatted and charmed for the short walk. They arrived at an unmarked white Bombardier 8000 with its engines idling at the edge of the tarmac. A pilot appeared in the doorway as they approached the stairway.

"Welcome 'board, Mr. Bartoli." His accent sounded Australian and he confirmed it when he asked his next questions. "So we're off to Uruguay, then, are we mate? No other luggage then?"

Howard settled into a dark green leather recliner, an odd color selection for a luxury private jet. But it worked. With the beige carpet, ceiling, and walls, the interior was welcoming and subdued. He stowed the backpack in a small compartment immediately below his reclining seat, and leaned back for a nap. He slept soundly until he felt the aircraft drop a few hundred feet and the engine whine, signaling the start of their descent.

The flight was less than eight hours to Montevideo, Uruguay's largest city and its capital. Though he'd rested, Howard's mind whirled the moment he opened his eyes.

Leaving Costa Rica so quickly had not been impulsive. It was essential. Someone was on his tail. First in Quepos, then in Jaco, and today in Cartago, they'd entered his room while he was out. He was pretty sure the second time, but after the third, he was certain it wasn't a coincidence. And the last folks had played the game seriously.

Only the FBI and the cosmetic surgeon should know he was in Costa Rica. He'd covered his tracks from Toronto well, and no one had bothered him for two months. The Bureau had no reason to spook him. But he could isolate only their phone as a common denominator. Now it was gone. Would the tracking stop? Or was The Organization involved? Fidelia still hadn't made contact, so it was unlikely she was behind the subterfuge. Was it from the dark net? Had his research attracted unwanted attention?

As the plane touched the ground again, Howard quickly checked his backpack's contents, making sure he hadn't overlooked anything. He stood to say farewell to the pilot the moment the jet came to a complete stop.

"Great flight. I slept the entire time. Thanks for the ride." Howard smiled while he spoke, but his curt tone signaled his haste to be on his way.

At the bottom of the staircase, another attractive young woman waited, trying to preserve her modesty as her short skirt blew erratically in the wind sweeping across the tarmac. She flashed a brilliant smile and hearty welcome. Then she walked beside him to the building and understood his question without a need to repeat it. His accent was improving. She showed no surprise with his request and led him out of the private jet section to a signpost for local transit.

A bus pulled up almost immediately, so he thanked the woman for her help and told her he'd be fine on his own. About thirty minutes later, he arrived in the Montevideo central terminal and filed out with the half dozen other passengers. Everyone wore face masks and avoided eye contact.

A giant electronic signboard in the waiting hall listed departures and platforms with brilliant colors changing continuously. Dozens of buses left the depot every day, even with the pandemic; though crowds were sparser than on his last visit there. Remarkably, people cautiously allowed adequate space between each other, just as they had in Canada.

He headed out to the buses and spotted one for Colonia del Sacramento. Instead of embarking right away, Howard wandered along the outside wall of the terminal, assessing the throng. He checked for familiar faces, scrutinized clothing and accessories, and looked for any interactions between people as they scurried from vehicles to doors or from the building to waiting taxis. It was unlikely he'd spot anything out of order. No, his intention was to memorize as many faces as possible—just in case.

The ride from Montevideo took about three hours. As in Costa Rica, buses stopped at the roadside whenever passengers wanted to get on or off. The giant signboard had confirmed that four more would pass that way before midnight, so he gamed the system.

While it was still light, he signaled to the driver that he'd like to stop at a rural crossroads just coming into view. There were signs of a small village, so getting off there shouldn't attract attention. From the top of the steps of the bus, Howard looked back at the remaining passengers. No one appeared interested.

He jumped down when it came to a stop and walked toward the rural settlement in case the driver or a passenger should check. When the bus disappeared over the horizon, he stopped walking, returned to the intersection, and waited for the next scheduled bus. One hour, he recalled.

To avoid attention, he sat on the ground, leaning against a large tree. There, he engaged in the next phase of his Google research. With a strong signal from SingTel's Uruguayan partner, he used his time productively.

When the bus came, more or less on schedule, Howard flagged down the driver like a local. He boarded and paid the fee to Colonia Valdense, a small town before Colonia del Sacramento and big enough to have an actual bus stop. It would raise less suspicion that way. He intended to buy a ticket only partway to his destination, get off this bus, and take the last one from Montevideo.

The strategy worked. No one paid him any attention as he got off in the small village, had dinner at a roadside food truck, and then boarded the last bus before midnight. It arrived in the UNESCO heritage town of Colonia del Sacramento in the wee hours of the morning.

He'd visited there once before but had had little opportunity to sightsee.

Still, he remembered the way from the bus station to a park next to the river, intending to hang out there until daylight. Walking along the uneven sidewalk in darkness, he watched his steps but took in the town's feel anew. He'd loved the place the last time he was there. The magnificent old buildings, huge and ancient trees overhanging the roadways, and the clear, salty air of the seaside all combined to invigorate his senses. He could hardly wait for first light to take it all in once more.

After he found a park bench to claim for a few hours' sleep, one last thought jolted through his brain. The reason he hadn't been able to see much when he was here before? He'd been recovering from an unfortunate encounter with a hooker. Bizarrely, from her, he'd caught the mumps—a disease all but eradicated in the US.

Maybe this time, he could finally disappear without all the drama.

TWENTY-FIVE

Düsseldorf, Germany, Monday July 20, 2020

Their goodbye had been perfunctory. Fidelia confirmed the account where she should transfer the twenty-five thousand owed for fuel consumed on the round-trip flight from Uzbekistan.

It seemed a little unfair after the more-than-special treatment she gave the guy, but she understood the drill. His ability to use the jet to bring her there cost money Zefar didn't have and could never justify to his superiors as a government expense.

She planted a peck on his cheek before the pilots opened the cockpit door on arrival, then flashed him her reassuring smile. That was the one she used to relieve men, implying their secrets would stay with her. She'd practiced it hundreds of times over her career.

His grateful grin promised loyalty. He'd continue to help her when needed, just as he had less than an hour before.

Klaudia had sent an urgent message a few minutes before their plane started its descent. She reserved a private jet out of Düsseldorf as Fidelia requested, but there was an issue now. A mechanical problem, the service company reported. And they couldn't get another long-range aircraft until morning.

Zefar needed to get the Government of Uzbekistan's plane back, so Fidelia had to find a way to stay in Germany for a couple days.

As usual, it took a single call from the well-placed state official to win special dispensation for her. Klaudia could meet her at the airport and drive her to her home in the nearby village of Angermünde. She had to promise not to leave the house for any reason and return directly to the private jet when it arrived on Monday. That favor cost Zefar. With a hearty laugh, he demanded Fidelia remember she owed him when they next met.

Klaudia drove her car right to the edge of the tarmac where the private jets landed. A ten-foot-tall chain-link fence separated them. A security guard stood waiting to open a gate with typical German efficiency so Fidelia need not enter a building. Klaudia waited on the other side.

Without a word, he opened the fence and motioned her through. After, Klaudia reached inside and slipped a twenty-euro note of thanks into his upturned palm.

It was only a fifteen-minute drive to Klaudia's secluded place at the northern edge of the charming village. Fidelia remembered the town fondly. Tall old trees still lined the winding road from the highway into the center. A tiny takeout joint was there on the right-hand side, operated by two young Turks selling the world's best pizza. On the left, commuters scrambled into the plain but functional Angermünde rail station.

A block later, customers filed in and out of EDEKA Steinert Getränkemarkt, the compact grocery that stocked more variety than supermarkets twice its size. She smiled as she noticed a traffic signal turn red, right in front of the store. Imagine a town so thoughtful its officials installed a light just to let pedestrians safely cross a little-traveled street to shop.

"Can we drive past the Schloss Heltorf? The castle?" She giggled like a young girl, but she loved the old, run-down structure in a field off the village's principal streets.

"Sure. But we won't stop. This is a borrowed car, and I don't want the COVID-19 police discovering us exploring around there." Klaudia laughed, but they both knew the German penchant for following rules. There just might be pandemic spies lurking about.

The castle drive-by added a few minutes, but they soon safely huddled inside Klaudia's functional two-story residence. When Klaudia had managed the escort business for Fidelia in Europe years before, they often met in the spacious house built behind a massive green hedge and another large home nearer the street. Her friend never felt the need for extra security because she believed an innocent intruder couldn't penetrate the place, and her sophisticated technology gadgets would deal with the less innocent.

Without her usual bodyguards, Fidelia wasn't as confident.

Determined to relax regardless, she asked for a cup of coffee. Like reunited girlfriends, they chattered about their activities since they'd seen each other in Australia, even managing a laugh or two among the ugly narratives. It didn't last as long as she wished.

Fidelia's secure phone rang. Its screen showed the caller was Luigi. He was still in Europe.

"Bad news. Found Sargetti. Throat's slit. Discovered the corpse inside a secluded bungalow on Lake Como."

She tensed. Alphonso Sargetti was the guy she'd named boss for Italy only a few months earlier.

"Any clues or messages?" Fidelia asked.

"Other than a sliced throat, na. The Russians used ta kill guys that way, but others have started to copy 'em. Can't be sure."

"Any word from Stan Tan or Duc Nguyễn?"

"My guys lost Tan. Watched his place twenty-four-seven for more'n a week. Didn't see nobody come or go. Yesterday, one of 'em posed as a city building inspector and got inside. Girl takin' care of the house said he wasn't there. Boys looked in every room and closet. Nothin'."

"Nguyễn?"

"Said he hasn't heard a peep from Tan—even when he didn't make his July payment."

"Alright. Tell Verlusconi he's in charge in Italy for now. Be sure he understands all the rules." Fidelia said. "Then send a technician into Tan's house. See what he can find. We need to get a lead on this Shadow character."

"Okay. Are ya still in Hue or talkin' from the plane?"

"Neither. I'm with Klaudia. A mechanical delay. We'll leave for Uruguay tomorrow morning."

"Everythin' still okay?"

"Things look fine here. But it seems my departure from Vietnam was timely. Nguyễn emailed me about a fire in the apartment only minutes after I left, plus a nasty call from a burner phone traced to Washington. Claims the woman said only that the Shadow was not pleased. Didn't know if it referred to him, me, or both of us."

"I'll organize a couple guys 'n Germany right now ta watch the place while ya're there."

She'd already shot him down once when she sent his people ahead to Uruguay. There was no point in refusing an extra layer of protection for the day.

In the end, it didn't help. Not five minutes after she finished the call, a massive explosion shattered the front windows of Klaudia's house. Instinctively, both women dove to the floor, fearing more. They heard screams and shouts in the street outside, and Klaudia dashed to see what had happened. When she returned, her face was ashen, her voice hoarse with fear.

"They blew up my friend's car! Come with me," was all she said as she yanked Fidelia's arm and tugged her toward an exit in the back. On the way, they grabbed her backpack. Klaudia motioned to put it on while she jammed a laptop inside another leather bag on the counter. Outside, she ran to a shed. Pulling a key from her pocket, she unlocked it and jerked the door free with a desperate tug before Fidelia caught up.

"Take that. Follow me." Pointing to one bicycle and hopping on another, she pedaled twice to reach a wooden gate in the backyard. Deftly, she slid the lock open and pushed it outward to let the bikes through.

Under cover of a densely wooded area, Klaudia led them left on the trail, along the road, and away from the airport. They pedaled furiously, like competitive racers with a finish line in sight. Fidelia's lungs burned with the exertion. Despite her runs and high level of fitness, at times her gasps for air drowned out the hum of passing cars. Although it was mid-morning, sweat oozed from her brows. Her thighs stiffened and throbbed. Her breathing became so labored, she was panting like a dog when Klaudia finally signaled to stop.

"There's a fueling station just off the trail. Stay here in the shade. I have some cash. I'll get us some water."

Many other riders were out that morning, so Fidelia wheeled their bikes a safe distance off the path and found a fallen log to sit on and recover. They'd ridden full out for more than a half hour. Every muscle in her body protested.

A few minutes later, Klaudia arrived with large bottles of water.

"I saw the aftermath on a TV screen inside," she began. "There's nothing left of my friend's car. Looks like a dozen or more emergency vehicles in the street outside my house. When I asked the guy in the store what he knew about it, he said the police thought it was some kind of terrorist activity."

"Where do we go from here?" Fidelia had regained her breath and composure enough to ask in a tone resembling confidence.

"We're almost at Duisburg. I think it's better to get out of Germany. If you're up for it, another couple hours riding and we can be in Maasbree, a little town in the Netherlands with an airport. It's just past Venlo."

"You'll arrange for the jet to land there?"

A half hour later and the arrangements were complete. They'd located a different Bombardier Global 8000, one freshly serviced in London. The provider could round up a crew and have it in Holland in about three hours.

The ride was longer than Klaudia first estimated, and the last five miles felt like torture. Despite regular rigorous exercise, it had been years since Fidelia had ridden for more than a half hour. And those rides were often on a stationary bike in a gym with no wind, bumps, or long, gradual slopes. When they finally arrived at the airport in Maasbree, her buttocks felt almost paralyzed as she stumbled off the bicycle right beside the aircraft staircase.

Tears blurred her vision. Sharp spikes of pain shot up her back with every step as jarring jabs crippled her thighs. Her arm muscles tightened and failed to relax even after stretching them upward for a moment. Fidelia checked her hands and expected to see blisters from tightly gripping the handlebars for over four hours. But, though overworked and sensitive beyond description, they were no worse off than any other part of her self-abused body.

Finally, she noticed a white unmarked jet sitting on the tarmac. A pilot stood at the top of the staircase and grinned down.

"Like me to stow the bikes on board?"

Without glancing at Fidelia, Klaudia told him that was a great idea then motioned to follow her up the stairs.

Inside, the plane was plush and welcoming. With two clusters of four seats surrounding fixed tables in the middle, there could be no doubt it once belonged to a corporation or wealthy business person who liked to work in flight. Someone had tastefully decorated the interior with beiges and browns that welcomed warmly.

The pilot wheeled the bikes to an area near the back of the jet, whipped a bungee cord from a drawer, and anchored them as though it were a usual pre-flight preparation. Given her current level of physical agony, Fidelia found it hard to imagine when next she'd feel like a ride. But they had them, just in case.

Another pilot arrived beside Klaudia's seat with a credit card reader in one hand, his left fingers poised to accept payment. After she produced a card from her backpack, he divulged their fee.

"It's billed in US dollars. It'll be forty-two thousand."

Klaudia nodded. That was the price they'd quoted. To make conversation, she asked how long the flight would be.

"You realize we need to refuel in Sierra Leone, right?" He looked down over his glasses to see her nod again. "We'll fly for about seven hours, almost due south, to get there. They're very slow on the ground, so figure two hours to top up. Then we'll have another nine hours across the Atlantic to Uruguay."

"Is there any food on the plane?" Fidelia wanted to know.

The pilot laughed.

"What, you don't want to dine in the workers' cafeteria at eleven o'clock at night in Africa?" He chuckled again at his poor joke. "There are two meals for each of you in the refrigerator. You can warm them in the microwave. There should be some for each of us as well, so we'll interrupt you a couple times in flight if that's alright."

Within minutes, the plane was airborne. As the wheels left the ground, Fidelia pressed the recline feature and leaned back as the seat flattened into a bed. Exhausted, she craved sleep. But Luigi needed to know about the change in plans. He answered on the first ring. She recounted the latest developments as he listened intently. Then she asked again if he had any news on Stan Tan's whereabouts.

"Na. Nobody knows where he headed. I've put the word out everywhere, but nothin' back yet. More bad news in the US, though." He paused only long enough for her focus to shift. "A Multima warehouse near Miami caught fire during the night. Extensive damage. Worse, the FBI picked up 'nother twenty-five of 'r guys before dawn. We're trying ta get access to 'em."

"Shit. We haven't been able to spring any from the first batch they arrested, have we?"

"They've dropped off the goddamned radar," Luigi said. His tone showed a mixture of remorse and anger. "Their families 'r desperate. My main guy down there's spendin' hours on the phone with wailin' 'n angry women. Some 'r talking about co-operatin' with the feds if we can't get their men back."

"Make sure your guy is giving them enough money. As long as they can feed the kids and pay the rent, they'll stay loyal. Anything else?" Fidelia rubbed her aching muscles as she asked, twisting slightly in her seat to shift the discomfort to another area of her pain-racked body.

"Ya remember when we were interrogating Ortez in Chile?" This was her primary protector's first mention of the traitorous former Latin American boss since his brutal torture and dismemberment months earlier. How could she forget? She had listened by phone to every scream of the agony Luigi administered.

"Of course, why do you ask?"

"Ya might remember I got 'im to divulge the name that went with that suspicious IP address 'n West Virginia. My people 'n Washington finally tracked the guy down but missed grabbin' him. Came within a hair of snatch'n him at Dulles International 'n hour ago. But he escaped. According to a flight plan filed with the FAA, he's on a private jet headed to Minsk. Ya wanna get 'im there?"

"Do we have anyone in Belarus?" Fidelia asked. She wasn't sure the guy was worth the chase. His connection to the South American traitor Juan Álvarez implied some link to the Russians. She hadn't seen any evidence yet, but Luigi was convinced the guy was up to no good.

"Got a team in Vilnius, in Lithuania. Can probably drive there 'n two 'r three hours."

"Your guys alright with the language and know how to intercept on the tarmac?"

"Everybody there speaks Russian. At least one of 'em knows his way 'round the airport. I think 'r chances of success 're good. Need to get the guy out of Belarus b'fore we interrogate, though. Haven't got a support network in the police or underground there." Luigi was thinking ahead and out loud.

"We still have that property in the countryside near Krynki in Poland, the place we used to hide the women we picked up back in the nineties; remember it?" Fidelia coaxed his memory. Luigi had been there several times with her before Belarus fell entirely under the control of the Russians.

"Yeah. Could drive there, but not sure I can tell the Lithuanians how ta find it."

"Get them to meet you somewhere near the border in Poland. You'll probably need them for the interrogation if Russian is the only language the low-life speaks." She wanted to cover all the bases.

"Guy's notta Ruskie. Just workin' for 'em. Name's Andrews, Joey Andrews. His English's just like ours. Born 'n raised in the Appalachians." Luigi's tone turned menacing. There was nothing he hated more than an American who sided with the Russians.

Fidelia took a long moment to process the new information.

"Be sure the Lithuanians have enough men and equipment. If this guy is connected the way I'm thinking, he might have significant Russian resources meeting him when he lands. It could get messy." She waited for him to assure her he got it before she ended the call.

She raised her seatback and stood up to ease the cramps in her legs. She stretched in several directions. Squatted a few times. Rubbed her thighs and calves. Then collapsed back in her seat, squeezing her knees up tightly against her chest as tears formed from the unexpected spasm. Her subsequent scream was loud enough to attract the attention of the pilots.

One dashed out from the cockpit and toward her when he saw she was in pain. Klaudia hovered nearby, uncertain what to do.

"Grab her other leg and rub like this," the pilot shouted to her as he pulled Fidelia's left leg straight and began deeply massaging it from her thigh downward. He ripped off her shoes and continued rough pressure as Klaudia imitated his technique on the right leg.

"There's a danger she's forming a blood clot," the pilot said as he worked his way down. "Over-exertion like your bike ride, combined with the high altitude and the sudden sedentary behavior, can do that."

Sometime later, Fidelia started to respond. She moved her toes and feet as he instructed. He helped her up and told her to walk. Unsteady at first, she balanced herself using a seatback but checked her movement. Everything still worked. The pilot examined her feet and ankles for swelling and reported all looked good. He managed a chuckle again.

"More bad news for you. No sleeping, at least until we land in Africa. You need to get up, stretch, and move around every fifteen minutes or so to be sure your blood continues to circulate well. We might want to have a doctor look at you there."

Fortunately, the impromptu massage and frequent movement combined to deliver relief. The pain abated. Her muscles became more flexible. Her heart rate returned to normal. By the time they reached Sierra Leone, Fidelia was confident she didn't need medical attention and told the captain when he came to check.

She slept for most of the time on the ground and until well after they were again at cruising altitude. The pilot generously woke her every half hour and even threw in a couple leg massages to be sure. Meanwhile, Klaudia arranged for the bodyguards to meet them when they landed.

About an hour before their estimated arrival, she reached one on his cell phone. They were in Montevideo, just off a commercial flight after approximately two days of traveling. Exhausted, they'd find a car and drive out to the landing strip in Punta del Este.

With luck, they should arrive about the same time.

TWENTY-SIX

Sainte-Agathe-des-Monts, Quebec Tuesday July 21, 2020

"I'm worried." A day earlier, Dan Ramirez had started his conversation with Suzanne simply, then paused for optimum effect. She noted the wrinkles in his forehead and waited until he carried on.

"I'd like you to consider leaving the country. It may be safer for you here in Canada than at home at the moment, but we're catching troubling undertones on the Internet and the dark net."

"There's always negative stuff on both. What's changed?" She softened her question with a smile.

"We still don't know who bombed your home. Maybe it was organized crime, but the FBI think maybe other culprits are possible. Messages suggest some underground elements are becoming unruly. Some of the vocal right-wing lunatics are mentioning you by name on the dark net. They're unhappy you require all employees to wear masks. On social media, rumblings from the disaffected are more misogynistic, with increased vitriol. It's all becoming weird. At the same time, personalities using pseudonyms urge followers to boycott Multima Supermarkets because our stores all have pharmacies. They imply you're in bed—at least figuratively—with Big Pharma. Separately, none of these mounts an insurmountable risk. Combined, I fear a caustic brew may erupt in violence. Like it or not, you're in their crosshairs."

It was an unsettling mouthful, but did it truly merit an escape from North America? Could there be other reasons he wanted her overseas? Suzanne took a moment to process his message before she responded.

"Okay. But isn't it hard for those types to get into Canada right now?" She had trouble making a connection between the malaise and her situation.

"Yes, but it's even harder for them to make it into Europe. And it would be almost impossible for them to reach you in a safe house in Lyon. That's where I'd like you to stay, at least until we have more clarity around the bombings and kidnapping. I've talked to Interpol. They're willing to provide a place and welcome having you close by."

For several minutes, he walked her through his rationale. She listened patiently but sent him away with a half-hearted promise to consider his recommendation. At first, she resisted the idea. She loved the magnificent rental home in the Laurentian Mountains. Not only an extraordinary find from the perspectives of scenery, comfort, and atmosphere, it also appeared adequately secure.

Of course, with the current Multima Corporation malaise, safe was a somewhat relative term—subject to individual interpretation. COVID-19 was not a serious threat. The team lived in a true bubble. Their engaging host, Florence Carpentier, ordered food and refreshments daily from a grocery store in the town of Sainte-Agathe-des-Monts. No one from the house ventured far off the sprawling property or had contact with other people.

With the addition of Dan's half dozen new bodyguards, she felt safe from whoever had attacked the Multima stores, bombed her home and kidnapped Jean-Louis Sauvignon. Stefan had expressed amazement at the massive array of weapons and ammunition the men had stored in the basement in neat rows, comfortably spaced for immediate access.

It wasn't a question of safety that changed her mind. Instead, it was Stefan's quiet comments as they took a stroll in the woods along the back property line. They walked relaxed, hand in hand, the silence punctuated with lots of deep breaths and contented sighs as they soaked in the greenery, fresh air, and a stillness she'd rarely experienced elsewhere.

"You know Dan has your best interests at heart, right?" Stefan used a gentle tone of voice to match their mood but left little doubt he expected an answer. She found it an odd alliance between her lover and chief of security and probed to satisfy her curiosity.

"Yeah. His sincerity is unquestioned. But what can we accomplish in France that the *gendarmes* and other government authorities can't do far better?"

"I don't think Dan intends for us to be involved with the investigation in any way; he just wants to keep you safe. But you always listen carefully. I'm sure you detected his underlying message. Why are you hesitant?"

It was a good question, a question that led her mind to wander a bit because she had thought about it for some time after their satisfying escapades in bed the night before. That few minutes had been idyllic while it lasted. The guy had such a magic touch. From foreplay to climax, he'd been tender and thoughtful. Mindful of her desires and needs. It'd been worth the trip to France to pick him up. After, while her companion slept in exhausted satisfaction, the plight of Jean-Louis weighed on her until near dawn. She owed Stefan an answer.

"The kidnapping terrifies me. My intuition tells me to stay as far away from the crime as possible. I'll soon have a terrible decision to make. It might become even more difficult if I'm closer. When John George Mortimer was still alive, he spent much of his last few months coaching me and sharing advice. He was a brilliant guy. It's almost as though he foresaw this kidnapping incident, as if he sensed the inevitability of it happening." She paused. Stefan was usually patient, always comfortable with her taking whatever time she preferred to choose her words carefully.

"You realize I'll have to make a decision that costs Jean-Louis his life. You understand that's the reason Michelle is so furious with me, right?"

"You're carrying a heavy load. Is it possible you're taking on too much responsibility?" Stefan asked.

"How do you mean?"

"Well, I think you can agree there was nothing you personally could have done to prevent Jean-Louis's kidnapping. He has no direct involvement in Multima, and he alone handled his security. Plus, there's no evidence his current dilemma relates directly to your company. Is it possible you're feeling responsible because of your close friendship with Michelle?"

"Yes. Our relationship is almost like family. Should I eventually choose to help her with the ransom—either with Multima funds or my own money—I'll have the same predicament. As CEO, I can't separate my personal decision from the company. Future risks to me and other Multima executives will increase."

"Are you prepared to risk your relationship with Michelle? Might you have a better opportunity to resolve your differences in person?"

They walked for another while as she considered his question. This time, he became more uncomfortable with the silence and added more for her to think about.

"I believe Dan also recognizes having you in Lyon, meeting face-to-face with the people at Interpol, adds an important dimension of urgency and importance. His experience in the FBI probably gives him unique insight into the personal components of policing that we outsiders don't share."

She had considered that aspect as she tossed and turned the previous night. She didn't reach a conclusion then and still had doubts. "You know how law enforcement resents meddling, and I think you recognize a rising tide of opinion around the world about the growing and disproportionate influence of business in government activity. What leads you to believe the police in France will interpret our engagement as anything more than unwanted interference?"

"If I read the minds of law enforcement at Interpol accurately, I imagine they'll welcome your involvement. Why? Because you'll be a convenient foil if they fail. If Sauvignon dies, they can reasonably argue they welcomed your perspective and information but couldn't persuade you to pay the ransom. They didn't have enough time to save his life."

"And that outcome helps my safety, my conscience, and overpowers a consuming sense of guilt in some magical way?"

"Perhaps. Dan Ramirez may anticipate that having you close to the action, helping to resolve the issue, and gaining some confidence you did everything possible before it became necessary to make a painful decision might soothe the agony quicker and more fully. These cops get to see human nature from unusual perspectives. And he is certainly one of the most insightful."

Stefan didn't suggest she decide. He just left his last comment out there for her to think about, and she thought about it often throughout the day.

By the dinner hour, Suzanne concluded Dan and Stefan were probably right. She should be in France. Within minutes, her security chief had the unqualified support of Interpol for their visit and clearance to land in Lyon. His contact even agreed to arrange ground transportation with an escort to the safe home they had in mind. Meanwhile, their host summoned a fleet of SUVs to transport them back to Mirabel airport, where the Multima Bombardier 5000 sat on the tarmac.

The pilots left with two of the bodyguards. A half-hour later, Suzanne, Stefan and the rest of the group hugged Florence tightly despite the public health recommendations and thanked her profusely for her help, hospitality, and camaraderie over the past few days. She promised to have the place ready for their return, which she hoped would be soon.

They slept through the overnight flight, touching down in France at the breakfast hour relatively refreshed. Interpol had the promised cars waiting beyond the gates of the private jet section, and they whisked the group to a secure spot just a mile or two from its headquarters on Quai Charles de Gaulle in the heart of Lyon.

Although they called it a safe house, it was actually an apartment on the third floor of a stately, gray building. Meticulously maintained outside, its lobby spoke of wealth with marble floors, ornate chandeliers, and gigantic mirrors enlarging the space. The painted sections were a subtle beige with white trim, and original oil paintings graced the walls tastefully.

A uniformed doorman greeted Suzanne by name and guided her to the elevator. It required a special card to reach her floor, and he squeezed it into her hand after passing it across the reader once.

Inside the apartment, they'd spared no luxury. Marble, granite, and other polished stones covered the floors and counters in the entrance, living space, and kitchen. More original oil paintings, some with subdued lighting above them, added warmth. An area outfitted with screens, printers and everything needed for work from home was larger than her corner office in Ft. Myers, with higher ceilings. Solid wood doors separated it from the other rooms.

Suzanne counted four bedrooms as she wandered through the place with Stefan, choosing the master with its king bed and a bathroom the size of many living rooms in the United States.

She giggled at the opulence. Wealthier than virtually every other woman on earth, she had never needed reassurance of her stature with elaborate and expensive quarters. Although her destroyed home in Atlanta and the house she'd inherited from John George in Fort Myers were luxurious, neither tried to match the display of wealth in this place.

Edouard Deschamps from Interpol knocked on the apartment door before they had completely settled in. He introduced himself as an assistant director of the agency, overseeing the rescue of Jean-Louis Sauvignon. Despite his elaborate efforts to project charm, his smile showed far too many teeth, making him resemble a tiny, slippery shark. He didn't bother to shake hands, blaming the pandemic.

"I don't wear a mask because they test Interpol leaders for COVID every day, just like your president," he said. His laugh sounded forced, lingering, and annoying, almost the sound of a braying donkey.

"I'll keep mine on and a reasonable distance between us," Suzanne replied. "We're not tested regularly, but we've been in a bubble for more than a week. We all feel fine and are grateful for the work you're doing to help Jean-Louis Sauvignon."

He acknowledged her preference to get down to business with a curt nod, then waited for her to offer a chair. She pointed to one well away from her as she chose a leather armchair for herself.

"Please have a seat. I'm not sure what we have here yet, but perhaps a bodyguard can rustle up a coffee from a shop on the street?" She watched him shake his head, not bothering to smile a second time. His forehead creased and he looked uncomfortable as he started.

"Monsieur Sauvignon is in peril. The people who have him are more ruthless than we first expected. When they severed his finger, it shocked us. We had told them Ms. Sauvignon would pay the ransom. We asked only for a little time to raise the money. Their answer was to cut off his forefinger and mail it to Farefour Stores headquarters. Ms. Sauvignon made a tearful public appeal on TV late last night. She begged them to not harm her father further. To contact her directly. Allow her a few more days to get the money."

"Did they respond?" Suzanne asked.

"Yes. Just before I came over, my colleague staying with her forwarded a text Michelle received today. It provided a mitcoyne address. The only other words were 'Before Saturday. No Delays or right hand will be mailed Monday morning.'"

Suzanne cringed and caught a grimace on Stefan's face from the corner of her eye. She took a deep breath before she asked her next question. "I haven't spoken to Michelle for a few days. Is she able to raise fifty million dollars?"

"I know. Ms. Sauvignon made us aware of the schism between you." Deschamps had the decency to make his words the least hurtful possible. "The quick answer is no. Her father is worth millions, of course. But much of that fortune is tied up in real estate in either his name or the names of companies he controls. Michelle has only uncovered about ten million in relatively liquid assets she can sell to raise cash quickly."

He left it there, figuratively passing the ball to her. Everyone knew Suzanne was the only person in the room who could produce fifty million in cash with the stroke of a pen. His apparent haste to pay a ransom raised concerns.

"I won't dismiss the possibility entirely," she replied in the most confident tone she could summon, not wanting the discussion to end before she could get more information. "First, I'd like to better understand what leads you have about Jean-Louis's whereabouts."

Deschamps nodded, satisfied with her position. He agreed to give her a full briefing personally that afternoon. Before that, he wanted to return to his office and consult with his team members to be sure the information he shared was the latest and most accurate. He stood and tipped his head toward the group as he headed out.

Suzanne shuddered involuntarily as Deschamps closed the door behind him. There was something unsettling about the man.

Unable to put her finger on precisely what she found discomfiting, she glanced at her watch. She had a choice. Either she could call Dan Ramirez at 4:00 a.m. to get his read on the Sauvignon matter, or Amber Chan in China, where it was 4:00 p.m. She hit the speed dial number for Amber.

"I saw the sales numbers for last week." She didn't mention how bad they were.

"The worst since I joined the company," her country manager groaned. "Our stores now have no pork or poultry anywhere in the nation. And they're threatening to cut off beef next Monday."

"How are discussions with the union going?"

"As expected. They're building a ring of iron around the membership. Labor union bosses vehemently deny any involvement in the protests, but my informants tell me several have shown up at the office bruised and battered. Some are not even well enough to return to work immediately. I haven't convinced their leadership to offer up a single sacrificial lamb."

"I doubt either of us really wants a sacrificial lamb. What's the latest on the democracy demonstrations? Are they making any headway with the government?"

"Another just started a few hours ago. Some reports say over four hundred thousand are in the streets clamoring about excessive use of force by the police. I expect Beijing's position will only harden."

"How about your personal safety and that of our workers?"

"I'm okay. The security plan Dan Ramirez put in place provides lots of protection whenever I go out. Candidly, I eat and sleep here at the office most days. Between the pandemic and the demonstrations, I feel better here on the top floor, looking down at it all. Our employees are also alright if they stay away from the action. But we know they won't. After every riot, at least ten percent of our staff call in sick for a day or two. In normal times, that percentage is less than one."

The women compared notes for another few minutes before they reached a mutual decision. Multima in Hong Kong would continue to resist the government's demands. They'd refuse to turn over any suspected insurgents or information about employees missing work because of illness or injury. Amber expected the bureaucrats in Beijing would soon demand she visit them for another unpleasant chat, so Suzanne offered words of support and encouragement she knew sounded hollow.

When her call with China ended, she thought Dan Ramirez might already be awake. If he wasn't, he should be. So guilt was not a factor as she waited for him to answer the ringing phone. As it continued to ring, Stefan wandered into the room, and she switched the device to speaker mode. With his clean background check, she and her security chief were both comfortable with him listening in and sharing his expert perspective.

"Was your flight to Lyon okay?" Dan asked before she could say hello.

"Everything is fine, and was your return to Ft. Myers uneventful?"

"Same. We have a bit of information from my guy at the FBI you might find interesting. They finished testing residue from the bomb that destroyed your home. One hundred percent match with the materials used for the bombs in both stores—the one we caught before detonation and the other in Ocala that exploded. They're confident we are dealing with the same people in all three cases."

"I'm not sure I find that reassuring." Suzanne used a tone of curiosity rather than concern.

"It's reassuring only from one perspective. If they track down the culprits, we're done. There aren't multiple groups of crazies we need to locate." Dan laughed uneasily before he continued. "But there are two new twists we didn't expect. A bomb detonated in a Jeffersons Stores location in Tampa early this morning. Lots of damage. Casualties. About the same time, the home of David Jones, their CEO, was also destroyed in Dallas."

Suzanne jumped to her feet as she listened to the news, tingling with shock. What in the world was going on? Her brain froze. For a moment, it felt like a useless block of ice suspended above her shoulders. She shook her head in disbelief several times before finally drawing in a deep breath. It was loud enough for Dan to hear.

"Are you alright?" he asked, his tone more intense and urgent.

"Yes. David Jones is certainly no friend of mine, and Jeffersons Stores is the competitor we love to hate, but this kind of violence is repulsive on every level. Was he in the house?"

"They think so. They recovered parts of two bodies, a male and a female. Of course, forensic tests will be necessary, but they expect to confirm one body is Jones."

Another long period of silence followed. If they confirmed the blast killed him, concern for her own safety grew exponentially.

Dan reinforced that worry when he continued. "I already sent messages to my men to increase their surveillance on you there in Lyon. From now on, they'll work in twenty-four-hour shifts. I recommend you stay in the apartment though."

"Thanks. I'll be careful. But what I'm really thinking about is what this all means. The FBI has been operating on the assumption The Organization is behind the bombings. That no longer makes sense. If Jeffersons Stores is owned by the Japanese arm of The Organization, why would they blow up one of their own supermarkets and their CEO?"

"You might be right. I've already pressed my contacts at the Bureau to enlarge their focus. But it's not unheard of for organized crime to create precisely the doubts you just expressed by sacrificing their own properties or people. Other factors could be at play. Maybe Jones wasn't following orders. Perhaps they simply want to collect a big insurance check on an unprofitable store. At this stage, nobody knows."

Their exchange of theories continued for another few minutes. When they hung up, Suzanne slumped back into the comfortable leather chair and looked upward at the rotating fan suspended from the high ceiling. She stretched out her arms to relieve the tension, then wrapped her hands behind her neck.

For some moments, Stefan let her absorb the distressing latest developments without interruption, sensing her unease and need for quiet to process increasingly disturbing news.

"You think they're on the wrong path?" He paced slowly in a large circle around the living room, his head down and hands clasped behind his back as he asked the question.

After her shocking call with Dan Ramirez, her mind raced in different directions. "Let's wait to hear what Deschamps says this afternoon. Dan's going to make sure Angela Bonner is aware of the meeting and attends. She has already met him and knows where to find him at Interpol. Still, my gut tells me we won't enjoy the briefing."

Stefan looked up from the floor and tilted his head inquisitively, silently coaxing her to continue. Instead, she stood up, stretched again, and then headed toward the kitchen to make another cup of coffee.

"Are you okay to chat a bit about work issues?" he asked as Suzanne stepped back into the living area.

It was Tuesday morning—still early in the week in the life of a CEO. With two major crises already sapping her energy, a pleasant discussion about topics more related to everyday business concerns might be therapeutic.

"Sure. What do you have?"

"I've been thinking a lot about your search for a new president at Multima Financial Services. I know some directors have been giving you grief about the time it's taking to identify a candidate."

"Grief isn't a strong enough word." Suzanne laughed. "I don't recall an issue the board has found more divisive. I thought delivering an outstanding replacement CFO might have eased the pressure a bit. Instead, I find more clutter in my email asking for updates or making suggestions than I imagined possible."

"Well, I have an idea you may like to consider." Stefan's face grew serious and his tone dropped an octave. "I can't promise you it'll do anything to make the board more cohesive, at least initially. And everyone will need to think outside the box, as you Americans say. But I might know your new president for Financial Services."

Suzanne looked at him carefully, saw his lips twitching to form a smile, and was intrigued. "Shoot. Who's the elusive unknown candidate?"

"As we worked through the resumes, discussed the candidates' strengths and weaknesses, then eliminated one after the other, I remained mindful of a personal characteristic you consider most crucial. Entrepreneurial skills." Stefan spoke slowly and deliberately, watching intently for her every reaction. She nodded slightly, so he continued. "Passion. Perseverance. Adaptability. Work ethic. Would you agree those are all essential components of a successful entrepreneur?"

"Sure. And I'd add resourcefulness. We need someone willing to invent new ways to do finance successfully. In the longer term, financial services might again become our most profitable business."

"Agreed. I think you have a candidate that closely matches those needs, and she's right under our noses. Natalia Tenaz."

Suzanne was dumbfounded and showed it. Her mouth was agape for several seconds before she recognized it and bit down hard. She reached for her cup of coffee and took a long sip to buy some time, then set the cup down. Too late, she noticed her toes and fingers were tapping nervously, so she casually crossed both arms and legs.

"You're at a loss for words. I think that's a first since I met you." Stefan grinned, then chuckled to ease the tension. He had detected her unease and didn't wait patiently for her to respond. "You probably wonder if I'm suffering from acute jet lag or perhaps temporary insanity, but I believe Natalia may have all the characteristics you seek except a current job title that implies she's ready."

His expression grew serious again, then he launched into a carefully structured summary of his thoughts that lasted over ten minutes.

He started with her education. She'd been top of her class every year of school, including in the prestigious MBA program at Harvard University. She joined Multima Financial Services after working with the renowned consultants McFinsey & Associates, where she mastered assignments on three different continents.

Natalia started at Multima in a marketing role, where she excelled and won annual performance reviews categorizing her as "exceptional," "extraordinary," and "inventive."

Then James Fitzgerald picked her to run his business intelligence unit, where she demonstrated an almost unbelievable ability to find useful information and keep her fingers on the pulse of goings-on with competitors, in the financial services division itself, and in other Multima operating divisions.

Since her promotion to credit director, transaction approval rates skyrocketed, the speed of those approvals increased dramatically, and bad debts had plummeted. Her performance reviews applauded her innovation, creativity, and willingness to explore unfamiliar concepts.

After James assigned her the responsibility of finding a replacement president, she had interviewed dozens of candidates, explored new avenues, and pursued every path with passionate dedication. That she hadn't yet identified an ideal candidate wasn't the result of either her effort or methods. It was solely timing and circumstance. People suitable for the position just weren't ready to move at this stage, reinforcing the stereotypical image of finance types as capable but unadventurous fiscal managers.

To add to that, Natalia understood the financial services business. She knew the players on the team. She had shown the specific qualities they were seeking in a leader. As a bonus, she belonged to a visible minority and offered an opportunity to promote both a woman and an internal candidate—actions close to Suzanne's heart.

"Obviously, it's your call whether you run my suggestion by the board," Stefan concluded. He showed no hint of a smile, no mischievous glint in his eyes. He was dead serious, and she respected his views.

"You've caught me by surprise. It never occurred to me you might think along those lines, but I hear you and will ponder your suggestion." Suzanne mirrored his gravity in both appearance and tone.

Stefan let his idea lie there and said he was going out for a morning run.

She needed time to mull over his unusual suggestion. She also wanted to learn more about James Fitzgerald's protégé before seriously considering the idea. Recent blind spots, tragedies, and betrayals had seared that reality into her mind. But Dan Ramirez and his team were already overloaded with the bombing and kidnapping issues.

A name from the past popped out from her memory bank. She hadn't seen him for a while but had maintained casual contact. He'd served the same role as Dan Ramirez for her in the Canadian supermarket chain she'd managed before John George Mortimer acquired that company almost two decades earlier. But his career path led to law enforcement when there was no longer a role for him at Multima. His choice had been a good one, and he now served in the upper echelons of the Royal Canadian Mounted Police, Canada's national police force.

Although the hour was unusually early, she took a chance. He answered on the third ring. After she explained her request, he said he'd do her a favor and discreetly undertake a background investigation of Natalia Tenaz. Of course, he couldn't provide any formal report but could let her know if there were any issues she should explore further. He'd get on it right away, and she could buy him an expensive dinner the next time she visited Montreal.

Just before she hung up—on an unplanned impulse—Suzanne requested he investigate the background of one more person. Her contact laughed and agreed to check out the second name for an equally expensive gourmet dinner. They both ended the call relaxed and laughing.

As the lunch hour in Lyon approached and hunger set in, Suzanne and her bodyguards discussed their options. Ordering in was the only practical alternative, as no one volunteered to cook and the refrigerator was almost empty at any rate. In the middle of their conversation, Suzanne's personal line rang. It was a local number.

"Is this Suzanne Simpson?" a woman's voice asked.

She confirmed it was.

"I'm Angela Bonner. You might recall me from the last time we worked together."

Suzanne remembered. They'd spent several hours on the company jet and in meetings less than a year earlier. Why the formality? She opted to reflect the same manner. "Of course I remember you, Angela. How may I help you?"

"I'm in Lyon and part of the team you're scheduled to meet at 1:00. Monsieur Deschamps asked me to notify you we must delay the meeting. He forbade me from giving you any other information at this point."

TWENTY-SEVEN

Colonia del Sacramento, Uruguay, Tuesday July 21, 2020

Howard Knight woke in darkness. A kink in his neck was the culprit. It took a moment to remember he was on a bench in South America. More precisely, he was on a hard park bench, using his backpack as a pillow.

He wiped his eyes, stretched, and sat upright. The sky was clear, stars sparkling brightly. But it was winter in Uruguay and the temperature had dropped significantly since he first fell asleep. With that realization, he shivered and rubbed his hands together for warmth as his brain slowly re-engaged.

At that moment, he experienced a memory flash that startled him. He sprang to his feet and started pacing around the park bench, as though chasing the idea might bring greater clarity. He had to act on the impulse immediately.

To be safe, he wandered over to nearby bushes and peeked through, behind, and over the vegetation to see if anyone was there. He returned to his sleeping spot and looked slowly in an arc from left to right, checking for any motion. Satisfied he was alone in the park, Howard opened his backpack and pulled out his laptop.

He leaned back on the bench and turned it on. It was 12:30 a.m. according to the display on the screen as the computer came to life. Closing the cover again, he tucked the laptop under his arm and wandered toward the main street. There, he opened and closed it as discreetly as possible as he passed each store until he detected an unsecured Wi-Fi connection.

In the recessed alcove of a natural foods store, he sat in a corner and googled Juan Presivo's name and found his Facebook profile. Howard vaguely recalled his name and associated him with odd political interests. The guy FBI Angela requested information about had no security protection at all. Tons of posts and photos appeared as he scrolled the feed, looking for either the face or name that had suddenly popped into his mind in the middle of the night.

Howard was patient. The fellow had hundreds of pages of entries on his profile, most ridiculing the American government, politicians, and anything deemed "politically correct." Other posts promoted conspiracies that sounded not only weird but outright bizarre. And the guy appeared to pose for selfies with virtually anyone. Scraggy beards, wannabe military outfits, and women using their bountiful breasts to promote almost any T-shirt message all made cameo appearances.

Howard was three years into the guy's feed before he spotted her. Lucy Andrews. Presivo's infatuation with her had halted abruptly his advancement in The Organization. As he looked at her photo, Giancarlo Mareno's explicit instructions to his Miami-based leader came back to him.

"She's a dangerous bitch. One of the radio talk show hosts. About a million people listen to her bullshit every day. She uses an American name, but she is really a foreigner. She pretends to be grateful to America for taking her in from somewhere in Eastern Europe, yet she hates everything about our country. And Presivo's screwing her. Leave him out to pasture."

That last sentence might have meant almost anything. His Miami crime boss could have killed Presivo, knowing Mareno wouldn't object. Or he could've assigned the guy meaningless errands that let him earn a living but assured he never came into contact with The Organization's head honcho again. The boss in Florida had chosen the latter.

Howard googled Lucy Andrews. True to form, she had a website and dozens of pages, articles, recordings, and photos. Of course, pictures. The woman was gorgeous. Bountiful black hair that flowed halfway down her back. Her grooming was invariably meticulous—even at a cookout or on a beach.

The picnic shots came from a political gathering where she mingled among a few hundred people who looked like they regularly visited Presivo's Facebook page. Almost every shot included someone wearing a T-shirt featuring an American flag or army surplus gear that didn't fit. Several had weapons strung from their shoulders. Lucy's beach shots showed her front and rear, perfectly proportioned, and her inviting smile was strangely seductive.

Before he scrolled through the pages, Howard checked to see what info she revealed about herself. As expected, almost everything was there. Most interesting to him was a revelation that she was married, and her husband's name was Joey. Joey Andrews.

Over two hours had passed. He stood up again, peeked out from the alcove, and surveyed his surroundings once more. He saw no motion, and the streets remained absolutely still, with not even the sound of a single car. It was eerie, and he shivered slightly in the chilly air but resumed his search.

Almost immediately, he spotted a post on Joey Andrews's Facebook page that merited more attention. "Soon to be fixed for life," the entry announced. Several likes and hearts decorated the post with a few comments wondering if this meant he had scheduled a vasectomy or was inheriting a fortune. Joey Andrews hadn't responded to any of them.

Howard moved to the "about" section of his profile to see what he could gain. Surprisingly, Andrews claimed to speak Russian. Curious. In her biography, his wife said she emigrated from Poland. She reported she graduated from the University of Warsaw. Why would Joey Andrews learn Russian rather than Polish? Wouldn't Polish be a more logical second language choice if he intended to communicate better with his bride and her family?

He found a possible answer when he tried Andrews's LinkedIn profile. He worked for a small technology company that did business with multiple Russian companies. His summary even declared that he had visited Russia over fifty times in the past ten years, a stellar reason to trust his relationships for opening markets and exploring new export opportunities.

Joey Andrews's social media profile suggested neither contact nor liaisons with the characters living on the outer margins that his wife mingled with. In fact, Howard checked both profiles twice to be sure the two were indeed married to each other. Photos and descriptions matched.

It wasn't much. He hesitated a moment as he weighed the security risks. The Wi-Fi from the alcove wasn't secure. He reached deep into the pocket of his jeans, then fished out and turned on the phone he'd bought from SingTel. It was only the second time he'd used it since leaving Toronto. A signal from roaming partner *Telefonica Moviles* appeared strong, so with cold thumbs barely cooperating, he typed up an email to share his curious observations with Angela at the FBI.

He really shouldn't have destroyed their phone, but it seemed only logical that the device was tracking his movements from Toronto—where they first gave it to him—to three different locations in Costa Rica. This little morsel of new info would show her there was no ill-will, give her a number she could use for texting him, and provide something to occupy her for a while.

He rechecked the hour right after he hit the send button. The laptop showed 5:17. That left another three hours to kill before the sun would rise this far south during winter. He used the time productively and searched for a place to stay. Howard had a specific location in mind but couldn't find it on the Airbnb site where he'd booked the last time.

He checked alternatives and investigated four different property rental sites before finding the spot on a website he'd never heard of called Tip-Key. It was a small dwelling on the outskirts of the town on an unfinished dirt road with lots of space between neighbors. Except for the barking dogs at night, it was a relatively quiet development, and the house met his needs perfectly.

He remembered the pool he hadn't been able to try out the last time. He liked the high wooden gate in front of the place that blocked unwanted attention. And the woman who owned the building was always friendly and accommodating.

So far, he'd been unable to load a TVB Bank Mastercard for his new Stuart McGregor identity and paused a few moments to consider the risks of using the Bartoli version. The only downside he identified was the possibility someone could track his location if they had access to the bank's computer systems. While he was with The Organization, they had tried to hack the mainframe and found it impenetrable. Five or six years had elapsed since those attempts, but he eventually satisfied himself the risk was low. He booked the house.

Although Howard used his Bartoli identification for the reservation, he expected she'd still be amenable to his proposal. Although she wouldn't recognize the name, she had accepted his same request using another identity the last time. Sure enough, as soon as the site approved his credit card, she texted that she would deliver a key and leave it in the mailbox outside the gate before nine o'clock.

Although it was still dark when he finished his tasks, Howard moved on from the store alcove. Staying too long in one spot posed risks. He headed toward the lighthouse. The narrow street zigzagged for a half-dozen short blocks before he passed the park again and eventually circled back to the main avenue.

He continued at a leisurely pace that killed time, kept himself warm, but wouldn't attract attention from anyone peeking out a window at an early hour. Eventually Howard came across a tiny plaza called Colonia Shopping. He'd bought groceries there on his last visit to the town. None of the stores were open that early, of course, but he knew his way back.

He checked Google Maps again and confirmed he was about halfway to the house he'd just rented. Shops or restaurants wouldn't open for another hour or more, so he opted to check out the rental home.

Sidewalks ended at that point, so he trudged along the side of the roadway, wary of the uneven ground, unexpected litter, and an occasional dead animal. The walk proved uneventful until he reached the top of Avenida Centrale, the poorly maintained road where the house was located. Dogs howled. He'd forgotten how annoying those mutts could be.

As Howard passed each property on the street, another dog growled, barked, and threw itself against flimsy fences and gates. They all sounded like mad German Shepherds or some other equally vicious breed deprived of both food and excitement for too long. He quickened his pace, but none of the beasts scaled a fence or broke down a doorway to finish him off.

To reach his rental house, it took about ten minutes. By the time he peered over the tall gate, there was just enough light from the rising sun to see it clearly. It appeared nothing had changed since his last unfortunate visit, so he moved on after only a brief survey and headed further along the street in the river's direction.

As Howard worked his way back toward the center of town to find a restaurant, he reassessed his priorities. He needed groceries, clothes, and other supplies. That would probably mean a half-dozen return trips walking from the house to the supermarket. A taxi might accomplish the task in one trip, but a curious driver could ask questions better avoided.

Before he reached his destination, he passed a shop that caught his eye. MotoRent, the sign announced. As its name suggested, the firm rented motorcycles, bikes, scooters, and an array of other gas-powered buggies. Perfect.

When he came across a restaurant opening its doors for customers a few blocks further along, he had a huge breakfast to replenish his energy. The owner appeared satisfied with his appetite and Spanish. They chatted between servings as he established a story for anyone inquiring about the town's new stranger. He was a Canadian financier taking an extended vacation and would stay for only a few weeks.

Howard left an appropriate tip as he finished and paid his bill. Then, with a spring in his step, he headed back to MotoRent.

TWENTY-EIGHT

Punta del Este, Uruguay, Tuesday July 21, 2020

To her pleasant surprise, the exhausted bodyguards driving over from Montevideo sat waiting outside the terminal where private jets arrived. One spotted her at the top of the staircase, then dashed inside as Fidelia stepped out of the jet and waved.

A moment later, a tall woman followed the same bodyguard out of the doorway, along the tarmac, and away from the building. She wandered toward another parked aircraft without looking in the direction of the new arrivals. The woman kept her gaze on the asphalt and disappeared behind the other jet as Fidelia and Klaudia met up with the bodyguards.

The guard named Carlos nodded wordlessly. The other led them through the empty terminal and out a rear entrance to a rented SUV. His name was Joe, and his eyes darted all around before he spoke.

"I gave her cash. The woman is onside. No record of the jet landing. No receipt for the fuel."

"Great. Thanks. Did you visit the house yet?" Fidelia asked.

"No. Just arrived ten minutes ago. You want us to leave you somewhere and check it out first?"

"We'll wait in the car when we get there. You guys can peek inside and be sure it's clear."

Joe nodded. Carlos slipped behind the steering wheel, and within moments they were on the roadway toward Avenidas Cannes, 20, near the center of the resort city and walking distance to the waterfront.

The trip took about twenty minutes, and she noticed the scenery was still like most other beach cities. Condos and apartments lined the street, with occasional breaks for supermarkets, shops, fuel stations, and the other necessities of life for vacationing tourists. In Punta del Este, most of those guests were Argentinian. In July, visitors were scarce and the city quiet. It was a good place to wait out the pandemic for a few months, avoid crowds, and find out what Stan Tan—and his friend the Shadow—were up to.

Fidelia recognized Playa Brava, the beautiful sandy beach directly

159

across the main roadway from their house. The home belonged to the recently deceased Manuel Ortez. Her former country boss for Latin America met an untimely end in Chile when she learned the bastard had betrayed her and worked for the Russian Mafia on the side. An unsettling shiver shot up her spine as she recalled the horrible screams she'd heard listening by phone from Australia while Luigi interrogated and dismembered the scum.

When Carlos brought the vehicle to a stop at the end of the driveway, he motioned for them to wait a moment. He casually drew a weapon from his jacket as the other guy unlocked the door. Fidelia and Klaudia waited silently in the SUV while they completed their inspection. Everyone looked exhausted from the previous eventful hours.

Rather than simply waving them in, Joe hurried back.

"There's a squatter in there. Young girl. Maybe in her mid-teens. Claims Ortez gave her permission to live there. You want us to throw her out?"

Fidelia considered her options for a moment. The young woman was probably the plaything she'd spoken with when she'd called Ortez about the Colombia problem a few months earlier. Not the brightest bulb in the lamp, she was presumably a kid from Ortez's escort operations. The house had enough space for privacy, so it was perhaps better to lock her in one room for a couple days until she could come up with a longer-term solution.

"Do you speak Spanish?"

"No. Carlos does."

"Okay, send him out."

Fidelia and Klaudia stayed in the vehicle while she gave him instructions. He was to treat the young woman courteously and gently.

"Take her to the small bedroom in the back corner on the second floor, far away from the master. Tell her we won't harm her if she cooperates, stays quiet, and doesn't cause trouble. Say nothing about Ortez's death. Let her know you'll bring her food and something to drink in just a few minutes. Signal when we're clear to enter."

Thankfully, Carlos waved them in a few moments later without further drama. Fidelia knew the layout of the place from a reward romp with its owner years before. Nothing had changed. The dark wood furniture was traditional Uruguayan with old Spanish influence, using ornate curves to create warmth and richness in design.

Chocolate brown drapes covering the windows looked like they hadn't been washed since her last visit. Thick, gloomy, and heavy to open, she had hated them from the moment she'd entered the house with Ortez. She yanked them wide to let light into their refuge for the coming few weeks or months. Sunlight made the interior more livable. The entire package evoked a fleeting flashback to her childhood home in Puerto Rico.

A quick inspection of the kitchen found an almost empty refrigerator and pantry cupboards equally bare. The young girl must have survived on food ordered in. Fidelia summoned her bodyguards and instructed them to write a list of groceries and supplies she started dictating while they scrambled for a piece of paper and pen. Within minutes, she had Carlos out the door with a prepaid credit card she used only for this type of errand.

Before she could assign Klaudia her sleeping quarters, Fidelia's secure phone rang. It was her primary protector.

"More problems at home," he said. "'Nother twenty-five guys disappeared overnight 'n an FBI roundup. This time 'n Jersey. Boys were swamped with calls from scared 'n angry wives 'n girlfriends."

"Be sure your people keep sending them money. That's what panics the women. Their only means of support dries up if their men are in jail, so make clear we'll get them what they need. Are you in Poland yet?" Fidelia kept her tone calm.

"Just arrived 'n Vilnius. Closest airport to Krynki we could find without landin' in Belarus. They check passports at the border. From Lithuania, we were okay. Guys here picked us up 'n we're a couple hours from the house."

"And the other Lithuanians you sent to Belarus to get the American?"

"Got him. 'Bout 'n hour ago. No Russians 'n sight and no resistance. Our guys drugged him to be safe and stuffed him in the trunk for when they cross the border. They should get ta the place in Krynki a few minutes b'fore us."

"Be gentle when you interrogate him. I need information, not retribution."

"Yeah ... yeah ... Still worried 'bout the FBI. Can't say why, but I've a hunch your old friend Howard Knight might be involved." Luigi chose his words delicately, but his tone was firm.

"Why do you think he's involved?"

"Every single arrest, the FBI mention they've someone feedin' 'em information. Might just wanna taunt 'r scare our guys, but I think they're braggin'. Since he disappeared from Stan Tan's place a few months ago, Knight's evaporated. No sign of 'im anywhere. But one of our moles 'n Canada thought he visited the US consulate 'n Toronto 'n April."

"Why is your mole letting you know this just now?" Fidelia used a tone more accusing than curious.

"She's the same gal who picked up that the FBI kept tellin' guys they had a source when arrestin' them. She found it strange. Day 'r two later, reminded her of a guy visitin' their Toronto office for a hush-hush meetin'. Guy covered himself in the hallways but didn't discover cameras in the meetin' room. She went to a file photo for a look at Knight. Thought it could be the same person. Let 'er know it pissed me she didn't report it right away. Claims she didn't know we're still interested in the scum. I know ya promised Knight you'd let him go. But I think ya may wanna track him down and have a chat."

More than once, Luigi had argued she shouldn't let Howard live. Initially, she'd wondered if it might be jealousy—even though she was confident he had no evidence of their previous intimate relationship. His danger antenna was usually good, so she took his concerns seriously.

Of course, after they'd eliminated Giancarlo Mareno in Martinique, she'd suggested Howard return to the safe harbor of the FBI witness protection program. Perhaps it was one of those rare occasions he'd followed her advice.

"Okay. I may be able to get a lead on his whereabouts. I'll let you know in a day or two. In the meantime, call me as soon as Joey Andrews—or whatever his real name is—starts to talk."

TWENTY-NINE

Lyon, France, Wednesday July 22, 2020

Delayed by a full day, Suzanne's promised Interpol briefing finally happened. Edouard Deschamps and Angela Bonner sat stiff and unsmiling in chairs facing her. No one seemed eager to begin the conversation, but the American forensic investigator eventually shrugged and waded in.

"I guess neither of us is sure where to start. It's volatile, fluid, and chaotic. Here's what we know. Your friend Michelle has become difficult. She refuses to communicate with the *gendarmes* in France or Interpol's people in Lyon. But it's worse than just communication. Edouard canceled our scheduled briefing yesterday morning because we learned her fiancé had arranged for Jean-Louis Sauvignon's ransom through his company. Les Entreprises Diverses borrowed fifty million dollars on its line of credit with a consortium of French banks, then loaned it to Guillaume Boudreau."

"They paid!" Suzanne gasped in shock.

"Yeah. They opened a mitcoyne account and followed the kidnappers' instructions. That was Monday. We know the transfer took place, but there's been no communication from Jean-Louis's captors since. No acknowledgment. No promise of release. Nothing."

Suzanne processed the implications in silence. Silence so long and profound she heard a faint tinkling of chimes from a balcony outside. Uncomfortable squirming in seats followed. Stefan spoke next.

"Is there any chance the funds went into a wrong account?"

"None." Finally, Deschamps said something. "Our digital experts checked. There's no doubt the money went to the right account. Angela has passed on the details to the FBI. They have a unit that has had some success tracking down recipients of payments despite the anonymity of mitcoyne. But it'll take time."

For a few more minutes, they discussed digital currencies, their strengths and weaknesses, and Interpol's optimism they'd eventually discover where Guillaume Boudreau's fifty million ended up. More pressing was the fate of Jean-Louis Sauvignon.

"Do you still think we can get him back alive?" Suzanne asked.

"Chances are slim, but we're chasing one possibility Angela passed on to us."

His choice of words and tone telegraphed his lack of optimism.

The American investigator threw it out there anyway.

"We've been getting some help from an FBI source. He's not officially in the witness protection program, but they tell me he's under the wing of a unit in the Bureau. I don't fully understand how it works. The Fort Myers office put me on to him. I know Dan Ramirez used to be with the FBI, so I checked with him to see if the tip was legit. He asked around with his contacts and confirmed I should have a dialog with the person in question. I've been communicating with him by email on a secure network."

She glanced about the room, taking the pulse of the group. To Suzanne, it all sounded truly farfetched, and she'd never been entirely comfortable with this forensic investigator turned FBI agent. However, Angela apparently considered her audience receptive enough to continue.

"His emails repeatedly cast doubt on The Organization's involvement in either the kidnapping or the bombings in the States. More than once, this source asserted these activities did not fit with the *modus operandi* of the gang. Still, he seems to have a remarkable recall for names that may be helpful." Angela paused again to see if everyone was following her explanation. Satisfied, she carried on.

"In one of his recent emails, he suggested we try to locate someone named Joey Andrews. Our informant thought there might be some connection between Andrews and someone in the lower echelons of The Organization. He remembered a fellow by that name had attracted the attention of Giancarlo Mareno because of his extreme right-wing political connections. Mareno thought the fellow a liability and had his role with The Organization diminished."

Although the story sounded convoluted, Suzanne forced herself to remain patient while the forensic investigator laboriously set up her conclusions. She kept her head tilted to portray interest and smiled a faint encouragement for the woman to continue.

"I know you guys aren't as interested in all the background details as I am, so here's the important point. Our source suggested I check the fellow out. I had the DC office of the Bureau do some digging. They confirmed Andrews speaks Russian and recently commented on Facebook that he was expecting a big payoff in the coming days. They did a routine search of the FDA's Advance Passenger Information System and learned someone named Joey Andrews left Washington on a private jet destined for Minsk just two days ago. The plane in question arrived as scheduled, but our person of interest has disappeared. The bodies of the plane's pilot and co-pilot turned up in a ditch in Belarus near the border with Poland."

"Is there any hope of tracking down this Joey Andrews?" It was Stefan who asked the question.

"Hope is about all we have," Deschamps replied. "But we sent an elite team from the national police force in Poland to the scene. They're traveling undercover because law enforcement in Belarus is notoriously hostile to perceived interference. They'll see what they can find."

To be polite, Suzanne continued to ask a few minor, clarifying questions before bringing the meeting to a close. Her furrowed brow and slumped shoulders reflected unease as the pair of investigators saw themselves out of the apartment. Still, she had a vast company to run and a demanding board of directors to satisfy. To an extent far greater than she preferred, the board's immediate satisfaction—and her own peace of mind— rested in the hands of James Fitzgerald and his girlfriend. So her next call was to James.

"Natalia still hasn't found a candidate we can take to the board." James always told it like it was, no sugar coating. "She hasn't given up. With help from Human Resources, she identified two new channels of prospects, particularly from Asian countries. Both show some potential, and they're filtering through those candidates as quickly as possible. You may need to ask for an extension, though."

"That's one option." Her answer was curter than Suzanne intended. Fortunately, her Mountie friend had come through with an overnight memo confirming Natalia Tenaz's background was so squeaky clean it was boring. She softened the message. "I'm not averse to asking for more time if we must, but Stefan suggested another avenue to consider."

She paused respectfully, knowing he probably wouldn't reply. After a second or two, she carried on. "An entrepreneurial mindset is crucial for the new president of Financial Services. We all agree on that. But it's the one weakness of every candidate Natalia has identified so far. Stefan wondered if maybe we haven't focused too much on academic qualifications and experience."

"Perhaps," James said when she hesitated a moment.

"All the people we've been considering are already vice-presidents somewhere or in other rewarding senior positions. He threw out an idea

I initially dismissed, but I'll share it with you to hear what you think." She paused again for effect and drew no response. "Brace yourself. Stefan thinks our new president is right under our noses. Natalia Tenaz."

Silence followed. A long silence with not even the sound of breathing. Suzanne looked at her phone to see if the line had disconnected.

"I didn't need to brace myself. I'm not surprised Stefan noticed her potential. I've watched her learn and grow over the dozen years she's worked with Financial Services. She's one of the brightest women I've interacted with and a born leader. If the decision was mine alone, I'd have moved her into the job without even doing a search."

James left his comment hanging. He knew how to manage conversations masterfully, but Suzanne was equally skillful.

"I hear a big, unstated 'but' at the end of that sentence."

"The decision isn't only mine. Nor yours. Some formidable egos on the board attach great importance to credentials and experience. I'm not sure we can easily convince them."

Interesting. The masterful executive showed no surprise with the suggestion Natalia might fit the bill. He only expressed concern about how to sell it to the other directors.

She tested her read. "Did I hear correctly? You think she's the best person for the role?"

"Best is a relative term." James laughed. "Can she do the job? Yes. Would she excel? I expect so. Is there someone even better out there? I don't know. I see her as stronger than anyone we've seen so far."

There, he'd taken a position. Now, was he ready to take a risk?

"You're in charge of the search and the recommendation to the board. Should we bring her name forward for consideration?"

"You're curious to see if I'm prepared to put my money where my mouth is?" He chuckled again. "Not yet. But here's what I suggest. Let me chair an ad hoc committee. I'll put Cliff Williams on it. He was even skeptical about giving her responsibility for the search. I'll add Abduhl Mahinder from The Bank of the Americas. Everyone respects his financial acumen. And I'll pick Ruth Bégin for her European perspective. We'll schedule a zoom interview with Natalia and see what that panel thinks."

The idea made sense, but could still be risky. Credibility with the board of directors was a CEO's most valuable asset and not one to be squandered. Everyone around the table knew James well. They also realized he wouldn't put forward such a radical recommendation without Suzanne's okay. She took her time to weigh the odds.

"I think you know it's counter-intuitive for me to give you the green light, but we're operating in unusual times and even stranger ways. I value your counsel. If you're prepared to carry the ball, I'll support you."

A shot of adrenaline jolted Suzanne upright with a sudden realization. Wasn't it odd both Stefan and James had spotted the same potential in the same candidate? Had she perhaps just played an expected role in a drama scripted much earlier?

THIRTY

Colonia del Sacramento, Uruguay, Wednesday July 22, 2020

By his second day with the electric scooter from MotoRent, Howard felt entirely at ease on the handy machine. He paid extra for a helmet and wore it every time, a decision made easy because they were compulsory in Uruguay. Three separate trips to the Supermarket, a clothing store, and Cellular Center, each with full bags on return, had polished his balance on the two-wheeler and built his confidence. Even deep potholes and unexpected dips in the road no longer caused his heart rate to quicken.

He stashed his laptop in his newly purchased backpack for safekeeping, then added bottles of water to the little pouches on either side. As an afterthought, he threw a couple apples and carrots into a compartment separate from the computer.

It was brisk that morning. A weather app on his phone showed it was just forty-five degrees. But he was better prepared than the night he'd slept for only a few hours on the chilly park bench. Now, he had a winter jacket, warm leather gloves, and a wool scarf he wrapped around his neck with a fashionable flourish.

Howard left that afternoon with a full stomach and expected to be out until early evening. With a snap of his helmet strap, he grinned. Then he locked the gate to the yard and revved the engine of the scooter twice before departing. With his blissful day out in a rental car in Costa Rica a week earlier etched into his memory, he sought more of the same.

Following his route from the previous outings, he navigated his way from the house to the main roadway cautiously and slowly, dodging the deepest potholes in the packed dirt road.

At the intersection with Highway 1, he made a careful right turn and twisted the throttle to its maximum. Within a minute or two, he achieved the machine's full speed of about thirty miles per hour and motored along the side of the roadway.

His helmet visor covered only the upper half of his face. That made it great to keep the bugs out yet feel the cool winter air sweep across the exposed skin. Other drivers were courteous. Faster cars and trucks pulled out to create wide berths between their bigger vehicles and his tiny, two-wheeled machine, and the pavement was well maintained—with a smooth shoulder of stones should he need to leave the asphalt in a hurry.

About twenty minutes from his rental home, Howard came to a major intersection and signaled his left turn to head inland. Highway 50 appeared on the first sign he passed, and it was clearly a secondary roadway. Its paved surface was mainly smooth, but the lanes were much narrower, and the shoulder inconsistent. It was the type of road that demanded constant attention to avoid a mishap with another vehicle, a rut, or some unexpected moisture on the pavement.

On the plus side, there was almost no traffic in the rural area. Large farms dominated the landscape on both sides of the highway. Some farmers concentrated on grains; others had cows wandering fields for dairy or meat. Overall, the air smelled fresh and his smile grew broader with every mile.

After about an hour, Howard had passed through the villages of Semillero, Tarariras, and San Luis. The first was no more than a collection of houses on a few tiny streets. The second was an authentic small town with a couple dozen roads and a compact Hospital Evangélico with a big banner on the corner. To follow the signs to San Luis, he had to leave the roadway for a bit. It became a gravel country road that finished at a large agricultural complex and not much else.

Back on Highway 50, Howard wound his way around more large farms and ranches until the road ended abruptly at Highway 54. Left led further inland, so he chose the opposite direction where Google Maps suggested he'd find a beach near the town of Juan Lacaze. It was too cold for swimming, but he usually liked coastal towns' casual, relaxed atmospheres no matter the season.

He cruised around the village, exploring street by street. Howard stopped when he saw a building of interest or needed more time to translate a sign. Houses were small, only two or three rooms in each, and maintenance of the structures was lax. Several were in disrepair, yet young children played in yards of places they considered home. Stores were tiny and sparse. Along the beach, shells of buildings housed restaurants in warmer weather, but now some were boarded shut.

Howard parked the scooter after a while and wandered the same streets he'd scouted on wheels. People returned his hellos when he greeted them. A few even stopped to inquire if he needed help or information. All were friendly and welcoming. After walking for an hour, he joined an informal, semi-circle seating arrangement of chairs on a patch of grass in front of a bar with four local guys who appeared out of work and perhaps permanent fixtures of the place. None wore masks.

They signaled a welcome when he asked in Spanish if he might join, and it took only seconds for them to pose questions, learning about the stranger.

Unaccustomed to such gatherings, he proceeded with caution. "I'm from Canada, a retired investor out to see a bit of the world," he answered to the first.

"You waited for a global pandemic to begin your travels?" a fellow asked before he laughed uproariously, prompting all the others to join. Knee slapping and hand clapping followed as one after the other joked at Howard's expense with morbid humor about COVID-19.

He took no offense and offered a wisecrack or two of his own. Apparently, he'd passed the admission requirements, and conversation drifted in various directions as they sipped on beers that reappeared almost magically when a bottle looked in danger of running empty. First, they wanted to know a bit about Canada. Then the focus narrowed to soccer in Canada, which Howard knew nothing about, so he switched the discussion to their homeland.

The guys took turns sharing good and bad things about their country for a few minutes before reverting to soccer. When Howard lived in the Netherlands, he'd followed soccer from time to time. European fans were as passionate about the game as his current companions, and he remembered a couple famous names of players from Uruguay. A mention of Luis Suarez and Edinson Cavani was all it needed to get them yakking for about an hour. The boys talked *fútbol*. He listened.

When they noticed he'd lost interest, the subject shifted to politics. Of course, Howard knew nothing about the government in Uruguay and little about current events in Canada. He used well-timed questions to keep the group animated and involved in their own limited world. He'd probably never have another conversation with any of the guys. Still, it was better not to create more lies than he could remember.

After his third beer, he glanced at his phone and realized he should head back toward his rental home in Colonia de Sacramento. Despite protests that it was too early to leave and offers to buy one more, he shuffled off to find his scooter. Thankfully, it sat in the same spot three or four blocks away in front of the only grocery store Howard had seen during his walkabout. He fired up the bike and sped off toward Highway 1.

The days were short at that time of the year, so he turned on his running lights just as he swerved left onto the thoroughfare. Traffic remained light, often with gaps of minutes between passing or approaching vehicles. Although cold, his heavy jacket, warm leather gloves, and the wool scarf around his neck and face kept him comfortable. The ride proved refreshing and relaxing.

His jaunt had been a good one. Some sight-seeing. Some fresh air. An opportunity to practice Spanish with a friendly bunch. Who could ask for more? All he needed was a fine meal to cap off the day. After a few minutes, Colonia del Sacramento appeared on the darkening horizon, so Howard checked his mirror before preparing to turn left onto a side street.

Bright lights reflecting off the mirror almost blinded him momentarily before he realized a vehicle approached rapidly. He nudged his two-wheeler closer to the edge of the roadway, leaving lots of space for the car to pass, and leaned forward to reduce the wind pressure on his face. When he glanced up again, a truck had streaked past, creating enough air turbulence that his scooter wheels wobbled.

He noticed more bright lights and another vehicle bearing down on him. This time, its operator showed no intention of sweeping around Howard and his motorbike. Instead, it looked as though the driver held him in his sights. He waved frantically to leave him space.

For an instant, time stood still. Searing heat from a car's engine. Deathly silence before a whine of acceleration. A fraction of a second before lights prepared to strike his fender, he veered desperately off the highway.

The shoulder of the road gave way, and the scooter's rear tire fishtailed out of control. It plunged downward into a deep ditch. He yanked back on the handlebars, but it was too late. Instinctively, his left foot touched out to the ground to maintain balance. In a flash of motion, his scooter swung sideways, hopped a short distance, and landed with a gigantic thud next to the pavement, throwing him off toward a ditch. When he hit the surface, the agony was immediate and excruciating. Then everything grew quiet.

Pain shot upward from his ankle to his hip. He reached down to touch the injured area, but found it impossible to move. His body felt anchored to the ground. When he glanced down, blood oozed from his leg, and something peeked out from a large tear in his jeans. It looked like a bone.

Another car stopped just behind Howard and activated its flashing lights. A door slammed and someone ran toward him, shoes scuffing on the gravel as they approached. It was a woman.

"Are you alright?" She pointed a flashlight beam into Howard's eyes, making him cringe instinctively.

Before he could answer, she noticed his leg and shifted the light.

"Call 1-1-2," she shouted to a companion. "He's injured. Seriously injured."

The good Samaritan dropped to her knees and leaned over him. She yanked a scarf from her neck and wrapped it tightly around the wound. Howard screamed out in pain even with the gentle touch.

"I'm sorry. I'm trying to slow the bleeding. It has to be tight. Be calm. My friend is calling for help. They'll be here soon."

Her voice was soft, almost soothing, although her manner didn't conceal her concern and urgency. It felt longer, but only moments later, the faint whine of a siren broke the silence at the side of the road. It grew louder quickly, and soon stopped with a crunch in the stones, bright blue lights flashing across the darkening sky. Seconds after its siren faded, another started faintly in the distance.

The paramedics asked only a few questions as they lowered a stretcher to the ground. With practiced skill, they hoisted Howard onto the device as he again screamed out in agony. Tears blurred his eyes. Despite the chilly night, his body became hot, then cold. Each tiny shift generated pain over and over in every part of his leg.

Inside the ambulance, one attendant jumped in behind the stretcher as the driver slammed the door shut. Almost immediately, the piercing sound of the siren blared out into the darkness and they were in motion.

"We'll get you something stronger for the pain as soon as we arrive at the hospital," he said as he held Howard's wrist to take his pulse. "Do you hurt anywhere else?"

"No," he finally said, amid groans of agony. "It's just my leg."

From the accident scene to the nearest emergency room was less than a five-minute drive with the sirens wailing and horns honking. Howard opened his eyes when the ambulance stopped and tried to reorient himself.

A rear door swung open before the paramedics pulled the stretcher outward. Despite their best efforts, it thumped solidly on the asphalt of the parking lot, evoking yet another scream of pain.

He saw a lighted green and white sign as an entrance opened and the attendants wheeled him through. Hospital Evangélico. Not the one he saw earlier on his scooter ride. He'd been inside this hospital before. Years earlier, he'd needed care when he collapsed in the same house he now rented, the time he caught the mumps. It wasn't important, but letting his mind wander, thinking about something other than his current injury, distracted him somewhat from the pain.

As soon as they had Howard inside, in a curtained-off emergency space with room for two separated patients, a nurse approached with an IV pole, a bag already mounted. She spoke with a soft tone as she explained she'd give him some medication for his pain. It might hurt his wrist for a moment. He nodded and continued to groan with every twitch of his leg.

His next visitor carried a clipboard. Middle-aged, tall, dark, and serious, she looked over eyeglasses perched on the edge of her nose as she asked if he had insurance. He shook his head.

"Our country provides health coverage for our citizens. I'm sorry, but we have to charge foreigners for treatment. Do you have a passport and credit card?"

"Yes. In my backpack. Can you bring it to me?"

Howard braced for the pain to come, but he couldn't let anyone else scrounge through his documents. There were two passports in there, one fake, the other legitimate. He needed to be sure they saw only the Bartoli one that matched his prepaid Mastercard. Silently, he also cursed his haste in leaving Montevideo. Belatedly, he'd learned it was the only city in Uruguay with a branch of the TVB Bank. He had a useful new identity but had no way to use the passport until he could load a new credit card.

It took more than a few minutes, but the woman returned with the backpack in hand and placed it next to him on the bed. Howard drew a deep breath and raised himself on an elbow. The morphine was working. Pain wasn't as severe as he'd feared.

The woman discreetly stepped away and chatted with an attendant while he looked for the documents. He fidgeted with the zippers and pouches until he found his wallet and the correct passport. The assistant took both from his hand and eventually returned. Howard slipped the card and fake document into a pouch just inside the backpack, near the top. It would be easier to find them quickly in case he needed to again.

A doctor came sometime later. He was young, probably recently out of medical school. He smiled first, pulled back a sheet that covered Howard's leg, then glanced at the injury for only an instant.

"You have fractures. No doubt about that. But we'll take X-rays to see how many and what we'll need to do to repair them. You were riding a bike?"

"A scooter, yes. I rented it. What happened to it?"

"Don't worry, you're not the first. The police will let the rental company know about your accident. They'll collect it from the scene of the crash. I understand you are a Canadian. I studied at U of T in Toronto for a year. What brings you to Uruguay in the winter in the middle of a pandemic?"

Howard thought a moment before he replied. A grunt of pain provided cover while he considered his response. It was better to keep his answers consistent. Others might ask in the coming days.

"I'm an investor. I've been traveling through Latin America looking for new opportunities. When the coronavirus numbers grew in this part of the world, I looked for the country doing the best job. Uruguay appeared to be a safe place to stay for a while. I didn't factor a crash into my calculations."

"Well, life is like investing. Sometimes we can't foresee all the factors needed to make an accurate calculation. That's why I will probably be practicing medicine for a long time." The doctor chuckled at his lame attempt at humor. "I'll see you after I review the X-rays."

As with everything in Latin America, the emergency room pace seemed slow and relaxed. Howard had little basis for comparison, but American hospitals must be quicker. Of course, they also cost exorbitant amounts. The costs might not be as high here, but would his credit card balance be adequate? Probably. He'd worry about it when his mind cleared.

Howard endured a fresh round of unwelcome pain from every shift and movement during the X-rays, and then the young doctor returned, his expression grave.

"It's a compound fracture. You've broken the tibia and fibula bones. The tibia will need surgery we can't perform here. I've called our headquarters in Montevideo. They can repair it for you. Is there anyone with you here in Colonia del Sacramento who might drive you there?"

Howard shook his head.

"Okay. I'll arrange for the same paramedics to take you in an ambulance. That's better anyway. They will keep the IV flowing and you'll feel less pain."

THIRTY-ONE

Punta del Este, Uruguay, Thursday July 23, 2020

It was five o'clock in the morning when a call from her primary protector woke Fidelia with several insistent rings. She was groggy and muscles she'd forgotten existed still ached. He agreed to hold the line while she eased her way out of bed and gingerly stumbled toward the kitchen.

Klaudia was already awake and seated at the dining nook, sipping a steaming cup of coffee. "Want one?" She pointed to the Keurig beside her.

Fidelia smiled, nodded, and clasped her hands in gratitude before she carried on with Luigi.

"What's up? Are you at the house in Poland?"

"In Poland. Not at the house. Long story." His tone usually signaled the direction of his thoughts, but this morning, it was impossible to detect what sort of complication he was dealing with.

"Let's hear it." She limped to a nearby chair and settled in.

"Guys from Lithuania snatched Joey Andrews as planned. No resistance. Pilots the only casualties. Dumped 'em in a remote area on the Belarus side of the border. Crossing into Poland, they saw only one immigration officer who waved 'em through."

"So why is it a long story?" She kept the tone of her interruption positive, but hoped it encouraged him to move along.

"When the guys got ta the place, 'twas occupied. Fortunately, they took off immediately and called me. One of the Lithuanians has a device ta detect the number of people inside the place. Slipped back on a path that crosses the farmland behind it ta get closer 'n use it. Just like that trail in England where hikers cross farmers' fields."

"I remember." Her curt response was to signal he should get to the point.

"Crawled along the path after dark 'n used the guy's trackin' equipment. Seven live bodies inside. From the trail, spotted two guys outside, front 'n back. Guardin' the place."

Fidelia motioned for Klaudia to come closer and switched on the speaker before she posed her question. "Any indication where the people are from? License plates, that sort of thing?"

"Couple Volkswagen SUVs parkt outside. Identical. White rentals. EU plates."

"Were you able to get close enough to read them?" Klaudia asked, pulling out her phone to take notes.

"Na. Too dangerous ta get any closer. No cover near the yard."

"Okay. I've got an app I'll download to your device while we're talking," Klaudia said. "When it arrives, activate the software and slowly move your handset across the house in an arc, like you're taking a video of the place. It should give us some more info."

Fidelia silently watched her friend, the technology geek, quickly punch a stream of letters and numbers into her phone.

"Okay. Did you get it?"

"Yeah, got it."

"Alright. We'll hang up while you use the app. Make a note of all the IP addresses that appear and call us back with that info."

The women sipped their coffee and chattered about their aching muscles, poor sleep, and recovery hopes until Fidelia's secure phone rang again.

"Texted Klaudia a screenshot of what I picked up with the app," Luigi started. "Guy from Lithuania showed me how ta do it." He snickered with satisfaction as he waited for her instructions.

"Great. Okay. There's eight of them. Two IP addresses originate in Belarus. Two others in Poland. The rest are Russian," Klaudia said as she peered at her phone.

"What's that tell us?" he asked with a trace of annoyance.

Fidelia answered. "We know you're outnumbered two to one, first of all. If the Lithuanian guy's app is right, there must be someone there without a phone. And it's an international gathering. Does it give us more than that, Klaudia?"

"Not immediately, but I'll try tracking the specific IP addresses. We might find exactly where they're from and be able to identify who we're dealing with that way."

"Alright, let's go with that to start," Fidelia said. "Luigi, I think you need to have a little chat with Joey Andrews, regardless. You can't use the house. Can you find a secluded spot to interrogate him tonight? Someplace his voice won't carry?"

It might be hard to locate somewhere that didn't attract attention. They weren't talking about the noise level of an ordinary conversation. There would be screams, and lots of them.

"We'll go somewhere. May take awhile. Now, question for ya, Fidelia.

Any luck findin' Howard Knight? Lost another fifteen men in an FBI round-up yesterday. This's gettin' real serious." Her primary protector snarled as he made his point, something rare in a conversation with her.

"Where last night?"

"Chicago. All important guys. Somebody's givin' the Feds information that's good as gold." His tone was more subdued.

"Alright. I'll keep looking for Knight and let you know."

Fidelia had barely slept the previous night. Despite her exhaustion, she had tossed and turned for hours, unable to get Howard out of her mind. Already, she had broken her promise to leave him alone when she'd had Tan ferret him out of Cambodia. Though reluctantly, he'd performed his vital part in the Australia operation exceptionally well and without complaint.

Long before that, he'd also been a decent lover for two decades, and he had always treated her with respect and consideration. In her line of work, she couldn't say that about many people.

But Luigi was probably right. It seemed no coincidence the FBI arrests were all guys with long tenure. Guys Howard would remember. He had already sold out The Organization once. Giancarlo Mareno, and Luigi, had wanted him dead; Fidelia had been more ambivalent. After all, his treachery opened the door to expand her influence and end up on top at The Organization. This time, it was different. If he fed information to the FBI again, it could be her ass on the line. It was painful, but she had to do it.

She waited until Klaudia left the room to shower, then found a project for the bodyguards to work on outside the house. For a second, she considered the girl they were holding upstairs, then quickly dismissed the thought when she realized her voice wouldn't carry that far.

First, she pulled up the email server Klaudia had created—the one that hid any return ID and scrambled the IP location after transmission. From her contacts app, she found the private email address. Finally, she attached the file with a photo she'd retrieved from her "special" files buried deep in a doubly protected cloud.

It pictured her target on his knees atop a table, nude and with two other men. One man's penis was in his mouth. The other was entering him from the rear. Above him, the two men were locked in a passionate kiss. She shook her head and turned away. People who thought only female escorts satisfied sexual fantasies had no idea. She had little doubt the guy would consider carefully her unusual demand.

She gritted her teeth and hit the "send" icon with a jab of her forefinger.

When Klaudia resurfaced after her shower, Fidelia put her to work on the IP addresses they'd picked up at the house in Poland. She asked her to start with the four from Russia. The woman was a true computer geek before she became an escort. If anyone could find the people behind those digital monikers, it was Klaudia. She was brilliant, even if her story was a sad one.

Although she'd lived the past couple decades in Germany, her friend was actually Russian. Years earlier, Klaudia had recounted bitter tales of misogyny, rape, and cruelty. From her days at university onward, she'd been part of a string of secret security agencies led by former bosses of the notorious KGB. Besides her legitimate duties, they expected her to service any horny associate without complaint and used threats and force when she hesitated.

They not only mistreated her on the job, they also paid her only enough money to afford a basic one-bedroom apartment. Unbelievably, she shared a toilet and kitchen with ten other people on her floor in the building. For Klaudia, escape to a life that earned wages twenty times greater appeared the only way out of her quagmire. That it meant trafficking girls and women was only a minor detail at the time.

She watched her friend tap the keyboard, intensely focused. Klaudia had lost no motivation to even the score with her former abusers. There was little doubt she could solve the mystery. But did they have enough time?

Two hours after she sent her secret, disturbing email, Fidelia left Klaudia with her search of IP addresses and motioned for the bodyguards to accompany her. She wandered barefoot from the house with only her secure phone in her hand. The guards knew the drill. They'd trail her a discreet distance behind, and well out of earshot.

It was too cold for people to use the beach for anything but a walk, so it was virtually deserted. It was quiet enough to carry on a conversation, but adequate background noise obscured her location.

"Did you receive an email, Mr. Fernando?"

"Who is this? What do you want?" The tone of his voice conveyed intense fear, not anger.

"It doesn't matter who I am. I have the original photo. You received it this morning, correct?"

"How did you—?"

"Never mind. I'll ask. You'll answer. If I don't like what I hear, Mrs. Fernando will receive a copy of the email I sent you earlier, and the CEO of TVB Bank will also find the photo in his inbox. Do we understand each other?"

He sobbed once. Fidelia waited. He drew a breath to say something and changed his mind. She gave him a few seconds to let his worry intensify.

"You have an important American customer named Mr. Smith."

"I have several American customers named Mr. Smith. Which one are you referring to?"

"The one who has over a hundred million dollars with you."

"Perhaps we have more than one person named Smith with more than one hundred million dollars on deposit with us."

Fidelia took a gamble.

"Cut the bullshit, Fernando. Answer my question, or I hang up and shoot out two quick emails. I have them ready to go. All I need to do is hit send."

"Okay. I think I know who you're referring to." His speech sounded faint, but she still detected its quiver of fear.

"That's better. He likes to use prepaid credit cards. He reloads about a hundred thousand at a time. Does that help your memory?"

"Yes."

"Where is he?"

"I don't have clearance to get that information." His voice trembled in panic.

Her reply was immediate, her tone unyielding. "Get access. Now. I'll hold."

"I'll try." His voice was now almost a whisper.

She held the phone to her ear as she walked along the beach. It took several minutes, and she encountered three or four other walkers before Mr. Fernando came back on the line.

"There was a transaction with the Hospital Evangélico yesterday in Montevideo, Uruguay."

THIRTY-TWO

Lyon, France, Thursday July 23, 2020

A spate of separate worries flooded her brain as Suzanne awoke with a start. Jean-Louis Sauvignon was still missing. Michelle refused to talk to her. Her company was misfiring in multiple crucial areas. Worse, she hadn't yet alerted her board of directors about her friend's abrupt verbal resignation, optimistically hoping she'd eventually change her mind and they'd reconcile. So far, the FBI had made little progress on the store bombings in the US or her Atlanta home, now sitting in rubble. And, on top of it all, the government of China was making life miserable for her country manager there.

Among that batch of concerns, she could do something immediately about only one. As she brewed a coffee in the Lyon apartment and performed her morning rituals, she prepared for another difficult conversation with Amber Chan. Her beleaguered president of the Farefour Stores subsidiary had texted requesting a call.

"Pork and poultry supplies are rolling again. One massive company in China controls all the pork shipments to Hong Kong. The main owner let a senior government official know they'd have to cut his 'dividend' because of the boycott of our stores. The cost of selling and delivering to thousands of small shops was far higher than selling to us." Amber's tone carried a tinge of sarcasm as she recounted the facts.

Suzanne liked how Amber always provided both background and recent developments so someone less familiar with China could easily understand. And she told her story well, so Suzanne listened without interruption.

"Once the government caved on the pork issue, the owner shared his success with the association of poultry producers. They, too, made a call. It's only been a few days, but shipments have started. Supply should be back to normal in a few weeks, but there's a new problem."

"What now?" Suzanne strained to keep her tone positive.

"Electricity. Someone is playing with the grid in areas where we have supermarkets. Without warning, our stores lose power. Our back-up generators only hold enough fuel for thirty minutes. When they shut down, we lose our point-of-sale technology, lights, and refrigeration. Everything crashes until we can refuel and restart either the power supply or the generators. I complained to Beijing, but they claim it's somebody offshore. From Macau, they think."

"Why would someone in Macau want to harass us?" Suzanne wondered aloud.

"The bureaucrats say it's probably a party sympathizer living abroad who 'realizes the damage Farefour Stores is doing to the people of Hong Kong by harboring dissidents.'"

"Do they really talk that way?" Suzanne had to stifle a chuckle at the absurdity.

"Yeah. They really talk that way. My technology team thinks they might be right."

"What? A foreign sympathizer from Macau is doing the dirty work for the Communist government?"

"It might be just a Chinese agent working offshore, but the local utility is convinced the signals that killed the power supply each time targeted only areas immediately surrounding our stores. The digital instructions originated in Macau."

"Any threats or demands?" Suzanne asked.

"Only one weird email from a server in Singapore, let me find it." It took a moment before Amber read the message with a tone of bewilderment. "Tell your American bitch-boss to show the Shadow some respect or electricity will be the least of your problems."

"Who's the Shadow?"

"I thought you might know," Amber said. "I have no idea who talks like that."

"Unfortunately, I know a politician who talks that way, but can't think of anyone known as a Shadow. Send that message to Dan Ramirez and ask his people to check it out. How long are these outages?"

"They vary from six to twelve hours. Enough that we have to lock the doors and take precautions. It's sweltering here. Fresh vegetables wilt on the counters without air conditioning. We have to throw out meat if we don't sell it immediately."

"Are the unions cooperating on the demonstrations issue?"

"We're still talking. They're adamant about protecting their members, and there is little doubt the uprisings involve some of the union leadership. Are you able to get us any help from the American government? Any pressure they can exert?"

"Alberto Ferer, our chief legal counsel, and Edward Hadley, who's responsible for government relations, have requested a high-level meeting since you first brought the concern to our attention. Unfortunately, this administration is so dysfunctional they're not getting anywhere. Let me talk with Dan Ramirez when he's available later this morning. Maybe his contacts at the FBI can help with technology or something."

After she finished her call with Amber Chan, Stefan wandered in from the bedroom and perched comfortably on a high stool at the dining island with a newspaper and coffee.

"Have you heard from Michelle's fiancé at all?" she asked.

"No. I left two voice messages, one at his office and another on his personal phone. Nothing so far, and that's unusual for Guillaume. I'll try again later this morning if he doesn't call before that. Speaking of feedback, any word from James Fitzgerald about the Zoom interview with Natalia Tenaz?"

"Curiously, no. He's usually prompt with follow-up. I'll check in with him today. If his ad hoc committee decided not to move forward with Natalia, we'll need to develop a viable strategy to keep the board at bay."

Suzanne clicked the remote for the wall-mounted TV. She liked to have at least a high-level awareness of issues around the globe early in her day. After turning on the newscast, the first feature she saw described Guillaume Boudreau's sudden ouster from Les Entreprises Diverses. His board of directors alleged the CEO hadn't obtained proper approval to use fifty million dollars of company money to pay Jean-Louis Sauvignon's ransom. His termination took effect immediately, and the board intended to launch legal action to recover the entire amount.

She glanced at Stefan. His attention was locked on the TV, his face showing an almost calculating expression. Shouldn't he look crestfallen instead? His long-time friend now had massive and expensive problems.

"That probably explains why he didn't return my calls." His face reddened before he threw an open newspaper on the floor in disgust, then spat out more. "Why did he make such a foolish move? He knew we were all doing everything possible to rescue the old man."

It was a good question—one she'd still like to ask Guillaume's fiancée. But Michelle also refused calls and even declined to talk with the Interpol emissary parked outside her apartment. Suzanne took time to process and assess her options once again. None were palatable.

"Let's round up the bodyguards and go for a run. Maybe that'll help us think more clearly."

He nodded and headed toward the bedroom to change. Before following him, she placed one more call, to Dan Ramirez.

"I just heard the news report too. It's a shame. But he made a truly stupid mistake that unnecessarily complicated this for all of us. I know Guillaume's your friend, but in my opinion, the guy deserved to lose his job." Dan was usually less judgmental and more understanding of human weakness.

She waited a moment or two and was glad she did. He volunteered more. "The situation in Belarus or Poland or both has become more muddled. They still haven't located Joey Andrews, the person of interest that Angela Bonner wants to talk to about the bombings. He was the only passenger on that flight from Washington to Minsk. However, we picked up one piece of info. A goon by the name of Luigi Fortissimo, who's high in The Organization, might be connected to the disappearance. The FBI got a lot of insight into the guy a few years ago from an informant. The Bureau arrested him back then in a roundup, but Giancarlo Mareno sprang him from custody within a few hours. So he's still on their radar."

"What's his role in all this?"

"We're not sure. The Bureau has a warrant out for his arrest on other matters. They've got a wiretap on his wife's number. The guy calls home almost every day to talk with her, and some sophisticated software scrambles their conversations. The FBI knows there's a call, they can track the length of it, but they can't usually decipher the conversation."

"What changed?"

"One of the FBI techies found a vulnerability on the woman's handset. To her, it appears everything is working fine, but the wiretaps are now actually decoding her conversations. They had a long chat two days ago. During that call, Luigi Fortissimo made three references to Eastern Europe. Another time, he mentioned Poland by name. Probably a momentary lapse. The wiretap guy immediately hacked the Polish service provider and learned Fortissimo was calling from a little town named Krynki. When he fed that info back to Quantico, somebody realized it was only a few miles from where they'd discovered the American pilots' bodies. The Organization might have more involvement in this mess than some earlier information led us to believe."

"Where do we go from here?" Suzanne asked.

"Angela Bonner's on the way to Krynki with a couple Interpol agents. She left during the night on a private jet, but it's a long flight. Over seven hours, I think. Then they have to rent a car. Candidly, I don't expect we'll learn much today."

Unease set in. Angela might well be an excellent forensic investigator, but did she have the skills necessary for fieldwork involving dangerous criminals? It was out of Suzanne's control, and a sense of apprehension was no reason to abort a mission undertaken by trained professionals. She mentally crossed her fingers and hoped for the best. She still had a company to run.

Minutes after her discussion with Ramirez, her screen lit up with a video-notification ring announcing James Fitzgerald. She waved for Stefan to move closer as she accepted the call.

She couldn't remember ever seeing her long-time colleague so dejected. He looked as though he hadn't slept, with large dark bags under his eyes, a deeply furrowed brow, and his hands clasped together to support his chin.

"The Zoom conference did not go well," James said. He cleared his throat before he carried on. "Cliff Williams tore Natalia apart. I never saw the guy so aggressive. If I didn't know better, I'd think he's misogynist. He interrupted her. He questioned her judgment. He even asked her if she seriously wanted the job!"

"That's odd. It sounds out of character for our friendly director from the Midwest. Was he having a bad day?" Suzanne sat bolt upright in her chair. That kind of behavior was not just unacceptable; it was offensive.

"Believe it or not, at one point in the conversation, I asked him exactly that. It relieved the tension for a few moments, but Abduhl Mahinder wasn't much better. Of course, he spoke more politely and acted as expected of a bank CEO. But the subtext of his questions implied Natalia needed to be prepared for treatment like that. He reminded everyone there were few female presidents of financial institutions. His queries and comments suggested she should expect to encounter the fierce resistance he had faced breaking into the all-white, male bastion of finance."

"How did Natalia react?" Suzanne tilted her head inquisitively, her tone conveying genuine concern.

"It would be fair to say she was shaken. She stumbled on a couple soft questions and visibly became tenser. I doubt she'd ever encountered such a tough audience." James shook his head and glanced downward. Evidently, he shared Natalia's discomfort.

"And how did Ruth Bégin react?"

"She was silent throughout. Few queries. Body language bordering on boredom and no defense of Natalia at all." James raised both hands in exasperation as he spoke, clearly bewildered by the French woman's behavior.

It was Stefan who asked the next question. "Did you have a wrap-up call to compare notes after the interview?"

"We did, and it was a short one. Williams made it clear at the beginning. He wouldn't support Natalia's appointment. He didn't explain his reasons but pronounced his position that she just wasn't right for the role. Before I could probe further, Abduhl echoed his comments. He, too, was not sure she could play with the "big boys" in the financial world. Ruth realized only a stalemate was possible. Rather bitterly, she claimed her opinion didn't matter and refused to share it."

Suzanne searched her memory in vain. In all her years working with James Fitzgerald, she couldn't recall him ever suffering such a clear defeat. That Cliff Williams caused the humiliation must have shocked him. James had argued tenaciously with John George Mortimer to appoint Williams and his friend, Chuck Jones, to the board of directors of Multima Corporation. She sought a way to soothe the wound to his ego.

"Thanks for bringing the idea forward. We all realized appointing Natalia would be an unconventional—and perhaps controversial—appointment. Though, I don't think any of us expected it to be so divisive. Let's set the question aside for now. Take a few days to consider appropriate next steps. What else is going on in the financial world of Multima that I should know about?"

As usual, he had a list ready to discuss, and he checked it off as they worked their way through it. Just before noon, they wrapped it up.

Entirely out of character, she walked over to Stefan and planted a big kiss on his lips before she drew him close and felt his body respond. Stress sometimes demanded unplanned and unexpected solutions.

"Let's change and go for that run before I'm tempted to take the afternoon off for recreational activities totally unrelated to the world of business." She looked into his eyes with growing affection and a mischievous smile of promise.

THIRTY-THREE

Montevideo, Uruguay, Thursday July 23, 2020

His throat was parched. He could barely swallow as he gradually woke. With some effort, he opened his eyes and focused. An IV stand towered over his head, with a plain white ceiling above and a slowly rotating fan in between. It took a minute for Howard to remember he was in a hospital in Montevideo.

Its name, Hospital Evangélico, came to him after a labored moment. He shifted his prone frame slightly, and a sharp pain shot from his lower leg to his hip, causing him to groan loudly. He minimized further movement as he tilted his head and scanned the small room. Behind him, light flooded in from an open window. In the distance, he heard cars, leaves rustling on a nearby tree, and the occasional cheerful chirp of a bird.

The ceiling needed fresh paint. Along its edge's, sections peeled, making the surface look rough and unfinished. He noticed a track for curtains that formed a U around his bed. Though it was open at the moment, someone could easily drag the curtain closed for instant privacy. Was there another patient in the room?

Howard arched his neck and raised his head enough to verify he was alone. In payment for his curiosity, violent pain rushed up his leg, forcing an even louder groan, almost a yelp. The sound of his discomfort attracted someone in the hallway, and a woman poked her head inside.

"Are you alright?" she asked in Spanish.

"No. I have a lot of pain," Howard replied, also in Spanish. He placed particular emphasis on the word "*mucho.*"

The nurse smiled warmly and walked up to his bed. She examined a gauge on the IV pole and squeezed the plastic pouch before she said more. Then she grasped his wrist and held it up. A cord hung limply.

"You have a button here. Can you see it?" She stared directly at him and waited for him to nod before she continued. "When the pain is too much to bear, push the button. A painkiller will release and give you some comfort. Don't abuse it, but use it when you need relief."

The woman offered a sympathetic smile again before she checked another monitoring device. She was shorter than average. She stood up on her toes to read the numbers on the machine. Her dark black hair wound tightly into a bun at the back of her head, and her skin tone was darker than Europeans' but lighter than most indigenous peoples. When she smiled, dimples formed in both cheeks, highlighting sparkling white teeth each time.

Satisfied with what she read, the woman made a trip around the bed, fussing with sheets. As a parting comment, she announced that someone would visit shortly to remove the catheter. He didn't understand the meaning of *catéter* at first. He'd never needed to use the word before, and he frowned to let her know.

"You might reach for the button for an extra shot when you see him coming," she said with a muffled chortle and wave as she moved on from the room.

He pushed it immediately. His left leg was already so painful that even shifting the sheets on the bed caused a jolt of intense discomfort. As he lay flat, looking up at the slowly rotating fan, his recollection was foggy, but the pieces began to fit together.

◡

He relived the crash from those horrifying seconds after he realized a huge metal bumper of a fast-moving vehicle was about to collide with his scooter. A vivid replay of the ghastly thump of his leg catching on the edge of a ditch caused another painful jolt that begged for more morphine. An image resurfaced of the sympathetic expression on the young doctor's face as he had explained the steps after the X-rays.

Fuzzy memories recalled an ambulance ride with drugs to ease the agony and induce slumber. Occasional glimpses of an attendant checking his pulse or reading monitors on equipment attached to his wrists appeared, then faded. Excruciating pain he felt with seemingly every bump in the road on the three-hour drive to Montevideo popped up again. Although, in reality, probably only a few occurred amid the drugs and sleep.

A picture formed of a masked woman leaning over the ambulance gurney when they wheeled him into a busy emergency room. A credit card was what she needed. They processed it only for the fifteen-thousand-dollar deposit, she assured him. Upon his release, they'd prepare a detailed receipt and adjust for any difference between the charge to his Mastercard and the amount required, she explained in a detached monotone.

When she returned later that night, she woke him to show him the card she had found earlier, before theatrically placing back it in the knapsack pouch. How much time he spent in the emergency room was impossible to estimate. He remembered hearing dozens of different voices murmuring through masks and almost constant movement around the area from squeaking stretchers, rattling IV poles on unsteady wheels, and occasionally barked instructions from doctors to interns or nurses to attendants or cleaners.

He never saw the surgeon's face. She wore a mask and green hospital garb covering every part of her body except a transparent shield over brown eyes and artfully trimmed eyebrows. Surgery would take a while, she explained. The tibia fracture needed a plate about a foot long to repair the damage and support his leg.

"You won't feel anything," he remembered her saying. "And we'll have you on your way in just a few days. Don't worry."

The morphine did its work, and Howard slept. For how many hours, he didn't know. He woke with a start and a direct jab of pain as a voice called out to him, and hands roughly yanked his bedsheets away.

"Hello. I'm here to remove your catheter. It will just take a moment."

With desperation, he grasped the magic button and pressed it furiously three times.

THIRTY-FOUR

Punta del Este, Uruguay, Friday July 24, 2020

Fidelia shuddered as she watched the Uruguayan all-news channel. The announcer rhymed off the day's statistics with the same tone of voice he used to recap yesterday's weather. Twenty-one new cases of COVID-19 in the country, bringing the total since the start of the pandemic to 1,117. One more person had died the previous day, making the total thirty-four.

A graphic changed to a map of the United States as the announcer explained it still led the world in COVID-19 cases. Grimly, he summarized that almost seventy thousand cases were identified, raising the number infected there to nearly four million. He paused dramatically, knowing his audience would instantly realize the virus affected more people in the US than Uruguay's entire population. American deaths now totaled over 142,000.

A shiver shot up her spine as Fidelia shook her head in dismay. Words alone could not express her relief over taking refuge in a country like Uruguay. For many years, America had been exceptionally good to her, but she no longer related to a growing and pervasive lack of concern for public health there. To her, it was curious why those same people thought The Organization had its values all wrong. Yeah, sometimes they brought wayward folks into line. But at least The Organization's misery was targeted. Those ignoring scientific health guidelines thumbed their noses at the well-being of everyone.

A phone call interrupted her mental critique of the American public's odd reaction to the pandemic. It was Luigi, and he was calling to update her on his success in modifying the behavior of one of those wayward types.

"Almost nothin' so far. Had ta stop. Don't have a doctor. Bastard lost a lot of blood 'n fainted twice. Had to slow it down." It was his shorthand version of the torture he and his goons had meted out to Joey Andrews, the guy they'd hijacked from a private jet in the Minsk airport.

"Is it his real name?" Fidelia wanted to start at the beginning.

"Yeah. We're sure of that. Definitely born 'n raised in the mountains of West Virginia. Documents all genuine US issue. Accent, phrases, speech pattern all American, even under 'xtreme duress."

"Duress, you call it now?" She laughed. "How many body parts is he missing?"

"Haven't gone that far yet. Started with fractures. Both knees. All the fingers and the thumb on his right hand 'r broken. Lost him for 'bout a half hour after the knees. Again after the fingers. Longer the second time."

"You've been through all his luggage, personal effects?"

"Yeah. Disabled his phone, an iPhone. No computer. Only clothes 'n his carry-on. Stripped him 'n checked body cavities. Nothin' hidden."

She listened intently and processed the information.

Klaudia sat across from her, joining in. She raised a finger. "Were you able to get the password for his phone?"

"Not yet," Luigi growled. "That's what we were workin' on when we lost him the second time."

"When will you start up again?" Fidelia asked. Her tone didn't mask her impatience.

"It'll be dark here in another few hours. The Lithuanians found a more secluded spot with an abandoned shed. We should be able to use it and turn up the pressure if the guy can withstand it."

"Focus on that password. He might be hard to break on subjects like who he's working for—or if there's any connection to the kidnapping they're blaming on us—but he could cough up the password. And try him on the Shadow. What does he know about him? Don't be as rough yet as you were on Juan Álvarez in Chile, but step it up. We're running out of time."

"Okay. How 'bout Knight? Feds ran in 'nother dozen guys 'n the midwest yesterday. Gotta neutralize him." Her primary protector's tone was angry.

She chose the words of her reply carefully. "I'm checking out a lead that seems promising. If it proves accurate, it's doubtful Howard Knight is feeding names to the Feds. I'll know more when we talk tomorrow."

After Klaudia returned to her scrutiny of the IP addresses captured from the phones around the house near Krynki, Fidelia started her own research.

Her list of contacts numbered in the thousands, and she had them organized two different ways. One database sorted names by country location, the other by job function. Her file for Uruguay was small compared to other countries. Still, she remembered most of the key people from personal visits and sporadic contact over her thirty years working with The Organization.

She called up the folder for Mateo Lopez. Middle-aged, with long experience in the outfit, Mateo pulled the strings in Uruguay. He used to work for Juan Álvarez and was now in line for a promotion after the traitor's demise in Chile. It took only a call and a three-hour drive before he knocked on their door in Punta del Este.

Her guards disarmed and frisked him carefully before letting him inside the house. Fidelia waited in the living room with afternoon light flooding in through one large window. She motioned for her guest to take the chair facing her, looking directly into that bright sunshine, before dismissing her bodyguards.

"You heard about Juan Álvarez, of course." She waited for him to nod. It came quickly with a tinge of fear. "You know why?"

He shook his head two or three times but maintained direct eye contact.

"He betrayed me. I learned he was working for someone else. I don't have to tell you The Organization doesn't tolerate traitors. Give me some good reasons you shouldn't suffer the same fate."

He rattled off three. Only followed orders he knew came from her. Paid his commission every month as instructed and never skimmed from the proceeds. Kept his subordinates in line and tacked in whatever direction The Organization ordered. The man was uncomfortable but seemed to tell the truth. He had helped her in the past without question or complaint, and she saw no reason she shouldn't rely on him now.

When he'd groveled enough, she cut him short with a wave of her hand and stood up.

"It's time for you to report directly to me. How long that continues depends on how well you handle an urgent matter. Tell me about the Hospital Evangélico in Montevideo."

For the next half hour, he explained how the hospital organized its primary facility in the capital with satellites around the country. He outlined the religious group underlying the medical organization. He shared the names of key administrators and doctors and their roles and responsibilities. Not surprisingly, he knew the financial underpinnings and summarized the strengths and weaknesses of the hospital's government-owned facilities and private competitors.

"Can you safely get someone inside?" she asked. "Inside a patient's room and inside the hospital's computer system?"

He simply nodded. She outlined her demands and asked him if it was doable. He nodded again.

"When?"

"Tomorrow, we should be able to penetrate their system. The guy will probably need an hour or two in the morning. Then I can have a gal check out the patient."

"Call me when you hear from the woman. Next steps depend on what she finds out, but tell your technician to eat an early breakfast and get inside the system quickly."

She stepped away to make herself a coffee while the bodyguards showed Lopez out and returned his weapons. Klaudia burst in from her room, laptop in hand, beaming from ear to ear.

"I may have a hit. One of the IP addresses in Russia looks promising." She continued to the dining island near the kitchen, plugged the computer into an outlet, and pointed to her screen before continuing.

"Here's a map of Moscow, and this is the physical location of one IP address we captured from Poland. I searched with Google Maps. The street and number sparked something in my memory, so I looked at the street view. It also tweaked some ideas. I was able to access the city records and learned the names of the tenants in those apartments. I recognized one of them. Yuri Federov. One of the meanest bastards in the outfit. One who demanded my services often." Klaudia's voice hardened with each sentence.

Fidelia looked into her eyes and saw what appeared to be a mélange of emotion. Anger. Hatred. Disgust. She elected to wait until her friend collected her feelings with a shake of her head and continued.

"This guy was one of the first to move towards the dark side of the secret services and embrace the mafia. He also has a sex addiction. He's always starved for it."

"Okay. But where do you see an opportunity?" Fidelia tilted her head and turned on an expression of puzzlement.

"He regularly reported to a guy named Boris Ivanov who's a major player in the mafia now, still working at the service, still using the same office. I called him today. His secretary answered as usual. I pretended I was calling for an official in the Federal Assembly. He wasn't available, but she expected him back soon and offered to take a message. I just hung up, of course."

Fidelia still didn't see where the conversation was going, but warded off a temptation to cut her short. Instead, she gave an encouraging smile.

"Before you wonder if I've simply had too much screen time, here's my idea. I've kept in contact from time to time with one of the Polish women we used to recruit the girls from Belarus. She lives in another small town near Krynki. She's the one who first recommended we buy that place where we stashed the girls for shipment to the West. Are you with me so far?"

Fidelia nodded. She remembered the woman and the circumstances leading to The Organization's purchase of the remote dwelling. Her interest piqued. "You think we might get her into the house?"

"I think so. We'll need to call her to be sure, but she's still in the business. For a few hundred euros, I expect she'll do it."

"Okay. But how do we do it?" Fidelia wondered.

"Leave that to me." Klaudia's expression swiftly shifted from anger to something resembling mischief, showing just the hint of a smile and brown eyes sparkling with excitement.

As her friend dashed back to the bedroom to make her call, Fidelia decided to take a walk. She summoned a bodyguard to follow her and slipped into sandals suitable for the beach. For more than an hour, she assessed the current situation.

Her guy for Italy had been murdered. They heard Alphonso Sargetti conspiring during an intercepted phone conversation with Stan Tan, so there was no doubt he was up to no good with someone in the background called the Shadow. But the Italian's throat was slit before they found out what he was up to. To complicate the issue, Tan had been missing from his home in Singapore for several weeks.

Meanwhile, the FBI continued to arrest essential players in The Organization and hold them in some secret location. Luigi's people hadn't been able to get lawyers to spring them or even talk to them. And her primary protector was sure Howard Knight was feeding the Feds information. She'd promised to leave him alone. Could it be the Bureau demanded something more to let him back into the witness protection program?

There was weird shit going on. No doubt about that. Luigi was confident no one from The Organization in the US had planted the bombs in Multima Supermarkets or Suzanne Simpson's Atlanta house. So who did?

And who snatched the French billionaire? Again, Luigi was positive none of his goons in Europe were involved. Her confidence in the big lug was absolute. Nobody performed better or with more loyalty. Still, someone had gotten to Sargetti and Tan, and that person must have deep pockets and powerful influence. And it became clearer by the day that somebody, somewhere, was trying to pin the bombings and kidnapping on The Organization. Why?

She couldn't shake a nagging sense that the root of all these issues was the Russian mafia. No doubt it pissed them off when she'd stolen a half-billion dollars from them in the shady transactions she engineered out of Australia. But she had eliminated both of the traitors who'd been colluding with them. Luigi took care of Ortez in Chile, and Aretta Musa handled Wendal Randal down under. Klaudia was confident they hadn't left any digital trail when they'd scooped the offshore bank accounts.

Was it possible the stuff happening in the US and Europe was not directly connected? Possible, but unlikely. One key to unlocking the mystery pointed to their captive, Joey Andrews. Luigi was certain the guy was a conduit between the Russians and her traitors. He had seen the guy's Virginia IP address on one of the digital transfers out of the Cayman account months earlier. More importantly, she needed to know who in The Organization was working with or for Joey Andrews. She realized it was a stretch, but might he also have some connection to the Shadow?

But he wasn't holding up well to Luigi's interrogations, so she made a mental note. Her primary protector needed to get the Lithuanians to bring a doctor over to their hideaway in Poland. A physician who could keep the scum alive until he filled in some of those blanks.

She felt better after the walk, her mind clearer, more organized. When she entered Ortez's former summer home, she punched the speed dial on her secure phone and reached Aretta Musa. It was about three o'clock in the morning in Australia. It took her country boss there a few seconds to wake fully.

"I was expecting your call, just not in the middle of the night. Did you get my email?"

Fidelia gasped silently. She hadn't seen a message from the woman but opened her laptop to its email app to check while she spoke. "I'm looking for it now. When did you send it?"

"Yesterday. Over 12 hours ago. It appeared clean on my side, no error messages."

"You better tell me about it. I can't find anything here." Fidelia slowly scrolled through her inbox, then circled back up again with a growing sense of unease.

"I had a visit from Stan Tan. He and two thugs arrived before dawn at the country house unannounced." Aretta's tone was calm, but Fidelia detected a tinge of underlying concern. She waited for the woman to continue after a pause. "He claimed they were there to collect the monthly contributions. Didn't want the payment to go to Macau this time. Wanted everything in cash as soon as the banks opened in the morning."

"That's bizarre. Even though your remittances are less than usual with the pandemic, you must generate a couple million a month, right?"

"Exactly. I told him there was no way to scrape together almost two million US dollars in cash in less than a week. It was all in the accounts, ready to transfer to Macau. He called someone and spoke to them in Chinese. I couldn't understand a word. When he finished, he handed me a scrap of paper with a digital code. Told me to send the entire amount there instead."

"Where were those accounts?" Fidelia demanded.

"In Sydney. A little-known credit union. I transferred everything there like he instructed, and he left. Didn't say more. But I had my guys tail him at a distance. One guy put a tracking device in the fender of his SUV so they could follow undetected. Sure enough, he went into that credit union wheeling a large piece of luggage and returned to the vehicle within a few minutes."

"Where did he go?"

"From there, they drove directly to the small private jet airport we used when you were here, just outside the city. A plane was waiting. They left the SUV in the parking lot, climbed aboard, and the jet soared off. It took a little persuasion, but my guys found the flight plan the pilot filed. It showed them headed to Honolulu. I figured you'd want that information."

"You said this was yesterday. Did you check to see if the plane arrived in Hawaii?"

"Yep. I guessed you'd ask that question too." Aretta's tone sounded a touch more smug than usual. "The jet landed at 4:51 a.m. on July twenty-fourth, today in your time zone, I think. It refueled and left an hour later. My guys understand the new flight plan showed its destination was Washington, DC."

"How many people were traveling with Tan?"

"When he came to the country house, he had two bodyguards. But the attendant at the airport told my people there was one more person who stayed with the jet—an American woman."

"How did the attendant know about the woman?"

"She got bored sitting alone on the plane, so she went into the terminal office and had a couple drinks with the pilots. The employee told my guys she talked loudly, definitely American. She wore a scarf on her head with huge sunglasses. Like she didn't want to be recognized."

Fidelia gave her an atta boy for the information and told her to report anything else suspicious.

Yet another alarming twist to the saga. Tan must have blocked or intercepted Aretta's email alerting her to his goings-on. The son-of-a-bitch probably had the technology to do it. An American woman was involved. Added to the mix, a couple million of her dollars also headed toward Washington. She banged her hand on the countertop in frustration.

The noise attracted Klaudia from her bedroom. "I reached her, the gal in Poland. She'll do it if we can get her into the house. Costing you two grand though—and in euros, not dollars." Klaudia giggled.

"Are you ready to make the call?" Fidelia asked.

Her friend nodded, slipped on a mask to distort her voice, and started punching numbers into a phone. She spoke Russian when someone answered.

Fidelia listened for tone and cadence, even if she couldn't understand the language. It surprised her the call took only a few minutes with limited back and forth.

"I told Yuri Fedorov I was calling to give him a message from his boss, Boris," Klaudia explained when she finished. "Told him they'd need to sit tight for two more days, so Boris was sending around a gift for him and the boys to share. They should play nicely with her. The jerk only wanted to know what name she'd use at the door and whether she was on loan or a permanent gift. I confirmed she was on loan."

"I'm missing the significance," Fidelia said.

"It's service code. 'On loan' means use her and let her go. A 'permanent gift' doesn't live after they're done with her."

THIRTY-FIVE

Lyon, France, Saturday July 25, 2020

Saturday mornings were typically more relaxed, even for chief executive officers. Suzanne hadn't set her alarm and woke an hour later than expected, thinking her body must have finally adapted to the jet lag. She stretched her arms and legs lazily and snuggled more tightly to Stefan. Both lay undressed on top of the bedsheets. After their passionate activities before sleep, their bodies and the room were still warmer than normal.

Gently, she touched his shoulder and nudged closer yet, looking over at his sleeping form. He stirred slightly, then blinked two or three times as he woke. Stefan felt her closeness and shifted toward her, a welcoming smile gradually forming, eventually dominating his face. He twisted, wrapped a muscular arm around her, rubbing the small of her back. His touch was delicate for a man. Testing, he squirmed tightly to her body and slid his fingers lower, stroking her upper buttocks seductively.

"Not this morning." She smiled, then lightly kissed him on the lips and rolled over toward the edge of the bed. "We've already overslept and I have work to do before my call with James Fitzgerald."

"We're good for each other, don't you think?"

Suzanne stopped her escape and swung around to read his expression. His smile looked more satisfied than mischievous. Blue eyes sparkled as brightly as the first night they'd met in Paris. The crease in his brow confirmed he expected an answer. She braced instinctively.

"We're great for each other. What prompts a question like that on a leisurely Saturday morning?"

"The university sent me an email yesterday. They're preparing for the fall semester. With the pandemic, they're polling professors to gauge preferences—lecture on campus or conduct sessions digitally."

"What did you tell them?"

"Nothing so far. These weeks with you have been wonderful despite the horrendous circumstances, but I don't want to wear out my welcome. Should I plan to stay here in France when you return to North America?"

"Hmmm," she replied, buying time. Suzanne liked his company and adored his love-making. It was refreshing to have a bright, articulate companion to bounce off ideas, enjoy intelligent conversations, and share special moments. Still, apprehension of distraction from her job and guilt about the amount of personal commitment the CEO role demanded made her pause.

"That's your call, of course. You've had a glimpse of my pace, the nonsense I have to deal with, and the sparse time that leaves for fun. I'm not inclined to change that for a while, no matter how much I enjoy our life together. I'm also not prepared to make a commitment or deepen our relationship. If you're comfortable with that, you're most welcome to return with me and teach online. If you're looking for more, I can't give it to you right now."

He didn't flinch. Instead, his broad smile not only held firm, it widened. "You're becoming quite predictable. I had guessed that was precisely what you'd say." He chuckled. "You said it more elegantly than the response I had conjured up, but it's what I hoped for. I'll tell the university I'd love to teach online."

Suzanne leaned over to his side of the bed, wrapped her arms around his neck, and gave him a long, deep, languorous kiss of appreciation. It tempted her to stay much longer.

Before they finished breakfast and their first cups of coffee, her phone rang. It was Michelle Sauvignon, experiencing great difficulty talking amidst sobs and audible angst.

"I need your help," she finally got out. Her best friend sounded more than desperate, which must have prompted her call after days of silence.

Suzanne bristled. Was she in physical danger?

"They've demanded more. They want more money to release my father." That's all Michelle could manage before another round of violent gasps erupted. She blew her nose and tried to regain control.

Suzanne asked the only questions she thought appropriate. "Where are you? Are you alright?" She hit the speaker icon, then leaned toward the phone, looking at Stefan's perplexed expression.

It took more than a few seconds for her friend to reply. "I'm ... I'm okay. It's my father. The kidnappers claim they never received the mitcoyne payment we made. They're still threatening to cut off his hand."

Time and lots of patience finally squeezed out more details—more than an hour's worth. Suzanne and Stefan, in turn, comforted, prompted, and pried for further information before they got a complete picture.

Before dawn, Michelle had picked up a call that lasted less than a minute. After the caller confirmed who she was speaking to, she bitterly accused her of "fucking them around." They never saw the fifty million in mitcoyne. Their patience was exhausted. She had five days to find the missing fifty million dollars or send another mitcoyne.

The woman rhymed off and repeated twice the account number where Michelle must make the payment, then snapped out that her companions were eager to sever the old man's hand or even more body parts.

On that gruesome note, the caller hung up. Sadly, the Interpol officer staying in the house didn't have enough time to trace the call, determining only that it was a mobile phone.

Michelle's voice trembled and wavered as she spoke, so Suzanne reached out.

"Stefan and I are in Lyon in an apartment near Interpol headquarters. Why don't you come with the policewoman and stay with us here? We have access to senior leaders and their protection. Together we can solve this."

She needed coaxing. Michelle was embarrassed about her behavior in the Laurentians and losing fifty million dollars. Clearly, she was fearful for the health of her father, and dejected that Guillaume had dumped her the same day he'd lost his job at Les Entreprises Divers.

Exhausted and bearing more stress and grief than before, time and patience elicited only a half-hearted promise that Michelle would think about her offer. Stefan approached after the call and wrapped a supportive arm around Suzanne's shoulders as he whispered reassurances she'd done everything possible.

When her spirit revived, she called Angela Bonner's phone. It rang eight times, then bounced into voice mail. Reluctantly, she dialed the number for assistant director Edouard Deschamps at Interpol headquarters.

This time, the call transferred to a woman after several rings. His secretary could only advise he wasn't in the office, but she would try to reach him and ask him to get back to her. Suzanne and Stefan exchanged glances, both recognizing the incongruity at the same time. Deschamps's assistant was at her post on a Saturday, but her boss was not. It seemed odd.

Regardless, she had little time to think about it. It was already time for a video session with their new CFO, Pierre Cabot. James Fitzgerald and Amber Chan also joined in to discuss the rapidly deteriorating profit picture of Multima's Farefour Stores subsidiary in China. James first outlined the concerns.

"China operations now represent over twenty-five percent of global sales in the Supermarkets division. Our fiscal quarter ends next week. Unless there's a miracle, we'll end it with revenue thirty-five percent lower than forecast and profits off by approximately fifty percent." Despite the worry, he kept a calm and factual tone and let the gravity sink in before continuing.

"That will drag down overall Supermarkets profit almost twenty-five percent from analysts' projections. Investors will skewer us in the stock market if we don't announce drastic cutbacks in operating expenditures for the next quarter."

She looked at Amber Chan, who was wringing her hands and squirming in her chair. Her country president knew well significant reductions in expenses meant Multima would need to lay off thousands of workers.

Suzanne had to reduce the tension. "I think we all realize Farefour China is going through a rough patch right now. This period will be a disaster. Maybe Amber can give us her best estimate of the profit picture for next quarter."

A good CEO knew the personalities of her team well. James Fitzgerald's objectives were entirely predictable when he'd requested the virtual meeting, but this was Suzanne's first video conference with Pierre Cabot. His direction was less certain. She'd already warned Amber and urged her to be ready.

Her country leader came prepared and painted a picture like a gifted artist with her characteristic high-energy enthusiasm, lots of charts and graphs, and a methodical delivery similar to Fitzgerald's own style.

Amber summarized the financial damage created by Beijing's interference with poultry and pork shipments. She used a colorful timeline to show how deliveries had improved since they lifted the temporary bans and highlighted the momentum with projections several weeks into the future. Her story made a compelling argument that Chinese customers hadn't abandoned their stores for competitors. She ended with an assurance her division would soon generate predictable, ever-increasing profits.

"You make a good case, Amber, but I'll put on my shareholder hat for a moment." James used his wise, fatherly smile to soften his next point. "Not only will it disappoint me that my small piece of the corporation might drop dramatically in value when we announce the results, but I'm also not hearing Multima management assure me they have acted on the earnings disappointment to reduce labor costs permanently. Do I want to continue to invest in a company that doesn't take advantage of these opportunities?"

Suzanne scrutinized Amber Chan's facial expressions on the monitor. She was rattled, and it was probably a cultural thing. Asian executives typically looked at laborers as a resource while American managers often considered labor a burden to profits—expenses to cull at every opportunity. She threw her China president an idea.

"What is Farefour China's cost of labor as a percent of sales right now?"

Amber grabbed the lifeline and ran with it. "Even with all the troubles this quarter, we kept our expense for labor at three percent. Our relationships with the unions are good. We've built a lot of trust. They work with us almost daily to adjust our employee schedules, adjusting costs up and down with fluctuations in business activity. How does that compare with the US?"

Suzanne knew the correct answer, and when Pierre Cabot changed the subject, he didn't surprise her.

"But our ultimate game plan must be to automate to the greatest extent possible. What is your strategy to eliminate cashiers and use robots to stock the shelves?"

Suzanne didn't wait for Amber to respond. She waded into the discussion, squaring her shoulders and staring directly into the camera.

"AI optimization is a conversation we should have another day. I understood the purpose of today's meeting was to discuss how we should announce the quarterly results to minimize negative shareholder reaction." Suzanne paused and softened her tone as she continued. "I think Amber provided a lot of good, helpful information we can build into the media story: Our expectation the earnings disruption is a single-quarter event. Our strong Chinese consumer loyalty. Excellent cooperation with the unions to manage labor costs. Doesn't that give us enough?"

Pierre Cabot realized he wouldn't win the battle for technology solutions that day and conceded. "You're right. We probably should set aside some other time to explore our automation opportunities, but I'd like to better understand Amber's sales forecast for the next quarter."

For the following several minutes, Cabot drilled down on the assumptions and numbers until it became clear he was comfortable building the earnings' announcement based on Suzanne's guidance.

"Okay, I get it. You're doing an impressive job there, Amber. I'll try to persuade our analysts and shareholders to agree with us."

Suzanne excused the Chinese woman as it was well after normal business hours in Hong Kong, and the subjects remaining on the agenda didn't directly impact her. Meanwhile, Stefan popped into the living room to find out what she fancied for a late lunch as they waded through the fiscal issues. They were back at it within seconds, and the issues became even more complex.

First, they tackled the European Central Bank's ongoing concerns about Multima Financial Services licenses that continued to drag with disruptions due to the pandemic. They discussed and agreed on the next steps and positioning of the issues with the coming earnings release. The executive team devoted more than an hour to a review of that announcement as Suzanne drilled down on the data—line by line—to be sure she understood even obscure nuances. Like a patient professor, her new CFO answered every question and provided the supporting background as needed.

"I'm impressed, Pierre. You've moved up the learning curve fabulously. You certainly sound well-prepared for analyst and media questions. And James, I realize you contributed significantly to Pierre's familiarization with the company. I'm indebted to both of you." She had another issue to raise with both men, one not included on the agenda they'd submitted. "Have you revisited our search for a new president at Financial Services?"

James Fitzgerald looked over at Pierre for an instant, then concluded he should respond. "Yes. We signed a contract yesterday with MacKenzie and Company. We weren't getting the right candidates through traditional human resources management, so we decided to be daring. It'll cost us about a hundred thousand in fees. But they're confident they'll have identified a half-dozen potential leaders that fit the bill before the end of August. I'll stick handle the issue at the board meeting to buy another month."

Suzanne didn't reply. Indeed, the idea was a novel one. MacKenzie and Company was legendary for innovative thinking and progressive consulting. The geniuses there might well identify the right person. And since James could probably "stick handle" the issue smoothly with the board, she nodded.

"One last question, if I may." James signaled for her attention the moment Pierre Cabot's face dropped from the screen. "Have you heard anything from Angela the past few days?"

His manner had at first appeared relaxed, but his posture stiffened as he leaned forward anxiously.

"No. We left a voice mail for her this morning, but she hasn't called back yet. I think she's in Poland, though." Suzanne's tone trailed off uncertainly.

"Yeah," he confirmed. "She headed there with two Interpol colleagues on Thursday. That night, she texted she landed okay. But she usually calls in every evening to chat, and I haven't heard a word from her for two days. No replies to my messages either."

THIRTY-SIX

Montevideo, Uruguay, Saturday July 25, 2020

Morphine helped. Sleep was sporadic for Howard, but the painkiller induced drowsiness that made it tolerable.

When a nurse dragged him from bed again about midnight, he had effectively negotiated the distance to the toilet in a corner of the room with minimal help. Unfortunately, deep sleep hadn't been possible since then, and his phone showed it was only 2:13 in the morning.

He took another sip of water. The other downside of the morphine was the constant thirst. It left his throat raspy. Swallowing was uncomfortable. Every sip reminded him it would shortly be time to ring the bell again, summon a nurse and hop over to the toilet on one leg, with both hands gripping the crutches. He hoped the soreness in his underarms would disappear quickly too.

Movement in the passage caught his attention, making him more alert. During the night, they dimmed lights in the corridor almost to darkness. Usually, he heard scarcely a sound as staff visited rooms only when required. Their footsteps were practically silent even when they entered.

The first noise wasn't from voices or traffic in the hallway. No, it sounded more like a gentle thump, maybe someone dropping a book on a table or knocking over a piece of equipment. Then only stillness for some time. He closed his eyes and tried to sleep once more.

Seconds later, another sound. Through the fog of the drugs, it took a moment to figure out what it might be—footsteps. Louder than usual. The noise became increasingly distinct and closer.

He shut his right eye, the one closest to the doorway, so someone passing wouldn't immediately realize he was awake. A shadow cast along the wall. Another appeared beside it. Were they looking into his room? He realized they were when the outline of a hand pointed in his direction. He closed his other eye and breathed deeply, his chest rising and falling as though he slept.

Whispers reached him, but it was impossible to decipher what they said—not even the language. Someone approached the side of his bed, breathing as little as possible and creating swishing sounds as they fiddled with something. There was no longer any point in pretending to sleep, and he opened his eyes. Abruptly, a guy slapped a broad strip of tape over his mouth.

It startled him as he took in a masked man pressing down on the adhesive roughly. Another pair of hands applied a second layer an instant later, silencing his attempt to protest.

One snatched the IV from his wrist with a violent tug, and Howard cried out from the sudden jab of pain. He produced nothing but a faint, muffled groan. He swallowed hard, and his body became rigid. This was obviously no hospital maneuver. No tests or X-rays. Someone was hijacking him from the ward.

Seconds later, the bed moved. Like seasoned staff, the pair swung the gurney out of the room and walked at a steady pace toward the elevator. Before they reached it, Howard tilted his head to the left, expecting to see into the nurse's station. It was dimly lit, but there was enough light to make out two bodies slumped forward on opposite sides of a tiny desk.

He gripped the raised railings of the bed and forced himself upward, twisting to free himself from the confines of the sheets.

From behind, an arm reached around and roughly ripped away the face mask they'd added, then slapped a cloth over his nose and mouth, making it a battle to breathe. Howard squirmed awkwardly for a few seconds, fighting back. Then he detected the same noxious odor he faintly remembered from Cambodia as everything went black.

A jolt of pain shot up his leg and woke him sometime later. He was groggy, his vision blurry, and his head throbbed. Hands reached for his shoulder without warning, then began shaking and rocking him viciously, repeatedly shouting, "Wake up!"

His eyes flickered. It was still dark as the arms dragged him from the rear seat of an SUV and demanded he stand up. With a single vicious tug, they yanked him to his feet while Howard screamed out in agony as his fractured limb bore too much of his weight. Nobody heard more than a muffled sound behind the layers of tape and a new mask covering his mouth.

He lifted his left leg, shifting the load from the injured one. He balanced there unsteadily while another pair of hands reached over his shoulder and passed him his crutches. Leaning briefly against the open SUV door, he slipped both under his arms and tested his balance. He stood on an asphalt tarmac and one man shoved him toward the stairway of a small jet.

As he advanced, Howard looked around and realized he was at the Montevideo airport, in the section reserved for private aircraft. He remembered being there briefly only days before when he'd arrived from Costa Rica. The SUV drove off, suggesting the two men left behind would probably board the plane with him.

The distance he had to travel was only a matter of feet. Still, Howard had just started using the walking aids hours before and only a few times for extremely short distances. The guy prodded him with a jab in the back to move faster. At the stairway, he didn't know how he could climb the steps with crutches. He tried to explain that to the fellow on his right by waving one in the air, shrugging his shoulders, and shaking his head.

The goon understood and suggested something to his companion. However, with the noise of the aircraft engine warming up and a mask covering the guy's mouth, Howard didn't understand. He wasn't even sure what language he spoke. The other fellow did.

As they approached the stairway, he mounted the first step and turned around to face Howard. The other guy stood behind him and put his hands on both shoulders. The first motioned for Howard to place both crutches on the bottom step first. Then he motioned for him to push himself up. He tried the maneuver and landed safely on the bottom step, the guy behind keeping him upright as he teetered.

The process took several minutes, although there were only seven steps. At the top, Howard ducked his head to clear the doorway and entered a palatial interior. There were about a dozen plush, white leather seats in the first section in clusters. Recessed lighting accented the luxury. Deep pile carpet felt soft underfoot and muffled the noise from the engines and outside.

One man gave another nudge, and Howard hobbled forward on his crutches to a second part. Equally opulent, this divided area had three comfortable seats, side-by-side, facing a huge wide-screen monitor on the opposite wall. He paused to check it out, but the goon jabbed his ribs again to keep moving.

Haltingly, he advanced to a final compartment. This section had a sofa large enough to hold three comfortably, with still another TV in the corner. As he turned slightly to his right, he saw a sizeable leather seat on the opposite side. Sitting in that chair, his back straight, legs crossed and hands clasped in namaste, Stan Tan tilted his head.

The Singaporean crime boss gestured to remove the tape from Howard's mouth, snapping a sharp command in Mandarin. His men reacted immediately and ripped the mask and bandages from his face, then motioned for him to sit. As he navigated the few steps to where they pointed, he heard a toilet flush and noticed it was feet away in the rear of the plane.

By the time Howard turned himself around and lowered his body delicately onto the sofa, a sound of running water stopped, a lock popped, and the restroom door opened. A tall, attractive female stepped into the compartment. Her long, dark, stylish hair first caught his attention. Then her eyes. Coal black. She wore a lot of makeup, perhaps a woman not entirely comfortable in her own skin. Her clothes were baggy and casual, the sort a soccer mom might wear on a chilly day, and not at all like her Facebook profile photo.

She looked at him for a moment, checking him up and down, her expression blank. When she'd seen enough, she carried on to the middle compartment.

"Welcome aboard, Howard Knight," Tan said after another minute or two of silence. "You've been a busy man since we last saw each other in Singapore. In a few minutes, someone will bring you some water. He'll also let you relieve yourself in the toilet before we take off. Unfortunately, we'll apply zip-ties to your wrists after that, and he'll move your crutches to the front for safekeeping."

While he spoke behind his mask, Tan scrutinized Howard closely. Like the woman earlier, his eyes flitted from side to side, and top to bottom, taking in every detail.

"We'll let you rest for a while. I realize you have some lingering pain from your mishap, but we're not equipped here with IV stands or other drugs. You'll have to manage. Our flight's a long one. We'll feed you during the trip, and the men will check in every hour to see if you need water. At some point, I'll return and we'll have a chat." He stood and prepared to retire from the compartment.

Howard blurted out a question just as Tan turned toward the front. "Where is my backpack? Where are my possessions?"

"Sorry. We had to leave your things at the hospital. But you won't need them where we're heading."

THIRTY-SEVEN

Punta del Este, Uruguay, Sunday July 26, 2020

"What do you mean, he's gone?" Fidelia demanded of Mateo Lopez when he called that morning.

"Just what I said. A Canadian named Mario Bartoli was a patient in the Hospital Evangélico, but he disappeared during the night. Someone took him."

She stood up and put the phone on speaker. This promised to take a while, and she needed a fix of caffeine. Urgently. While loading the Nespresso machine, she noticed her companion had come out from a ground floor bedroom to check out the commotion. She addressed both.

"Klaudia has joined me, Mateo. Tell her what you just told me, but give us as much detail as you can."

"Okay. I sent a gal over to the hospital early this morning to find Knight. She knows the facility well, and I also gave her the name 'Bartoli' you mentioned he might use. When she showed up, she noticed the place swarming with police. Uniformed guys. Detectives. Twelve or more investigators. She called and asked if she should bail out, but I ordered her to ask our questions and learn what she could."

"So this gal knows the hospital well and agreed to do what you requested?"

"Yeah. She actually worked there for a while and knew an attendant in the reception area. That person told her someone drugged two nurses during the night. A security guard reported finding them about four in the morning. When management checked, they discovered a patient was missing. She confirmed it was Mario Bartoli."

"Did he just walk out of the hospital?" Klaudia wondered.

"No. He couldn't have. That's what's so weird. He had surgery the day before to fix a severely fractured leg, from a motorcycle crash or something. The dude could hardly move."

"Okay. So what happened?"

"The security guard was away from his post at the front entrance having a cigarette break. Of course, the guy didn't admit to it, but he was probably taking a nap. Anyway, he vaguely recalls seeing two men—both wearing medical garb—load someone, presumably Bartoli, into an SUV from a hospital gurney, then jump in the vehicle and speed off. He couldn't get there in time, but he clicked a photo as it drove away."

"So he got a license plate?" Fidelia asked.

"Yeah. And he reported it to the front desk. They initially thought a patient had skipped out without paying the bill and called the police. Of course, the *cana* didn't treat it as a priority. Coincidentally, when a cop arrived to check out the non-payment claim, the administration staff learned about the two drugged nurses and all hell broke loose."

"Do they have any notion where Knight is or who grabbed him?"

"Our gal says neither the *cana* nor the hospital has any idea who it was or where they've run."

"Has she talked with the security guard?"

"No. He split before she arrived."

"Here's what you need to do." Fidelia gave him time to focus or make notes or whatever he needed to do to be clear he understood her message.

"First, send your woman to find out if they left behind any of Knight's, or Bartoli's, personal effects. Be sure she gets anything left. Second, track down that security guard and look at the license plate number of that SUV. Get back to me *immediatamente*. If I'm not available, give it to Klaudia. She'll tap into the government database to identify the owner, but I'm guessing it'll be a rental car. Send a couple of your best guys out to the airport poking around for anything strange that people might have seen. If I'm right, they'll be in the perfect place when Klaudia verifies the vehicle ownership."

After Fidelia hung up, her accomplice nodded and set off to the bedroom. She likely wanted a head start on cracking those data files so she'd be ready when Lopez provided the plate number.

She flipped open the lid of her laptop and began to work. Whoever snatched Howard Knight probably had no intention of keeping him somewhere in Uruguay. Kidnapping by locals was improbable. She doubted he had family or friends in the country who might have intervened. Oddly, this all sounded like an FBI or CIA operation. Perhaps they suspected Luigi's sense that Knight was feeding info to the Feds and spirited him away before she could find him.

She located the secret number for The Organization's mole inside the Bureau in DC. At the end of her call, the terrified gal understood what Fidelia needed, and how urgently. She promised to deliver the information as quickly as possible.

Her plant at the CIA was equally responsive when Fidelia spoke with her minutes later. If the Agency had played a role in Knight's abduction, she'd find out.

Seconds after completing those calls, her phone rang again. Expecting the call to be Lopez, she grimaced to see her primary protector's name appear on the screen.

"Got nothin' from that guy, Andrews. He's an asshole. Seems ta know nothin' 'bout the French billionaire."

"What happened?"

"The Lithuanians brought a doctor last night like ya wanted. Doin' a great job. Andrews's still conscious, but barely. Stashed him in an abandoned shed far from any nosy neighbors. Started removin' body parts, 'n he began talkin'. But none of it makes sense."

"Try me."

"Guy says he came to Belarus ta meet his wife. Claims she's bringin' him a couple million dollars. Don't compute. Wife's 'n American radio announcer. Lives in Virginia. Why the fuck would she fly all the way over here ta give him money?"

Luigi rarely cursed in conversations with Fidelia. She didn't really care, of course, but it showed his exasperation. And it sounded bizarre.

"What else did you learn?"

"Claims ta know only what the media reported 'bout the Sauvignon kidnapping. Everythin' he told us we seen on TV. Didn't waiver, even under duress."

That word again. "Duress" had become Luigi's new term for horrible and excruciating torture. She had listened while his guys removed body parts from Ortez in Chile. Duress definitely didn't adequately describe the suffering.

"Why does he speak Russian?"

"Nonsense again, even after he lost three fingers. Claims his wife is 'n love with Russia. Travels there often. She insisted Andrews learn the language. Seems like more bullshit to me."

"Are you giving up?"

"I'll keep at it if ya want me to. He's still alive, but I doubt we'll get more from 'im."

Luigi sounded defeated, but it wasn't like him to give up.

"Let's keep him alive for now if you're in a good, secure location," Fidelia instructed. "Here's what I need you to do. Klaudia got a woman inside the house in Krynki. Take one of the Lithuanians back there with you after dark and monitor the place from afar. Let me know if you see anything unusual. I'll share what I hear from her. You might wanna find a thermos and some coffee. I expect she'll be there all night."

"Okay. Any word on Knight yet?" Her primary protector's tone hardened as he asked the question.

Fidelia grimaced before she answered. "It's complicated. We thought we had a lead on him, but it didn't work out. I'm trying other avenues."

"I don' need ta tell ya how nervous that guy makes me. Had 'nother twelve arrests overnight. Top enforcers in 'Frisco. Few knew 'bout them, but Knight did."

"You know I share your urgency, Luigi. But I think our best bet, for now, is the Polish gal Klaudia brought into the house in Krynki tonight. Let's see how that pans out."

"Okay. I'll do what ya tell me ta do. By the way, 'bin wondering a bit about your German friend. Known her a long time 'n you're close. But she's really Russian, right? Used ta be part of the KGB there, right? Any chance she's a mole?"

THIRTY-EIGHT

Lyon, France, Sunday July 26, 2020

Suzanne expected the early morning knock at her apartment door to be a bodyguard requesting permission to enter. When the door opened, it stunned her to see her friend and colleague, Michelle Sauvignon, standing in front of a giant woman who looked as if she could play professional basketball.

Her friend was a mess. She'd abandoned her meticulous grooming routine and appeared as though she hadn't slept in days. Her green eyes were bloodshot, with red rings and heavy dark bags. Approximately the same height as Suzanne, she looked shorter that morning with slumped shoulders and a slightly bowed head. Her long hair straggled in all directions, begging for a brush. When she looked upward, she wept silently, making no effort to wipe away the tears trickling down her face.

Suzanne moved forward, spreading her arms in welcome, wrapping them tightly around her friend's upper back and pulling her closer. She had no idea what she should say, so she simply closed her eyes to fight off her own threatening tears and hugged tenderly but firmly.

Michelle gently pushed her away and stepped backward. "I'm so sorry! I should've listened. I should've been patient like you suggested. It's even worse for my father now."

Suzanne waited a moment to reply. Michelle was her closest friend but also a vital subordinate. The words she chose next could have a lasting impact on their relationship.

"Step inside. I was hoping you would come this morning. Let's have a coffee together and decide where we go from here." Suzanne took her hand and led her toward the dining area.

"I'm Reta Fournier, with Interpol." The tall woman said, then waited awkwardly for an invitation to enter the suite.

"My apologies. I must have forgotten my manners when I left my bedroom this morning. Please, come in. Join us for a coffee."

Suzanne recovered her most charming smile and pasted it on. Surely the woman would realize she usually wore makeup and didn't dress in

212

only a fluffy white robe. She led them to the dining area and offered chairs while organizing the coffee machine and mugs. When a suitable amount of time had elapsed, she excused herself to put on more clothes and ducked back into the bedroom.

Stefan woke briefly to ask what was happening. She told him and suggested he sleep longer, thinking Michelle might relax more without a guy in the room for a while. He got it, nodded, and was breathing deeply to induce slumber as she applied a dash of lipstick before slipping out again fully dressed.

Their conversation started uncomfortably. The agent from Interpol felt obliged to first bring Suzanne up to date. She would have preferred instead to attend to her friend and assess her current mental state. However, she listened politely and was glad she did.

"We received another call demanding payment," the French woman started. "Our technology people used sophisticated software they just brought over from headquarters. Before, we needed ninety to one hundred seconds to pick up both the number and the precise location of a caller. The new version lets us capture both in less than half a minute." The agent paused and smiled broadly before continuing, her pride in recounting the story obvious.

She took a deep breath before she carried on. "We coached Michelle to wait a bit after she picked up the call before she said anything, then urged her to say hello slowly and softly. We wanted to throw the caller off balance and buy a few moments. She did it fabulously. It was over ten seconds before the flustered suspect blurted out his demand for her to pay fifty million dollars into the mitcoyne account before midnight tonight. Or they'd sever her father's hand."

The woman paused once more and glanced toward the grief-stricken daughter, sensitive to the impact of her words. Michelle nodded for her to continue.

"She bought another few seconds by asking the suspect to repeat the number of the mitcoyne account. He had to first find it on a piece of paper and she brilliantly read it back to him at a snail's pace to be sure she had it right. As soon as Michelle asked to speak to her father, the guy cut off the call. But our technician was jubilant. He had a hit."

Suzanne strained to maintain a neutral expression. So far, she didn't share the Interpol officer's delight with their technological achievements. From Michelle's dejected appearance, she wasn't sure her friend found it positive either. Suzanne nodded an understanding and said nothing.

"Here's where it gets interesting. The telephone had an IP address in Belarus like the last time, but when we accessed the service provider's records, we identified the physical location of the handset as only blocks away from the Sauvignon residence. We asked the local *gendarmes* to pay a visit."

The tall woman nodded and paused dramatically to be sure her audience grasped the significance of the recent development. "They took him into the Avignon station for questioning and found out he was a landscaper. His identification and work papers confirmed he worked for a nearby business. On a hunch, the interrogators checked with the custodian at Monsieur Sauvignon's estate and learned it was the same company who provided their gardening services. The local police called Interpol, and we immediately sent a highly skilled negotiator to interview the suspect."

The woman needed a sip of coffee before she continued. Suzanne took a gulp, too, then noticed Michelle sat silently, barely moving, and continuing to look downward in apparent despair. The agent cleared her throat and resumed after a moment.

"The person of interest is not a hardened criminal. He broke within minutes. Claimed not to know who issued the orders. Knew only that they transferred two hundred euros into his bank account immediately after he confirmed he had delivered their message. How did he confirm it with them? By phone. In less than an hour, our technicians had the number and service provider for the fellow our suspect communicated with. They determined the individual giving him the orders called from an area near the airport in Minsk, Belarus. Luckily, we have a team nearby. They'll visit the location soon and try to apprehend whoever's calling the shots."

"That sounds encouraging," Suzanne said. "But do we have enough time left before their deadline?"

Michelle lifted her head slightly but still had to look up to meet Suzanne's gaze. Her face contorted in pain. Tears filled her clouded eyes as her lips quivered. She was so pale she appeared almost lifeless.

"That's the problem. It will take a miracle for all the pieces to fit magically together before they cut off my father's hand at midnight tonight. I have to find fifty million dollars somewhere, urgently."

THIRTY-NINE

In the air, over Northwest Africa, Sunday July 26, 2020

Without pain-numbing drugs, the word discomfort took on an entirely new meaning.

Howard curled up on the jet's sofa because he couldn't stretch out fully. His tall frame was a foot longer than the space available, and solid walls on either end confined him. Worse, his injured leg swelled painfully inside the cast the surgeon had applied to support the fractures in his limb. His body became damp despite the air conditioning and he shivered.

Several hours at high altitude probably contributed to the swelling, and Howard's eyes filled with tears as he grimaced and groaned. Each time one of Tan's goons brought him a bottle of water, Howard pleaded for cushions to elevate his limb. Nurses had done that at the hospital and told him inflammation at the fracture in the boot would reduce if he kept his leg higher than his heart. The Asian guys either failed to understand his pleas or merely ignored them.

They flew for several hours with varying degrees of air turbulence. Howard tried to buckle himself into the sofa during one prolonged session when they must have passed through a storm. But with his wrists secured by zip ties, he couldn't attach the connections while lying prone. Sitting was even more uncomfortable. Instead, for what seemed like an hour or more, he gripped the bottom of the seatback to avoid falling off during the most violent drops in altitude.

Stan Tan came to visit moments after the plane began its descent. He stepped into the compartment and closed privacy curtains behind him before he plopped into the chair opposite. The Singaporean crime boss checked out Howard at some length, then took in the sofa and walls on either side, even peeking up at the ceiling for a moment.

"Are you alright, Howard Knight?" he finally asked.

"I'm not okay at all." He seethed as he spat out the words. "My leg feels like it's about to explode. The pain is incessant, with spikes every time I move. I've begged your guys for cushions to get it up higher, but they do nothing. Are you trying to kill me here?"

Tan understood immediately and left the cabin for a moment. He returned with one goon in tow and pointed toward Howard's limb, issuing instructions in Chinese. The guy roughly hoisted the injured leg in the air, threw a half dozen tiny pillows in the space below, and dropped it onto the heap.

The Singaporean instructed his man to arrange the pile neatly, one cushion on top of the other, to get Howard's foot above his heart. That was good, a clear sign they weren't hoping for him to expire on the plane from a blood clot or cardiac arrest.

"Better?" Tan inquired after his thug had left the compartment and closed the curtain again.

"Marginal," was all he could muster.

"We're going down for fuel. We'll only be on the ground for about an hour, but my guys will find you some food and painkillers at the airport. It's late though. I'm not sure what will be open."

"Thanks," Howard said, gritting his teeth. "Can you at least get rid of the zip ties? I think you know I can't escape, and I'm hardly a threat to your goons when I can't walk and they've stashed my crutches somewhere."

Tan considered, his face impassive, eyes probing. "I'll tell the guys to remove the restraints after we refuel and take-off again. Your reputation for resourcefulness and creativity precedes you." He chuckled to himself for a moment or two. "How did you injure your leg?"

"I suspect you already know the answer to that question. I'm guessing it was someone working for you that ran me off the road." Howard watched Tan's face and thought he noticed a slight pursing of his lips. "I'm also thinking you were very unhappy when you learned your goon hadn't entirely finished me off."

Tan formed a tight smile. The hint of a nod confirmed it. "You're partially correct. Unfortunately, since I helped Fidelia and accommodated you in Singapore, it's become necessary to alter my plans far more often than I would have liked." His exaggerated politeness grated. "This entire mess she got me into has been expensive, dangerous, and annoying. But that's my issue to clear up."

Howard waited. Two fingers arched over Tan's nose, giving the impression he was still thinking about the best way to resolve that issue. Or it might have just been a gesture to think about what he would say next.

"Some people are furious with Fidelia and The Organization. They lost an enormous amount of money when she hoodwinked them out of a half-billion dollars. Unfortunately, your ex was extremely careless. She left too many digital footprints. One of those clues also led them to me, so I have no choice. Either I deliver you to them or they tear a strip off of my hide. I think that's the correct American expression. Do you understand me?"

Howard knew its meaning, but the pain he felt overwhelmed his capacity to process, so he didn't try. Instead, he groaned again and studied the plain aircraft ceiling for about the hundredth time. Like the other times, he found no satisfaction or relief from the agonizing, continual, and throbbing misery.

Tan sat silently in the chair, waiting for some form of response. After several minutes, he stood up, stared down at Howard, and made only one more comment. "The guys will bring your food and whatever medication they can find in Freetown." With that, he left and yanked the curtain closed behind him.

Freetown. That's in Sierra Leone. In Africa. What on earth were they doing refueling in Africa?

FORTY

Punta del Este, Uruguay, Sunday July 26, 2020

Mateo Lopez was efficient, even if the information he shared with Fidelia wasn't entirely satisfying. He drove from Montevideo that morning to deliver the backpack. He guessed she'd want to check the contents personally.

Together, they scrounged through each of the pockets and zippered compartments. When they came across the phone and laptop, she summoned Klaudia immediately.

"See what you can find and let me know as quickly as possible."

She shifted her attention to Mateo as he flashed two Canadian passports, one of them found in a "secret" compartment camouflaged well in the sack's bottom. As expected, one identified Mario Bartoli. When Fidelia held it up to better light and scrutinized it, she concluded it was the same document she'd seen in Singapore weeks earlier.

The one from the secret compartment was new. Stuart McGregor? The photo was unquestionably Howard's, but someone had done extensive work on his face, ears, and hair. She examined the new one in the same light. Very official. She couldn't spot any mistakes. That meant somebody with access to genuine passports created it. Only the Canadian government itself, the CIA, or the FBI could issue a legitimate document.

Meanwhile, Mateo had rummaged through a wallet and produced two more bits of interest. First was a Mastercard issued by TVB Bank with Mario Bartoli imprinted on its front. The other card was an Ontario driver's license carrying the name Stuart McGregor. It, too, appeared to be genuine. So Luigi was correct. The FBI seemed like the most likely source of the new documents.

"What did you find out from the security guard?"

"We found him at home. When we got the photo of the SUV, we confirmed your hunch. It had Hertz clearly marked in one corner, so we didn't call Klaudia. Our people went directly to the counter at the airport."

Fidelia nodded, and Lopez glanced down at a tiny notepad before he continued his report. "A company reserved and paid for the vehicle from Singapore. A couple Asian guys picked it up and returned it. The Hertz office was closed when they brought back the car. They left it in the parking lot beside the tarmac used for private planes, with the keys in the ignition. They must have taken off in a hurry."

"Do you have connections in air traffic control?"

"Of course. One of the guys I sent to the airport knows someone there. It was a quiet night. The pandemic has killed the number of flights. Only two private jets landed overnight, and one of them was still parked out there. The other was a plane registered to a company in Macau. It arrived from Hawaii. Before that, it was in Australia. A really nice airplane, my guy said, a Bombardier Global 8500. It came in after midnight and was on the ground for about four hours. It refueled, then took off about an hour after the incident at Hospital Evangélico, destined to Sierra Leone according to its flight plan."

The plane sounded like the one described by Aretta in Australia, but it was unlikely Stan Tan had connections in Africa. His territory was Asia. Howard Knight had no connections there; Fidelia was sure of that. Unless he staged the entire affair as a diversion, the jet's passengers probably planned to refuel and carry on northward toward Europe— the same stop her trip with Klaudia had made traveling in the opposite direction. But something didn't compute.

Aretta's people thought the flight originally headed to Washington after Hawaii. Did they simply change their plan and fly to Uruguay instead? Or did someone order Tan to abort the stop in DC? Or did it imply the need to hunt down Howard Knight in Uruguay was a new one for Tan—or whoever was pulling his strings at that moment?

"Get to your contact with air traffic control again. See if they've registered a forward plan from Sierra Leone. If they have, where? And then find out if they filed any further flight plans from that location."

Mateo reached for his phone and headed off to a quiet corner as Klaudia bounded back into the room, whooping with joy. Waving a handset, she squealed and beamed with delight.

"One message to a woman named Angela at FBI headquarters, using the name Mario Bartoli from a Singaporean email address." She noticed Fidelia's puzzled look. "I imagine he bought the phone in Singapore and set up his email with SingTel's server."

"What's it about?"

"I'll read it to you," she replied. She cleared her throat and read aloud. "I've been followed. Had to move on. Destroyed your phone before I realized you guys probably weren't the culprits. Still see little connection between The Organization and those bombings. Not their style. Here's something to investigate. Not part of The Organization but connected indirectly to a lower-level guy. Maybe just a sexual dalliance. But Joey Andrews and his wife seem odd. Check these links to LinkedIn and Facebook profiles, particularly the comment about coming big payday. Not much, but all I've got. Let me know if you're okay with these less secure emails or if you prefer I wait for a new phone."

"I'm not sure I share your excitement," Fidelia said.

"It confirms Howard was cooperating with the FBI but didn't throw The Organization under the bus." Klaudia's tone was mildly defensive. "I checked the profiles he mentioned. The guy seems to be unremarkable and a little weird. Smart enough to learn Russian, though. It's his wife you want to focus on. I've seen her face before. Twenty years ago, we were in the same English language training program of the Russian secret service. She was the top student."

Fidelia didn't make a link immediately, but with time, it gelled. If Klaudia remembered the woman as a secret service trainee, she could confidently rely on her brilliant friend's memory. The husband must have a connection to someone in The Organization. Patiently, she searched her memory for a clue. Suddenly, she recalled part of a casual conversation years earlier, with Howard Knight of all people.

He once mentioned that he'd watched a guy's career progression evaporate instantly because of his fascination with a talk-show radio host. It took another few moments before the name came back. A low-level drug runner from Miami named Juan Presivo. He might also have access to people who made crude bombs. Joey Andrews's Facebook comment about expecting a big payday could mean anything. She needed to make a couple calls.

First, she connected with their DC mole in the FBI. When the woman tearfully explained she hadn't been able to find any current information about Howard Knight, Fidelia showed sympathy. She calmed her down by promising she'd keep their little secret a while longer if the agent performed better with a new request.

Fidelia wanted everything the Feds had in their files about Joey Andrews; everything, she emphasized. She also demanded to know what the FBI knew about Stuart McGregor, a Canadian. The woman had first protested that she didn't have access to any data on foreigners, but acquiesced to her demand when Fidelia reminded her of their secret video. Still sobbing, she said farewell in tears, with a promise to do everything possible.

After a quick search in her contacts, Fidelia pulled up the info for the number five guy in Miami. She shook her head in dismay as she thought about her leaders numbered one through four. They were already in FBI custody without access to legal representation, probably somewhere offshore. She keyed in the phone number and the fellow responded on the second ring.

"Find Juan Presivo and bring him in for a chat. Find out what he knows about a guy named Joey Andrews in Washington. Also, find out what he knows about making explosives or anyone he knows that makes bombs. I have information these guys might be related to all the recent arrests. No need to be gentle, and don't let him loose until you check with me."

The fellow asked for only a few more details and some background before he assured her he'd call back later that day. Before she had time to go for a run, Luigi called.

"Ya won't believe this," he whispered. "Somebody's out there."

"What do you mean?"

"I returned ta the little place near Krynki with one of the Lithuanians. Followed the same trail we used yesterday ta spy on the place. Suddenly, the Lithuanian stopped and motioned for me ta be quiet. He pointed ta somethin' that looked like clothes on the ground ahead. I couldn't make out what it was at first. When he whispered 't was a person, I saw he was right. Male or female, can't be sure. But someone's lyin' out there with binoculars trained on the house."

"Are you certain it's safe to talk?" Fidelia asked

"Yeah, I'm a few hundred yards away. A wooded area. Left the Lithuanian back there ta keep an eye out."

"Use that app Klaudia downloaded to see if the person has a mobile phone. That might help us."

"Okay. I'll need ta get closer. I'll do that, then send it ta her. Any word from the woman ya sent ta the house?" Luigi asked.

"Not yet. Be sure you text or call when you see her leave."

FORTY-ONE

Lyon, France, Sunday July 26, 2020

The tall woman from Interpol tactfully disappeared outside the apartment. And Stefan graciously offered to keep himself occupied behind the closed doors of their bedroom as Suzanne sat with her friend and talked. To be more precise, she listened while Michelle alternated impassioned sobbing with oblique answers to questions.

Despite heartfelt sympathy about her dire circumstances, it wore thin. Minutes ran on as Suzanne struggled to gauge the depths of her friend's despair. Michelle recounted the discussions she'd had with her ex-fiancé, Guillaume Boudreau, which led to their decision to borrow from his company to pay the ransom demand. She used terms like love, compassion, and gratitude as often as words of desperation, such as anxiety, fear, and heartache.

It became apparent she would do almost anything to muster fifty million dollars again, despite her horrible experience with their first deposit to a mitcoyne account. A different side of her friend emerged. Her thinking became far less critical and totally reactive. Eventually, it proved impossible to find a plausible path to persuade her to process her grief more dispassionately.

After more than an hour, Michelle suddenly demanded action. She asked Suzanne—simply and directly—to lend her the money. She'd repay it with whatever rate of interest was necessary within days of her father's release. Their family fortune was in the billions. She would persuade her father to liquidate assets to offset the loan. Of his profound gratitude, there would be no doubt.

Finally, Suzanne promised to explore the possibility.

Her broker was away until Monday when the stock markets opened in the US. Then it might be possible for her to sell some of her personal holdings of Multima shares. Even that posed problems. Assuming she sold equities worth fifty million, she wouldn't actually get the cash until the settlement date two or three days later. If the kidnappers were demanding payment by Friday, they were cutting it close.

Although she'd agreed to nothing more than investigating the possibility, Michelle appeared satisfied. Oddly, she became almost cheerful and relaxed despite her failure to get Suzanne's commitment. It was both curious and out of character. Suzanne chalked it up to some bizarre combination of grief and anxiety.

At the first opportunity, she excused herself to rouse Stefan from the bedroom. He was sitting in bed, reading when she entered. Suzanne quickly summarized her conversation in a whisper, including her curiosity about Michelle's unexpected acquiescence.

"She's under a lot of strain," Stefan said. "Logic and reason are often the first victims of extreme mental pressure. Would you like me to talk with her?"

"Dan Ramirez is expecting my call," she continued to whisper. "Can you be a darling and take Michelle and a couple bodyguards for a stroll outdoors? I'd like privacy for the chat with him."

His eyes shifted uncomfortably for an instant before he nodded.

When they returned together to the living room, Stefan turned on his considerable charm to persuade their friend to join him for a walk around the block. The fresh air and sunshine would be good for them both, he proclaimed. Then he chatted quietly with her outside of Suzanne's hearing. After a while, Michelle acquiesced with a trace of a smile.

Dan Ramirez was at Multima's US headquarters in Fort Myers and alone in a large conference area with a wide-screen monitor when their Zoom connection activated. He dove right into his briefing.

"There's something fishy about this entire Sauvignon affair. The FBI technicians in Quantico now believe fifty million dollars *weren't* sent to a mitcoyne account."

He gave her time to process his allegation, then carried on. "The folks digging into the cryptocurrency world are unbelievably capable. If they raise a red flag like this, we'd best pay attention."

The claim surprised her, of course. Curiously, the sensation wasn't shock or amazement. At this stage, nothing was impossible. Still, she needed much more. "That's quite an allegation. What led them to that conclusion?"

"I won't pretend to understand the bits and bytes and ins and outs of crypto technology. They're way beyond my computer skills. But, here's what they tell me. The Bureau developed an app to help them track money laundering. It's not foolproof to be sure, but they can connect all the dots from the time a cash transfer leaves for a mitcoyne account and through the stages they call mining. The software's clumsy but efficient. They don't want the bad guys to know they have this capability, so they haven't started using it to press charges. Meanwhile, they're still learning."

"Fair enough, but what caused the concern with this specific transaction?"

"Michelle's boyfriend gave the French police details about the transferred cash. After spending a lot of time in mitcoyne mines, someone checked the bank's records and gained access to their mainframe computer, legally we'll presume. They learned the money never arrived in a mitcoyne account. Instead, in milliseconds, it moved through dozens of accounts in France, and then to Gibraltar, to Cayman, to Singapore, and finally to a bank in Macau. The FBI plucked fifty million from that account this morning."

"Wow," was all she could say.

"I understand Michelle is there with you, and a team from Interpol is on its way to have a chat with her."

"She's out for a walk with Stefan. Let me check if one of the other bodyguards can catch up to them."

"No, it's okay. I'm sure the police woman is with her. She had instructions not to lose sight of her. Let's not raise any alarm bells until we sort this out. You should see the investigators there soon." Dan's tone remained calm but emphatic.

That conversation demanded another caffeine boost. The coffee maker hadn't finished brewing when James Fitzgerald's name flashed in a FaceTime alert on her private phone. When she accepted the call he appeared on edge.

"I heard from Angela. She sent me a text. Said she couldn't speak freely, but just wanted to let me know she was alright and on a surveillance mission. How are things there?" Although he asked casually, he looked uncharacteristically flustered and ill at ease.

Her posture straightened as she braced for what was to come. She needed to learn more about Angela's text first. "Okay, so far. But you look uneasy this morning. Was there something in Angela's message that caused concern?"

"Nothing specific, but it isn't her message that has me worried. It's information that Natalia Tenaz uncovered. I'm not sure how to break it to you."

"Directly is always the best way. You know that."

"It concerns your friend, Michelle Sauvignon. Natalia did some research and learned some shocking news. That woman is not Jean-Louis Sauvignon's daughter. She's his wife."

FORTY-TWO

In the air, somewhere over northwest Africa, Sunday July 26, 2020

As promised, Stan Tan's thugs brought Howard some food and medication while the jet refueled. It had been dark when they landed and took off, so he saw little of the airport activity. The place appeared almost vacant, so it would not have been surprising for the guys to return empty-handed. The pain intensified by the hour, with shocks so sharp he cried out for relief more than once.

They removed the zip ties after takeoff. Immediately, Howard stretched down to the area around his boot cast and gently massaged his leg, hoping to improve circulation and ease the continuous throbbing agony. He'd always considered his threshold for pain higher than most, but the constant tears struggling to burst free suggested otherwise.

For a moment, one thug hovered over Howard, watching. Soon bored, the fellow tossed a paper sack on the sofa and left. Inside the bag, cold sandwiches wrapped in cellophane contained some sort of meat with wilted lettuce on top. At the bottom of the sack, he found a few condiments in plastic containers. Next to the food nestled a bottle of water and a small vial of ibuprofen. He reached first for the painkillers.

He expected they'd do little to soothe the pain, but quickly snapped open the container and shook three tablets into his hand. With the other hand, he twisted the bottle cap and promptly flushed the pills down his throat. He deliberated about eating the sandwich for some time. Its appearance surely wasn't appetizing, and health standards at an African airport in the middle of the night were as close to a wildcard as anything he might imagine.

Sometime later, the rumbling of his stomach and a realization he hadn't eaten for several hours won out over his better judgment. He smelled the meat; no foul odors. Nibbled a bit on the corners; the taste was bland but not offensive. Within minutes, the sack was empty, with the ultimate outcome still unknown.

About that time, Stan Tan returned to the compartment, calmly drew the curtain closed, and plunked himself down in the corner chair opposite Howard again.

"How is your discomfort now?" His expression and manner suggested genuine interest.

"Marginally better. Where are you taking me?" Howard's tone was more abrupt and aggressive than he intended. It must have been the pain, but he made no effort to soften it.

The crime boss's chin jerked up slightly, and his eyes suddenly became animated, then softened, before he chose to continue their conversation.

"Giancarlo Mareno always spoke highly of you. He often said you were the brains of The Organization, then he'd add with a big laugh, at least the financial brains." Tan's smile broadened while his shoulders relaxed, clasping his hands innocently in his lap. "I wonder, how did a bright guy like you find himself in this mess?"

"You know. It was one of your people who hounded me out of Costa Rica, then ran me off the road in Uruguay, breaking my leg in two places. Now, you've kidnapped me from a hospital. What else is there to understand?"

The Singaporean threw back his head and chuckled, but his body soon coiled again. He resembled a surly snake about to lash out in attack and sprang upright to deflect Howard's intense scrutiny.

"I know nothing about Costa Rica or your unfortunate accident. You'll probably need to talk to the Shadow about that. If my men had intended to harm you, we wouldn't be having this conversation. So cut the crap." He stood menacingly over Howard as his demeanor changed from polite to sinister. His voice was low as he spat out his question. "What did Fidelia and you do to anger the Shadow?"

"I have no idea. And who the hell is this Shadow?" It was risky to rebel. However, he knew nothing about the Shadow and had to make that clear.

"In a few hours, we'll touch down in Gibraltar. Between now and then, I'll choose. Either I will leave you there and let you live a little longer, or I'll turn you over to the people who are harassing me. It's up to you to convince me there's more in it for me letting you survive than there is tossing you to the other guys."

He didn't respond, and instead assessed the fellow from a different perspective. After a while, he stared downward sullenly to test Tan's reaction. It was swift. In a motion he barely detected and couldn't avoid, the Singaporean walloped the side of his face viciously. The impact left Howard teetering on the edge of the sofa, wiping away a cruel sting that competed with a sharp stab from his injured leg. He peeked up again.

"Now, how much did she swindle from the Russians during her little escapade from Australia?" Tan demanded.

Howard tried to calculate the relative risks quickly. We weighed the probability of another violent reaction against the retribution Fidelia might impose if he divulged the approximate value of her total haul. His decision favored the immediate danger.

"I'm not aware of the specific amount. My role was to get the Multima executives to behave the way we needed. Suzanne Simpson purchased shares for her personal account at the price we requested, and Wilma Willingsworth bought back equities for the company at an inflated value. Your boy did all the trading, so he'd know better how much she shortchanged the Russians."

"He thought it was a half billion or more. Where did she hide it?"

"I don't know. You can beat me until my brain is frazzled. I can't tell you a thing. I've been out of The Organization for five years now." He looked at Tan without blinking, underscoring his honesty.

"Rumor has it you skimmed a sizeable chunk of money from Mareno. He wanted revenge and posted a reward for your capture." The Asian leaned in so close to Howard's face he could smell the ingredients in the guy's lunch. "Where are you hiding it?"

"Fidelia asked the same question. I told her and I'll tell you now. I truly do not know. I skimmed the cash to ease my conscience about the miserable way The Organization treated women. Human trafficking. Beatings. Degradation. I filtered all the money to a woman on the west coast of the US who built an app that circulates it around the world continuously from account to account. Only the software knows where it is and pays out a small amount every month to a couple agencies that help girls. Again, you can beat me to a pulp, but I can't give you anything because I don't know."

He maintained eye contact with Tan as he told the story. That part of it was true. There was no need yet to share any details about the other millions he had skimmed and parked in the Caymans.

The Singaporean thought about it for a moment, weighing the benefits of using his guys to test Howard's tolerance. Then he shook his head as though he'd decided it wasn't worth the trouble.

"Have it your way. I'll just follow the Shadow's orders. Should the Russians ask, you might want to fine-tune that story, though. Enjoy the rest of your flight."

FORTY-THREE

Punta del Este, Uruguay, Sunday July 26, 2020

Her skin carried a potent scent of perspiration, and huge, damp blotches on her T-shirt attested to a long, demanding run along the tranquil beach on a cool winter evening. But a quick peek into an entryway mirror as she entered Ortez's former home confirmed she looked fit and trim.

That glance was Fidelia's last moment of relaxation.

While she was outside running, her primary protector had called Klaudia and uploaded a screenshot from the secret app. To everyone's surprise, the IP address for the phone of the person lying on the ground behind the house in Krynki was American. Klaudia matched it to a Verizon number registered in West Virginia and was already looking for a way to hack their customer records and get a name.

Minutes later, Mateo Lopez called. His guy at the airport had wangled from his contact a flight plan for the Bombardier Global 8500 that had left Montevideo earlier, presumably with Howard Knight on board. It showed five passengers, the same number as the leg from Uruguay to Sierra Leone, and it was due to arrive in Gibraltar in about eight hours.

Luigi called again. He'd received a call from his guy from San Marino who was keeping an eye on the leader who'd replaced Sargetti in Italy. Under cover of darkness, Antonio Verlusconi had loaded two large pieces of luggage into an SUV and was driving into Linate Airport in Milan as they spoke. He wanted instructions.

"Let him go. But when he gets on a plane be sure your boy gets the aircraft ID. Phone me back immediately with that information." Fidelia barked out orders like a marine sergeant. "Any sign of that woman we sent to the house in Krynki?"

"She's headed toward her car right now."

Fidelia summoned Klaudia and relayed the news; they should expect word soon. In the meantime, she took a quick shower and changed from her running gear. Her companion pounded away on her laptop keyboard, determined to penetrate the Verizon shield of security in West Virginia.

The call came on Klaudia's phone.

"You owe me another thousand euros," the Polish woman blurted out first. "Those assholes weren't only randy, they were monstrous. They violated every orifice of my body multiple times. It aches everywhere. I never should have accepted the goddamned job."

They let her vent, knowing too well how miserable she must feel. They had been there and done that too often. Eventually, Fidelia spoke.

"We understand. Klaudia will transfer another three thousand euros once you give us the scoop on who's there and what they're doing."

"There are two Poles, four Russians and a couple from Belarus. The pigs each went twice. Not one of them had any class, and their cocks weren't even impressive. Thankfully, none of them had staying power and half dropped their loads within a couple minutes, like schoolboys."

Fidelia refocused her attention. "Were there any other women there or any other people who didn't partake in the action?"

"No females. I can't imagine any girl could survive more than a few hours with that bunch. There was an old guy. He called out from the bedroom once. Three of the goons blocked the hallway from view while he went to the toilet. I couldn't see his face, but he was naked. I saw veins and wrinkled skin on his legs. I was on my hands and knees on the floor so you know I was looking for some distraction to get my mind off the bastard ramming my ass."

Fidelia looked at Klaudia and cringed. Both understood the woman's repulsion for the men and their miserable treatment. They gave her a moment to compose herself again before the next question.

"You speak Russian and Belarusian, right? Did you hear any conversation about the old man?"

"They said little. I had the impression none of them would be there much longer. They all sat around like pigs, chatting and watching while each took his turn with me. A couple squawked about the time their job was taking. One complained his wife was threatening divorce if he didn't get his ass home by the weekend."

"Did they mention the old guy's name?"

"No. I heard something once that sounded like it could be French but didn't hear it clearly enough to be sure."

"What do you think the guys were doing in Poland? Did anyone say anything that hinted at that?"

"At one point, I thought they might be preparing to rob a bank or something. When the guy was complaining about his wife, another said 'Let her go. With your share, you'll be able to buy one far more beautiful.' Of course, the scum all found that funny."

The instant Klaudia finished the call, Fidelia pressed speed dial for her primary protector. She trusted his judgment and valued his perspective as a male. With Klaudia's help, she recounted the conversation and the woman's observations without missing a detail. Luigi listened carefully, asking clarifying questions from time to time.

As they talked, Klaudia pounded furiously on her laptop, determined to crack the security wall and learn the name that matched the IP address for whoever was lying on the trail behind the house in Krynki.

"No bank worth robbin' in a hundred miles of this place," Luigi said. "It's gotta be the French billionaire they have 'n there. It's gotta be."

"Maybe," Fidelia allowed. "Let's check a couple more things before we jump to any conclusions. Leave the Lithuanian to watch the person lying on the ground out there and the goings-on around the house. Be sure he alerts you to any movement at all. I want you to go to wherever you're stashing Joey Andrews and change your questions."

"Whatcha lookin' for?"

"First, drill down on that guy, the Shadow. The one Tan and Sargetti talked about when this mess started. I just remembered Nguyễn commenting that Tan told him the Shadow was a politician, and another time he traced a threatening call from a woman referring to the Shadow to a phone in Washington."

"Funny ya should mention the Shadow. Caught somethin' on the dark net last night. A guy braggin' 'bout gettin' a bonus from the Shadow for lightin' up a car in Düsseldorf. Sounds like maybe he was the one tryin' to git you 'n Klaudia."

"Let's see what he knows. Then focus on his wife. Klaudia has good reason to think Lucy Andrews might be Russian, not Polish, as she claims."

Only minutes elapsed before the crime boss from Miami called with his report on Juan Presivo. "The punk was involved in three bombings—the supermarkets in Naples and Ocala as well as a Multima warehouse in Florida. Didn't have the intelligence to even realize how badly he screwed up and the mess he caused."

"Give me the story, the full story." Fidelia gritted her teeth, her blood pressure rising and face warming.

"Andrews approached Presivo. Claimed to be working secretly for some part of the government. He wanted our guy to arrange the bombings under the pretense Multima Supermarkets CEO Suzanne Simpson was fundin' some fuckin' cult called QAnon. They intended for the explosions to trigger some fuckin' public inquiry, leading to the woman's arrest, and saving the country from takeover by fucking cannibalistic pedophiles."

Fidelia's jaw dropped as she listened. One of her people had the stupidity to fall down such an obvious rabbit hole? She shook her head slowly and drew a deep breath before she confirmed it scornfully. "Have I got this right? Presivo agreed to place bombs in three different locations as a public service?"

"Not exactly. He signed on to the jobs at fifty grand a hit. Naples. The store in Ocala. And the Multima warehouse. At least he didn't plant the fuckin' bombs himself. He found an illegal Mexican willing to do it fer a grand each. He bought the supplies on the street and taught the fucking beaner how to put 'em together. That's why each time worked better. The guy learned and fuckin' Presivo kept forty-nine grand per job minus his cost of materials."

"What about bombing the Jefferson's store and the explosion at their CEO's home?"

"He didn't know who did it. Claims Andrews offered 'im the jobs but he turned 'em down 'cause he thought The Organization had some connection. Didn't want to anger the higher-ups. Says Andrews was fuckin' pissed 'cause some guy called the Shadow wanted 'em hit."

"So the guy had some smarts. Anything else your genius had to share with you?"

"Asked him about Andrews's wife, Lucy. Presivo bragged she was another reason he did the jobs. Claims the radio broadcaster has the hots for him and Andrews shares her. Agreed to throw in a night with her if Presivo accomplished all three hits within a month. Fuckin' idiot even boasted he'd already claimed his bonus. Woman told him it was the last time, though. She was leaving on some trip and didn't expect to return."

"What's his current condition?"

"We did little more than threaten to get the fucker talking. Like I say, he's not our sharpest knife in the drawer."

"You still have him?" Fidelia asked.

"Of course. How do you wanna dispose of him?"

"I'll make a call and ask someone we have inside the FBI to contact you. She'll use the name Sheila. Force the bastard to tell her what he told you. If she wants him, break both knees and leave him wherever she instructs. If she has no interest, feed him to the fish."

It never hurt to help a mole win a new promotion. Every step up the ladder assured easier access to more files.

FORTY-FOUR

Lyon, France, Sunday July 26, 2020

The team from Interpol showed concern from the moment they burst into the apartment their agency had loaned to her. Suzanne had expected maybe two guests after her conversation with Dan Ramirez. Instead, a half-dozen people—some heavily armed—barged in the door and fanned out instantly in all directions and into every room.

She froze, swallowed hard, and tried to absorb the activity. A blur of action on a Sunday afternoon in an apartment in Lyon. The scene mesmerized her, and her chest tightened in angst.

She found her voice after a moment or two. In French, she loudly demanded to know what was going on. A tall agent with a sprinkling of gray in his hair and wearing a dark blue suit smiled apologetically before he responded.

"I'm Inspector Franboise. Sorry to alarm you, but we needed to verify you're alone."

Other agents nodded or raised thumbs as they stepped out of the apartment's several rooms and signaled to Franboise. After surveying the room and appearing satisfied with the response, he turned back to Suzanne and suggested they take a seat.

He plunked down his large frame at one end of the sofa and motioned for her to sit at the other. Before he began, he took a long, deep breath, and his dark eyes softened as he looked directly at her.

"A citizen discovered our colleague, Reta Fournier and an American bodyguard, lying on the sidewalk in a recessed entrance outside a store two blocks away. She's badly injured. An ambulance rushed her and the American to the hospital. Both were incapacitated, and both remain unconscious. What can you tell us?"

Her mind went completely blank. An icy shiver shot up her spine, and her body felt numb for a second. Her mouth was agape and dry when her brain finally processed the implications.

"Where's Stefan? Where's Michelle?" Her voice squeaked so feebly she didn't recognize the sound and shook her head several times. She repeated her questions at least an octave higher and loudly enough to qualify as a scream.

Franboise reached out to touch her hand, then quickly pulled back. He sized her up carefully before he answered. "We don't know. Please tell us what you can. Did they all leave together?"

"Yes. More than an hour ago. I asked Stefan to take them so I'd have a bit of time alone. What happened?"

The detective nodded in understanding and ignored her question. "What is your relationship with Michelle Sauvignon?"

"She's a friend and colleague. We've been close since we were students at Stanford. She became one of my most senior executives when we acquired Farefour Stores from her father three years ago. Where is she?" Her tone was more assertive.

Still, he ignored her. "How about the male, Stefan?"

"I've known him about a year and a half. Michelle introduced us to each other in Paris in 2019. We've seen each other on and off since then."

Suzanne stood up and looked down at the detective as she posed her question once more. "Monsieur Franboise, I understand you have a job to do, and I want to help you if I can. But I insist you answer. Where are they?"

He remained seated, confident enough to withstand a look most would consider withering. "We don't know. Local police have scoured nearby streets. They started the moment we discovered Reta Fournier and the American bodyguard. They checked a radius wider than anyone could reasonably have walked or run. They also checked all available videos for the Metro. So far, they've found no sign of either."

Suzanne sat down again. Franboise inquired if he might make a coffee for each of them and dismissed the rest of the Interpol agents from the room with a wave and nod. Then the inspector stood up and headed toward the coffee machine. Returning with two full mugs, he pulled a notepad and pen from his pocket and asked more questions.

She lost track of time as Inspector Franboise posed one query after the other. What was Michelle's job with the company? What did she do in that role? Where did she go for business? How did she travel? Whom did she report to? Who reported to her? Why did Suzanne appoint her friend to the chief operating officer position? The interrogation stretched on, and Suzanne's furrowed brow reflected her puzzlement about why the information might be helpful to Interpol.

Just when she thought he'd finished, Franboise started seeking the same details about Stefan. Some questions she found intrusive, almost offensive. Had she met his family? Did she ever accompany him to École Polytechnique? Had she verified he actually worked where he said? Had she checked into his background? Did she know how much money he earned as a professor?

Her replies became more vague with each invasion of her privacy related to Stefan. She glanced at her watch and stood up again.

"I'm sorry, Monsieur Franboise. I have a video conference scheduled with a colleague in the US. You'll have to excuse me." Her tone left no room for discussion. She softened it slightly. "I expect to be on the call for about an hour. I can make more time for your queries later if needed."

The inspector hoisted himself from the sofa with a neutral expression and stared at her before he locked his jaw firmly. He spoke quietly, but his eyes flashed. "I understand. I'll wait outside in the hallway until it's more convenient for you, but I have several more questions to ask."

FORTY-FIVE

Gibraltar, Monday July 27, 2020

As the Bombardier Global 8500 jet started its gradual descent into Gibraltar, one of Stan Tan's thugs brought his crutches back to Howard's compartment and pointed toward the restroom. They'd stop in the tiny British Protectorate at the southern tip of Spain for refueling, the Singaporean crime boss had said before he closed the curtain behind him after his last visit.

His confidence in using the crutches on the plane had grown after three or four trips to the toilet. Howard navigated turns without gripping a seat back for balance, learned to spin on the heel of his right foot to save steps, and no longer banged his injured leg into walls or seats as it hung dejectedly to the side. But the suffering never ended.

Since their stop in Sierra Leone, he'd taken three pills about two hours apart on at least four occasions. His stomach didn't feel great either. Sleep had been impossible, with sharp pangs of pain a product of every movement and constant swelling beneath the cast, despite elevating his foot above his heart.

On the horizon, the sun rose just as the plane landed and followed a runway marking toward the private jet terminal at the end of the tarmac. From his seat, Howard saw a sign for the bus depot immediately across the road from the airport. There were no commercial passenger airplanes in sight. In fact, there were only two planes parked near the building and they had claimed the spots nearest the lobby, forcing the pilots of Tan's jet to make a broad sweep around them to find a space.

A fuel truck waited beside one, and workers wearing black clothing and ear protection appeared ready to perform their duties. When they came to a complete stop, Howard swung off the sofa and planted his right foot on the floor. He stood up on his good limb and stretched.

Before landing, Tan's goons had again reclaimed his crutches and carted them off to the front. Without them, he couldn't travel far. Still, he hopped unsteadily on his healthy leg a couple times while reaching for the seat in the corner. There, he plunked himself down just in time to see the stairway lowered to the tarmac. Seconds later, Tan's thugs ambled down the stairs and headed toward the office, probably in search of food to bring back to the plane.

They took only three or four steps before Howard noticed a flash of motion from beneath the aircraft. Clad entirely in black, two forms suddenly materialized and grabbed both Asian men from behind. With hands over their mouths, neither cried out, but both struggled a few seconds before their bodies fell limp. While their attackers dragged their prey under the jet, another pair scrambled up the stairway with two more on their heels.

Howard shifted his position in the seat to look down the aisle toward the cockpit. The first men neutralized Tan and the female passenger in the front compartment. As though watching a movie in slow motion, one man screamed obscenities and pointed a weapon with a silencer directly at Stan Tan's face. Blood and gore splattered everywhere in the cabin immediately after the sound of a loud pop.

The second attacker grabbed the woman by her throat and threw her to the ground. She lost consciousness. In the background, assailants three and four had reached into the cockpit and attacked the pilots from behind their backs. He couldn't see precisely what they were doing from his seat in the corner, but there was a flurry of motion as arms waved in desperation.

That left only Howard untouched in the tail compartment. With no weapon, no crutches, and no means to defend himself, he breathed in, his pulse racing frantically, and prepared for the worst. Inexplicably, he reached again for a cushion from the sofa as though it might somehow soften the blows to come.

Leaning across the aisle attracted the attention of the man holding the firearm, and he pointed it menacingly, shouting *alto*! Howard stopped. The pillow dropped to the floor while the attackers continued their bustle at the front.

The thug taking care of the woman had zip ties wrapped around her upper and lower body. She still appeared lifeless. The two who had first focused on the pilots hoisted her up—one grabbing her knees, the other wrapping his arms under her shoulders. They all quickly disappeared down the staircase while the guy with the gun approached Howard, yelling for him to raise his hands where he could see them.

As the attacker drew near, he noticed the bright yellow air cast.

"Do you understand Spanish?" he asked in Spanish.

Howard nodded, then started to speak, but the assailant cut him short. "Can you walk on the bad leg?"

"No. I'm in severe pain," he replied. "Who are you? What do you want? Where are my crutches?"

The aggressor ignored his questions and shouted out to the others for help. He stashed the gun in a pocket, then reached out and grabbed Howard's shoulders, shoving him forcefully back into the corner seat. His head banged against the window on the way down. Then the man in charge turned around and ordered his goons to drag him out of the plane.

"Wait!" Howard screamed. If the thugs pulled on his injured limb, the damage might be irreparable. "Don't touch my leg. I'll come with you if you help me along the aisle."

They paused. After a quick consultation, the leader appeared to accept his suggestion and pointed to the tallest guy, ordering him to assist Howard. The others dashed ahead. The big fellow yanked him to his feet with ease and wrapped Howard's arm around his neck. He leaned toward the burly man for balance and hopped on his good right foot as quickly as the confined space allowed.

Desperately, Howard looked for his crutches. He twice shouted out *muletas,* the Spanish word, but the goons ignored him in all their commotion.

At the top of the staircase, the big guy pulled Howard forward, flopped him over his shoulder, and simply carried him down. As the goon swung sharply at the bottom, Howard noticed a helicopter had landed directly behind the jet during all the violent upheaval, its rotors still idling. In a few long steps, the burly man covered the space from the aircraft and hoisted him upward to waiting arms that drew him into the chopper and threw him into a seat.

As a pair of hands buckled him in, he felt another hand shove a putrid-smelling cloth down tightly over his nose and mouth. The last thing he heard was someone shouting into a phone. "Mission complete. Got both. Heading out now. Pilots secure in cockpit. I'll call you when ..."

FORTY-SIX

Punta del Este, Uruguay, Monday July 27, 2020

Fidelia called his private number despite the early hour. Deschamps could figure out for himself what he'd tell his wife. In the end, it turned out there was no problem. The Interpol assistant director himself answered.

"Looking to be a hero today?" She didn't expect a reply, but gave him enough time for her voice to trigger his recall. "Can't be a hundred percent sure, but we think the guys who captured Sauvignon are holed up in a small house near Krynki in Poland."

A murmured command to hold on, motion in the background and footsteps on a stairway presumably meant he'd scooted out of bed for more privacy. A moment later, still speaking barely above a whisper, he resumed. "Why do you think so?"

"We have resources in the area on another matter. They stumbled on a home and found lots of people there. We thought someone we were looking for might be inside and covertly penetrated the place. Two Poles. Four Russians. Two Belarusians. And an old guy."

He didn't need to know she was trying to deflect unwanted attention from The Organization. Or to hear the entire story about why they had nabbed Joey Andrews. Or to realize her criminal element owned the dwelling in question.

"You've got the wrong gang. Our people here arrested a local two-bit landscape worker in the affair. He led a team to a gravesite in a wooded area near Avignon yesterday. The body is missing the forefinger on its right hand. It has a badly mangled head and face, but we'll do tests later today to confirm identity. The culprit claims it's Sauvignon."

That was startling new information. The business tycoon dead in France? Who might the old guy in the house near Krynki be then? And why would he need eight guards around the clock?

"I'll leave it to you to decide. If the body turns out to be someone else and the thugs in Poland get away, it'll be you who deals with the fallout. Frankly, I don't care. Just trying to return a favor."

He considered it for more than a moment. She'd touched a nerve.

French *fonctionnaires* were all cut from the same piece of cloth regardless of their role in society.

"Where's the house? I have some resources a couple hours away. We can check it out."

"Tell your people to be careful. They're heavily armed with lookouts twenty-four seven."

She called her primary protector next. "Deschamps is sending a team. It'll probably be two or three hours before they arrive. Any developments?"

"One of the Lithuanian's still watchin' the place. No changes 'round the property. He's also keepin' his eye on the woman watchin' the house. Sure she's a woman now 'cause she needed ta relieve herself. Guy got a good view of her squattin' b'side the trail. She's lyin' flat mosta the time with her binoculars pointed at the building."

"A woman? Interesting. Klaudia matched the IP address to a phone number in West Virginia owned by someone named James Fitzgerald. I wonder if that's the Multima James Fitzgerald and if she's connected to him some way."

"Was talkin' ta th'other Lithuanian. He wondered if there was a connection 'tween the woman and that jerk Joey Andrews we're interrogatin'. Asked him nicely. Claims not. Says his wife's flyin' in ta bring him his share. At any rate, she'd never be lyin' on a trail with binoculars. Not the type."

"His share of what?" Fidelia asked.

"Can't get it out of 'im. Maybe he doesn't know. Under duress, he insisted she was probably plannin' to dump him, just bringin' money to soften the news and shove him outta her life."

"Why might he think that?"

"Says she's always had the hots for some dude 'n Russia. Remember, confessed yesterday his wife was originally Russian—not Polish, like she claimed earlier. Maybe he's tellin' the truth. After all, we severed his right hand. Still in agony from the broken knees. Lithuanian doctor's kept him alive so far, but I don' know how much more value he has."

"Has he divulged any other details? Anything minor you haven't shared with me yet?"

Luigi was smart. He took his time thinking about her question. When he replied, his tone was tentative. "Well, there's one bit I didn't consider very important. Said his wife was travelin' to Minsk with a Chinese guy, some big shot from Asia. Couldn't tell us the guy's name, so we figured he might have been delusional. Jus' b'fore he passt out again."

"I think I know where we can confirm that detail. Stan Tan was on the plane our boys from Spain hijacked today in Gibraltar. Howard Knight may have been with him. Tan's no longer with us, but they've got the woman. I'll figure out who she is," Fidelia said.

"Did the Spanish guys nab Antonio Verlusconi 'n find out what was in the bag he was carryin'?"

"No. Apparently Verlusconi, or one of his pilots, saw the commotion on the ground from the air. The Spaniards reported a jet aborted landing seconds before touchdown, while they were busy stuffing the woman and Knight into the chopper. I've got someone trying to find out where he went."

"Whattaya wanna do with Andrews?"

"Give it one last try. Focus on his wife. Try to get the name of the Russian she supposedly has the hots for. And see what he knows about some cult called QAnon."

"Got it. Do my best. B'fore ya go, guys here think the Lithuanian doctor is alright. Won't talk. They've used him b'fore. Has stock market debts he's tryin' to pay off with 'r sharks there. Ya okay sendin' him back when we're done today?"

"If the Lithuanians believe he's safe, no problem. But call me to let me know what you get from the Andrews guy before you return to the house."

FORTY-SEVEN

Lyon, France, Monday July 27, 2020

"I asked her to explain precisely what she found," James Fitzgerald said to Suzanne. "Oh, there she is now."

Natalia Tenaz's face appeared on the wide-screen monitor. She looked less distraught than James. Her expression projected calm, her large brown eyes alert despite the extremely early hour in Chicago.

"Go ahead." Suzanne tried to muster a smile but realized she'd failed when she caught her own image on the screen. She looked flustered instead, redder than usual, and dark bags under her eyes made her look older. Regardless, she focused her full attention on the young woman and what she had to say.

"When James called to tell me I wouldn't get the job as president, he also shared the news about Michelle Sauvignon's father. It horrified me." Natalia shook her head and shoulders to emphasize the depth of her concern before she carried on.

"It was Saturday, and I had little planned, so I googled Sauvignon to learn more. Before I realized it, I'd fallen down a rabbit hole on the Internet, as happens sometimes." She smiled sheepishly. "I'd always known his name as a rich Frenchman, but why kidnappers would target him in particular intrigued me."

"What did you find, Natalia?" It came out with a tone of exasperation Suzanne tried quickly to correct. She softened the follow-up, mindful of the Canadian Mountie's "squeaky clean" assessment of the woman's background. "I mean, how did you conclude Michelle Sauvignon is Jean-Louis's spouse, and not his daughter?"

"Okay. I'll get right to the facts. Sauvignon's wife, Bernadette, died in Avignon in 1980 at age forty-four in a hospital for the mentally ill named Centre Hospitalier de Monfavet. For the following seven years, he had quite a reputation as a playboy. He dated dozens of women and generated a sizeable amount of negative publicity for himself and Farefour Stores. During that time, he also made many trips to Russia, ostensibly to expand his business to a country undergoing political

241

pressures that led to the tearing down of the Berlin Wall. Are you with me so far?"

Suzanne was hooked. She nodded.

"In January 1983, he married a much younger nineteen-year-old Russian woman named Michelle Sokolov, who returned with him to France as Michelle Sauvignon. I can't find a reason, but immediately after they arrived, she adopted the persona of his daughter, not wife. Shortly after, she moved to the United States to study at Stanford University and graduated with an MBA in 1988. I think you know the rest of the story."

Suzanne was aghast. Like someone had just punched her directly in the stomach. She breathed, but her chest constricted and her lungs felt trapped. Below the table, her knees knocked together furiously, as though trying to run from an awful truth. Why would a college student befriend her and maintain that friendship for decades—all the while misrepresenting herself as a daughter instead of a spouse? And why would Jean-Louis Sauvignon participate in the charade?

James and Natalia waited patiently while Suzanne visibly struggled to process the story. She looked unwell. On the screen, she appeared shocked, pale, and confused. She grabbed a nearby glass and swallowed a large gulp, then forced herself to stand erect to be sure she was fully in control. Leaning on the chair's back, she faced the camera.

"Natalia, how did you find that information?"

"I have to make a confession. I hacked some records in Avignon. They were sealed digitally in the early nineties. I admit my curiosity got the better of me, and I found the digital seal wasn't that sophisticated. Once I decided to hack it, I only needed a few minutes. It was ancient technology, after all."

"Do you speak French, Natalia? Is there a chance you misunderstood something you read?"

"I did my MBA work at the École Polytechnique. As I say on my resume, I converse in French as well as English." Natalia's tone reflected surprise—or perhaps disappointment—that Suzanne hadn't noticed that information. After all, they had recently discussed her credentials as they considered her potential promotion to president of the division. But that could wait for another day.

The bitter news was undeniable. Once again, some mysterious blind spot had ambushed Suzanne's judgment about friends and colleagues. Unpleasant memories flooded her mind as she paced restlessly behind the chair while the others waited silently for her response.

In earlier years, she had overlooked the sordid connections of Hiromi Tenaka until he was brutally murdered outside the door of her room in a Hawaiian hotel. For a decade, she had relied upon her colleague Wilma Willingsworth. Then her trusted CFO committed suicide the same day she paid inflated prices for a share buyback, costing Multima shareholders hundreds of millions.

Now, the bewildering revelation that a close friend since college was a complete fraud. More disconcerting, if Natalia had uncovered the truth with relative ease, how had Dan Ramirez's ace security team missed it?

James Fitzgerald finally broke a silence uncomfortable for everyone. His tone radiated empathy, almost tenderness. "Would you like some time? Would it be better to call back later?"

Suzanne shook her head twice and sniffled, fighting to suppress tears. She reached for a tissue, turned away from the camera, and blew her nose. When she faced the monitor, her composure returned. She even pasted the outline of a smile on her face.

"Thank you both for giving me a moment. It's all a massive shock and took a bit to process. But I have a sense you have more surprises in store. Let me hear them."

Natalia raised her eyebrows uncertainly. Her forehead furrowed, with lips pursed tightly together. She formed the picture of a woman desperate for guidance. James Fitzgerald bailed her out.

"Your intuition is correct, Suzanne. There's more. But we don't need to get into it right now. We can let Interpol complete its investigation. They might reach different conclusions."

"No. If you have something else, I want to know what it is." Her voice sounded strong as she braced for any eventuality.

James nodded into the camera.

"Stefan Warner is also not who he seems. He lived in Germany only as a child. His parents were Germans who worked for the KGB. They fled to Moscow well before the Berlin Wall fell, and his education and professional grooming all came from the Russian secret service. That spy agency engineered his appointment at École Polytechnique. Contrary to his resume on LinkedIn, other than an internship at McLindsey and Associates in Moscow, his job as professor appears to be the only position he's ever held. There's no record of his employment at any of the other companies he claimed."

FORTY-EIGHT

Unknown location, Monday July 27, 2020

Howard smelled a noxious gas as he gradually awoke. His throat was so dry he could barely swallow. He couldn't open his mouth because they had sealed it shut with some sort of tape. Swallowing was almost as painful as the dull throbbing in his leg below the knee. They'd used something that rendered him unconscious, and it had been some time since he'd taken the ibuprofen or anything else to reduce his pain.

When he checked for movement in his arms, he realized they had clasped his hands behind his back with zip ties or some similar restraint. The slightest squirm sent shots of agony up his leg and spine. Had they dropped him at some point?

Gingerly, he opened his eyes. The bright sunlight forced his eyelids to flutter reflexively, seeking relief from the intense heat. He closed them and listened instead. Seagulls occasionally squawked in the sky above, and he detected a faint but unmistakable sound of waves gently caressing a sandy beach further away. He took a deep breath through his nose and mentally confirmed the undeniable scent of saltwater in the air.

Muffled voices caught his attention. Howard rolled his body to the other side and noticed large picture windows blocked by dark brown drapes. He couldn't hear the conversation well enough to distinguish whether male or female or both, or what language they spoke. He remembered a woman lying on the floor of the helicopter when they threw him in.

He raised his head slightly to see if he was alone. He was. Several lounge chairs sat scattered around an area that looked like a patio. Small red tiles covered the surface, and painted white walls, about three feet high, surrounded the bright spot. With a determined grit of his teeth, Howard tried to hoist himself to a seated position. He failed, but caused enough movement of the lounge chair that it squeaked loudly in protest.

A sliding door opened a moment later, and he shifted toward the noise. The big fellow who'd tossed him over his shoulder on the jet stairway had poked his head outside.

Howard seized the opportunity to shout out a muffled cry as he wriggled painfully in the recliner, demanding attention. The big guy slid the door all the way open and stepped onto the patio with another man right behind him. It was the goon who'd used the gun on the plane, but he appeared to be unarmed now. It was he who talked.

"Our orders are to treat you humanely and keep you alive, if possible. Personally, I'd be quite happy if you gave us an excuse to eliminate you." He spoke in Spanish with a slow, almost taunting, style. "We'll remove the tape only for you to eat or drink. If you say a word, we slap it back on your face and you can starve for all we care. Understand?"

He waited for an acknowledgment, so Howard nodded after a decent interval.

"First, we'll take you to the toilet. Neither of us cleans up piss or shit, so you better do it when you have the chance. We'll remove the restraints while you do that. Then we'll leave them off while Francesco here gives you some food and water. When you're finished, the tape and zip ties go back on, and you return out here. If you behave, we'll give you an umbrella."

With a flick of his wrist, he motioned for the big guy to take over. He grabbed Howard by the front of his T-shirt and hauled him up in one effortless motion, causing him to land awkwardly on both feet. He almost passed out with the sudden pain and stumbled as he shifted his weight to the good leg. His captor steadied him without emotion, then lifted him roughly over his shoulder again.

He was upside down. As the big fellow twisted his body to redistribute his load, Howard looked over the ledge of the wall. He realized where he was. His eyes darted from side to side as he checked to be sure he was right, then muttered a muffled, frustrated "Goddammit" behind the tape.

It was the patio of Giancarlo Mareno's condo in Ayamonte, Spain. That left little doubt the thugs in control of his fragile life were from The Organization. And they were undoubtedly following orders from Fidelia Morales. Pain screamed from every part of his body.

When he finished hopping from the bathroom to the kitchen, Francesco pointed for him to sit at a dining area just inside the sliding patio door. A bottle of water sat on the table. Beside it was a half loaf of local bread, a large orange, and a dark black liquid that resembled coffee. He was alone at the table and glanced around. Nothing had changed in the place since he was there almost two years earlier.

That time, he'd escaped from watching thugs by exploiting their greed, his conniving, and an ability to swim across the bay when he caught them unawares. His leg injuries and heavy boot made a repeat escape impossible at this stage.

Howard broke the bread into bite-sized morsels and slowly chewed each piece, making it last as long as possible until none remained. He peeled the orange with the same slowness. He took a sip of the black liquid and immediately spit it out in a spray that covered the surface in front of him. The taste was too vile to be considered coffee, so he shoved the rest to the center, removing any temptation to try it again.

In several gulps, he drank the bottle of water. It rinsed his mouth and cleared away the awful residue of whatever that cup contained. The last sip reminded him he hadn't brushed his teeth for almost a week, prompting a grin at the absurdity of concern about oral hygiene when he might not live to see another day.

What happened to the woman from the plane? He knew he saw her in the helicopter, and he thought he recognized her from his social media research for Angela.

The brown drapes on the window were drawn, but he noticed the two guys sitting on the patio. They looked relaxed. Both sipped from bottles of beer and chatted amiably with each other. He couldn't hear their conversation with the door closed, but guessed they were probably trading stories about their favorite soccer teams. It seemed the preferred pastime of all Spanish men.

Howard raised himself to a standing position on his healthy leg. He watched outside and observed no interest from either man. Neither glanced at the window nor interrupted their conversation. On his journey from the bathroom, he'd noticed the doors to the three bedrooms were all closed. From the table to the closest of those doors, he calculated six good hops.

He used the dinner table to help his balance for the initial two, then gave it all he had for the next four, grabbing a wall to stabilize his arrival. He tapped on the door, heard nothing, and turned the knob to peek inside.

The woman from the plane lay on the bed, naked and battered. Her eyes were swollen shut, her face bled in several places, and ugly bruises covered her entire body. He was about to call out to her when the brute with the gun screamed out for him to close the door or he'd use the weapon.

Howard turned toward the sliding patio entry and looked into a revolver poised to fire. The guy behind it was angry, with a red face, glaring black eyes and his arm waving the handgun erratically. Using the sides of the open doorway for balance, Howard swung round on his good foot and studied the man.

Francesco suddenly appeared over the guy's left shoulder and responded when his companion ordered him to go around him and into the living room. Then he shouted in Spanish for Howard to get his ass back to the table, making it clear he couldn't care less about his injury or pain.

He hopped the same way he came, where the big fellow waited, holding zip ties and tape. Francesco yanked his arms backward and secured his wrists. This time, the adhesive went entirely around Howard's mouth, face, and head, assuring its subsequent removal would cause another spike of intense discomfort.

The giant grabbed his prisoner by the elbow, balancing him as he hopped toward the lounge chair outside. His armed companion set the gun on the table, took out his phone, and punched in a speed dial number. When someone answered, the man let loose a diatribe in Spanish.

Their visitor saw the woman, he explained loudly. Just for a moment, he thought. No, he didn't think the captive talked to her. What should he do next? Tomorrow? Yes, he'd do his best to keep them alive until then.

At that point, the guy pulled closed the sliding door. Francesco shoved Howard roughly into the lounge chair and turned away without saying a word. He tried to protest behind the tape, but the big lout ignored him. As the sun beamed down with mid-day intensity, he guessed the temperature was already in the nineties. Meanwhile, the bastard left the only umbrella for shade on the other side of the patio.

FORTY-NINE

Punta del Este, Uruguay, Monday July 27, 2020

Fidelia told Mateo Lopez he'd performed like a magician.

However, when she first demanded he find a long-haul private jet to fly her from Uruguay to Portugal non-stop, he came up short. There wasn't a private plane capable of traveling that distance. But he found a Bombardier 8500 on the ground in Buenos Aires that could leave immediately, pick her up in Punta del Este, and have her in Faro by the following evening. They'd land only in Sao Paulo for about a half hour to refuel.

Within minutes, Fidelia ordered Klaudia to pack her things and get ready to depart. Mateo drove them to the airport, where they waited a few minutes for the jet to touch down and park just outside the rear terminal.

Waiting was productive. She had the opportunity to review how Mateo would eliminate any record of their flights with his guy in air traffic control. There should be no trail of their travel. They chatted about finding another place for the young woman still locked in the upstairs room at the Punta del Este house.

Last, she rewarded him for his help by elevating his status to country boss for Uruguay. Mateo carefully noted the account number and all transfer details he should use to send her 20 percent share of his total take each month from that date onward.

Once they had settled into the plush leather seats on the private jet, Fidelia hit the speed dial for Luigi on her phone. It was four in the morning, but he was out in the field at the house near Krynki.

Her primary protector wasn't happy to learn she was about to leave for Portugal. "Guys in Spain got that woman they're waiting for here. If yur suspicions are right, there'll soon be some furious goons looking for 'er. Ya might walk inta a situation where 'r guys can't protect ya."

"I'll take my chances." This was a non-negotiable, and her tone reflected it. "What's happening there?"

"One Lithuanian took the doctor home. Found a place to bury Joey Andrews. With luck, it'll be years before anyone finds the remains." He paused. "You're using the secure phone, right?"

When she confirmed it was safe, Luigi carried on with his update. "That American woman's still out in the field watchin' the house. Lithuanian's a couple hundred yards away from 'er in the bush. I'm in the woods at the side of the property, watching for any activity. Any word from Deschamps? Interpol gonna rescue the old guy?"

"Haven't heard a thing. I gave him the tip. We'll have to wait 'n see what he does. Tell me more about Lucy Andrews." Fidelia spoke louder as the jet engine revved and raced down the runway for take-off.

"Joey Andrews claims he met 'er in a singles club 'n Washington. Slept with 'er from the git-go. Was shocked when she proposed marriage a few months later. She promised to pay all their living expenses and keep 'im a happy man. In return, demanded he perform jobs from time ta time for her and a government agency she worked for. Never asked which. Her politics were 'xtreme right wing, so the idiot always assumed it had somethin' ta do with the Republ'can Party."

"So civics must have been a keen interest for him in school," Fidelia mocked.

"Didn't ask. My guess, the guy didn't go far 'nough to see a civics class. Never uses a proper sentence. Claimed ta be an entrepreneur. Probably meant he hustled a few bucks wherever he could." A pause followed.

Suddenly, Luigi raised his voice in alarm. "Holy shit! A chopper's approachin'. Gotta find better cover. Call ya back."

Fidelia heard the helicopter clearly in the background.

She hit another "recent" number and waited for Deschamps. She hung up after seven rings, lingered a few seconds, and tried again. This time, the phone rang more than a dozen times. A crying woman finally picked up but said she didn't know where her husband was. Fidelia quickly disconnected, leaving her question about the rescue of Sauvignon unanswered.

Luigi got back to her once more before they reached cruising altitude. She could barely hear him as he spoke into the telephone while helicopter blades thrashed the air some distance away.

"Deschamps's guys 're gonna be too late. Both SUVs just roared out the driveway. Chopper landed in a field behind the place. Accordin' to the Lithuanian, it's Russian. Now, people are racin' toward it like it the house was on fire. Six of 'em 'n an old guy stragglin'. An' holy shit! Now, the 'merican woman from the field is rushin' toward the copter too, wavin' and screamin' out."

"Is she trying to be a hero and take them on herself?" Fidelia wondered.

"No. She just ran up b'side the chopper. Threw her arms around the old guy's neck. They're kissin' for chrissake. Now, one goon's yellin' at 'em ta get inside. Chopper's lifting off. Two of the guys just dragged the woman 'n old guy into the chopper. Still no sign of Deschamps's boys. What ya wanna do?"

"Nothing. If Interpol can't get their act together quickly enough when we give 'em a tip, they'll just have to keep their file open." Her calm belied her annoyance. There was now little doubt the Russian mafia was playing a major role in this entire charade and drawing much unwanted attention toward The Organization. Her efforts to land them in even more hot water had simply unraveled. Still, it was what it was. Time to move on. She'd look for another way to make the bastards pay.

"Has your enforcer in Italy figured out where Antonio Verlusconi is?" she asked. "His July payment didn't arrive in Cayman. So we can guess what was in those two pieces of luggage he took with him to Gibraltar."

The helicopter racket reached a crescendo as it lifted. Luigi delayed until it faded and it was easier for him to be heard.

"My guy said the plane belonged ta one of Verlusconi's runners. Got a call from a pilot during the night. From Cyprus. Pilot unloaded the bags 'n took 'em inside a hangar like the bastard instructed. Waited for Verlusconi ta return from some delivery. Bugger fell asleep in the terminal waitin'. Three hours later, someone workin' inside the terminal woke 'im up. Told him Verlusconi had paid him to load the luggage onta another plane much earlier. It left right away, 'n its flight plan showed Minsk in Belarus."

More treachery to serve the Russians. The pair schemed furiously, and within minutes, it was decided.

Luigi agreed to take the Lithuanian with him to intercept Verlusconi. By his calculation, they'd arrive perilously close to the time the Italian would arrive, but there was little traffic that early in the morning. Fidelia told him there was a bonus of 25 percent of whatever he recovered. If he needed motivation to drive slightly over the speed limit, that amount should provide it.

"By the way, video your little chat with Verlusconi. I want every country boss to get a personal copy of what happens for cooperating with the Russians," she said.

While Fidelia's heart was still racing, Klaudia finally provided some welcome news. She had discovered a path into Howard's secure laptop. The FBI probably knew about the violation almost instantly, but didn't delete the computer's stored data quickly enough. She always carried a USB drive in her pouch and backed up the entire file in a matter of seconds.

Since they had climbed into the private jet, Klaudia had worked furiously in a seat opposite Fidelia, searching for clues. She found his Facebook research first. It was easy to follow his history on the site, and she discovered the profiles where Howard learned about Joey and Lucy Andrews, plus all the background behind his alerting the woman at the FBI. She shared her findings with surging enthusiasm.

Eager to channel her friend's excitement productively, Fidelia narrowed her focus.

"I'm intrigued by this mysterious figure Stan Tan and Alphonso Sargetti referred to as the Shadow. We overheard them use that term in their telephone conversation right after Luigi rescued me from the Singapore jail. See what you can find in Howard's files."

FIFTY

The dramatic story James Fitzgerald and Natalia Tenaz recounted to Suzanne raised more questions than it answered. According to his school records in Frankfurt an der Oder—the town where his family had lived until he was twelve years old—Stefan Warner was a genius.

Communist party loyalists, Stefan's parents were rewarded with excellent jobs in the Russian bureaucracy after moving to its capital, while their son attended the most elite schools in the city. He graduated from university before he was twenty and worked as an intern in the Moscow office of the world-famous McLindsey and Associates consulting firm until he became a professor at École Polytechnique.

"I'm still not sure what the relationship is between Michelle and Stefan," Natalia explained. "Clearly, they met often over the years. Even when she was living and working overseas for her father's company, Stefan made several extended trips to China between teaching semesters. I presume he spent some of that time with her. Strangely, there is no record of Jean-Louis Sauvignon visiting Asia, at least by commercial airlines."

Natalia had promised to keep digging while Suzanne marveled in silence about the woman's ability to learn so much, so quickly. It was easy to see why James considered her such an asset. Still, she made a mental note to connect again with her Mountie friend. If Stefan's background had evaded Multima's security scrutiny entirely, was it farfetched to wonder if the guy's scheme to promote Natalia had some underhanded goal?

Suzanne's day didn't improve right away. She had a few minutes to gather up her thoughts and soothe her battered ego before Dan Ramirez called from Florida. Although it was still early morning there, he had rousted his contact in the Fort Myers FBI office and squeezed out a few more details.

"You know I'll never say I told you so ..." The temptation to say it just this time was so great he allowed it to hang there for a moment. "Let me mention how happy I am the Bureau got some people from the consulate over there to keep an eye on you. I didn't want to disturb your sleep last night to let you know, but this story gets more complicated by the hour. Deschamps, from Interpol, is now under arrest."

"Deschamps is mixed up in this?" Suzanne asked.

"We're not sure to what extent yet. He tried to have the autopsy results changed for the corpse they discovered near Sauvignon's estate in France. The coroner concluded the body belonged to another older man who lived in Aix-en-Provence. They had received a missing person report for the fellow about the same time as Sauvignon's kidnapping. The first thing the coroner checked was fingerprints. None of the prints matched Sauvignon's. They all fit the missing person."

"How did Deschamps get involved?"

"Internal Services at Interpol had been monitoring Deschamps's phone for a few weeks. They'd received a sexual harassment complaint from a former low-level employee. It seems the Assistant Director has, shall we say, a proclivity for young women and girls. The complainant's story was convincing enough to justify a wiretap, and they were listening when he ordered a subordinate in the coroner's office to get the report 'adjusted.' He offered the assistant one hundred thousand euros to have the document changed. A team then watched that subordinate pass an envelope to the coroner hours later and arrested all three of them."

"I confess, you've lost me. If I heard you correctly, the landscaper accused of involvement in Jean-Louis's kidnapping led police to a body and claimed it was Sauvignon. But fingerprints prove it's someone else. Is Sauvignon alive? Are they still making ransom demands?"

"The answer to your first question is we don't know if he's dead. They have no reports of any other corpse matching his description. He may be alive, and a captive of kidnappers, but there has been no communication since Michelle and Stefan suddenly disappeared."

"What's the new theory?"

"There are a couple, but the most plausible suggests Sauvignon fled after cooperating with people who staged his kidnapping to collect the ransom. If he shared in only a percentage of that ransom, the old guy could still live well for his remaining years."

"Why would he do that?"

"He needed the money. Seems he owed a fortune to interests in Russia. Forensic investigators just discovered the hundreds of millions you paid him for the Farefour Stores slowly trickled to offshore accounts thought to be fronts for the Russian mafia."

Suzanne swallowed her pride and shared with Dan her earlier conversations with James Fitzgerald. She recounted Natalia's revelations about Michelle and Stefan both coming originally from Russia and mustered enough confidence to reveal how thoroughly her long-time friend had deceived her when actually she'd been married to Jean-Louis.

Stunned, Ramirez cut short their call to get this new information to his contact at the FBI, leaving her to mull over her muddled past and future.

How bizarre her life had become! In the five years since she'd left a relatively carefree job as president of the Supermarkets division—working under John George Mortimer—her world had evolved into a prison of angst.

The malaise started with John George's cancer diagnosis. Before she had time to grasp the role of CEO fully, he and the board of Multima promoted her to succeed him. His death only months later had devastated Suzanne. And her grieving was more complicated and intense because only a short while earlier, he had revealed that she was his daughter.

Then the attacks started on the corporation she'd inherited—relentless assaults on Multima and her character that sapped valuable time and energy. For the past several months, she had led her businesses through a global pandemic that redefined commercial operations. Vicious characters had planted bombs in her supermarkets and destroyed her home. Now she faced harassment from the government of China and the haunting mysteries surrounding her lifelong friend. Throw in for good measure deception by her most recent lover and a kidnapping. How were these people able to evade Dan Ramirez's background investigations?

It didn't seem possible this chain of events was the product of random misfortune. All looked crafted to destabilize her and the mammoth enterprise she led. Someone, or some entity, still wanted to wrest money—and perhaps even control of Multima—from her. She understood why The Organization might want to use the phenomenal cash flow her company generated around the world to hide and move illicit money. She was also aware of hostile takeovers of department stores to repurpose their valuable real estate.

But why would Multima interest the Russians? Might they simply be helping someone else? The Organization? Or could it be a powerful person with connections to both Russia and the underworld pulling the strings?

Regardless, they had sapped every ounce of her energy. It was time for rest. Complete relaxation wasn't achievable until she shed the mantle of leadership of Multima Corporation, but her crushed spirit begged for a temporary reprieve, at least.

Choking back tears and trembling as she keyed in the numbers on her phone, she called Eileen. She needed the company jet to pick her up and deliver her to Montreal as soon as possible. Regardless of the risks of the pandemic, criminal stalkers, and government rules, she required an escape from it all. That wonderful rental home in the Laurentian Mountains was the perfect spot to sort it all out.

Then, another call to her friend the Mountie. He needed to dig deeper on Natalia. And he still owed her a report on the other one.

FIFTY-ONE

Ayamonte, Spain, Monday July 27, 2020

Broiling. That was the best word to describe the current state of Howard's skin. Every so often, he turned sideways on the lounge chair as far as his hands bound behind his back allowed, but any relief was only temporary. His throat grew drier and swallowing became a chore. When he called out beneath the tape covering his mouth, only a feeble growl escaped. Of course, with the thugs both inside the air-conditioned apartment, no one heard his plaintive cries.

Initially, the seagulls sounded far away, closer to the beach and ocean, a quarter-mile from the condo. As the sun rose higher in the sky, the birds ventured nearer, checking his baking progress to see if a promising meal was ready to consume. Lapping waves in the distance were first therapeutic, then became an annoying irritation. His Mediterranean heritage served him to some extent. Although his skin was burning, it had only a tinge of red as its tanned hues darkened by the hour.

Of course, the stress on the outside of his body only exacerbated the pain from his broken limb. It had swelled badly in the heat. For a while, he tried elevating it by balancing his left heel on the toe of his extended right foot, but that extra weight was also painful. The injured leg fell off the good one continuously, each time causing more jabs of agony. Besides, it wasn't elevated enough to help.

Finally, the thugs came outside and dragged Howard back into the condo just as the afternoon sun began to dip. The big fellow plunked him at the table inside the door. To his amazement, the woman from the bedroom now sat on a chair facing him. He could no longer be sure her face was the one he thought he remembered.

She was a mess. She looked worse than he felt. Her eyes swelled almost entirely shut, with blue, purple, and black shades of bruises covering her face. Matted long hair appeared as though someone had extracted whole clumps, leaving bald sections with blood coagulating among the strands left behind. Her broken nose flopped lazily to one side, with ugly clots still filling her nostrils. He tried to block out of his mind the only other time he had seen a female so badly battered.

The thugs studied Howard's reaction and looked satisfied with his inability to avoid a cringe at first sight.

"One word to the woman and your face will match hers," the lout who held the gun said. "Francesco will remove the tape from your mouth and the zip ties while you eat. If you say a single word, he'll rearrange your high-priced cosmetic surgery. Do you understand?"

Howard hesitated a moment, then nodded. It made no sense to ask for pain relievers if the thugs were simply about to administer more agony.

With a deep-throated laugh, Francesco ripped the tape off his mouth, and a searing throb tracked the motion across Howard's face and around the back of his head, yanking out hair stuck firmly to the adhesive. With practiced polish, the enforcer reached down and cut the zip ties.

Howard lunged forward to grab a plastic water bottle and drained the entire contents in two or three long, greedy gulps. He started to ask for more, remembered the "one word" threat, and instead held out the empty with an expression pleading for more. The guy with the gun nodded his assent.

The food offered was the most basic possible—the smallest loaf of Spanish bread Howard had ever seen. It was a *barra*, a crusty baguette-type slab. It sat on the table's wooden surface alone, unappetizing, lacking even butter for flavor. The woman watched him as he broke off a morsel and raised it to his mouth. She did the same with the piece in front of her, revealing a bloody mouth and a broken tooth as she ate her portion.

As Howard nibbled at the *barra*, he schemed. With the last mouthful, he had an idea. Slowly, he lifted a finger in the air to get the attention of the one with a gun. He elevated his left hand and held it flat while he made a motion of writing with his right arm. The guy eventually shrugged and told Francesco to find a pen and notepaper.

In neat letters, Howard printed a basic message:

Need shade, painkillers, more water & cushion to elevate leg

He passed the note to Francesco, who carried it over to the fellow with the gun on the other side of the room. The jerk simply laughed, scrunched the piece of paper into a ball, and threw it away.

Regardless, his request had some benefits. Instead of shoving him out to the patio and the still intense afternoon heat, Francesco motioned for Howard to hop toward an empty bedroom. Once again, the guy applied tape, but only over his mouth. The zip ties went around his

257

wrists, but this time in front, and before the big man left, he tossed three large cushions at Howard.

A constant hum from the air conditioner and improved circulation in his lower leg eventually lulled him into a restless sleep. Sometime later, he awoke to angry shouting from the living area. There were several voices, male and female. He couldn't understand clearly what they were saying, but the conversation was loud, furious and animated. When it stopped, he heard the creaking of an elevator, then the sliding door to the patio opened and closed.

Total silence followed for a few minutes before the sliding door sounds repeated. Clicking heels on the tiles, indicating a woman's shoes, advanced down the hallway and stopped outside his room.

When the door opened, Fidelia Morales poked her head inside.

He froze. His spirit sagged. Blood vessels to his brain sped up their work like cars on a raceway, roaring in protest to the added stress and strain. He imagined the rest of his life could be measured in minutes.

"Are you decent?" She smiled with the question, then her expression became more somber as she looked Howard over from top to bottom. When she noticed his leg resting on the mound of cushions, she grimaced, then stepped forward and gently pulled back the tape from his mouth.

"You needed surgery, I heard. Is it still painful?"

"On a scale of one to ten, I'd rate it about eleven and a half." He groaned to add emphasis. "Any chance you have painkillers in your bag?"

"No, but we can get you some. I think the pharmacies stay open later at night here. But first, let's have a little chat to decide if it's worth making the investment." Her tone turned stone cold. With nothing more to say, she spun on her heel and left the room.

A short time after, Howard hopped toward the patio under her bodyguard Carlos's watchful eye. Eventually, they stopped at a straight-backed outdoor chair directly opposite Fidelia. It was no surprise Klaudia Schäffer sat in a similar chair in the same quiet corner. Voices didn't carry far with cement walls on two sides.

Fidelia pointed for him to sit. "We know you fed information to the FBI. Over fifty of The Organization's guys have disappeared after arrests. Give me one good reason I shouldn't eliminate you."

Howard tensed. He'd never heard her tone so threatening and was unsure what direction to take. He opted for candor. "If you know I gave info to the FBI, you also must realize I didn't give them anything that would warrant arresting anyone, other than maybe Juan Presivo from Miami. I had to offer them something for chrissake. It was the only way I could get back into the witness protection program. Your suggestion, remember?"

His expression matched her coldness. The future didn't look promising at any rate.

"Presivo was a problem, and that's fixed. Your investigation also linked the troublemaker to Joey and Lucy Andrews." Her tone sounded sarcastic until she paused. "That was good. You know she's your roommate in the bedroom down the hall, right?"

"Your guys didn't make any formal introductions, and I didn't get the connection. In fact, if my memory serves correctly, they took offense when I attempted to introduce myself." He allowed the hint of a smirk, then quickly shed it to match Fidelia's manner. "I thought it was her until I saw the woman's maliciously re-arranged face. Now, nobody could be certain."

"Who is the Shadow?" Fidelia's tone was abrupt and demanding.

"No idea."

Then it dawned on him. Capitalized as "The Shadow" on one of Joey Andrews's Facebook posts, the words had struck him as odd. But he dismissed it when he found no other reference or connection to the content he reviewed. Still, he had to give her something, so he told her about the post.

"When I read that name, I immediately thought about a metaphor of the Shadow as perhaps the dark side of human nature. Then I realized the dude didn't have enough intelligence to understand symbolism and concluded it probably referred to one of the weirdos his wife appealed to in her radio broadcasts."

"Stan Tan used the term once in a conversation we overheard." Klaudia took a turn, her tone soft, almost warm. She played the good cop in their interrogations. "Did he use it at all when he spoke with you?"

"He asked me what you did to anger the Shadow. I told him I didn't know who the Shadow was, let alone how you might have offended him. He smacked me in the head and left it at that." Howard rubbed the side of his skull as though the pain had reappeared.

"Why did Tan snatch you in Uruguay?" Fidelia changed her tack and manner. She even showed the hint of a smile as she asked.

"Somebody in Moscow—or mixed up with the Russians—is pissed with you. Probably directly related to that half billion you stole from their offshore bank accounts. They figured out Tan's involvement with you. Then someone persuaded him he might extend his life expectancy if he delivered me and a few million dollars in cash to them in Minsk. I suspect Lucy Andrews delivered those instructions." He threw in the last bit to temper his angst, sound less cavalier, and plant something else for her to ponder.

She reacted as expected and mulled it over for a moment before she spoke. "Klaudia, tell the bodyguards to give us some space. Dispatch them to the pharmacy across the bay to get some pain relievers. The strongest possible. Then have that nice private chat with Lucy Andrews we talked about."

Fidelia waited while her friend executed her instructions. Once she heard the doors close, followed by the hum of an elevator, she resumed. "Of course, the Russians are pissed. I expected retaliation. But this doesn't feel like it has Ruskies planning it and calling the shots. This is sloppy, unprofessional, disorganized."

"There's clearly some American involvement and maybe French, too," Howard agreed. "And it's somebody who either hates you and Multima Corporation or wants to control you both, eventually."

"Why might the Russians want to control Multima?"

"Same reason any greedy, run-of-the-mill property developer would want them. Their stores sit on some of the best suburban real estate in the world. Or, if they're just interested in the business, Multima generates hundreds of billions in revenue every year with huge profits after expenses. And during uncertain times, everyone must eat. Remember, when I worked for Mareno, he wanted Multima so he could launder money almost everywhere. The company processes more cash every year than many banks. And they have the power to move markets—stock markets and food markets."

She considered his reply for a moment. "So you think someone is playing the Russians to get at either Multima or me? Or both?"

"It wouldn't surprise me if eventually you learn this guy they call the Shadow is trying to quarterback the game."

"So I need somebody to find out precisely who the Shadow is?"

"Maybe. But that person isn't me. I want to be rid of all this shit."

Fidelia didn't reply at first. Instead, she stood up and paced the perimeter of the third-floor patio, slowly and deliberately. Deep in thought, her head bowed, hands clasped loosely in front of her, she displayed her typical manner when weighing a significant decision. When she was ready to talk, she remained standing and looked down at Howard coldly. He expected the worst.

"It tempted me to let Tan continue on and deliver you to the Russians, or whoever. But there was still the issue of several million of The Organization's money the worthless scoundrel would have likewise delivered to them. So I saved your ass ... again. You no longer know much about our activities, but the Russians don't know that. I think you can visualize clearly how it would have ended for you."

She swept back her hair and bent close to his face before she finished her ultimatum. Her brown eyes flashed, her expression devoid of emotion. A poker player requesting another card could not have looked more unattached. She pursed her lips and chose words designed to rattle him.

"You have one choice to make. Full stop. You agree to stay with me in The Organization as my financial advisor—and you do it without grumbling or complaint. That's my preferred outcome. If you're not prepared to do that, I'll save the medication the boys went to buy for a future nasty headache. I might need one after they cart you out to the marshes and quietly drown you. Your choice."

Without blinking, she stared directly into his eyes, watching him wilt.

His tongue swelled inside his mouth, unable to move. His dry throat felt on fire, but he couldn't muster a swallow. His brain raced in dozens of different directions, reaching a finish line that spelled defeat.

He'd watched how coldly she pulled the trigger to execute Giancarlo Mareno as he pleaded to be spared. Her current expression displayed the same nonchalant contempt it had that day. There was no alternative, and that horrible realization took a few moments to crystalize as she continued to glare at him.

Unwavering. Calculating. Daring.

His voice was hoarse when he finally replied. "How may I be of service?"

Howard dared not think the words "for now" or allow his expression to convey anything other than fear. As effortlessly as a snap of her fingers, she had once more sucked him back into The Organization's chaotic and ruthless depths.

An hour or more after the guys left for the meds, Fidelia received a call from the basement asking if it was okay to bring them up. In the interim, she had bounced ideas, theories and questions off Howard in rapid-fire sequence. What did he know about the Sauvignon family in France? Could there be a link between the Shadow and Sauvignon? Why would they drag Suzanne Simpson personally into the retribution? Why would the Russians cooperate with any of them?

When the guys finally delivered some Ibuprofen, he gulped down double the recommended dosage and a bottle of water. Then he watched Fidelia send the bodyguards downstairs once more as Klaudia pulled up her chair to rejoin them on the patio. Slumped dejectedly in his corner, his expression undoubtedly reflected his chagrin.

"Lucy is ready to switch sides." Klaudia ignored him and focused entirely on Fidelia as she spoke.

"She is the woman I knew from the Russian services. Just never left. I told her she could use your compound in Muynak, Uzbekistan, if she comes over to our side and shares everything she knows. It took a while. Your savage Spaniards did a lot of damage—emotionally as well as physically. Eventually, she agreed. She'll talk with us now."

Fidelia stood up and headed toward the living area inside, waving for Howard to follow. Klaudia hesitated and bent over to give him a tug to his feet ensuring he was balanced before setting off hopping. Then she called out to Fidelia's back. "Oh, I also promised her a million of your euros for expenses." Then she muffled a subdued giggle.

Lucy Andrews explained it all in granular detail, patiently responding to occasional gentle probes from either Fidelia or Klaudia. Howard sat on a sofa off to the side and listened. Despite his agonizing pain, he found her story fascinating.

Like Klaudia, she had joined the Russian secret services during her high school years, and her education came from several successor branches of the former KGB. They groomed her to be an American, helped land her first job in broadcasting, and manipulated her career progression through media outlets they influenced or controlled.

Also, as with Klaudia, they treated her like dirt. Superiors expected her to submit to every command. That control included messaging for her talk radio broadcast and most aspects of her personal life. They picked Joey Andrews to be her husband because they wanted an uneducated goof who couldn't think for himself and responded to the most infantile bribes to support his lavish lifestyle. They told her who to sleep with, apparently believing ratings and listeners increased exponentially if some hick could claim on his social media that she serviced him after some event.

She'd never escaped like Klaudia. Instead, she remained trapped in the lure of eventual power and influence that flowed from her subservience to the Russian masters. It all had changed only a few weeks earlier.

With no prior planning or warning, the bosses in Moscow had

ordered Joey Andrews to plant bombs in Multima Stores and at Suzanne Simpson's private home. He contacted a second-rate felon named Presivo in Florida. They'd forced her to sleep with him a couple times as a reward. The guy accepted the new assignment willingly.

A few days later, she received a message she was being recalled. No other explanation. They'd find a role for her in Moscow, but her mission would finish after a trip to Singapore. Someone named the Shadow had arranged a jet to get her there to deliver an ultimatum to Stan Tan.

To ensure Tan carried out the instructions she had relayed, her responsibility was to accompany him and see that he performed as expected. Or kill him.

The kidnapping of Jean-Louis Sauvignon was a ruse. The money Tan hi-jacked from Aretta Musa in Australia—and the bags of cash Verlusconi planned to deliver to Gibraltar—were all for delivery to the French tycoon and his latest lover in Minsk. In gratitude for decades of service, Moscow agreed they could disappear and live off the few million stolen from The Organization.

But that plan—hatched by the Shadow—was botched because of poor planning and execution. Moscow, Sauvignon, and the Shadow originally plan to split the fifty-million- dollar ransom. Unexpectedly, someone intercepted the cryptocurrency transfer from Michelle's fiancé. Moscow suspected The Organization was the culprit once more, which had triggered the demand for the Shadow to summon Tan.

For good measure, someone at the top decided to force Tan to also bring a few million dollars to finance Sauvignon's escape.

"Moscow was prepared to let the French billionaire and some other American operative disappear, but refused to pay for their retirement," Lucy Andrews told them. She never explained who the female American spy was, but Howard saw no compelling need to clarify. It didn't affect him.

Lucy Andrews continued to talk well into the evening. The bodyguards had called up several times, confirming everything was okay in the suite, requesting permission to take dinner breaks, and muttering discontent about hanging around in the underground parking lot of the complex.

Fidelia waited until the exhausted woman's voice became hoarse, and could barely speak, to ask about what weighed most heavily on her mind. "Who is the Shadow?"

Lucy took a long, deep breath. Then she collected her thoughts, squirming in her chair. Finally, she chose an answer. "I don't really know.

I have only suspicions. We spoke only a few times. All communication used a voice synthesizer that scrambled his identity. I had never heard of the Shadow until about three years ago. His calls all came either from inside the White House or near it, using a burner phone. Moscow made it clear the Shadow was tight with our top guy and his orders and requests were not only to be reported but also followed and respected."

Lucy shrugged but offered no more, her body language suggesting she might share more later.

Fidelia's expression was grim, but she remained calm and appeared deep in thought for a few moments.

"Klaudia, tell the bodyguards we need two cars immediately for Faro. Then help Lucy get dressed and ready to travel. We'll meet them downstairs in five minutes. Howard, start hopping toward the elevator door." As she issued her orders, she pressed a speed dial and started walking as she barked into the phone, "Are the fuel tanks full? Okay. We'll be there in an hour. File a flight plan for Minsk."

FIFTY-TWO

Fort Myers, Florida, Tuesday September 8, 2020

Suzanne woke up in Florida that morning grateful for the five previous weeks she'd spent in Canada at the magnificent home in the Laurentian Mountains. Of course, she had to work every day, but the experience kept her physically away from any danger of contracting the dreaded virus. Still, more than once on an afternoon hike, she asked herself if it was all worthwhile.

Early in her stay, her friend from the Royal Canadian Mounted Police met with her at the house in the mountains to deliver his detailed reports and collect on her promise of a good dinner together. His "deep dive" into Natalia's background had reinforced his earlier positive image of the young woman, and he heaped praise on her as he explained his reasons to Suzanne.

When the conversation shifted to her other request, her friend in law enforcement grew stern and uncomfortable as he shared his findings. At first, Suzanne didn't believe him, declaring there must be some mistake. He shared the evidence he had at that time and told her there was little chance of error, but he'd get more proof.

That dinner meeting led to more sessions and dozens of phone calls, some on high-security lines used by the RCMP and FBI, for her friend felt professionally bound to share the discoveries with his contacts there. After the third meeting she flew her chief legal counsel to Quebec to deal with the betrayal. Alberto Ferer stayed with her at the home in the Laurentian Mountains for more than two weeks as they grew resigned to the accuracy of the evidence and plotted a strategy to deal with it.

Alberto had returned to Florida a week earlier so he could prepare for the inevitable confrontation. Suzanne used the remaining time alone to question herself, consider her future, and wonder if she truly wanted to keep the role of CEO at Multima. As time passed, her mind cleared, and her perspective grew. She became more determined to not only carry on but achieve new heights for Multima Corporation and herself.

That morning as she drove along McGregor Boulevard from John

George Mortimer's former home toward the company's US headquarters in the heart of Fort Myers—the wind blew her hair in all directions. It had been many months since she'd driven John George's sporty Nissan 370Z, and it was not a convertible. Instead, Suzanne had lowered all the windows and let the warm, salty air from the nearby Gulf of Mexico flow through the car to prepare her spirit for a difficult day.

It wasn't yet time for the tourists, so the streets were quiet and traffic sparse. Of course, that was also due to the reduced mobility for many people during the pandemic. Still, it hadn't affected sales at Multima Corporation. The day would start alright because she planned to review the quarter-end results with James Fitzgerald and her new CFO, Pierre Cabot, right after her first coffee.

At headquarters, as she walked down the hallway to her office, the quiet struck her once again. True, they'd moved a dozen positions to the new corporate offices in Montreal, but most of the remaining staff had worked from their homes for the past nine months. The business not only functioned with people spread out in all directions, it flourished.

Eileen greeted her with a welcoming smile and handed Suzanne a cup of coffee as she passed her assistant's desk. It was the first they'd seen each other in person in a while, and the worry lines had intensified on Eileen's forehead and her posture appeared a little less erect. They needed an informal chat about stress management, and she made a mental note to schedule lunch on a patio together later in the week.

Suzanne and James spread out in the sprawling meeting room, more than the recommended six feet. They didn't wear masks, but had months earlier agreed to maintain distance and avoid handshakes or hugs. Pierre Cabot was a Canadian and unable to visit the US headquarters. Airlines could get him there alright, but his government insisted all travelers quarantine for two weeks when they returned. Instead, he joined by videoconference.

Her new finance expert walked them through the numbers for the fiscal quarter in less than an hour. As Suzanne anticipated, the performance figures were stellar in both the Supermarkets and Financial Services divisions. She joked Cabot would look like a superhero to investors and analysts during his first fiscal quarter on the job, and complimented him warmly for his grasp of the data before he shut off his video connection.

She looked at James for a long moment after Cabot's face disappeared from the wall-mounted screen. It was the first they had met in person since the shocking news of Angela Bonner's mysterious disappearance, and Suzanne needed to take good measure of the toll it had taken on her most valued confidant. She started slowly.

"I had an independent third party put Natalia's background under a microscope." She watched as he tilted his head in curiosity without revealing a bias. "She's a remarkable young woman. My source couldn't provide a written summary, but he told me about her outstanding scholastic achievements. They extend far beyond what she lists on her resume. I found it touching she still sends half of what she earns back to Puerto Rico to support extended family." She waited to assess James's reaction.

"She's modest too. I could have shared all that with you, except she asked me not to. I credit luck, not prescience, for hiring her. But a little good luck never hurts ..."

Suzanne looked into his eyes as his voice trailed off. It was time to switch to her purpose. "Still no word?"

They both knew she referred to Angela. It wasn't necessary to mention her name.

He shook his head and gazed downward at the table, avoiding eye contact. James's hands resting on the tabletop trembled slightly, and his nervous fidget telegraphed discomfort. She shared his pain. Angela Bonner had been the love of his life in recent months and she had disappeared entirely, leaving not a trace.

Stefan Warner had become extremely important in her own universe over the same period. He'd also been missing since the day he left the apartment in Lyon for a walk with Michelle Sauvignon.

"I'm moving on," he finally managed. "Her last text said she was doing surveillance at a remote country home in Poland, but you know the story. When the Interpol reps she worked with returned to that house, it was empty. They checked the entire surrounding fields and nearby woods a dozen times with people, dogs, and technology. No sign of her, her clothes, or a corpse. According to Dan Ramirez, the folks at Interpol know a chopper landed there that day. They assumed everyone inside the dwelling used it to escape. It looks as if she, too, climbed into that same helicopter."

Suzanne nodded as he talked. It was a time for empathy, not judgment. Words couldn't adequately describe her own broken heart, and she doubted they'd console James. When it was her turn to speak, she chose her message deliberately and delivered it slowly and softly.

"Moving on sounds almost insensitive, but it's what we both have to do. Questions and doubts may haunt us for some time. But in the mountains of Quebec, I came to understand that grief must have its limits or it will destroy us. You've grieved these past weeks, and I admire your strength and tenacity in performing at such a high level despite the burden. You probably realize the reason I asked you to stay behind after the videoconference is to let you know I still desperately want you to continue with Multima."

He nodded, struggling to create a modest grin, and sat more upright in his chair. Ever the shrewd negotiator, he tipped the conversation back to her with a simple, "What do you have in mind?"

"Where you decide to live is immaterial to me. The corporate jet you're using will remain assigned for your exclusive use as long as you work for this company. Where I'd like to ask you to hang out for a year or two—or longer if you wish—is at Financial Services in Chicago. You were correct. Natalia Tenaz is the right person to become its next president. But neither you nor I can make that happen immediately."

He inhaled more deeply, his resting hands on the table showing more confidence and poise as his body visibly relaxed. She waited for his nod before continuing. "Take on the role of president for a while. Groom Natalia for the position, and build the support we'll need to elevate her to the job in a year or two. We can't pay you the same fee we're paying for the temporary assignment, but I'm sure we can get both you and our board comfortable with remuneration. Will you consider it?"

To Suzanne's immense relief, James had already given it some thought and outlined a modest, simple compensation package. She accepted his offer on the spot. They both knew ratification by his fellow directors would be only a formality.

From the conference room, Suzanne popped back to her office, where Dan Ramirez sat waiting on the sofa of her meeting area. She drew a last deep breath and swung open the door to enter. He pulled up his mask until she waved it was okay, then jumped right into the update she'd requested.

At long last, they'd found out who was behind all the power outages in Farefour stores in China that began after prior harassment by the Chinese government.

"We already thought someone in Macau was responsible. My contacts in the FBI had identified an IP address associated with a casino there. One of their techies kept chasing it and found the Macau IP address linked to one in Singapore. They didn't solve it until Interpol sent over recovered computers and electronic devices hidden on a private jet that was hijacked in Gibraltar, of all places. They traced those to the corpse of a Singaporean named Stan Tan."

"Can I assume Tan had a connection to organized crime?" Suzanne asked.

"We think so, but we don't know exactly which gang he was associated with. Sources in Asia suggest he was a regional crime boss for The Organization. Data on his devices show he had communication with, and was taking some instructions from, someone known as the Shadow. Another passenger on the same jet is still missing. She was an American citizen named Lucy Andrews. Facial recognition software picked her up in Australia, with Tan, a day before they arrived in Gibraltar."

"Wow! Can this story get more complicated?" Suzanne forced a chuckle but didn't see where it all headed.

"Yes, it can." Ramirez looked grim. "They found the body of Lucy Andrews's husband Joey—also an American—in Poland, only a few miles from the house where Interpol suspected they'd find Jean-Louis Sauvignon before the gang escaped."

"So ... people in America directed Jean-Louis's kidnapping?"

"Perhaps. Everything the FBI or Interpol have learned about the Shadow points a direct line to the US. More disturbing, the peripheral pieces point not only to a criminal element like The Organization, but they also implicate Russian interests. Most troubling of all, the Bureau thinks it might involve someone very tight to the White House. Are you ready for one more update?"

Suzanne nodded but held a sense of dread before Dan Ramirez began his story. Her stomach tightened, and her throat felt dry.

"The FBI techies made some progress on the fifty million dollars that disappeared in France. They're now sure the cryptocurrency didn't leave the country back in July. Someone had the technology smarts to hijack the transaction and move it around within the country for more than a month. They tracked it to over one thousand different accounts in French banks, then lost it again on the thirty-first of August to an account in Russia. From there it digitally divided into thousands of smaller amounts in hundreds of unique entities the Bureau can't trace."

She listened with the most impassive expression she could muster, bracing for more.

"When Interpol couldn't find Stefan's computer anywhere in the safe house they loaned to you, they realized he must have taken it with him when he left for his walk with Michelle. It still hasn't shown up, but someone finally made a critical connection. One of the guy's primary research subjects at the university was cryptocurrencies. They now suspect he had the knowledge and motivation to re-route the transaction from Michelle's boyfriend."

That didn't sound right. Dan had already told her the FBI had recovered fifty million that followed another track through multiple countries.

"Where did the fifty million the Bureau snatched in Macau come from?" she wondered aloud.

"Nobody's sure. There was a mysterious transaction created in Düsseldorf. It stole smaller values from a dozen different brokerage accounts controlled by a handful of numbered companies. There's no record of any reports of thefts received from any of those brokerages. However, the FBI knows unauthorized amounts were taken. Later, someone consolidated the fifty million and launched it on its track around the globe."

Suzanne relaxed momentarily and took a deep breath. It wasn't as bad as she'd feared, but it still didn't promise closure. "Can we consider these attacks on me and Multima finished?"

"There's always hope," Dan Ramirez said with an unconvincing shrug.

She nodded perfunctorily, took another long, deep breath, and squared her shoulders to project maximum authority. She chose a calm yet assertive tone.

"I need to ask for your resignation now."

Ramirez snapped upright as though she'd physically attacked him. His eyes darted in all directions, and his face reddened, the veins on his neck bulging.

"What did you say?" he asked, his voice meeker than before.

"I think you know why." She pointed toward two men standing outside the glass door to her office, and his eyes followed her finger. "One is from the CIA, the other from Quantico. They'll arrest you after you sign this letter of resignation, releasing Multima Corporation from any and all obligations. They've pieced together your long history of selling intelligence to the Russian government—first state secrets, more recently confidential Multima information."

She slid a typed document across her desk and left it sitting on the surface, facing up at him and awaiting his signature.

"There's some mistake, Suzanne." His tone became more desperate. He had trouble forming words and his hands trembled visibly. "They've got something wrong. I'm not signing anything. This isn't right!"

She shook her head slowly, taking no pleasure from either her decision or action.

"No, Dan. There's no mistake. When a friend first revealed your crimes to me, I spent dozens of hours challenging his evidence and arguing for your innocence. I also initially found it impossible to believe the man John George Mortimer and I trusted unequivocally could be guilty of such a betrayal. But no doubts remain and there's little chance a jury won't reach the same conclusion. If you won't resign, then I hereby terminate your employment for cause."

She stood up and handed another document to him. In his shock, he reached out and accepted it. At that moment, one of the men outside stepped into her office, but she finished her thought looking directly at Dan Ramirez.

"And, knowing they were using the information you stole to undermine our company and to curry favor with someone I despise, cuts even more deeply."

With her last words, the first man through the door began to read Dan Ramirez his Miranda rights.

FIFTY-THREE

Punta del Este, Uruguay, Tuesday September 8, 2020

Of course, they didn't follow the flight plan Fidelia had first instructed the pilots to file when they left Faro. About an hour out of Portugal, she made her way to the cockpit and huddled with the aviators. Instead of Minsk, they needed to submit promptly a revised plan to land in Düsseldorf. The reason for the change was a passenger on board had changed her mind.

She had hoped to persuade Klaudia to stay. She had even offered obscene amounts of money to lure her in. But her long-time friend was adamant. She wanted to return home immediately and focus again on her growing technology security business. Insistently, she reminded Fidelia of previous broken promises to let her escape The Organization.

Fidelia had given some careful thought to the possibility Klaudia might one day become as dangerous as Howard Knight in the wild. In the end, she decided her intimate friend was far more drawn to the mysteries of technology than any malice toward The Organization. Still, it would have been better to have her closer at hand.

Fidelia's insistence the escort and human trafficking businesses would continue unabated—despite Klaudia's protests—didn't help her cause. There, they agreed to differ, though her friend had abandoned temporarily her efforts to stymie the trade. Despite the complexities of their relationship, their farewell at the top of the plane's staircase was a little teary. Their friendship was genuine.

With a hug and goodbye, Klaudia scooted down the stairway and crossed the short distance to an opening in the chain-link fence that surrounded the complex. An SUV with protection waited, and with a last energetic wave, she slid into the rear seat, gone once again.

Fidelia chatted with the pilots as a ground crew refueled their jet. She wanted them to file a flight plan for Minsk in Belarus next. However, about an hour before landing, they should change that official plan to land instead in Vilnius, Lithuania—where they'd take on an additional passenger and baggage.

The co-pilot nodded, made the calculations and told her they should touch down again in about three and a half hours. With a reciprocal nod, she popped back to her comfortable leather seat facing Howard. There, she hit the speed-dial number for her primary protector and asked if that gave him enough time.

"Yeah. Should work. We're 'cross the border already."

"Everything go okay with Antonio Verlusconi in Minsk?" Fidelia asked.

"Yeah. Snatched him off the private plane right after he landed. The Lithuanian has great connections. Got us on the tarmac 'n parked beside the aircraft b'fore the stairway lowered. I neutralized the pilots. Lithuanian grabbed Verlusconi. Didn't take much. Shit his pants when he saw us. Stunk up the car for the rest of 'r trip."

"I don't need the background color; just the facts will do."

"Once we had him in the SUV, we loaded his two bags. Both jammed full of euros. Lithuanian drove while I started askin' questions. Told us quite a bit b'fore we needed ta use any persuasion tools."

"Like why he was ripping off money from The Organization?" She laced her tone with sarcasm.

"Scum was in it as deep as his former boss. Alphonso Sargetti told 'im they were doin' a favor for the Shadow—that bastard we've been tryin' ta find. Verlusconi said he never met the guy but knew he was 'merican. Very close ta the White House."

"How close?"

"Verlusconi didn't know but said Giancarlo Mareno first introduced the mysterious character to Sargetti a few years ago. Thought this 'Shadow' character looked ta have connections ta both the Russians 'n' The Organization."

"Okay. So who was he supposed to meet in Minsk?"

"Stan Tan an' some 'merican woman. They were gonna bring the money 'n' deliver part of it somewhere. Didn't know where."

"What else did you get?"

"Lithuanian found a spot in a deserted barn near the border. Intensified the interrogation. But got little more—even after severin' a few fingers. Verlusconi knew the woman was Lucy Andrews. Knew she was a radio talk-show host. Thought she also had some connection to the Russians. But didn't know how."

"No problems crossing from Belarus?"

"Immigration guy asked a question. Lithuanian slipped him a hundred euro note 'n he waved us on through."

A few hours later, the rented Bombardier Global 8500 touched down in Vilnius. Luigi and his Lithuanian waited on the tarmac, precisely where air traffic control had instructed the pilots to park. It was a secluded corner where a row of jets blocked the view from any curious eyes in the tower or terminal.

Within minutes they had the bags of money on board, stashed in a compartment at the rear of the plane beside those collected from Tan in Gibraltar. Fidelia used the time to inform the pilots Minsk was no longer part of the plan. They should head to Uzbekistan once they were ready to fly again.

Before the aircraft was refueled, one pilot asked if they could delay departure for a few hours. They desperately needed some sleep. Fidelia quickly weighed the risks. Sitting on the ground anywhere with a few million in cash wasn't a great idea. Who knew who might develop a sudden curiosity?

She suggested an alternative. Could they risk flying with one captain for a while after take-off while the other slept? They talked it over in the cockpit, and one emerged to give her a cursory nod and instructions to buckle up. They left as soon as they signed the fuel bill.

It turned out neither became so exhausted he needed to join them in the cabin for a nap. In fact, they arrived at the small airstrip near her compound in Muynak in just over three hours, then made the brief twenty-minute drive with bodyguards.

Her friend Zefar Karimov had quickly assembled a security convoy of five vehicles and a dozen armed men to ensure they traveled from the airfield to her complex without interference. He greeted Fidelia and her companions with a greedy grin, his hand out for her promised twenty-five thousand dollars.

Lucy Andrews immediately fell in love with the compound. Her manner reflected joy that Fidelia had agreed to let her stay there with armed protection. Once settled in, she slept, exhausted after the torture and turmoil of her last few days.

Howard still hopped painfully on one leg, though she'd ordered a bodyguard to find him a set of crutches somewhere in town.

Luigi and Fidelia counted the money. Between the bags of American dollars and the euros in the luggage, it totaled over ten million. He claimed his share as soon as they finished. She had to smile at how little it took to satisfy the guy.

She stashed the fee Klaudia had promised Lucy Andrews for living expenses in a secure safe larger than some bank locations used. Then they all rested.

The pilots slept for a full night and woke up ready to fly. She coaxed Howard from his bed in a makeshift room on the main floor and called out to Luigi in the bedroom next to her. With all the movement and voices, Lucy Andrews awoke and joined them for a small breakfast of breads and fruits the resident chef had prepared before any of them were awake.

By the time the sun rose completely, they had bid a farewell to grateful Lucy. Fidelia knew the woman would be a useful ally in the coming years and left her rich, contented, and comfortable. Although she lived there alone, bodyguards would always be available for fun and recreation. She also had the latest digital toys and devices for communication, entertainment, and information. Of course, it was all connected to the secret apps Fidelia used to monitor every conversation or contact.

Many years earlier, Giancarlo Mareno had taught her to always apply the old Russian proverb made famous by an American president: "Trust, but verify."

Their long flight south that day took them first to Nairobi for a two-hour refueling stop. It also included some food for the three remaining passengers—Fidelia, Luigi, and Howard. She smiled as Knight tried out his new crutches on the runaway, circling the plane for more than a half-hour, honing his skill and exercising latent muscles.

She noticed a hint of a smile appear on his face a couple times as he realized she was watching. Her primary protector took care of the food. When he returned to the airplane, he had loaded his arms with sandwiches, salads, breads, and fruits. There was enough to feed a dozen people, she said, laughing.

The long flight from Kenya to Punta del Este was uneventful. They ate, slept, and occasionally talked awkwardly. Luigi had learned of her secret, multi-year liaison with Howard, but she left him uncertain where the former fugitive fit in their current arrangement.

On the other hand, she was sure Knight did not know her relationship with Luigi was anything more than crime boss and that boss's primary protector. Since he'd rescued her from the Singapore jail with the help of Zefar Karimov, she'd rewarded him with only the single night's romp under the sheets in Hue, Vietnam. And he hadn't asked for more.

During the flight, she watched Luigi closely. She saw nothing in his eyes suggesting mischief, as they often had before the Chilean massacre. Understandably, it had changed him, and she silently vowed to let their sexual relationship lie dormant for a time.

Mateo Lopez and his team waited for them beside the private aircraft section of the airport in Punta del Este and whisked them to the house. The girl had vacated the room upstairs, so Fidelia delegated her former space to her primary protector. She gave Howard the ground-floor bedroom.

Once they settled in, she began rebuilding The Organization. First, they sprang the dozens of guys the FBI had snatched off the streets in July. She hired a couple ace attorneys to lead the charge. Within a few days, they penetrated the never-ending American news cycle and made it uncomfortable for the Bureau. Civil liberties missionaries soon picked up their messages.

After another week, Luigi started to hear from guys who'd been released with no charges laid against them. They confirmed the FBI had spirited them off to Guantanamo but forced them to sign documents saying otherwise as a condition of release. The civil liberties people wanted to create a fuss, but Fidelia chased them away. The boys had only a few bumps and bruises and didn't seem unduly inconvenienced. It certainly wouldn't merit a war with law enforcement.

Her primary protector relaxed once his men started returning, and she refocused his attention on plugging the other gaps. First, she rewarded the Spanish country boss by giving him Gibraltar, a territory he'd long craved, but that had previously been part of the Italian span of control.

With the arrest of Deschamps, she ordered the crime boss for France to infiltrate Interpol at the most senior levels. She gave him a ninety-day deadline to complete the task and threatened financial punishment if he failed. Luigi had been so impressed with the Lithuanians she added Poland to the stables of the top man there. He now controlled all the Baltics plus Poland, and cheerfully agreed to add 5 percent per month to the monthly commission he sent her.

She toyed with giving Singapore to Aretta Musa in appreciation for her support, but Howard advised against it. Instead, he recommended she expand the influence of the boss in Macau so they could optimize their take from the casinos. Both countries had become powerhouses in the growing Asian gaming business, and linking them solidified The Organization's iron-clad control.

By mid-August, things stabilized. She changed her routine to run on the beach every day with one or two of the bodyguards. While she ran, her primary protector caught up with his wife on new, secure phones. They spent more time talking week-by-week.

Howard gradually did more than listen. His first advice on Singapore and Macau alone made having him around worthwhile and paid the expense of his feeding and housing many times over. He increasingly offered more ideas and suggestions, each carefully thought out and artfully explained.

It was also he who persuaded her to set aside revenge on the Shadow—temporarily. "We might know who the Shadow is, but there's an election in a few weeks. The American people might throw out some of the scum in and around the White House. Save your ammunition until he might not have the same access to power and influence. Your revenge may be sweeter."

Of course, with Howard close by to offer grounded advice, she also didn't have to worry about him mucking up some golden opportunity to win favor with the Feds.

By Labor Day, things had changed.

"I heard from our mole at the Bureau in DC. They've withdrawn the arrest warrant for you and dropped all surveillance." She noted how broad Luigi's grin grew as she shared the news. "Are you ready to go back to New York?" She knew the answer, but waited for him to give a confirming nod.

"Then it's time for you to go." And it was also the moment to give him a boost. "We're going to change your job back there. I've no desire to return to the US. I want you to run the show there. Send me ten percent of your take every month and you keep the rest. It's time for you to move from being my primary protector to become my country boss." It better described his true role, and her take was adequate compensation for her needs. She had little ego to massage.

She gave Luigi a hug and perfunctory kiss on the cheek as they said goodbye at the doorway before he and the American bodyguards left for their rented private jet waiting at the airport. They agreed to keep in touch, and she saw no need to provide greater motivation. He looked happy with the outcome, too. At least now, his wife would ease the pressure for him to return and eliminate an unnecessary distraction.

Earlier that morning, Mateo had driven Howard to Montevideo for x-rays at a private clinic. The surgeon from Hospital Evangélico agreed to meet secretly there to assess his fracture and determine if the air cast had adequately done its job.

Meanwhile, Fidelia prepared for her next mission. She booked—for the entire day—a spa she'd visited on previous trips. The whole facility, with no other guests permitted.

She ordered the works, and a team of three worked on her diligently until late in the day. A massage, sauna, manicure, pedicure, plus a radical new cut and style rounded out the afternoon before she returned to the house.

It smelled terrific when she stepped inside. Her resident chef was in the last stages of preparation for a gourmet feast, and her phone rang before she closed the door.

"Just calling like you asked," Howard said without a hello. "The leg's fine. She wants me to use crutches for another two weeks, but the cast is no longer necessary. Mateo says to tell you we should be back at the house by dinnertime."

It had been a slow process. But, once again, she had gradually come to realize how useful it was to have Howard around. The guy was brilliant in all matters financial. He understood intimately how major corporations functioned, and she needed his expertise to grow The Organization to its next level of success. There was also that recent unexpected tinge of a growing desire.

She decided it was time to shift her curmudgeon's outlook from ambivalent captive to motivated participant, and she plotted to use the method that had succeeded at every stage of her life.

When Mateo later texted to advise they were thirty minutes out, she dressed for dinner. She chose her only transparent top, a pale green button-down that accented the brown of her eyes nicely. She left three buttons open and squeezed into the shortest skirt in her wardrobe, a white one that drew attention to her darker skin tones. Of course, she slipped on stiletto heels and added a squirt of perfume.

Five minutes before Howard's expected arrival, she lit candles, switched on romantic background music, and dimmed the lights.

ACKNOWLEDGEMENTS

Collaboration is important for my writing. Once a manuscript draft is complete, fine-tuning begins with a genuine welcome for criticism, feedback and suggestions from two excellent professionals.

Paula Hurwitz and Val Tobin helped me polish this novel with incisive editing and proofreading. Their valuable input improved my story meaningfully, and any remaining shortcomings are entirely mine.

Early on, I asked a few people to read an initial draft and give me feedback on content and style. Cheryl Harrison, Heather & Dan Lightfoot, and Cathy & Dalton McGugan offered observations and comments about the characters and plot that added significant value.

And I can't thank Kim McDougall of Castelane too often for her advice, cover design, and pleasing book layout. I truly admire her expertise, pulling it all together with unmatched professionalism, good humor and attention to detail.

Readers, family, and friends spread across the globe: I appreciate your reviews, support and encouragement. You provide unlimited inspiration.

ABOUT THE AUTHOR

Gary D. McGugan loves to tell stories and is the author of *Three Weeks Less a Day, The Multima Scheme, Unrelenting Peril, Pernicious Pursuit,* and *A Web of Deceit.*

After a forty-year career at senior levels of global corporations, Gary started writing with a goal of using artful suspense to entertain and inform. His launch of a new writing career—at an age most people retire—reveals an ongoing zest for new challenges and a life-long pursuit of knowledge. Home is near Toronto, but Gary thinks of himself as a true citizen of the world. His love of travel and extensive experiences around the globe are evident in every chapter.

FOLLOW GARY D. MCGUGAN

Subscribe to Gary's VIP Readers List:
https://www.subscribepage.com/garydmcgugan

Facebook
www.facebook.com/gary.d.mcgugan.books

Twitter
@GaryDMcGugan

Gary D. McGugan Website
www.garydmcguganbooks.com

Instagram
Authorgarydmcgugan

LinkedIn
https://tinyurl.com/rmbhfzer

CPSIA information can be obtained
at www.ICGtesting.com
Printed in the USA
LVHW022039041222
734570LV00003B/229